FALLING FOR JUNE

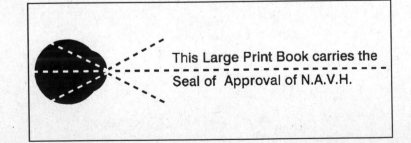

This Large Print Book carries the
Seal of Approval of N.A.V.H.

FALLING FOR JUNE

RYAN WINFIELD

THORNDIKE PRESS
A part of Gale, Cengage Learning

GALE
CENGAGE Learning·

Farmington Hills, Mich • San Francisco • New York • Waterville, Maine
Meriden, Conn • Mason, Ohio • Chicago

Copyright © 2015 by Ryan Winfield.
Thorndike Press, a part of Gale, Cengage Learning.

ALL RIGHTS RESERVED

Thorndike Press® Large Print Basic.
The text of this Large Print edition is unabridged.
Other aspects of the book may vary from the original edition.
Set in 16 pt. Plantin.

LIBRARY OF CONGRESS CATALOGING-IN-PUBLICATION DATA

Winfield, Ryan.
    Falling for June / by Ryan Winfield. — Large print edition.
      pages cm. — (Thorndike Press large print basic)
    ISBN 978-1-4104-8248-8 (hardcover) — ISBN 1-4104-8248-0 (hardcover)
    1. Large type books. I. Title.
  PS3623.I644F35 2015b
  813'.6—dc23   2015019398

Published in 2015 by arrangement with Atria Books, an imprint of Simon & Schuster, Inc.

Printed in Mexico
1 2 3 4 5 6 7 19 18 17 16 15

For those who have been hurt in love
yet still dare to fall.
And for Christine, dahling —
the bravest of them all.

1

All I ever wanted in life was a condo in Florida with a pool to lie beside in the sun, and I was closer than ever to getting it when I met David Hadley and fell for his wife. But it's not exactly how it sounds, so let me explain.

First, I think I should tell you a little about me and how I came to know David Hadley. I promise not to bore you with too many sad, personal details about my childhood, especially since this is, after all, a love story — or, if things work out the way I hope, two love stories in one.

I grew up on a muddy street in a tiny backwoods timber town called Belfair. The sign on the road that led into town claimed it was Washington State's Best-Kept Secret, but it said nothing about the dark cloud that seemed to hover above it year-round. My father was a high-climbing tree topper by day and a wine connoisseur by night —

those two things sound like they shouldn't mix, I know, but they somehow did in him — and nearly every afternoon I would ride my bicycle out to the work site and holler up a "Hello!" just to see his purple grin beam down on me from atop a big Doug fir or Pacific red cedar. He was a kick, my old man was. And that's how I'll always remember him, that lofty purple grin.

My father took pride in his longstanding memberships with a half dozen mail-order clubs for exotic wines from around the world, and he considered himself a great collector — even though his collection consisted mostly of saved corks and empty bottles. He also considered himself the town sommelier, which was the only French word he knew, and one he proudly used. That was my dad, Belfair's tree-topping sommelier. All month long he'd take orders for friends, and on delivery days, he'd load up the cases in my rusted red wagon — we never had a car; too much wine to buy, I guess — and tow them down the muddy streets, making his rounds and waving hello while flashing his purple grin to everyone he passed. He had a lot of friends, my old man did. Especially on delivery days.

Belfair had four bars and one church back then — the bars are still there, but the church was torn down years ago — and while it was not uncommon for my father to visit all four of the bars on any given Sunday, he never once set foot inside the church. Well, at least not until he entered it headfirst to be displayed at the front for an afternoon. The pastor claimed the Good Lord had called him home to heaven, but I knew my father had bought himself a ticket there one bottle at a time. I had to bury him on credit. I was nineteen. I'll never forget looking down at him in the cheap, plastic-coated casket and seeing his lips frozen in his signature purple-toothed grin, an expression so a part of his being that not even the mortician's cunning could erase it from his face. I had seen photos of his father, and of his father's father, and it was a drunken smirk that ran in our family just as strongly as our small ears and big hands. But despite his purple smile, life had been hard for my old man — especially after my mother ran out on us.

Her name was Oksana and she was beautiful. But she was never meant for Belfair. She had only been passing through on her way south from Vancouver, stopping just long enough to make the mistake of getting pregnant with me. She tried to be a mother for a little while, she really did, or so my father told me, but then she left for cigarettes and milk on the eve of my third birthday and just never came home. A package arrived six months later from California with a bottle of Napa wine for my father and a Mickey Mouse T-shirt and belated birthday card for me. Inside the card was a Polaroid of her standing in front of MGM studios, and that's the only photo I have of her. She sent two more letters that year — one from San Diego, one from Houston, and both addressed to me, as if I could read at the age of three — but she sent nothing after. And that's fine with me. It really is. But I still keep her photo just the same.

My father never married or even seriously dated after my mother left. I remember several neighborhood women helping out with me early on, many of them single, but if my father showed any romantic interest in any of them, it was never serious enough, and soon they drifted away and it was only the two of us left on our own. I'll tell you straight up, though, he was a gentleman all the way, my old man was. Despite my mother's having run out on us the way she did, he didn't hate women at all. Not one bit. He did, however, hate the idea of love. And so do I, to tell you the truth. Or at least I did, before I met David Hadley and heard a love story that would change my life. But I'm getting ahead of myself. Back to my old man.

I remember asking him about love once. I said, "Do you think you'll ever get married again?" He laughed. "I'd rather fall from the top of old man Snyder's tallest Doug fir." Then he looked up from the TV just long enough to lift his wineglass, as if toasting to his own comment. When I pressed him about it, he set his glass down and switched off the TV — a rare and serious occurrence in our little trailer. Then, what was even rarer, he called me over and pulled me down and sat me on his knee, just like I'd sat when I was a boy, except now I was twelve and already a man, were you to ask me. But the reason I'll never forget it is because he looked right into my eyes and for once he wasn't grinning.

"Don't you ever believe anything you hear about love, Son," he said. "Love is nothing but a snake with a head on each end, and it'll bite you coming and going. You hear me? Fools play with love like they do fire, but you and me, we know better than to believe in love because we've been burned by love. Best lesson I ever learned, your mother taught me. Love will run right out the door just as soon as you begin to feel a little comfortable. Love's hot as the sun but cold as a star. You hear me, Son? You don't need love. You don't need it at all. Tell me you understand."

I nodded that I understood, and I thought I did. But I was young and scared, and he was old and scared, and together we didn't know enough about love to fill a wineglass.

"This doesn't mean we disrespect women," he added, reaching up and cupping his hand around my neck and looking at me sternly. "You treat women like a gentleman does. And that's an order from your father, Son. Respect women but keep them at a distance or else you'll get burned badly. Just like your mother did already, to you and to your old man."

Then he released my neck and eased me off his knee before picking up his wineglass again. I was still rerunning the conversation in my head when I heard the TV switch back on. But I never forgot it. Not a word. It was the only serious conversation we ever had about anything, and it was the only direct advice he ever gave me. I guess maybe that's why I took it to heart the way I did. But despite adopting my father's opinions about love, I disagreed with him wholeheartedly about Belfair. For him Belfair would forever be home; for me it was nothing but a hell I couldn't wait to flee. Truth is I was already dreaming of escape long before I'd asked my old man about love. Hell, I was dreaming of escape before I even learned to read.

On Sundays my father would sometimes take me down to the Silver Spruce Saloon for a hot cocoa while he impressed his friends by describing various wines at the bar. Talking tannins and nuttiness and all that garbage nobody really understands. But I loved going because they had one of those real estate brochure racks there in the corner, and I was so mesmerized by the glossy, sun-dappled pictures that I'd let my cocoa go cold just flipping through them again and again. They seemed as far away from Belfair as Camelot to me.

When I got a little older, I'd ride my bicycle fourteen miles to the ferry terminal to load up on the magazines that passengers left behind on the free shelf, then ride back and pass cold winter evenings cutting out my favorite beach houses and hanging them on my bedroom wall. It looked like my room had been papered over by *Town & Country* and *Coastal Living*. Not an inch of wood paneling was uncovered, I swear. My father came in once and saw it and just shook his head and walked out again. I

13

think he thought I wanted to be an architect or a travel agent or something. But I didn't. I just wanted the hell out of Belfair.

I know I said this was a love story, and that I promised not to overwhelm you with childhood travails, but this will all make sense when I tell you about David and June and how I came to be the caretaker of the greatest love story I've ever heard. And I don't want you to think I'm looking for any sympathy here, either, because I'm not. I don't even think my childhood was all that bad. Certainly it wasn't compared to some others I've heard about. I told that to a concerned guidance counselor once, that my childhood wasn't so terrible, and she said that each of us has experienced the worst childhood we will ever know. And even though I remember thinking at the time that she was kind of pessimistic to be a counselor, she was right. But that means that each of us has experienced the best childhood we will ever know too. So, on balance, I guess mine was all right. But still, I couldn't wait to bail out of Belfair.

My plan was always to leave the day I turned sixteen. Of course, my father was fully in his cups by then and partially disabled from a fall that broke his left hip, so I put my dream on hold and got a job at the local planing mill instead. And then three years later my father died, as I mentioned already. Our trailer was a rental, and there was nothing in it worth selling that hadn't already been sold, so after I'd worked long enough to pay off the funeral debt, I packed a bag and made the rounds saying good-bye.

The manager at the mill laughed when I told him I was leaving for Seattle. He said the city would chew me up and spit me out like a twig tossed into a wood chipper. He was always calling me a twig on account of my being skinny. But he wasn't a mean-spirited man; he was just afraid. All of Belfair was afraid, I guess, since no one ever left. But I wasn't afraid. Truth is, I had nothing to lose except a suitcase full of clothes, my favorite Miami condo clipping torn from my bedroom wall, and sixty-four dollars and ten cents. I remember the exact amount because I counted it on the ferry four times before I made my first investment in my future by tossing the dime overboard with a wish. I wished for that condo in Miami, but I told myself I'd settle for dying anywhere other than Belfair, and without the drunken family grin on my face.

The city did chew me up, but I refused to let it spit me out. I slept on the streets beneath the viaduct until there was space in a men's shelter. Then I jumped between hostels, taking a job sorting donations at the Salvation Army and working my way up to cashier. I was always good with figures, even though I had dropped out of high school to work at the mill. I studied nights for my GED and got it, along with a better job and a studio apartment. Then I enrolled at Evergreen Community College. When I received my associate's degree, I went back to the cemetery in Belfair and showed the diploma to my father — "Look, Dad, I did it; the first in our family to graduate college." Then I went to show it to the mill manager, but it turned out I'd missed him already at the cemetery.

I was on my way to enroll at the University of Washington extension campus when I met a man on the bus who saw the financial aid application in my hand and laughed. For some reason he felt the need to warn me that going into debt for a useless degree would be the worst mistake of my life. He said the real money was in mortgages. He said he'd made piles of cash selling loans, enough in fact to buy his first home before he was even twenty-five. He said he damn near had a real estate empire. Although, looking back, I never thought to ask him

16

why in the hell he was still riding the city bus if he was so wealthy. But whether he was full of bull or not, I promptly forgot about school and enrolled instead as an assistant mortgage broker at Washington Mutual.

The bank was growing fast, gobbling up smaller banks all around the country, and I watched the mortgage brokers I was working for get fatter and flusher by the day. Then it was my turn. A simple test, a minor background check, and at last, I was a licensed broker ready to take on the world one mortgage at a time. But as it often does, the world had other plans. The housing market crashed, the bank went belly-up, and almost as soon as I had earned my promotion I was out of a job. I looked for work, I did, but there was no place for a freshly minted mortgage broker with no experience, even if he did have an associate's degree. Some luck, right? Back to the Salvation Army for me, or so I thought, until a new plan presented itself in the form of a stolen newspaper.

I don't like a thief at all. And I've never been one, except accidentally. My alcoholic neighbor got the paper, but he never was up before noon on a Sunday, so it was my habit to borrow it to read with my coffee. I'd always fold it up neatly and have it back at his apartment door before he even knew what day it was. Except this one particular Sunday when I forgot to give it back. I forgot because there was a front-page article about people defaulting on their home loans faster than they had signed them. That in itself wasn't news. What was news was farther down in the story, about how a local firm was handling foreclosures for the big banks. They employed reps to go out on house calls to discuss options with the homeowners. The paper called them "vulture visits," of course, while the big banks spun them as "pre-foreclosure counseling sessions." Everyone else called it "cash for keys." But I didn't care what they were called. All I cared about was the claim that a good rep could earn six figures. That, and they were hiring.

I ran out right there without even finishing my coffee, taking the paper with me. I bought a new suit on credit at Macy's — they'll give anybody a card, I swear, even if you don't have a job — and changed in the store before heading uptown. Then I walked into the offices of Foreclosure Solutions Inc., wearing my new suit and a confident smile, and walked out employed. My business card read "Housing Transition Specialist," but really my job was convincing delinquent homeowners to leave their properties voluntarily in exchange for a little cash toward a fresh start. It isn't the type of career one is proud of, I know. But don't judge me, please. Someone had to do it. Plus, it was a whole lot better than shoveling sawdust at the mill.

The way I saw it, I was helping people. And it wasn't just win-win, either, it was triple-win all the way: the banks didn't have to go to court to foreclose, the homeowners walked away with a little dough, and most importantly, I got paid. Before long my closing ratio was the highest in the company, my payout average the lowest, and I was training new foreclosure counselors and cherry-picking my own cases. Things were good for me, even though I was still a long way from Miami.

The housing crisis dragged on longer than anyone could have imagined, and business was booming because of it. I moved into a nicer apartment, bought better suits, and taped that old condo clipping from the glossy pages of *Penthouses in Paradise* magazine to my shaving mirror.

By the eve of my thirty-third birthday, my dream was about to become a reality. I had a mortgage preapproval in hand; I had a promise of a job from my employer's sister company in Florida; and I had a Realtor in Miami scouring South Beach foreclosures for just the right condo. It was a good day to be turning thirty-three. It also just happened to be the day that David Hadley's letter landed on my desk.

I only opened it myself on account of the stamps. It was addressed to Mr. Ralph Spitzer, as was all the mail that made it to my department, and it was posted with forty-nine carefully placed one-cent stamps. I had no idea they even offered those still. But maybe they don't; they could have been old, now that I think about it. Anyway, the stamps had bright red birds on them, and an entire flock stared at me from both sides of the envelope. There was hardly any room at all for the address and it was so heavy with all those stamps I was surprised it even got delivered without more postage, although there would have been nowhere to put the additional stamps.

I opened the envelope and withdrew a single sheet of ruled yellow paper, neatly folded and covered on both sides with shaky handwritten script. I'll spare you the struggle of reading it by retyping the letter here:

Dear Mr. Ralph Spitzer:

Your name reminds me of a man on CNN. I hope it isn't you. Sometimes I watch cable news and I think if there is a God, He or She should tip this whole world like a dinner plate and send us tumbling off of it like so many useless crumbs into space. I just don't see the point. But then I think about my wife, June, and I remember her saying that maybe there is no point to anything except falling pointlessly in love. Of course, she said it just before she jumped off of a seventy-six-story building, which at the time had me questioning her sanity. But that doesn't mean she wasn't right.

My name is David Hadley, although you probably know me as Case Number 524-331, or perhaps as 772 1/2 Whispering Willow Lane, Darrington, WA 98241. I never have been quite sure where the 1/2 in the address comes from — especially since the property is just north of forty-two acres — but the postman never seems able to find us without it so I always make sure to point it out. Actually, I should probably get used to saying postwoman now, since our new one is a lady. But that's neither here nor

21

there, and then the address doesn't tell you much about this place anyway. What's important for you to know is that less than two hours' drive northeast from Seattle, in a valley at the base of Whitehorse Mountain, 772 and 1/2 are the numbers on the mailbox at the entrance to Echo Glen. Now, I'll admit the mailbox is rusted, and the wooden gate it's attached to is half-rotted and leaning worse than the house or even the barns, but I swear to you and to postwomen everywhere that you ought to be able to send mail here simply by addressing it to the Center of the Universe, which it is. Or at least it was for June and still is for me.

I'm writing to take you up on your offer to discuss my options before you foreclose. Please come by anytime. But don't come before *Good Morning America* is over in the morning. And don't come after *Jeopardy!* starts at four. Maybe come late morning if you can. I seem to have more energy then anyway. And besides, there's nothing on television at that time except cable news.

Sincerely,
David Hadley

After reading the letter, I looked up Mr. Hadley's loan in our system, but there was nothing unique about it. Plus, to tell you the truth, being that far out in the country, it wasn't a huge loan by Seattle standards and the potential commission wasn't enough to get me excited — especially not on the eve of my birthday.

I keyed the correspondence into the computer, stamped the letter RECEIVED, and tossed it in the bin to be assigned to a more junior foreclosure counselor. Done and done, on to other things. My intention was to never think of it again. But, as I've since found, sometimes fate has plans of its own.

2

Because I spent most days out in the field making pre-foreclosure house calls, or "sits," as we called them in the biz, it was my habit to catch up on paperwork by spending evenings in the office. Most nights I stayed until the janitors showed up. Then I'd head to the corner bar near my apartment. The bar is called Finnegans, with no apostrophe, although I never knew why. It isn't even an Irish place at all. Estrella thinks it was named for the writer James Joyce. But I haven't told you about her yet, have I?

This particular night, I sat at the bar dividing my attention between the television and the clock on the wall beside it. As soon as the clock struck midnight, I waved Estrella over and asked her for a glass of their best cabernet. She spells her name with an R and two Ls, but it's pronounced es-TRAY-yah. It's a cool name. It means "star of heaven" or something in Spanish. She didn't tell me all that; I looked it up.

"I need to see your ID," she said.

"Really?" I asked her. I'm italicizing it because I said it really cheekily. "I only come in here for dinner all the time."

"Yeah, so what?" she said, flashing me an equally cheeky smile. "You always drink club soda and lime."

She was just messing with me, I knew she was, but I could tell that she wasn't going to let up so I pulled out my wallet.

"You're probably just trying to get my address," I said.

She took my license but she didn't look at it right away. Instead, she kind of held it for ransom against my attention and hooked a hand on her hip and smirked at me. She did it cutely, of course, but it was still a smirk.

"You wish, mister," she said.

She's younger than I am, but not by enough to be calling me mister.

"But I am wondering why you haven't asked me out yet," she added, getting suddenly shy, or at least pretending to. I know she blushed for sure; I saw it. Anyway, then she looked down at the bar and coyly said, "You've been coming in here for almost a year, and it can't be for the food."

25

"I like the atmosphere," I replied, making a big show of shrugging nonchalantly as I looked all around the bar. It really did have a good vibe, this place. But I knew that wasn't what she wanted to hear, and it wasn't really the truth either. I was just stringing her along a little. "And I like you too," I added after what felt like a long enough pause. "I like you a lot."

"You do? Then why haven't you asked me out?"

I knew she wouldn't understand this next part, but it was true. "Because I only ask out girls I don't like," I said.

When she heard that she let her hand fall off her hip in a cute but defeated gesture, and she bit her lower lip a little. She was always doing that, biting her lower lip. Usually when she was carrying a tray or something. Sometimes, after serving my meal, she'd linger awhile and watch the baseball game on TV with me, maybe just for a few minutes, but she'd bite her lip then too. And if our team was at bat, she had this nervous way of twisting up a strand of her hair in her fingers as she watched. It really was cute.

"So, you only ask out the girls you don't like," she said. "Well, that doesn't make one ounce of sense, even for a man, does it?"

I've noticed that women are always saying things that sound like questions even though they're not questions at all. Why is that? I suspect it's because they know they're right but don't want to hit us men over the head with it, since it happens so often.

But anyway, in this case she was wrong.

"It makes plenty of sense," I said. "And I'll tell you why. Love is fun at the beginning, but it always bites you in the end."

"I'm sorry," she said, "I must not have known that you were such an expert about the immutable nature of love."

"Immutable?" I asked, raising a brow.

"It was the word of the day on my vocabulary app."

"Well, my point is if I asked you out we'd have a great time, I'm sure of it. For a while anyway. Then we'd get bored with one another, and one of us, most likely you, would move on. And then I'd be all tore up and brokenhearted and where would I go for my dinner? I couldn't come here any longer after that. And as I said, I really like this place."

I couldn't tell if she looked disappointed or just amused.

"There are only like three other bars that serve food on this block," she said.

I didn't dare tell her, of course, that I

couldn't eat in most of those bars for the very reason I had just spelled out. I didn't tell her because while I might have taken to heart my father's sage warnings about love, I also remembered his stern advice about being a gentleman and all. Plus, the declining state of my local dining options wasn't really the point, because although I did like the place a lot, I liked her a lot more.

"And besides," she added, "your little hypothetical scenario assumes I'd say yes if you did ask me out."

We had kind of flirted before, but nothing this direct. Now she was biting her lip, which drove me crazy, and coiling her hair, which made me feel like I was one of those ballplayers up at bat.

"Wouldn't you?" I tossed out — meaning *Say yes,* of course. And as I asked it, I laid on her what I considered to be my most charming smile yet.

It was dim in the bar, but I swore I saw her blush again.

"Maybe," she said, holding my stare for a beat. Then just like that the moment passed and she released her lower lip and let her hair fall. "But then you're moving to Miami anyway. At least that's what you keep saying."

"See," I said, "love is already turning on us."

"Hey, it's your birthday!" she exclaimed, finally looking at my license. "Why didn't you say so? No one should drink alone on his birthday."

What is it about people and birthdays, anyway? It's just another day, really. But she had hardly handed me back my license and she was gone. She came back with the glass of wine I had asked for and two shots of Jack Daniel's, one for each of us. But I don't ever touch liquor, so I had to let her down as easy as I could on the shot. Besides, even though it was technically my birthday, I wasn't really celebrating. And I wasn't drinking alone either. I was paying my respects to my father the only way I knew how.

It had been our tradition to have a glass of wine together on my birthday. It started when I was just three, with a finger of cabernet sauvignon in my bottle to quiet my crying when my mother didn't come home, and it continued until he died. And now I allow myself one glass of cabernet every birthday, just to remember him by. My old man, the sommelier of Belfair. So if I'm counting right, and I'm pretty good with figures so I think I am, that makes thirty-one drinks in my entire life, one for every birthday since I was three, but not one sip of alcohol on any of the days in between. And I'll tell you straight up, if you could see how white my teeth are, you'd know I was telling the truth.

Estrella was a good sport about the shot, of course — she seemed to be pretty easygoing most of the time — calling over the busboy and giving it to him so the three of us could toast my birthday. Then she left me to attend to her other customers and I sat watching the TV while the cabernet worked its way from my belly to my head. And then something happened that seemed simple enough at the time, even though it would forever change my life.

What happened was one of those commercials for anti-depressants came on. You know, the one where the cloud is following the lady around. But then she takes this pill and of course the sun comes out and the grass gets suddenly green and this little red bird flies down and lands on her head and starts singing. Perched right there on her head, I swear. Silly as hell, even for an anti-depressant commercial. And that red bird got me thinking about those stamps, and the stamps got me thinking about David Hadley's letter.

Hadn't he written something about God tipping the world like a dinner plate? Wouldn't that be something to see? I was pretty sure he'd also written that his wife had jumped off of a building. And now he was being foreclosed on. Talk about tough luck. Something in the tone of his letter had come across as endearing, though, and it made me curious about him.

And that's all it took — that sappy pill commercial and a little lousy curiosity — because the next thought I had was that maybe I would swing by the office in the morning to get his file and go out and meet with him myself after all. I sure wouldn't mind seeing the Center of the Universe, I thought, and a drive into the country sounded like a much better way to spend a birthday than cooped up in the office waiting for some clown to show up with a cake.

Just about the time I had made up my mind to go, Estrella reappeared with a huge cupcake, crowned with a candle. She was singing "Happy Birthday," and the busboy and then the rest of the bar joined in. It could have been from my once-a-year glass of cabernet, but I felt my cheeks flush. I know, embarrassing, right? People really do insist on making a big deal out of birthdays.

Estrella wouldn't let me blow the candle

out until I made a birthday wish, even though I reminded her I was turning thirty-three, not three. But she insisted, so I did, and since I liked her so much I didn't even fake it. I closed my eyes and made a real wish. It was easier than I thought, too, because it was the same wish I had made back in Belfair when I was just a boy, the same wish I had made nearly every day since.

3

There's something very relaxing about driving north out of the city, especially in fall. Maybe it's the almost imperceptible fade from the gray sidewalks and glass skyscrapers to the golden leaves of turning trees; or maybe it's the smell of clean, moist air spilling in through the cracked car window; or maybe it's just the simple relief of knowing that you're leaving the hustle of the city streets behind for an afternoon. Whatever it is, I felt my mood lifting the farther north I drove.

It was raining like hell when I left Seattle, and hailing by the time I hit Marysville, but when I finally exited the interstate, I came out from beneath the dark clouds and dropped into a wide sunlit valley, surrounded by pine-covered hills. It was nice, it really was. A rainbow even followed me. I got my first glimpse of Whitehorse Mountain as I rounded a bend. It stood framed between two heavily forested peaks and its shady folds and sawtooth summit infused me with a sense of mystery. I wondered if it was possible to feel nostalgia for a place one had never been before. The mountain played peekaboo on the hilly skyline, appearing here and then there as the road twisted through the valleys of eastern Snohomish County, until at last it was above everything else on the horizon and lit by shafts of morning sunlight piercing through the dissipating clouds. I was beginning to feel glad that I had decided to come. So glad, in fact, that as I passed through the small timber town of Darrington, I was not nearly as bothered by the sight of a lumber mill as I thought I should be, even though the smell of damp sawdust reminded me of my childhood home.

I consulted my map until I found Whispering Willow Lane. The sign was nearly obscured by the overgrown willow trees, and the overarching willow branches hung so low above the roadway in places that I could see them in the rearview mirror rustling in the breeze created by my car as I passed. I sure felt a million miles away from the city, even though I had left it just an hour and a half before. The road took me across a river on an old covered bridge, and then about a quarter mile past the bridge I came upon the address. His letter had not misled me. The mailbox was red with rust, and it was attached to a weathered-timber archway that leaned so precariously above the gravel driveway that I almost hesitated to drive beneath it. There was a wooden sign hung on chains that read:

ECHO GLEN

The property was densely overgrown, and as I drove through it I caught glimpses of its prior glory through the brush — peekaboo orchards scattered with unpruned apple and cherry trees; snapshots of barns and stables in various stages of dilapidation, losing their quiet battles with brambles and brush. I had the sense I was entering a place shrouded as much in mystery as it was in shade. The property opened as the drive turned to follow a fence line up toward the house. The house was white. At least it looked like it had been before years of weather had stripped most of the paint away and turned the wood siding a silvery gray that stood out against the dark trees rising up the mountain behind it. There was a quiet stubbornness to the house. As if it had long stood there at the base of that

35

mountain, guarding the valley against the advancing forest that seemed to press against its back, or perhaps served as a final gateway to the wilder, enchanted lands beyond.

As I got closer I saw that the house possessed a strange cheerfulness too. Despite the faded paint, it was well kept and bordered by green, freshly cut lawns. Rhododendrons flanked the covered porch, and bright flower baskets hung from hooks in the low porch eaves. The contrast between the manicured look of the house and the wildness of the surrounding property created the impression of a slow retreat by the caretaker to the confines of the home and its four walls. As if he maintained what he could as an act of defiance against the advance of time. I parked in front of the house — backing in for a quick exit if necessary, as was my habit on these visits — and got out of the car. I could hear a creek running somewhere unseen and I paused to breathe in the country air. Who knew the Center of the Universe smelled like wet grass and pine trees?

The steps to the house had been built over with a wheelchair ramp, and I wondered if Mr. Hadley was disabled. I'd been on a few appointments with homeowners who were and it always made my job much harder. That, or if they had young kids or anything. Or if they had lived there a long time. Actually, it was never easy telling people they had to leave. But as I said before, even though it wasn't the kind of career one was proud of, I was good at it. And if it weren't me at their door offering them a check to vacate now, it would be the sheriff in a few months offering them nothing.

I knocked on the door. I've learned to ignore doorbells and instead always knock lightly three times. It's the least intrusive, I think. I waited, and then knocked three times more. I was just raising my hand to knock a third time when the door flew open as if it were on springs and an old man stood in front of me squinting into the light. He was noticeably shorter than I am, but he had a presence about him that filled the doorway. I guessed him to be in his late seventies or early eighties by the look of his thinning gray hair and the white stubble on his cheeks. You could tell he was really old by his clothes too. He wore brown corduroy pants and a colorful patchwork sweater that appeared to have been knitted by someone who was blind. The door opened so fast it kind of surprised me, though, and I was still taking all this in when he spoke.

"If you've come to preach to me about Jehovah, I'll kindly tell you as I have the others that I'll be finding out the truth a lot sooner than you will, young man."

His voice was gravelly and gruff, but it was also kind.

"I'm from the bank," I said. "I've come about your letter."

I opened the file I had carried with me from the car and held up his letter. There were two enormous breast pockets sewn into his sweater, made of what looked like leather and both bulging with the weight of whatever personal possessions he felt necessary to store there, and he reached into one of these pockets and pulled out reading glasses. Then he took the letter from me and looked it over, as if verifying that it was in fact his handwriting. When he appeared satisfied, he handed the letter back and said, "I didn't expect you to come so soon."

"Well, I just had to see the Center of the Universe," I said. "And meet the man who can lick forty-nine one-cent stamps." Then I stuck out my hand. "I'm Elliot Champ."

He didn't shake it right away, asking instead, "What happened to Mr. Spitzer?"

I didn't want to tell him that he'd written to a fictional person and that Ralph Spitzer was just a made-up name for our computer-generated form letters. But I didn't want to lie either. In the end, I fell back on my training and ignored the question altogether, shrugging and saying, "I'm Elliot Champ, sir, your housing transition specialist."

My arm was getting heavy by this time, but I kept my hand out for him to shake. He dipped his head a little so he could look at me over the reading glasses. Then he retrieved a small notebook and pen from his other sweater pocket and wrote something in it. I had the feeling he was taking down my name. Now my arm was really getting heavy.

"Elliot Champ, you say? Sounds more made-up than Spitzer to me." He tucked the notebook away in his bulging pocket. Then he finally shook my hand, and when he did, it was as if everything had suddenly changed. He smiled and stepped aside, pulling me into the foyer. "I'm so glad you've come, Mr. Champ. You have no idea." He caught me too off guard for a response. This certainly wasn't the welcome I was used to on these visits. "May I take your coat?" he asked as he closed the door behind me.

I thought it was nice of him to offer, but I still told him no. I'd learned long ago to keep everything with me on these visits. You just never know when you'll need to clear out in a hurry. I took a moment to look around the small house. All the visible walls were hung with watercolors in homemade frames and several windows had been covered with old stained glass, infusing the rooms with soft, colorful light. It sounds funny to say, but I thought the whole place kind of matched his sweater. Or maybe his sweater matched the house. Anyway, when he brought me into the living room, I thought it even more.

The living room looked about as lived-in as a living room can, with rainbow-colored afghans draped over old leather chairs, a red sofa so faded it looked pink, and books and newspapers spread everywhere. There was an old tattered recliner parked in front of the TV, and I got the sense he spent most of his time there.

"I'm glad you're not that Ralph Spitzer fellow anyway," he said, stepping over and switching off the TV. "Every time I get a letter from him his name reminds me of that man on CNN. Such doom and gloom. I don't know why I even watch it, except maybe to remind myself that I won't be missing much when I'm gone."

But I was hardly listening to him because I was looking at a brightly painted wooden rooster standing in front of a window bay

— and not just any rooster either, but one that was five feet tall with a seat carved into its back. The old man saw me looking at it and smiled. Then he broke into a kind of tap dance right there on the living room floor — as best he could anyway for being so old and all — and as he danced he belted out a corny campfire refrain that went:

We had an old hen that wouldn't lay eggs, until that sly old rooster flew into our yard and caught our old hen right off her guard. But we're having eggs now, soft-boiled and poached hard, oh we're having eggs now, ever since that sly old rooster flew into our yard.

The whole song-and-dance display really was strange, and I wondered if maybe he wasn't quite right in his mind. I'd been on sits like that too, and they weren't easy either. But then he finished the song with a laugh, as if it had been a perfectly ordinary thing to do, patting me on the arm and asking, "Can I get you some coffee or tea, young man?" When I told him coffee would be great, he said, "I actually don't have any coffee. The doctor tells me I can't drink it with the medicine I take. But I do have tea." I told him tea would be just fine, but I was still wondering why he had offered me coffee when he didn't even have any as he shuffled off toward the kitchen.

When I was alone, I stepped over to inspect the rooster. It looked hand-carved and old as hell; the paint was all cracked. I love that sort of thing, though. Anything with history. I could have admired that rooster all day, but then the view outside drew my eye. The window was wet yet from the earlier rains, giving the backyard a watery, faraway appearance through the old leaded glass. The creek I had heard earlier came down from the mountain and turned and ran along behind the house. A narrow footbridge crossing it was covered with wisteria. It really was a great view. The land on the far side of the bridge was quite wild, of course, but a well-worn footpath was visible disappearing along with the creek up into the shaded wood. I wondered who used the path often enough to keep it clear. Surely not the old man.

"I hope you didn't have a big breakfast." I turned at the sound of his voice and he handed me a steaming mug of tea. "Smooth Move," he said. "I'm afraid it's the only tea I have left. It's supposed to loosen you up, but I'm sure it's mostly marketing. The bathroom is just down the hall on your left, however, just in case you need it."

Perfect, I thought, since I'd had a bran

muffin and a latte before driving out. He indicated that I should sit in an old leather chair, saying something about its being the most comfortable. But he must not have sat in it himself for a long time because I sank so low into the worn cushion I wondered how I would ever get up out of it again. The old man took quite some time getting himself settled across from me, and I sipped my tea and watched him with idle curiosity.

After setting his mug on the end table, he turned the chair to face mine. Then he retrieved his cane from the corner and used it like a handrail to lower himself into it. When he went to retrieve his tea, however, it was just out of his reach, so he hoisted up the cane again and used its curved handle to hook the mug and pull it across the table toward him. I'm not sure why he went to all the trouble, though, because he lifted his tea and blew on it, and then set it back again without taking a sip. Then he sighed. We were easily six feet apart, with the book-covered coffee table between us, but I could clearly see that he was sizing me up in the silence. After a while, he reached into his sweater pocket and consulted his little notebook. Then he looked up at me and said, "Elliot Champ, eh?" I nodded and he slipped the notebook back into his pocket.

"Is it chilly in here, Elliot? I can light the fire."

"No," I replied, "it's fine."

"Are you too warm then? I could hang your coat."

I told him I was actually quite comfortable — which wasn't exactly true on account of being sunk into the damn chair so deep — and he just nodded and let another silence pass. Then he cleared his throat. "This is very embarrassing for me, you know."

Sometimes I ran into this on sits.

"There's no need to be embarrassed," I said.

"I've never failed to pay a bill in my entire life," he replied, pausing to look down at the rug before adding, "I used to be an accountant, you know."

This was the part of my job I hated most — seeing this sadness, this shame. It was always the same. And the worst part about it was that the judgment was all theirs. No one I ever knew really cared two cream puffs whether or not anyone else could pay their mortgage. They were too damn busy working to pay their own. And I sure as hell wasn't judging him. I was still in the habit of borrowing newspapers so I could save enough dough just to buy my first place.

"Well, sir," I said, "everyone falls on hard times now and again. No shame in that."

"Yes," he said, nodding. "I guess everyone does." He was still looking at the floor, or maybe even through it, and his voice seemed to be as distant as his gaze. "But it's not falling that's hard," he said, almost under his breath. "It's holding on."

"Holding on, sir?" I asked, repeating him. "How do you mean?"

He looked up at me and I saw that there was sadness in his eyes. I remember thinking at the time that it seemed like a deep and unreachable sadness, something altogether too heavy to be caused by losing just a home, even if it was the Center of the Universe. I wouldn't find out until much later that day what his sadness was really about.

"Sir, are you okay?" I finally asked.

His head jerked slightly at my question, as if he had been jolted out of a trance. The melancholy seemed to drain from his eyes, replaced by confusion. It almost felt as if he'd forgotten that I was there and was surprised to see me, and I wondered if maybe he didn't have a touch of dementia. He fished a hearing aid from his pocket and screwed it into his ear.

"Should we move the chairs closer?" he

asked. "I'm afraid I might be talking too quietly again."

"No, you're talking fine," I answered. Then I gestured to my own ears to make a joke and ease the tension. "I just have small ears is all."

"Your ears look fine to me," he replied.

But he was just being nice. I know because I really do have small ears. They run in my family.

"But I will say you do have large hands," he offered. "That's my wife's two-handed mug — she made it herself from Spanish clay — but it nearly disappears in your mitt."

I looked at the mug in my hand, really for the first time. It was glazed this beautiful deep blue that you could kind of see the brushstrokes in. Then, probably because I was looking at her mug, I was reminded of something he had written about his wife in his letter.

"This is probably none of my business," I said. "And I don't mean to pry. But you mentioned in your letter that your wife jumped off of a building . . ."

I said it kind of gently because I was aware it might be a touchy matter, but I was not at all prepared for him to laugh.

"I'm sorry," I said, opening the file in my

46

lap to consult his letter. "I must have read your letter wrong. The handwriting was . . . well, I just must have read it wrong."

His laugh slowly worked its way into a nasty cough and he leaned forward in his chair, struggling to breathe. I attempted to rise to help him somehow, but I had my tea mug in one hand and the file open in my lap — plus, I had sunk so low into that damn chair cushion that I could hardly get out to save my own life. Fortunately, he held up his hand to halt me, anyway, taking deep, gulping breaths and waving me off.

"Sit," he said. "I'm fine. Just give me a moment."

I watched him with concern. It was quiet for a minute, the both of us just looking at one another and breathing. When he had finally caught his breath, he sighed and said, "Now, what were we talking about?" I didn't answer right away. There was no way I was going to bring up his wife again. But then he must have remembered on his own because he said, "Oh, yes, June. My wonderful wife. She did jump off of a building all right. That's how I met her. But that was nearly thirty years ago."

Now I was really confused, and once again, I opened the file in my lap. Did he just say thirty years ago? Then how had they both signed on to a loan in 2005? But then I remembered the wheelchair ramp, and I looked around at the uncluttered hallways, the wheel-worn hardwood floors. I panicked a little, thinking maybe his wife was crippled from the fall but was still around, that maybe she was there somewhere, in one of the bedrooms or something. That would really make my job harder. I was trying to think of a gentle way to ask him her whereabouts, but he beat me to it with his own rather personal question.

"Do you get paid commission, Elliot?"

I had been asked this before, so I gave him my customary answer. "I get a base salary." I usually left it at that too, but then he raised one bushy eyebrow and looked at me kind of quizzically, so I added, "And I get commission, yes."

"How much commission?" he asked.

"I'm sorry, sir, but that's kind of a confidential matter."

"So says the man from the bank with my financial obituary in his lap. And one who just asked me about my wife jumping off of a building too."

I remember thinking right then that he was a sharp old dodger, and he sure did turn out to be. I warned myself to be on my game with him when it came time to negotiate. But for some reason I kind of liked him. Plus, I think I might have been in a good mood too — on account of being so far away from the city, and the fresh air, and it being my birthday and all. I decided to answer his question.

"I earn about fifteen hundred for each deal," I finally said. "Sometimes more if it doesn't cost us too much to get the homeowner to leave."

He nodded. "Thank you. I appreciate your honesty, Elliot." And he did seem to genuinely appreciate it, but of course he hit me right away with another personal question. "And what will you do with mine, if you don't mind my asking? Assuming I agree to leave."

"Your commission?" I said, knowing full well that's what he meant, but asking it anyway to buy myself a minute. I briefly considered making up some worthy cause for the funds but decided instead to just tell the truth. It was usually easier. "Add it to my savings, most likely," I said.

"And what are you saving for?"

I felt like the meeting was heading in the wrong direction, like our roles were reversed or something. Wasn't I supposed to be asking the questions? Then again, it was nice to have someone taking an interest in my plans.

"I'm saving a down payment for a condo in Miami."

He laughed so hard I worried he might start coughing again, but he didn't. "Why of all the places on God's green earth would you want to live in Miami?" he asked.

It was a silly question, so I gave it a silly answer.

"Because it's the Sunshine State."

"Filled with crowded beaches," he shot back. "And too much sunshine."

Now I was kind of getting irritated, I'll admit it.

"You can't have too much sunshine," I said.

"Sure you can," he retorted right away, obviously disagreeing with me just because he hated Florida for some reason. Then he doubled down. "The sun is nothing but a weapon without clouds and trees to shade you from it."

"If that's how you feel, I guess," I said.

"I'm missing a chunk of my nose to prove it."

"That aside, you'd feel differently if you grew up in Belfair, where I did. I don't think I knew what the sun was until I left town at nineteen."

"Well, forget about the sun for a minute then," he said. "What about the bugs and humidity? They've got alligators down there too. And snakes that swallow dogs. And brain-eating amoebas. I've seen it all myself on cable news."

"Cable news. Geez. I'll tell you what, if you keep crapping on my dream, maybe I'll send your friend Wolf Blitzer down here to deal with your delinquent loan himself, instead of me, Mr. Hadley."

As soon as I mentioned the delinquent loan, he straightened a little in his chair and the twinkle sort of disappeared from his eyes. Suddenly everything seemed more formal between us than when I had first arrived even. Looking back, it really wasn't fair of me to change the subject off of Florida by bringing up his loan. It was a cheap trick and I knew it. Sometimes I could be a jerk.

"I'm sorry," I said. "I was out of line."

"No," he said somberly, "I'd rather get it out of the way."

"Okay, let me just cut to the chase, Mr. Hadley. Peel it off like a Band-Aid, if I can. The bank will let me offer you up to three months' worth of mortgage payments in cash, and no recourse if the property is sold for a loss. And all you have to do is sign a deed in lieu of foreclosure and move out within the month. How does that sound?"

He nodded, as if it was about what he had been expecting.

"Is that the deal you offer everyone?" he asked.

I had been on hundreds of sits, and this was always the part where they tried to get a little more money. Usually I started lower and held out longer, but as I've said, I kind of liked this old guy.

"For you, I'll make it four months' worth of payments," I offered. "But that's the best I can do. The absolute best. It really is."

"That's not —"

"Actually, for you, I'll sweeten it a little on my own," I said, cutting him off. I couldn't stand to let him beg. I just couldn't. "As I said I get a flat commission of fifteen hundred. I'll kick you back a thousand of it, since we're being so personal and all. That should at least help with the moving expenses, yes?"

"What I wanted to ask you," he said, once I finally allowed him to get a word in, "is how much do you need to get that condo you're saving for in Miami?"

"Miami? I thought you said I'd be foolish to move there."

"I never said that. There never was a fool

who followed his dream, even if it does lead him somewhere as silly as a swamp. How much do you need?"

He was hard to peg, this old dodger. One moment he looked almost senile, kind of lost in his own thoughts, and then the next he'd have a keen twinkle in his old watery eye, as if he were leading me along the whole time. But how could you not like someone with a wooden rooster in his living room and a song and dance to go with it? I decided to answer his question.

"All told, I need about twenty thousand more dollars. And at the rate I'm saving I'll be able to buy in six to nine months."

He put his reading glasses back on, pulled his notebook and pen out again, and wrote something down.

"What are you writing in there?" I asked.

He grinned at me over his glasses. "You have your file; I have mine." Then he took the glasses off and tucked them away along with the notebook, back in his big sweater pocket, before swelling up in his chair. It's hard to explain what I mean exactly, but he inhaled a deep breath and straightened his back and about twenty years seemed to drop off of him. He smiled like he was about to solve the winning question on *Jeopardy!*. "Elliot, my new friend," he said, "I'd like to make you a proposition."

"A proposition?" I asked.

"That's right."

This was not the first time a homeowner had attempted to lay some outlandish scheme on me to save their property, but I decided to humor him and play along.

"Okay, sure. I'm listening."

"What if I offered you a deal that would net you the twenty thousand you need to get your place in Miami in just a couple of weeks?"

"Twenty thousand's a lot of money."

"Yes it is," he replied.

"Two weeks, you said?"

"Give or take."

"What would I have to do to earn it?"

He shrugged, rather coyly, but in a masculine way. "Nothing illegal."

"That's fairly vague for someone who used to be an accountant," I said.

I swear I saw him smile, but I couldn't tell whether it was because of the accountant comment or because he knew I was taking the bait.

"So, you would be interested, then, I assume," he said.

I sat quiet for a minute, looking at him and wondering if he was serious or if he was messing with me. I was interested, of course. Who wouldn't be? But then how could an old man who couldn't even pay his mortgage come up with twenty grand? And what was I in a position to do for him to earn it? And in two weeks, no less. Plus, I worried if I heard him out it might be harder to turn him down, which I surely would have to do. But curiosity was killing me, and I just had to hear what the old dodger had cooked up.

"Okay," I finally said, "they might be small, but I'm all ears."

He kept quiet, eyeing me like a cunning old storybook wolf, silent and dangerous, just sitting for a full minute or so and not even saying anything.

"Well, what is it?" I asked, swallowing the hook whole. "What's the deal?"

He leaned forward and rubbed his hands together, speaking conspiratorially. "I can't tell you any details about the offer until you hear the whole story," he said. "It'll take a little time, but it will be worth your while, I promise."

I'd like to have been able to claim I had something better to do on my birthday than listen to an old man reminisce, but I didn't. And besides, there wasn't much I wouldn't sit through for a chance to earn twenty thousand clams.

"So, you'll sit and listen," he said, watching me as I mulled it over.

"All right," I said, after hesitating just long enough to get back a little hand. "But only if I can switch to a different chair. This one is swallowing me."

After I had dislodged myself from the chair and settled on the sofa to listen, the old man brought his hands together prayer-wise in a kind of satisfied and grateful gesture. Then he interlaced his fingers, closed his eyes, and inhaled one long, calming breath, as if deciding where exactly he should start. When he opened his eyes again, he began:

"I suppose I should first tell you about how I met my wife. And I can't tell you about her unless I tell you how I came to be standing on the roof, ready to jump. It's a little embarrassing now, and I'd like to say I was young, but compared to you I was already an old man at the time. It all began in the winter of 1986 . . ."

4

Halley's Comet was passing overhead somewhere, obscured by high clouds, the night David Hadley's mother passed away. She had been too young to see it when it had last visited in 1910, so despite its having returned twice in her lifetime she had never set eyes on it and never would.

And neither would he, David thought, standing at the care center window and not yet knowing that his mother had drawn her last breath on the bed behind him. She was seventy-eight years old. David was fifty-one. When he turned and saw her open mouth and blank stare, he did not call for help. Cancer had done what cancer does and there was no help to be had. He simply closed her eyes and sat beside the bed, holding her hand until the last bit of warmth had drained away, leaving her fingers cold in his.

Well, he thought, I guess I'm next.

And he really couldn't wait to join her in that dreamless sleep. Besides his having just lost his mother, David's life was a first-rate mess. He was divorced, exhausted, out of shape, and depressed. He had been diagnosed with an anxiety disorder, but he suspected, at least in his case anyway, that this was just a vague label they used instead of diagnosing him as a terminal loser. He had told the doctor as much — asking why he shouldn't feel anxious when something terrible seemed always about to happen and usually did — but his doctor's answer had been another prescription for Noveril, which David added to the others lying in his desk drawer, unfilled.

David worked for a Seattle accounting firm in the newly constructed Columbia Seafirst Center. It was the tallest building on the West Coast, yet David's seventh-floor cubicle had a view of nothing except the office bonus board, which showed him behind everyone else in billable hours each month. He liked to tell himself it was because he was thorough in his work; he knew it was because he hated his job. David spent his days auditing inventory reports for the firm's industrial clients, pursuing numerical representations for various pieces and parts he would never see and didn't care to

58

understand through an incalculably large labyrinth of colorless spreadsheets. But there was no spreadsheet big enough to add up his regret, and after work, on nights when David did not visit his mother, he would stop into the state-run liquor store on his way home and buy a bottle of Southern Comfort.

"You know it's cheaper if you buy the fifth or the half gallon," the clerk would almost always say as he rang up David's usual pint and stuffed it into a paper sack. But David was an accountant and he knew this wasn't true — because he'd drink however much he bought and be back for more tomorrow anyway. He wasn't an alcoholic, though — no, he was a failure even at that — because he had quit before and he knew he could quit again at any time. It wasn't his drinking that worried him, not at all. Rather, it was what he might do for relief instead of drinking once the booze stopped working.

With the bottle tucked deep inside his coat, David would walk through the Seattle drizzle the rest of the way back to his apartment, looking down at the sidewalk and avoiding the eyes of passersby. Once home, he would settle into his chair and watch the rain slide like sadness down his window, sipping his SoCo straight from the bottle to slake his thirst for freedom from his own miserable thoughts, a welcome, albeit brief, relief.

Sometimes he would turn on his small TV and watch *Cheers* or *Miami Vice*. Later, he might stumble outside to the all-night convenience store for a half gallon of ice cream and a pack of cigarettes. It was not uncommon in those sad and lonely days for him to wake the next morning on his sofa with the television still on and his naked chest covered in a sticky amalgamation of Southern Comfort, Breyers Mint Chocolate Chip ice cream, and Marlboro ashes. On especially depraved mornings, there might be a finger or two of melted ice cream left, and he would pick out the cigarette butts, tip the container to his mouth, and drink it for his breakfast.

In addition to antidepressants, David's doctor had been suggesting cardiovascular exercise for years, and he ignored this prescription just the same as the others. There was a gym across the street from his office, but the people inside always looked like hamsters in a cage to him. Plus, as he reminded himself each morning as he passed it by, there was no reason to put his humiliation on display. It was David's mother who convinced him to finally take his doctor's advice. "Please, Davy," she had pleaded from her care center bed. "If you won't do it for yourself, at least do it for me. I couldn't go on without you." He knew by then that at the rate her cancer was advancing he would outlive her even if he took up dodging city buses for exercise, and she knew it too, but he agreed anyway just to ease her mind.

His doctor had suggested climbing stairs, and what better place to find them than the seventy-six-story Columbia Seafirst Center, where he worked? So while Halley's Comet was still working its way around, and while David's mother was still alive, David began dragging himself off his couch each morning, knowing that when the workday was over he would change in the office bathroom, ease into the stairwell, and begin his daily torture routine. His doctor was thrilled when he found out, of course. He even said it would help with David's depression. And his doctor was right, but not in the way he thought.

David had hoped the stairwell would be empty and he had not counted on the health-conscious employees descending from the lower floors on their way to the garage or out to catch buses in the street. But by the third week he had progressed to higher floors, where he discovered a wonderful solitude, having the entire stairwell there to himself — nothing but his own steps echoing off the concrete walls and his own thoughts echoing in his throbbing skull. The fact that he was getting progressively healthier brought him no peace and seemed rather like an accidental side effect of the promise he had made to his mother. Something did change however: he began to look forward to his workouts, if for no other reason than a subtle but growing form of sadism. He even began to relish his nightly drinking again, sometimes taking the clerk's advice and swapping his usual pint for a fifth, simply for the extra bit of suffering the hangover added during his afternoon climbs. It was pure torture — and in his mind, he deserved it.

The exceptions to this routine were the days he went to see his mother. It was reading to her in her bed — usually "Laughter, the Best Medicine" from *Reader's Digest* or "Letters to the Editor" from the Sunday *Seattle Times* — that spared him on weekends when he might have otherwise had no stairs to climb and nothing at all to interrupt his sorry self-loathing and bingeing on ice cream and booze. But comets are always on the move, and so is cancer, and then his mother died, and with her died the last of his reasons to do anything at all, including climbing his stairs. Or so he thought.

Much to his own surprise, just four days after he laid his mother next to his father in the family plot, David was back in the stairwell again. Maybe because he didn't know what else to do, or perhaps because he had come to enjoy the company of his echoing steps and the hollow pounding of his tired heart, which seemed to beat like a drum calling him toward death. He often begged with every third or fourth step for his heart to give out, for the pain to be through. But the human heart is hearty, even when broken, and his was stronger than he knew.

Despite his heart's commitment to cling to life, David often thought about suicide. The idea had occasionally crossed his mind over the years. He had even written a suicide note once, a decade prior when his wife had filed for divorce. But that had been little more than a cry for help and a poor pass at punishing his wife for wanting a child so much she'd leave him for a man who could give her one, especially a man who had supposedly been his friend. But this time was different. The death of his

63

mother and the absolute loneliness he felt afterward, along with the fact that he had no one left to even write a farewell note to, made the odds of his seriously attempting suicide much greater. And as the idea grew daily in his thoughts, so did a strange and dangerous ritual.

Each day, around half past five or so, David would find himself standing on the top stairwell step of the Columbia Seafirst Center, drenched in sweat and wondering if today was the day that he would finally die. You see, he had begun checking the roof access door, hoping to find it open. Each time he lifted his tired foot onto that last step, he'd reach for the handle, close his eyes, and make a silent promise: if he ever found it unlocked, if the door ever actually opened, he would walk straight to the roof's edge and jump off. It was a silent wish for freedom, a kind of personal and daily prayer for relief. And if nothing else, it was a coin toss to see if he really did want to die.

When David was a young boy, before the accident that killed his father, every Friday evening they would all three pile into the front seat of his father's pickup and go downtown to eat together at the local diner. "Life is too damn short to not splurge a little now and again," his father would always say. And each time after dinner David would find himself torn between his two favorite desserts on the menu: baked chocolate pudding or the "world famous" Riley's marshmallow pie. It was a tough decision for a boy with a sweet tooth, but other than once on his eighth birthday when his mother had allowed him to order both, he had to choose one.

His father would haul out a quarter and toss it into the air, then catch it and slap it down on the worn yellow Formica tabletop, keeping it covered with his flattened hand. "Heads or tails for pudding, Son?" But the point was not to order the dessert that won the toss. The point was to find out which dessert he really wanted. "Because," his father would tell him, "if you say tails for pudding and tails wins, you'll always know by your first gut reaction if you really wanted pie."

And so it was now with suicide. Each time David reached the top stair, he'd put a hand on the roof access door lever and close his eyes, taking a deep breath and telling himself that if it opened he would jump. And each time it didn't open he felt a surge of disappointment. The coin toss never lied. But because the door was always locked, he could not be entirely sure how he would feel were it to ever actually open onto the roof. Until the day that it did.

A little over two and a half months after his mother's passing, while his coworkers rushed home to huddle around their TVs and watch news coverage of the Chernobyl meltdown trickling in reluctantly from overseas, David was having his own meltdown in the stairwell he had come by then to haunt. His mind was racing faster than his heart, and not one thought was good. He felt panic taking over, the stairwell closing in, and his claustrophobia got so bad he stopped off on the fifty-fifth floor to puke in the bathroom. He hid for several minutes in the stall, just sitting on the toilet with his head down between his knees and chanting, "Enough, enough, enough."

When he finally got up from the toilet to leave, he caught his reflection in the bathroom mirror and stopped to look at the stranger he had become. His face drooped, more from hopelessness than from age. It was not an unhandsome face, but he could not see this at the time. Nor could he see that it was a thoughtful face, with features almost too delicate for a man. His face, the one that lived inside his mind and heavy heart, was the face of a thirteen-year-old boy.

Prior to thirteen his features had not existed to him at all — other than as a means of seeing, smelling, hearing, and tasting the world, of course. But with puberty blossoming at thirteen, he began spending long mornings in front of the bathroom mirror, warring with pimples or hunting for the first signs of a whisker, and he came to know his face. And that was the face he expected now to see. That was the face he had been looking at in the truck's rearview mirror when the other car came into their lane. That was the face he had been looking at when he should have been looking ahead at the road. That face became the face of a regret he could never outgrow, staring at it ever after with shame and silent judgment in countless subsequent mirrors, and hearing again and again his father's final words: "You drive, Son. I'm tired."

He and his mother had taken over his father's small antique business then, once David had recovered and his father was in the ground. His mother handled the sales and restorations, and young David handled the accounting. It was this tragedy, in fact, that had led him to his current career. Strange how little in life we actually choose for ourselves, David thought.

And now, all these years later, standing in

a bathroom on the fifty-fifth floor, David knew with equal conviction that he had gone terribly off track. He was certain he had taken a wrong turn somewhere, perhaps on that fateful day, but the tangled intersections of the past would yield no clue as to how he might right his course, and the relentless march of time offered him no hope of ever returning to start again. So here he was, standing in the mirror and looking at a stranger.

These were just some of the thoughts rattling around in David Hadley's tortured head as he looked in the mirror. They were still on his mind when he returned to the stairwell, and they grew in amplitude with each floor. When he reached the last step and grabbed for the handle of the roof-access door, his mind was an echo chamber of regret. But by this time David had come to expect that the door would be locked, and he no longer bothered making his silent promise. The result of neglecting this, of course, was that he had no idea how he really felt when the handle turned and the door swung open.

It was a damp and dreary Seattle afternoon and all he could see outside the door was a wall of gray. It seemed like purgatory waiting. His heart pounded in his heaving chest, and he was suddenly aware that he was soaked with sweat. Is this a wake-up call or a gift? he wondered. He thought back to all those days when the door had been locked, and he remembered how disappointed he had felt each time. Then he thought about the stairs leading down, the walk home, the liquor store again, the empty apartment, the mindless TV. Finally, he thought about the stranger's face in that mirror. "This is your chance," he told himself. "You may never find this door open again."

David lifted his foot and stepped across the threshold onto the roof. There was not nearly as much wind as he thought there should be at such a height, and he walked slowly and methodically, crossing the rooftop toward the edge. He had doubts, of course — who of even the most depressed among us wouldn't? — but each step was a silent vote for following through. And although he had expected to feel nervous, his breathing and his heart rate actually calmed the closer to the edge he came. Then suddenly he was there, with a woozy head, wobbly knees, and a whirling stomach. There was a wide, foot-tall rail, a kind of bulkhead covered with metal flashing, and he sucked up his fear and stepped up onto it and looked straight down into the gray.

A thick fog had rolled in from the sound, and only the tops of the highest buildings rose above it, piercing the fog and creating the impression of a disconnected ghost city floating on a cloud. But the city was not floating, and he knew that were he to lift his foot once more, just one easy step after all the others in his life that had been so hard, the ground would come rushing up through the fog to meet him, putting an end to his imponderably pathetic life. And in a mercifully short amount of time too, he thought. He guessed about six seconds. And because he was an accountant, he was close to being right.

He closed his eyes and imagined he had already jumped:

One one thousand — the roof falling away — two one thousand — accelerating fast — three one thousand — exhale your last breath — four one thousand — faster yet — five one thousand — fractions of a second left — six one thou— Cut to black!

Then that would be it. No more seconds; no more regret. Just death. Just endless nothingness. Just the absence of living. Nothing to be fearful of at all, he thought. It was, after all, a state he'd existed in, or not existed in, for billions of years before he had been born. A little voice inside his head rose up from some dark and baleful place where it had been hiding his entire life, apparently waiting for just this kind of moment. "Here's your answer at last," it said. "Here's the one thing at which you cannot fail. The one decision you cannot second-guess. Take the step, my man; accept the relief. I know you're nervous. Don't be. It's easy. Trust me. Just lean forward and physics will take care of the rest."

David felt his quads twitch and flex as he leaned out, as if his muscle fibers themselves knew what was coming and were protesting. Second thoughts fought to save his life, but corporeal doubt was no match for the certainty of his spiritual pain, and feeble reason was no match for the voice. "You're brave, my man. I always knew you were. That's it. Just a little bit farther."

Then his head went quiet and calm washed over him. For the first time in a long time he felt fine. So this is all it took, he thought. Freedom had been waiting here all along. All he had needed was an opportunity and the resolve to follow through.

He leaned out, attracted by the gravity of relief and the promise of a rush toward quiet bliss. His eyes were still shut, his knees trembling — *no, maybe, yes*. He knew he had decided when the chatter of his thoughts stopped altogether and his lips curled into a smile. He had found a solution at last.

Now willfully, he inhaled his last breath.

Leaning out into the void.

No fear left.

He felt his stomach lift, his legs going limp. Then he heard another voice, this one quite different from the other, and coming, it seemed, from outside his head:

"You can't change your mind halfway down."

David opened his eyes, saw the fog beneath him, and panicked. His arms came out instinctively and began flailing in the cool damp air, the gyroscopic thrust arching him, pulling him back, steadying his precarious stance on the ledge. Then he looked to his left, from where the voice had come, and saw a woman standing next to him. The adrenaline coursing through his system had his brain firing double speed, but even so, or maybe because of it, time seemed to have slowed, or perhaps stopped altogether, as it sometimes does for those who have come to the end of a life and have only moments left with which to contemplate it. And although David was mildly aware in some remote corner of his mind that he was still standing on a roof ledge nine hundred feet plus above the street, all he could think about was this curious creature standing next to him with the peculiar and enchanting smile.

It was the most mysterious smile David had ever seen. Although it was not so much upon her mouth as it was contained within her eyes. It was a smile at once intimate and elusive, familiar yet strange. Her irises twinkled with ironic exuberance from within the folds of the tanned and crinkled skin that surrounded her eyes. He could not tell their color. He could only tell that they seemed to be illuminated from within and altogether too bright for the gray light in which they both stood, side by side now, on the quiet roof. She was gazing idly out at the city below them, as if the two of them were nothing more than old friends enjoying the view. She was slight of frame, almost birdlike in her build, and yet she was somehow anything but small. He could not have guessed her age. She appeared both impossibly young and utterly timeless. There were deep lines etched on her face, but they contrasted so sharply with the youthful energy in those sparkling eyes that he would have believed her had she claimed to be either side of seventeen or seventy-five.

All of this ran through David's mind in mere moments, of course, and when he finally realized that he had not actually jumped, and that this woman was not an apparition come to visit him in death, he opened his mouth and in a nervous, high-pitched voice that sounded very out of place considering the circumstances, asked her the only sensible question that came to mind: "Do you work here in the building?"

"Only today," she replied, very conversationally.

His gaze dropped to the Building Maintenance logo on the breast pocket of her jacket. The jacket was blue, and she wore a blue backpack that matched it so perfectly he only saw it because the straps crossing her chest bisected part of the white lettering. None of this would have seemed out of the ordinary had he not glanced farther down and seen that she was not wearing any shoes. She had on khaki cargo pants, the kind hikers often wear, and their bottoms were cinched tight around her thin ankles, showing off her sockless feet. David noticed that three of her toenails were pink, as if she had started painting them but had given up.

"Are you planning to jump?" she asked.

David lifted his gaze back to her face. She was looking directly at him. Her eyes were still smiling, but they seemed to him to contain something else now too. Possibly concern, he thought, or perhaps just curiosity.

"Ah, well, not really," he stuttered. "I was just looking."

He wasn't quite sure why, but he stepped back down off of the ledge. Her head turned to follow him, but she did not move. She was eye level with him now.

"It's nothing to be ashamed of, you know."

"I'm not ashamed," he said. "I have no reason to be ashamed."

This was an enormous lie of course, because he was ashamed about everything and he wore it like a neon safety vest. But she did not challenge him. She only smiled more deeply with her eyes and said, "Good."

Good. The way it rolled from her mouth gave it much more meaning than the word itself. *Good.* As if she were telling him with that single syllable that he was right to not be ashamed, and that he never should be, ever. *Good.* As if the word itself was a reason to live.

"Are *you* planning to jump?" he asked.

"Oh, I never know what I'll do anymore

75

until the moment comes and I've done it. Although I guess it did take a little planning to get the door unlocked today, so it would seem a shame to waste all that effort."

He felt his heart sink. Part of him had thought that maybe she had come to convince him that jumping was a bad idea, and his realization that she might be as suicidal as he was stripped him of even this little glimmer of hope.

"So, you do mean to jump." It was a statement more than a question, for he already knew the answer. Somehow, he knew.

"I sure as hell don't want to hike down all those stairs," she said. "It was a real trek just getting up them. No, I think jumping seems the faster way down."

He began to panic. Was he talking to a lunatic? Should he restrain her? Call for help? He knew he was in no position to give advice on the subject, but at least he hadn't been so cavalier about jumping to his death.

"You mean to tell me you'd rather jump than walk down stairs? That's your reason for wanting to die. Are you mad?"

"Why of course not, silly," she replied. "I'm not jumping because I want to die. I'm jumping because I want to live."

"You want to live?"

He was feeling rather confused, naturally.

"Yes, I want to live," she said. "And so should you."

"I should?"

She nodded. "I think so. Don't you?"

"But you don't even know me," he said.

The smile in her eyes deepened. "I think I know you better than you think."

Something about the way she looked at him made him believe that maybe she did.

"But what if there doesn't seem to be any point to living?" he asked.

He detected a subtle nod of her chin, a momentary look of sadness, as if she understood his statement all too well. But then her lips curled at the corners and her eyes took on their sparkle again. "Maybe there is no point to life," she said, "except falling pointlessly in love."

This caught him off guard, and for some reason he blushed. Then he felt the old resentment rise, the one buried deep in his guts that he only took out on special occasions when he wanted to simultaneously feel sorry for himself and hate his ex-wife.

"I know for a fact that love has killed more people than it's saved," he said.

As an accountant, of course, he knew damn well that this likely wasn't true and certainly couldn't be proved, but he said it anyway. But if she disagreed with him, she chose not to argue over it. She simply shrugged it off and said, "You're so cynical." As if that were news. As if he hadn't just been about to kill himself. "Besides, what if life and death aren't separate things anyway?" she asked.

"What do you mean, 'aren't separate'?" His mind was working overtime to keep up.

"Well, what if they're just sides of the same thing? What if death is not the opposite of life, but rather the one part that gives all the rest of life its meaning? I'm not saying it's so. But what if it is? What if you have to let go of your life to truly live it? Wouldn't that give you an edge on the rest of the world, knowing that, now that you've looked into the abyss and stepped back from the ledge?"

On some subconscious and metaphorical level David thought maybe he understood what it was she meant. As a suicidal accountant standing on a roof, however, her words confused him greatly.

"Let go of life to live? That sounds a little clichéd and a lot hopeless."

"Maybe," she said. "But hopeless can be a good place to start again."

A cold wind came up and pressed against his back and he suddenly felt unstable, and surprisingly, especially to him, afraid of falling. They were after all on the edge of a very high building. The wind seemed not to worry her, however. In fact, it hardly seemed to touch her slight frame, and only the ends of her hair danced in the cold breeze. His mind raced to make sense of what was happening. He glanced behind them at the open stairwell door, then back to her. He wanted to say something thoughtful, but words betrayed him. Then he realized that while they had been talking she had actually stepped closer to the edge and her pink toes were hanging over. He recalled her first words to him, and as if his having taken that one small step down off the bulkhead had somehow reversed their roles, he repeated them now.

"You can't change your mind halfway down."

Her face lit up once again with her mysterious smile, and she held him suspended in her eyes. He knew then that she would jump, and that he was powerless to stop her.

"Make me a promise, will you, darling?" she said.

David was lost for a response, hung up on the intimacy of the word *darling,* but she went on without waiting for an answer anyway.

"Don't make a choice today that your future self can't undo. Please, promise me. We all owe ourselves that. We all owe the child inside of us at least a chance to be forgiven by the man or woman we're destined to become."

He was shocked by her familiarity and her insight. Had she been in the bathroom with him when he looked into that mirror? Had she been reading his mind here on the roof? Perhaps he had jumped after all, he thought, and this was just some crazy imagined conversation occurring in the last milliseconds of brain activity as he smashed at a hundred miles an hour into the sidewalk below.

"Promise me," she said again.

"Promise you that I'll give myself another chance?"

"Yes, exactly that."

Something about her eyes made it impossible to do anything but agree — and not just agree for the sake of agreeing, but to actually agree and follow through.

"I promise," he finally answered.

"Good," she replied, the simple word filled again with hidden meaning.

Then, having secured his promise, her

eyes released him. One moment her smiling eyes had offered the intimacy of a lover — "darling," she had called him — and the next moment they had withdrawn into themselves as quickly and coolly as two flames being turned down in their lamps. She was still standing there with him, but he felt suddenly helpless and alone on that roof. Then she turned her eyes away.

With one quick and powerful motion that reminded David of the uncoiling of a spring, she leaped away from him and out into the gray. He lunged forward to grab her, but he was too late and only the bulkhead saved him from falling over after her. His heart sank and he felt like puking again. He was afraid to look down. Then he heard a thick whoosh of air followed by a sharp snapping sound, and he leaned over and saw a bright-yellow smiley face grinning up at him from the top of her parachute canopy as it disappeared into the fog.

"I'll be damned," he said aloud.

Then she was gone, and he was once again alone.

5

I had been reclining on the sofa with my legs crossed, and the old man's tale had held me so captivated that I hadn't even noticed that they had fallen asleep until I took advantage of a pause in his story to stretch and nearly fell onto the floor.

"Are you okay?" he asked, seeing me stumble.

"I'm fine," I said, shaking it out. "Where did you say the bathroom was again?"

"Just down the hall there on your left." He reached for his cane and started to rise. "I'll make you some more tea."

"No thanks," I said. "The one cup seems to be working as advertised."

I didn't think I was away that long, but when I returned from the shitter the old man was gone and there was a glass of water and a plate of sliced apples on the coffee table in front of where I had been sitting. When Mr. Hadley reappeared, he was carrying a plate of apple slices for himself and a glass of milky liquid that I could tell tasted terrible just by how it looked.

"I thought you might like a little snack," he said, indicating the apples with a nod. He set down his plate and took up his cane to lower himself into his chair again. "I'm supposed to take my medication with food, but an apple's about all I can stomach any longer before noon. That and MoonPies."

"Thanks," I said, biting into an apple slice, then adding quietly, "Just what I need after that Smooth Move tea too, more fiber."

I said it under my breath but I could tell he heard me because he laughed. I guess those hearing aids worked pretty well. Then he said, "It's a lovely sound, isn't it? The crunch of an apple. Have you ever heard a horse eat one?"

"No, I don't think I have."

"Well, maybe later we'll go out and feed one to Rosie."

"You have horses here?"

"Just Rosie. I've managed to place all of the other animals elsewhere, but Rosie's blind and she's been rather bad off since her seeing-eye horse passed away. She can't eat a whole apple at once any longer, on account of her missing teeth, but she still loves them. June spoiled her something terrible

83

and she almost expects one every day. Won't touch a carrot, but she sure loves apples."

"If you don't mind my asking, where will Rosie go?"

I didn't say it exactly, but by "where will Rosie go?" I meant when the bank foreclosed. He seemed to understand, though, anyway.

"She'll be gone by then," he said.

"Yeah, but where?"

"Who can say until they get there," he mused, with a bit of a twinkle in his old eye.

He pulled his bridge from his mouth and picked a piece of apple peel free that was caught in its wires. Then he smiled at me with no front teeth. "Don't get old if you can help it, kid. You start losing pieces of yourself. What doesn't fall out, they want to cut out. Of course, of everything I've lost I probably miss my mind the most." He laughed at his own joke and slapped his knee. Then he reinserted his bridge and picked up his drink. He winced when he sipped it. I knew it tasted bad.

"Are the apples enough for you?" he asked. "I have some microwave dinners."

I assured him that I was fine, and he leaned back in his chair. Then he smiled again, this time with all his teeth.

"Shall I continue with my story then?"

"Sure, but I do have a question. I'm assuming that was your wife, June — the lady on the roof with the parachute. But I'm curious why she wasn't wearing any shoes."

"That's a good question, Elliot," he replied. "A good fine question. And I wondered the same thing. Especially after I found her boots . . ."

6

He found her boots sitting neatly together on the top step just inside the roof access door, with the socks stuffed inside. Why she had left them there before jumping he could not have guessed at the time. Perhaps they had been part of her disguise, he mused, or perhaps she had planted them as a kind of false clue. They were old worn hiking boots in men's size nine, and they were much too large for her feet as he remembered them. He was quite shaken by the encounter, and it eventually occurred to him as he squatted there that he should probably disappear before being discovered, so he scooped up the boots, tucked them beneath his arm, and hurried off down the stairs.

The headline in the morning newspaper read:

DAREDEVIL DOLLY
BAREFOOT BASE JUMPER
STRIKES AGAIN

Witnesses on the street had watched her land. A few claimed to have seen her running around the block and climbing into a waiting car, although what make or model none could say. She was described by some as being extremely short, and by others as being unusually tall, but all could at least agree that she had been barefoot, appearing like a vision from the overhead fog and touching down in the street with the nimble grace of a sparrow, before gathering up her parachute and vanishing just as quickly as she had appeared. Speculation in the article ran wild: "She's a communist spy." "She's doing it for nuclear disarmament." "No woman would dare it, I say; she must be a man wearing a disguise." "She's a fame seeker." "Thrill seeker." "She must be Scandinavian; only a Swede would be crazy enough to jump from a building in the fog."

The next day the papers had moved on.

But David Hadley had not.

Their rooftop encounter had rattled his psyche more than a little, and no sooner had he descended to his office cubicle, concealing her boots quickly beneath his desk, than he found himself already obsessed with finding her again. He wanted to see those smiling eyes; he dreamed already of hearing her call him "darling" one more time. Plus, he should thank her, shouldn't he? She had, after all, narrowly saved him from suicide. But mostly he wanted to seek her out because he found himself pondering what exactly she had meant when she had said, "What if you have to let go of your life to truly live it?"

She had said much more in their brief talk, he knew, but these were the words that had echoed in David Hadley's mind as he stood on the ledge, watching her drop away into the fog. And now he had to know how it felt: falling like that, rushing toward certain death, then choosing at the very last second with the pull of a cord to live. And, like everyone else, including the news-papers, he also had to know why.

If there was a positive side to his new obsession, it was that David no longer thought about suicide. Nor did he stop at the liquor store on his way home ever again. Instead he would walk to the library after work and spend evenings with his face pressed close to the blue screen of the microfiche machine, searching for a picture or a name. There were several prior jumps reported in the newspapers — one from the Space Needle, after the painting crew had inadvertently left the roof access hatch unlocked; one from scaffolding on the famed Smith Tower; and another from a communications antenna atop Queen Anne Hill — but no one had a clue as to her identity. Investigators had only recently decided, after several eyewitness accounts and the aid of one hastily shot and grainy tourist photograph, that the jumper was actually a she. Which left them to wildly hypothesize as to why a pair of men's size-nine boots were left behind at the scene of each jump — with the exception of the most recent one, of course, since David Hadley had those boots sitting now beside his bed.

He was not proud of it, but because he had no one in his life to hide anything from he was not ashamed either, and each night before going to sleep, David would take the socks from the boots and hold them to his nose as he drifted off to sleep. The fragrance was of wool and leather and a hint of something else too — something subtly sweet that reminded him of summers as a boy. He was not sure why he smelled her socks like this. Many months later, when it was almost too late, he would come to understand that it was because he already loved her. He had resigned himself that day on the roof to falling nine hundred feet to end it all, but he never would have guessed he'd fall much farther in less than the time it took to turn and look into her smiling eyes. All he knew for sure was that he had to find her again.

An awkward visit to the Seattle police department armed with a poorly concocted lie about an old college friend he was trying to locate landed him the number to a local sketch artist. He went to see her the following day. But although he sat with her in her studio for most of an afternoon, all he seemed able to recall were the stranger's eyes.

"And you say you knew her well, huh?" the artist asked.

"I guess not as well as I thought," David replied.

He walked out with a sketch of her eyes floating on a page, a wise and knowing smile without a face. It looked less like a portrait sketch than it did a rendering of a Buddhist symbol someone might have wanted tattooed on his or her arm.

David would sit in his bed at night, propped up against the headboard with her socks in his lap, holding the sketch before him, staring at the eyes and trying to animate her from his memory upon the page. And as with anyone who looks for any one particular thing long enough and doggedly enough, he eventually came to see not what was there, but what he wanted to be there instead. He saw her so clearly one evening he retrieved a pen and began tracing in the rest of her features. By morning, of course, his sketch looked nothing like the way he remembered her, and he quickly whited the pen lines out, making a promise to himself to only mark it from then on with pencil. Which he did each night as day by day his obsession with finding the Barefoot BASE Jumper grew.

Being an accountant, he made a spreadsheet outlining what it was he knew about her. She was an expert with a parachute. She had a disregard for the law. She had a thing for men's shoes. He guessed her age to be close to his own, but of this he was still unsure. She had had tan toes. Tan toes, yes, and three of the toenails were pink, he remembered. He wrote it all down. Anything beyond these general facts, however, he hadn't any clue. And he seemed to be losing hope of ever learning more. Then late one night, while his list-in-progress rested on his nightstand and her socks rested in his sleeping arms, he woke from a dream and sat bolt upright in his bed.

"The door was unlocked!"

Early the next morning he was in the building maintenance office, waving his drawing in front of the super's face.

"I know it was you," he said. "Who else has a key to that stairwell door?"

"Lots of people do," the super replied, casually sipping his coffee and looking over the mug's brim at David with an expression somewhere between curiosity and fear.

"I'm not with the cops, I promise," David went on. "And I'm not interested in telling the papers who she is either. I work at Caldwell and Strong on seven, and you can verify that in the directory. Look, here's my building access card."

The super waved the offered card away, reaching instead for a clipboard on the desk and holding it out for David to see.

"This here's the list of everyone with keys to that door. You can see yourself there's two dozen companies. Whoever your Daredevil Dolly turns out to be, her little stunt just made my job a lot harder. From here on the locks are changed out and everyone wanting up has to come to me. I hope you find her, fella. And when you do, you tell her I ain't at all happy. You hear?"

That was on a Friday. Saturday he found himself at a parachute center housed in a small airport north of Seattle. He spent an hour there harassing the woman who maintained the flight manifest with his drawing. "Sir," the woman finally said, her patient eyes melting slowly into pools of anger, "the weekend's our busiest time, and I'm afraid I've told you four or five times now: nobody here knows anything about the Barefoot BASE Jumper."

Just for good measure, he held the sketch up one last time.

"You're sure you don't recognize her?"

"Looks a lot like a young Bette Davis to me," she said. When David sighed, she added, "Or maybe Cybill Shepherd."

"Those two don't even look anything alike," he said.

"Hey" — she shrugged — "it's your drawing, buddy."

Another weekend, another parachute center, another disappointment. He was quickly running out of hope. Despite causing him frustration, however, David's obsession was improving his life. He was out meeting new people, even though it was to harass them with his sketch; he was sleeping more, because dreams were the one place he could clearly see her face; and he was becoming more efficient at his work, if only to be able to leave the office early in order to continue his quest. He even saw his name slowly climbing up the office bonus board for the first time. But none of this mattered to David. All he could think about was finding her.

But not even the strongest of attractions can be maintained in a vacuum, and as the scent faded from her socks, his enthusiasm for the search began to wane. He found himself feeling lonely again, spending long evenings cooped up in his apartment with only the TV for company. He had replayed his rooftop conversation with her in his head a thousand times, recalling the promise she had extracted from him to give himself another chance. And it was this promise that kept the thought of suicide from crossing his mind again. But he was sinking into a depression just the same.

Then one evening he saw an ad for the local humane society on TV, and he began to cry. He wasn't quite sure why; maybe he saw himself in the sad puppy's eyes. The next day, a Saturday in early June, David was driving home from having his first colonoscopy — which had left him feeling more than a little vulnerable, even though the prognosis had been all clear — when he passed by the humane society and recognized its sign from the commercial. He pulled over and went inside. The dozens of sad faces staring out at him from their cages immediately overwhelmed him. No way could he do it, he told himself. No way could he be responsible for another living creature. He could hardly take care of himself and he knew it. But he also knew that his shrinking from anything that resembled responsibility had been a recurring theme for him since the day his father had died.

The woman at the front desk looked defeated when he told her he had changed his mind. So defeated in fact that David asked if there might be some way other than adoption that he could help. He had meant something along the lines of a financial donation, and had even taken out his checkbook, but much to his surprise, she waved the check away and asked him if he had a driver's license instead. And so he began his days as a doggy driver, taxiing terriers and chauffeuring shih tzus all over the city, logging long hours each weekend on the road, delivering the little yapping companions to new, if sometimes temporary, homes. He hated it, or so he claimed. But in truth it was the best thing

95

to ever happen to him.

He would address the little faces in his rearview mirror as they looked out through the bars of their carrier doors. "You want to listen to the radio?" he'd ask. "Do you prefer classical or jazz? Neither? Okay, stop barking. I turned it off." He went as far north as the Canadian border, and as far south as Portland, and even though he was loath to admit it, he began to look forward to these drives, and to his furry companions, finding it more and more difficult each time to say good-bye. Then one day a doggy delivery forever changed his life.

It was on a Friday, the fourth of July, when he left the office to pick up a cocker spaniel, having no idea that he would not return to his job for several weeks. He picked up his yapping companion and drove it south to Puyallup, fighting traffic to reach his destination before the fireworks began. Arriving at the puppy's new home, he lingered for just a moment in the foyer, being welcomed by the licks of a half dozen dogs, when he once again laid eyes on the face he had been dreaming about all this time. He walked without a word into the kitchen and stood staring into those smiling eyes.

The flyer was hung from the refrigerator by a fruit magnet, and it read: "Even racehorses deserve a happy retirement." It was an advertisement for an animal rescue called Echo Glen, and in the picture on the flyer she had her arm around the neck of a horse as it ate grain from the palm of her hand.

David reached into his pocket for his wallet and pulled out the worn and tattered sketch he had carried with him all this time. He unfolded it and held it up. Yes, he thought, if nothing else, he had in fact captured her smiling eyes.

"It's lovely work they do up there at Echo Glen," the homeowner said, appearing beside David at the refrigerator. "And it's not just horses. They rescue dogs, cats, goats, and all sorts of other animals too. Have you been out there yet?"

"Do you know who she is?" David asked.

"Of course," the woman said. "Everyone knows June."

June. So that was her name. June. June. June. Yes, it even sounded right.

"May I take this?" David asked, reaching and pulling the flyer free from its magnet without even waiting for a response.

He drove home beneath the colorful bursts of fireworks, but he hardly saw them at all; his heart was bursting with an excitement brighter still. He was half tempted to keep going when he reached Seattle and drive to the address on the flyer, but he decided against it and spent a near-sleepless night in his bed, reaching countless times for the lamp so he could pick up the flyer and look again at her face.

The next morning he was up before dawn and in the freeway fast lane, heading north out of the city. In the seat next to him he had the flyer and a map. When he finally arrived at Echo Glen, the gates were open, but he hesitated in the street with his blinker on, too nervous to turn up the drive and too committed to turn back. But as so often happens, fate made the decision for him in the form of a honking lumber truck barreling down on him in his rearview mirror. He turned in and drove through the gates.

It was a beautiful property, with gorgeous orchards and sweeping fields cut through by a clear mountain creek. The road turned at a fence line and led him up past barns and stables to a circular drive at the end of which stood the house. He took a deep breath, climbed the steps to the porch, and rapped on the door. He must have stood there for a long time; he must have felt his courage draining away with each unanswered knock. Maybe it wasn't meant to be, he thought. Maybe she wouldn't want to see him.

He was returning to his car when he heard voices from beyond one of the barns. Deciding he'd come too far to turn back so easily, he went to investigate. When he rounded the corner, his heart leaped in his chest. But yours would have too.

Beyond the barn was a barren circle of dirt and in the center of the circle stood a man on fire. The man was staggering about like a fire-engulfed zombie, helicoptering his flaming arms. But he was not alone. There were other people circled around him, watching. Watching, but not helping.

David rushed into the circle, stripping off his coat as he pushed through the idle spectators and wrapping it around the burning man to smother the flames. It was a heroic image, the two of them embracing there in the dirt circle with flames licking up between them. Then someone tackled David to the ground and he heard the hollow *whoooosh* of a fire extinguisher. Then someone yelled, "What's hot?" And he heard the reply, "Nothing. Nothing. I'm fine." And then someone was pulling him to his feet and shaking him by the shoulders, asking, "Are you crazy, comrade?"

David could smell gasoline and his own burned hair. He was standing in the center of the circle and all eyes were on him. Slowly, very slowly, the way a Polaroid picture might develop, he began to see what was happening.

The man who had been on fire was peeling off his protective clothing and mask. Men beside him held fire extinguishers. The rest of the group stood staring at David with smug, satisfied expressions, as if they were enjoying his discomfort — looks David recognized from decades ago when he was in school; looks that could have only belonged to students.

"What were you thinking, comrade?"

The man asking him the question had a firm grip on David's shoulders and was looking right into his eyes. He was tall and thin, with dark eyes and dark skin. He spoke with a slight accent. David thought he might have been Mexican, but he was Spanish.

"I wasn't thinking," David said. "I just saw someone on fire and I acted."

The man appeared as if he were about to chastise David, but then he caught himself with his mouth half open and cocked his head, as if considering David's answer. Then he smiled. "You know, comrade, that's a satisfactory answer. Most satisfactory." He released his grip on David's shoulders and reached up to take his face in his hands, just for the briefest of moments. It felt like a sign of affection to David. Then the man turned and addressed the gawking crowd. "Students, what you have witnessed here was courage in action. Action devoid of thought. The body and the mind fused into one. You have seen displayed the very nature of what I have been teaching you."

The students all began to nod, as if they'd known this all along. There were nearly a dozen of them, mostly men, with a few women sprinkled in, and they all looked to be half David's age. The young man who had been on fire was just getting his last leg out of the burn suit, and he stepped over and shook David's hand.

"That took real courage, dude. Sorry about your jacket."

David looked down and saw his coat smoldering on the ground. "Oh, it's fine," he said. "That old thing."

"Students," the instructor said, "you've seen true bravery, a rare thing in this world. Now, please help me welcome our new student."

"It was nothing, really," David said, blushing. "Wait. Me? A student?"

The instructor stuck out his hand. "I'm Sebastian."

"Okay. Yes. Sure. Hello. I'm David."

Sebastian's handshake was firm but friendly, and he didn't immediately release David's hand. Instead, he held on to it and said, "There can be no indifference between courageous men such as us. We will either be great enemies or good friends."

David had no idea at the time just how true this statement would become. All he knew was that he was very, very confused.

"But for now," Sebastian went on, "we are student and teacher. Come with me and we will get your paperwork sorted out." Then he turned to address the students again. "Practice your high falls, but keep an eye on one another. We'll be back *en un momento.*"

Before David could even protest, Sebastian put an arm around his shoulder and led him away toward a trailer. "It's nice to have a mature student," he said once they were inside and sitting down across from one another at the small desk. "The others will look up to you. Especially after your fiery entrance."

David looked around the cramped trailer. There were diagrams and drawings of falling dummies and choreographed fights and detailed car crashes covering the walls. Sebastian opened a desk drawer and took out a pack of cigarettes. He offered one to David, but David declined. Sebastian shrugged and lit one himself. "We had begun to worry you wouldn't show, like the others," he said, blowing out smoke. "It means a lot to the camp and the sanctuary that you've come. We need the press desperately to help us raise money."

"I'm sorry," David said, "but I seem to be a little confused. Do you happen to know the woman who runs the animal rescue? Echo Glen, I mean." He pulled the flyer out of his pocket and unfolded it on the table. "Her," he said, tapping his finger on the picture. "Do you know June?"

Sebastian took a drag from his cigarette. The way he had his elbow on the table and his cigarette held up near his head looked very European to David, if not a little pretentious. He barely glanced at the flyer. "But of course I know June," he said. "How could I not?" Then his eyes hardened and his face dropped into a frown, as if he had suddenly tasted something sour. "I can see that you're like every other newspaperman, chasing the easy headline. Too good to talk with me I suppose. You only want June because she's the one in the Stuntmen's Hall of Fame." He took another drag, then leaned forward and blew smoke out his nose as he spoke. "I will be inducted someday, comrade. You can bet your lousy newspaper career on that."

David was more confused than ever. *Newspaperman?* Surely not him. *Stuntmen's Hall of Fame?* He hadn't any idea that there even was such a thing.

"I'm sure you will be," he said. "But if I could just maybe talk with her for a moment, with June. That would be great."

"That's quite impossible now," he said, stubbing his cigarette out in the ashtray on the desk. "But she will be glad to see you finally arrived when she returns." Then he opened the drawer again and took out a packet of papers and laid them on the desk in front of David. "Please, sign these waivers."

"Waiver?" David asked. "You need a waiver?"

"Of course. We want you to have the real experience, don't we, now? Everything from a student's point of view. Besides, you'll need to be enrolled before you can see June. She's much too busy to talk with a reporter who isn't serious this time. We've had others not follow through, you know. Now, please sign if you would. I must be getting back before one of those monkeys breaks their skull."

David looked down at the papers on the

desk in front of him. Printed on the top in bold capital letters were the words: ECHO GLEN HOLLYWOOD STUNT SCHOOL, LIABILITY WAIVER. Below the title there was an italicized quote: *"Let go of your fear and live your dreams."* He couldn't have explained at the time why he did it. Maybe because Sebastian had mentioned several times how June would be glad to see him, even though David knew it wasn't really him she was expecting. Or maybe it was the quote about letting go of fear, which reminded him of their rooftop conversation. Or it could even have been the adrenaline from his brush with the flaming man that was still clouding his mind. Whatever the reason, David picked up the pen, printed his full name on the form, and then signed it. That was easy, he thought, even though he was now impersonating a newspaperman.

"Very well," Sebastian said, pulling the signed form back across the desk. "Now, about your payment for the three-week course."

"My payment? And did you just say three weeks?"

"We wouldn't want your reporting to be biased, now, would we? The authentic student experience. And, after all, comrade, about the fee: the whole point of the story is raising money for the animals, you see."

Five minutes later David was two thousand dollars poorer and already second-guessing his decision to play along as Sebastian showed him the bunkhouse where he was supposed to sleep. They had converted an old barn into barracks with what looked to be foldout army surplus cots lining the walls. David suspected the cots were as uncomfortable as they looked since it appeared that many of the students had taken to sleeping on a giant pile of hay. Their blankets and bags were strewn everywhere.

"You know what," David suddenly said, "I completely forgot my bag. Would it be all right if I drove home to get it and returned tomorrow?"

Sebastian shrugged. "Suit yourself, comrade." Then he patted his shirt pocket, where he had tucked away David's check. "You paid already. We start an hour past sunrise. *Nos vemos en la mañana.*" He walked off and left David standing there, pausing only briefly to turn back at the barn door. "And, comrade," he said, "don't forget to bring your mouth guard and your cup."

"Mouth guard. Cup. You mean, like a personal drinking cup?"

Sebastian laughed. Then he reached down and grabbed his crotch. "No, comrade, a cup to protect your tender *cojones.*"

7

I laughed so hard at that last part that I almost fell off of the couch — mostly because Mr. Hadley had half risen from his chair to grab his crotch and deliver the *co-jones* line with a Spanish accent. He really could be quite theatrical. Between his storytelling and that crazy rooster song-and-dance he'd put on earlier you'd have thought he was an old vaudeville man long before you'd have ever guessed he was an accountant.

"You didn't go back, did you?" I asked, once I'd gotten over my giggle fit.

"You'll have to be patient and hear the whole story."

"Okay, okay," I said. "But at least tell me who they thought you were."

"A reporter for the *Times*," he said. "June was expecting one, although he never showed. She had hoped a newspaper story would help boost enrollment."

"So, the stunt camp was like a business she ran?"

He nodded. "But its main purpose was to raise funds for her true passion: rescuing animals. Well, animals and people. She had arms big enough to hug the entire world. Say . . . you didn't finish your apples. Aren't you hungry?"

I looked down and saw that my apple slices were all brown. Truth is, I was hungry as hell. I'd just been so wrapped up in the story that I'd forgotten all about them. There was a cat clock on the wall and it meowed just as its tail pointed to noon.

"Tell you what," he said, seeing me glance at the clock, "if you don't mind moving into the kitchen I'll make us some lunch."

The kitchen was on the south side of the house and it had a little dining room nook built right up against the window. The sun was coming in. It was nice. Mr. Hadley went to work, taking down pans and dishes and opening drawers and generally just making a lot of noise. He did everything pretty slowly and methodically, like old people sometimes do. I noticed that his hands shook a lot. I offered to help, but he shooed me away, so I walked around and admired the watercolors that were on the walls.

They were all over the house. Some of

them looked pretty good; others looked like maybe a child had painted them. I really liked one of them a lot, though. It was a painting of a waterfall coming down a mountain glen. There was a little hill with an oak tree on it that overlooked the whole scene. The sun was hitting the hill. It really was a gorgeous painting.

"Who painted this one?" I asked.

He had the stove going and was opening a can of soup. He didn't even look up to see which painting I was asking about. He just said, "My wife."

It made me wonder who had painted the other ones, the ones that looked kind of like they'd been done by a kid. They weren't bad, just sloppier. But I really liked that waterfall.

By the time he finished preparing our lunch, he had made a royal mess out of the kitchen. I got the impression he didn't cook for two that often. I asked again if I could help him, maybe by cleaning up before we sat down to eat, but he waved dismissively at the mess, as if it were no big deal. He really was a character, this Mr. Hadley. He had made us grilled cheese sandwiches and tomato soup.

We had just settled into the nook — which was no small task given that he had to go back to the living room to fetch his cane first; you could tell he didn't like to use it with company around, but he really did need it — when he took one look at my bowl and said, "Shoot." Then he went through the whole process of hoisting himself up again. What he'd forgotten was the garnish. I'm not kidding. He went into the kitchen and came back and dropped a tiny sprig of fresh thyme or something into each of our bowls. "There we go," he said. "Perfecto." Then he lowered himself into his seat again. I didn't dare fish the thyme out and put it on my plate like I usually do with that stuff. Instead, I had to push it around in my soup the entire time to avoid eating it.

But forgive me, please, for boring you with the travails of uneaten garnish. We have a love story to get back to.

8

When David arrived the next morning, with his mouth guard and his cup, it was still very early and the camp had not yet woken up. There were several old picnic tables near the bunkhouse and he sat at one of these with his duffel at his feet and contemplated the likelihood that he was making a huge mistake. He didn't have any paper to do a proper spreadsheet, but he could hazard a fairly educated guess.

The sounds and sights of the farm were very different from those of the city. He heard horses neighing in their paddocks across the way. Smelled a tinge of manure. A rooster crowed. The sun was up. Birds were singing. Oh, come on, David, he thought, stop being so negative and cynical all the time. After a while an old three-legged Labrador retriever trotted over from somewhere and licked his hand. It sat at his feet and he leaned over to scratch its belly.

Its leg started kicking. Then David spoke to it using the puppy voice he'd honed while driving for the humane society: "You like your belly scratched, boy? Is this how June does it? Does she scratch your fuzzy wuzzy belly just like this? Maybe she'll show up any minute and scratch your belly, and mine too! Wouldn't we be a couple of lucky old dogs?"

Then, all at once and without warning, the dog got up and hobbled away, the bird-song ceased, and everything got quiet, even the horses. It was as if they had sensed it was coming. The chanting, that is. Suddenly, speakers mounted in the bunkhouse eaves blared to life — "Ooga-chaka ooga ooga ooga-chaka!" It was deafeningly loud, and David nearly jumped up off the picnic table where he sat. It was the intro to "Hooked on a Feeling," of course, and the music would have been enough. But there was more.

The exterior hayloft door in the gable end of the bunkhouse swung open and Sebastian stepped out onto a makeshift balcony and began singing along into a battery-operated bullhorn. It reminded David of a crazy clock he'd seen on a German palace during a year he'd studied abroad, except Sebastian was singing with a Spanish accent and the figure on that clock had been wearing more than just underwear. Between the underwear and the look of his wild, slept-on hair, David assumed that the hayloft must have been Sebastian's apartment.

The music blared on, Sebastian sang along, and the students began appearing one by one from the bunkhouse, blinking into the sun and rubbing their tired eyes. The following morning David would be among them as they emerged, and he would wake up to this same crazy ritual — only the song seemed to change daily — three more times before he'd even set eyes on June. And then, when he and June did finally come face-to-face again, David would be in such an embarrassing and compromised position that he'd almost wish that they hadn't.

It was a Thursday, his fifth day in stunt camp, and his fourth day calling in sick to work — which he didn't feel too bad about because although he wasn't really sick, he had told his boss that he felt like he'd been dragged behind a horse, which he actually had. No amount of stair climbing could have prepared him for stunt camp, and he ached in places he hadn't even known could ache. So far he had jumped from a scissor lift onto air-filled mats, beginning at three feet and working his way up to thirty; run a gauntlet of smoke and been launched from a piston-fired platform over an old burning car; fought off swashbuckling opponents with a broadsword that weighed more than he had when he was young enough to have been playing at such games; and even jumped through a breakaway window into a big pile of hay. Plus the horse-dragging incident, of course, which was too embarrassing to ever fully tell of. About the only thing he hadn't done yet was be set on fire, unless you counted that mix-up when he had first arrived. But it wasn't his singed brows that had him feeling embarrassed when he finally saw June. No, it was much worse than that.

Sebastian called it stunt camp's crowning act. "Wire flying, comrades," he said. "It's the future of stunt acting. Flying fighting, coming everywhere to theaters near you." But if it was flying fighting they were supposed to be learning, then David wondered why in the world he needed to wear a Peter Pan costume. Worse yet, a Peter Pan costume that was four sizes too small. David figured it must have been a kind of initiation — in fact, that was the only reason he didn't object — because each of the students had to put on the silly tights and green vest, hat too, before being hoisted up into the rafters of the big red barn to fly from the hayloft. The goal was to swoop down and grab an egg from a basket of them balanced on a classmate's head. The trouble was, you had to rely on the person, or persons, manning the wires.

It took David so long to squeeze into the costume — finally giving up on the belt altogether and settling on closing just one button on the vest — that everyone was waiting and watching as he reentered the barn for his turn on the wire. Even more embarrassing, it took two of them to hoist him up. When he was finally in position, he stood on the edge of the hayloft and looked down at the basket of eggs on the unlucky girl's head. Her expression was no show of faith in David's dexterity, and her eyes were half closed already as if she were preparing to be yolked.

"Sing the song, comrade," Sebastian called, holding his arms aloft. "Sing the song and fly."

David frowned down from the hayloft, shimmying around in the harness to try to take a little pressure off his already aching legs. He was wearing his cup and his mouth guard, just in case.

"Do I really have to sing?" he mumbled.

"Come now," Sebastian replied from below. "You are my comrade in courage."

"But what does the song have to do with Peter Pan?" he asked with a noticeable lisp due to the mouth guard. "And what does Peter Pan have to do with eggs?"

Sebastian looked insulted. "It's a stuntmen's tradition, comrade. And besides, Peter Pan is my own personal addition. The costume belongs to June. She's played him many times."

"Well, thank you for the extra layer of humiliation," David mumbled to himself, wrenching down the vest to cover his belly where it had come exposed. He didn't want to do it, but the tights and harness were cutting off the circulation in his legs and he feared if he didn't get it over with he wouldn't be able to go at all. So he flapped his arms as he'd been instructed and sang as best he could with a mouthful of plastic.

We had an old hen that wouldn't lay eggs, until that sly old rooster flew into our yard and caught our old hen right off her guard . . .

When he had finished the song, David plucked up his courage and sort of half-stepped, half-dove from the hayloft platform. He was surprised at how easy it was and how great it felt. He had dreamed of flying, but here he was really doing it.

117

The students manning the wires guided him deftly through the air, and he swept in a gentle arc across the barn, passing over, although just out of reach of, the basket of eggs. But that was fine. The first pass was practice anyway, he reminded himself. He'd have another chance when he swung around. Or so he thought.

Because he had passed over everyone on his first flight and was now facing away from them, all he saw was daylight from the opening barn door reflected on the wall ahead of him, and all he heard was Sebastian saying, *"Hola, señorita!"*

The two students manning the wires must have gotten caught up in the excitement of whatever was going on, because they ceased what they were doing altogether, and instead of making a nice swooping turn and coming back around again, David stopped midflight and swung there like a pendulum, hanging from the rafters in the center of the barn. He heard a conversation happening behind him, although not well enough to make any of it out, since he was busy flailing his arms and kicking his legs to turn himself around on the wire so he could see what was going on.

When he did get turned around, he saw the backs of the students' heads, including the one with the basket of eggs he'd been aiming for, and he saw the back of Sebastian's head too. In fact, the only person facing him was June. She was listening to something Sebastian was telling her, but her eyes kept darting above his head to where David was hanging. Then she began to giggle. She even lifted her hand to her mouth to try to contain it. Sebastian turned around and looked up at David. He appeared surprised to see him still hanging there.

"Oh, my apologies, comrade," he said. "I forgot you were still flying." But rather than instruct the students to let him down, Sebastian turned back to June. "This is your reporter, *señorita*. This is David Hadley." He held up his hand in a broad theatrical gesture, as if to present David to her, where he hung in his tights, bulging in the harness and the silly Peter Pan vest. The hat had fallen off somewhere during his flight, thankfully. David's face flushed. He felt like a piñata hanging there, and he half wished the students would pick up sticks and start hitting him. It couldn't have been worse.

He opened his mouth to say hello, but somehow during his flight, or perhaps just because he was hanging nearly upside down, the mouth guard had shifted considerably and what came out instead sounded like, "Heh-whoa dare."

But at least June didn't laugh at this final humiliation. And if she recognized him from their encounter on the roof all those months ago, she showed no sign of it. She didn't even let on to Sebastian that he wasn't the reporter she had expected, if in fact she knew it at the time. Instead, she just smiled up at David with her wise and knowing eyes. He thought he saw a sparkle of recognition in them, perhaps a hint of humor too, and the intimacy of the shared look was so enchanting that for a moment, anyway, he didn't even care that he was hanging from the rafters in tights.

"Charming to meet you, David," she said, bowing slightly and extending her hand. "You do make a very lovely Peter Pan. Now, if only you had appeared at my bedroom window like I wished when I was a little girl." Then she turned back to Sebastian and said, "I realize it might be tempting for you to hang our reporter out to dry, since they do it to us all the time, but for the love of Wendy, please put the poor man down." And then she turned on her heel and strode from the barn.

David watched her go with a mixture of embarrassment and glee. They did eventually let him down, of course, and he spent the next several days stalking June as she worked with the animals around the farm.

He would wait for an opportunity — usually when one of the other students had done something unsafe and was being scolded by Sebastian, most often in Spanish, which nobody understood — and then he would slip away and try to find her. It was a large property with many outbuildings; the stunt lessons took place away from the rescue animals, so when he found her David would have to pretend he'd been sent by Sebastian on some errand. He suspected that June was onto him, though, since he'd returned on this particular afternoon to the stables to ask for various bits of tack more times than could have possibly been necessary, even if they had been working with horses that day, which they weren't. But he did finally manage to strike up a conversation with her.

A yearling filly that had been born blind and abandoned by its owner had just arrived, and June was spending quite a bit of time acclimating it to its new surroundings. She was brushing its coat and humming to calm its nerves when David crept back into the stable.

"Need another halter there, do you, darling?" she asked.

"This one you gave me wasn't big enough," he said.

He was a terrible liar.

"Oh, is that so. You must be working with Scamp then, since that halter's plenty big for any of the others." When David nodded, she grinned and added, "Well, perhaps you should bring Scamp up with the halter then since he's in the stall there next to you."

David just nodded again. "Oh, sure," he said, hardly hearing a word she had said. "Sounds good."

She was captivating to watch. He could have stood there and looked at her forever, despite feeling like she saw right through him — although she still hadn't acknowledged whether or not she recognized him. She hadn't mentioned anything about his supposedly being a reporter either.

June giggled quietly and shook her head. "The halter's over there, darling. In the tack room. Just swap them out."

When he came out of the tack room with the bigger halter, June had settled the young filly down and was feeding it grain from her hand. She caught David watching her and waved him over to her side.

"Do you want to pet her?" she asked.

"Don't be shy, she needs to be socialized."

David shook his head, but June ignored it.

"Give me your hand."

She took his hand in hers and placed it on the filly's head. The black velvety hair was soft and warm against his palm, but it was June's hand on his that made him shiver with excitement. He couldn't explain it exactly, but he felt magnetism in her touch. There was life churning inside of her, fighting to get out, and it made her vibrate with a sort of contagious energy. She was looking at the filly, but he was looking at her. He couldn't seem to look away for a moment.

"See," she said, "there's no reason to be afraid."

"No reason to be afraid?" he asked, coming out of his trance to realize that her hand was still on his, guiding him as he stroked the filly's head.

"That's right," she said. "Especially not of horses."

"Maybe if you haven't been pulled through a six-foot pile of fresh cow shit meant for fertilizer, like I was by that crazy quarter horse the other day," he said.

"Oh, Lord" — she let a chuckle slip — "I heard. That was you?"

He could tell she was trying to contain

her laugh. He had noticed while watching her that she was a little vain about her teeth. They weren't terrible, just somewhat crooked, but in a cute way, he thought — although she seemed to try to hide them. He wondered if maybe this was partly why her smile was so much in her eyes. He had first noticed it as he watched her talking with a visiting veterinarian the afternoon before. They were telling one another jokes, he assumed, and whenever June laughed she kept her lips sealed tight, holding it back, keeping it in, until her head would finally tilt back and her mouth would open and let loose the most captivating laugh he had ever heard. It was a beautiful thing to hear and see. So beautiful one might follow her around just waiting for it. Which, of course, was exactly what he had been doing.

But this laugh she seemed to contain as much for David's wounded pride as she did for her own vanity, and when it had passed, she said, "Don't feel too bad. That Billy's a five-gaited horse: he's got Gallop, Stop, Turn, Buck, and Drag. Our comrade Sebastian put you on him for some fun, I suppose. You just have to get back on and let him know who's boss."

"Oh, I plan to," David said, trying his best to sound rather brave. "And if he tries to buck me again I'll play a round of horseshoes while he's still wearing them."

June laughed, out loud this time.

"You should put that line in your newspaper article," she said.

His hand was still on the filly's head and June's hand was still on top of his, and she looked up at him with a closed-mouthed grin, waiting for a response. Did she recognize him from the roof? he wondered. Or was she only aware that he wasn't the reporter he had claimed to be? He couldn't be sure which; she was impossible to read.

He decided to risk it, although what he ended up saying sounded more cryptic than he had planned.

"It wasn't just a cry for help, you know."

"Oh, I know, darling," she immediately replied. "Who would have heard you from way up there anyway?"

So, she did know. She knew and she had just been waiting this whole time for him to say something; she'd been watching him follow her around from barn to barn with his seemingly endless need for lead ropes and halters and bits, but knowing all the while that what he really wanted was to speak with her about that day on the roof.

"I'm glad you're keeping your promise," she said.

125

She even remembered their conversation.

David nodded. "I guess I'm lucky you were there."

Her smile deepened, this time making its way down to her mouth. "Maybe lucky. Or maybe you were exactly where you were supposed to be that day, and perhaps I was too."

A moment of understanding passed between them. At least David thought it did. But then she removed her hand from his and stepped over and turned on the hose to fill the watering trough of a neighboring stall. His hand was still on the filly's velvet head, but June's was gone, and he felt as though she were gone too.

He turned to say something to her, something more about that day on the roof, but her back was to him now, and in addition to monitoring the water, she was busy scooping grain into feed bins. It was almost as if she had gone directly back to work, forgetting their conversation as quickly as it had happened, forgetting that he was even there.

David lingered for an awkward half minute or so before he took up the halter from where he had hung it and eased out of the stable without a word. He thought about their conversation a great deal that night.

He would have thought about it more the following day too, except that was the day the busload of hippies with a wounded ostrich arrived, and the day he first learned what it felt like to really fly.

9

It was a terrible place to leave off telling the story, it really was, but I'll be damned if the old man hadn't fallen asleep right there at the kitchen table in midsentence. He had just segued quite eloquently from his encounter in the stable with June to telling me about a bus full of young hippies who had arrived to drop off an injured ostrich they'd been traveling with — you'll have to wait for the story; I was just as curious as you are — when his chin dropped to his chest and he started snoring.

I was worried at first, before I heard him snoring. Like maybe he'd up and kicked the bucket on me or something. I've had a lot of crazy stuff happen on these pre-foreclosure visits, but no one's ever died. One guy in our office had a homeowner set the house on fire, then try to lock him in it. But that's a story for another day.

With Mr. Hadley snoring, I didn't know

what to do. I noticed he had hardly touched his sandwich, although a drying ring of tomato soup clung to the white whiskers surrounding his lips. Sleeping like that, with the soup around his lips, he looked more like a little boy than an old man. I decided I'd try to clean up the kitchen, if I could do it without waking him. It was kind of out of character for me, but I really had wanted to help when I'd offered before.

I carried our dishes to the sink and began washing them, stealing glances at my sleeping host and being careful not to make too much noise. There was a window over the sink and it looked out on an apple tree beside the house. If you had to wash dishes it was a nice view. I was looking at the tree, focusing on being quiet, when the phone rang. I nearly dropped a plate. I turned around, but Mr. Hadley had not woken so I stepped over and caught the phone off the wall midway through the second ring.

"Hello." I cupped my hand over the mouthpiece to muffle the sound.

"Yes, hello, Mr. Hadley," the voice on the other end of the phone said. "I'm calling from the department of planning about your cemetery inquiry."

"Oh, no. I'm not . . ."

Just then the old man opened his eyes and

looked at me. I felt more than a little awkward standing in his kitchen on his phone speaking to someone who thought I was him. He looked down at the table, as if searching for the missing dishes. Then he looked back at me.

"Hello . . . ," the phone said in my ear. "Mr. Hadley?"

I hung it up. I'm not sure why, but I just did. I guess I panicked.

"Who was that?" Mr. Hadley asked, fully awake now.

I didn't want to lie so I answered as honestly as I could. "I don't know, he didn't say his name. I didn't want to wake you. I'm sorry I answered your —"

"It's fine," he said. "I get wrong numbers calling almost every day. And people selling siding or awnings or Lord-knows-what. They really are pushy. Sometimes I talk to them if I'm bored. You might be surprised to know that you can keep one of those time-share salespeople on the line for a good four hours before they'll give up and call someone else. She never did send me my prize, now that I'm thinking about it. Say, where'd my sandwich run off to?" he asked. "I hadn't touched it yet."

After we had finished cleaning up the kitchen together, despite his trying to shoo me off again, he softened an apple in the microwave and chopped it into slices. I was worried that they were for us — I'd had quite enough fiber already — until he squeezed on a little lemon juice and said, "She's blind as a beetle and can't really tell if they're brown, but I prefer them to look nice when I feed them to her."

Then I thought maybe they were for June — since her whereabouts were still a mystery to me. But he dried the apple slices in a paper towel and handed them to me to carry, then grabbed his cane and walked me out to the barn.

The barn was across the drive and down a bit, at the edge of a field. It was even more weathered than the house, with only a few remaining flakes of red paint clinging to its exterior walls. The big door was already slid half open on its tracks and I followed him inside. It was dim and smelled of hay and moist dirt. Shafts of sunlight filtered in through old skylights that had been mended and covered over with green tarps.

"I don't bother to turn the lights on anymore, since Rosie's the only one left and can't see a thing anyway," he said. "I came out here once in the middle of the night to check on her in a storm, and every bulb was burned out, it had been so long since I'd turned on the switch. Have you ever heard a thunderstorm from inside an old, empty barn? You don't know whether to feel awestruck or forsaken. It's quite a sound. June and I spent the night in a barn once, waiting out a rainstorm. But I'll get to that later."

By the time he finished talking we had arrived at the last stall. He hung his cane on a hook and slid the stall door open, almost without thought, as if he had done it a hundred times before, even though the effort appeared to take a lot out of him. An old black mare was lying on her side in the back of the stall. Her head was lifted, as if she'd heard us coming. Her eyes were milky white. David entered the stall and signaled for me to follow. I held the apple slices out on the towel and he took one and fed it to the old horse.

"Not exactly the crunch of a fresh-picked apple, is it?" he said, feeding her another. "But then she hasn't got many teeth left, have you, you old dame, you? Just like your partner here. Gumming up our boiled apples until we return to fertilize a new crop."

Then something happened to me: a revelation of sorts, or, more accurately, a massive realignment of the world as I knew it, occurring in just an instant. It had only happened a few times before. One of them being when my father opened that package from my mother, the one with her picture, and I suddenly knew, even at that young age, that she wasn't ever coming home. The other being when my father died and I stood looking at him in his casket. There have been very few moments as momentous as these in my life, but this was one of those times.

I was standing there with that paper towel and those apples in my hand, watching Mr. Hadley feed them to Rosie, and I suddenly knew this was the yearling filly that June had laid his hand on in his story, and I knew this was probably that same barn too, maybe even the same stall. Now here they were, all these years later, the old man and the old horse. It was the first moment I truly grasped that time will catch up to each of us, as it must with all things, and I wondered where I would be standing thirty years on, what I would be doing.

I stood in the trance of this epiphany, this revelation swirling around me with the stirred-up dust, and when I came to my senses, the old man had his hand on Rosie's head and they were both watching me, although she could not see.

"Here, you feed her one," he said, nodding toward Rosie.

I stepped closer and squatted to feed an apple slice to the old mare. She slurped it up, then licked me as if to get familiar with this new hand delivering her treat. Then she sighed a heavy, hollow-sounding sigh, and I could see her ribs in the low light, beneath the slick black coat.

"This is the same horse that June was caring for, isn't it?" I asked. "All those years ago. The filly in the stables."

"Yes," he said, nodding. "She was just a yearling then."

I was suddenly curious about June again — maybe because I was getting impatient; maybe because that call I'd answered about the cemetery was still on my mind — and I turned to Mr. Hadley and said, "Is your wife . . ." I almost said *dead,* but I caught myself and changed it at the last second: "I mean, is she still around?"

The old man closed his eyes for a moment, sighing, not unlike the horse. "Sometimes I think so," he finally said. Then, as if suddenly very tired from standing, he stepped over and reached outside the stall for his cane and used it to lower himself onto a bale of hay in the corner. He looked as though he wanted to speak, so I sat on the hay next to him. It was quiet for a minute. Dust swirled in the dim light. The horse let out another heavy sigh.

"She really was something," he said. "My June was. I wish you could have met her." He had his hands folded over the cane where it stood in front of him, his moist eyes turned up to the skylight. "I wish everyone could have met her. She had a contagious optimism."

"What happened after your conversation with her here in the stables?"

"Is that where I left off telling the story?" he asked, glancing over at me.

"Actually you had just started to tell me about a busload of hippies with an injured ostrich. But mostly I was curious about you and June."

He laughed. "I'm not surprised. Even hippies with an ostrich are hard-pressed to compete for attention when it comes to June. Everyone who ever spent five minutes in her presence was ready to follow her to the end of the Earth. Or, I should say, off the edge of a cliff, as was the case with me that night those hippies arrived . . ."

10

Sunday was wild-card day at stunt camp and the students had voted to do high jumps. A young woman they called Hollywood Heidi was up on the scissor lift and saw it first. She pointed and said, "There's a pink bus tearing up this way."

They all turned to watch as the bus barreled up the drive in a wild rush of spitting gravel, followed by a cloud of dust. It came to a rocking halt in front of the house. The windows were covered over with old curtains and cardboard signs with slogans like LOVE IS A WAY OF LIFE, and you could not see inside. But you could sure hear.

There was a wild ruckus emanating from the bus's interior. It sounded like someone was being murdered. The noise progressed from the rear of the bus toward the front, and the students all stood watching the door and wondering what on earth would emerge, David among them. As the noise grew even more absurd, Sebastian stepped in front of his students and held out his arms, as if he would protect them. His courage, as it turned out, was not just talk.

When the bus door finally opened, a man popped out with a kicking ostrich in his arms. Although from David's point of view, it appeared more like an ostrich popped out with a kicking man clinging to its back. The bird was that big. The man had long dreadlocks and was dressed in a tie-dyed robe with tassels, and he came away from the bus turning in wide circles like some kind of carnival dancer, trying to keep ahold of his crazy catch. Several pale and dirty faces appeared in the bus's doorway, looking out. "Help him," one of them called. "That giant turkey's tryna kill him."

There was blood on man and bird alike, although it was hard to tell from which it had come, and David didn't understand why he didn't just set it loose. He was about to suggest as much when Sebastian said, "This is our time, comrade. Men of courage must act when called upon."

The next thing he saw was Sebastian rushing in to save the day. He came alongside the hippie, getting his arms into the mix and helping to subdue the fighting ostrich. Of course, as so often happens when one tries to help, the hippie took advantage of the offered aid by passing off his problem entirely, and he let go and stumbled back toward the safety of the bus, leaving Sebastian holding on to the wild bird.

"Help, comrade!" Sebastian cried. "Help me!"

David looked around at the other students, but he knew it was him Sebastian was calling. Oh, what the hell, he thought; it can't be worse than being dragged by a horse through manure. But in that he was wrong.

Just as David stepped up to lend a hand, Sebastian unknowingly spun a half turn and brought the ostrich around to face him. Sadly, it was a very frightened bird, and David was met with two kicking claws that shredded his pants and opened a nasty gash in his thigh. Fortunately for all involved, the door to the house opened and June came rushing out.

She bent briefly over David to check his wound — he was now sitting on the gravel drive, bleeding — then she stripped off his shoe and peeled his sock from his foot. He was wearing knee-high cotton tube socks and he thought at first that she was going to use it as a tourniquet for his leg, but she left him sitting there and turned instead toward Sebastian and the still-thrashing ostrich. She threaded the sock quickly over her hand. Then she reached and nabbed the ostrich's writhing neck and pulled its head down to her level, snatched its beak, and slipped the sock over its head. Almost instantly the hooded ostrich went still. And just in time too, because at that very moment Sebastian succumbed to exhaustion and sat down with the giant bird trembling in his lap. The pair of them made such a peculiar sight that David couldn't help but forget about his injury long enough to laugh.

"What's going on here?" June asked, turning toward the bus and addressing the faces peering out. "Where did you get this bird and why are you molesting it?"

"We were only trying to help," a quiet voice replied from the shadows of the bus interior. "Tell her, Clarence."

Then the man with the dreads and the tie-dyed robe stepped, or more likely was pushed, out into the light.

"Yeah, man," he said. "We didn't know. We just found it lying on the side of the road. We thought it was dead, you know, but I guess it was just knocked out or something. It woke up and went bat-shit on us, man. Right while we were rolling down Springer Finch Road. Beatrice there was

139

driving and she knew about your place. Her mom lives in Arlington and she said you saved a baby fox or something once." Then he turned to look back into the bus. "Was it a fox, did you say?"

"No," the voice from inside the bus replied. "It was a pig. From Teddy's farm."

"Well, I was close anyway," he said. Then he turned back to June. "So, can you help it? I think maybe it fell out of a truck or something."

"Isn't he a lucky bird to have had you come along to save the day," June said.

David did not entirely understand her sarcasm, but he would later when he learned why they had picked up the ostrich to begin with. But as it turned out, the ostrich had done more damage than it had received, and by the time Sebastian and David got back from the urgent-care clinic — David sporting six fresh stitches, Sebastian just a bandaged needle prick and an earful about the dangers of tetanus — June had the big bird penned and peacefully eating sunflower seeds from the palm of her hand.

"I thought for sure you'd have gone home," she said when David joined her at the fence to watch. "Maybe given up on the idea of stunt camp altogether."

"And let my comrade Sebastian down?"

he replied. "No way. And besides, I thought you said there was nothing to be afraid of."

She laughed. "I said there was nothing to be afraid of with horses. I never told you to try to ride an ostrich." Then she reached into her other pocket and handed him back his sock. It was bloodstained and torn. "Sorry," she said.

"They come in packs of six," he said, shrugging. "But it reminds me," he added a moment later, "I've got a pair of yours at my apartment in the city."

"Is that right?" she asked. "You kept my socks."

He didn't tell her he'd been sleeping with them for months.

"And a pair of your boots too," he answered. "At least I think they're yours. They were a men's size nine . . ."

She nodded but didn't say anything.

The ostrich was pecking at her empty palm now, and she scooped another handful of seeds from her pocket.

"You want to feed him?" she asked, offering the seeds to David. "Kiss and make up maybe."

David held up his hands and shook his head. "No way. I've had enough wildlife encounters for a few days."

She laughed and tossed the seeds into the

141

pen. Then she turned around and leaned against the fence.

"I know you're not a newspaperman," she said, looking at David. "And I'm assuming you don't have any real aspirations to be a Hollywood stuntman either, even though Sebastian tells me you're getting quite skilled at high jumps."

"No," he said. "I'm just an accountant."

After several quiet seconds had passed, she said, "Well, I think it's a pretty safe bet you didn't end up here because you wanted to return my boots . . ."

He sighed, looking at the ground. "I know I haven't . . . well, I just didn't . . . I mean, okay . . . you want to know the truth, then?"

"Is there ever anything else worth knowing?" she asked.

"The truth is I've been trying to find you since that day on the roof. I even hired a sketch artist. Here. Look." He pulled the sketch from his pocket and unfolded it. The paper had been worn as soft as thin cotton and the ink was already fading. "I know it's just a pair of eyes mostly, but doesn't it look like you? I mean, kind of, right?"

She took the sketch and looked it over. But whether she saw the resemblance or not, she didn't say. David thought she looked slightly fearful as she handed it back.

"And you went to all this trouble why?"

Keeping her socks and hiring a sketch artist had not seemed at all excessive or strange to David in his solitude, but now that he had said it out loud and been asked by the object of his obsession why, he felt somewhat creepy.

"I'm sorry," he said, tucking the sketch away in his pocket. "I guess after you jumped from the roof that day I just had to know who you were."

"You don't plan to tell them, do you?"

"You mean tell the papers? The police? Of course not. No way! You think that's why I looked you up? Is that what you're worried about? Oh Lord, no. I've been searching for you because I wanted to thank you. You saved my life."

She was wearing rubber boots and she looked down and kicked some of the dried mud off against the fence. Then she hooked the heel of her boot on the rail and looked up at David again.

"No, you saved your own life," she finally said. "You're the only one with that power."

"Maybe. But until our talk I really did want to die."

"Oh, darling," she said, gently shaking her head. "Is that what you think your problem was? You think you wanted to die? That wasn't it at all."

"It wasn't?" he asked.

He had, after all, been standing on a roof ready to jump when they had met, hadn't he?

"No, dear, it isn't. If you truly wanted to die, the solution would be easy. There are a thousand ways one can die before breakfast. Your problem is that you want to live, David Hadley. You want to live but you just don't know how."

He looked at her quizzically, wondering how she knew so much about him. Then, as if reading his mind again, she answered his unspoken question.

"I once stood on a roof, just like you. I know what it's like not wanting to go on. Alone in the world, looking for relief."

"Is that why you jump with a parachute? BASE jump, or whatever they call it? Do you have some kind of death wish?"

"No. I told you already, I jump because it makes me feel alive."

"It does? But how? I mean, what's it feel like?"

"Jumping? It's like life boiled down into seconds. It's freedom. It's dying unless you choose to live. And when you do choose life, you value it. I think we all value the things we choose more than the things we take for granted, don't you? And unfortunately some people take life for granted. I was one of them."

The way her eyes lit up as she talked about jumping made David not only want to jump himself, it made him want to kiss her. But he didn't, of course. Instead, he asked, "Is that what you meant when you said I had to let go of life to truly live?"

"Did I say that?" She asked it as if she were hearing it for the first time. Then she did something so simple and so intimate it made David's heart skip a happy beat. She reached up and gently touched his cheek. "Whatever I said, I'm glad. Because you lived and you're here. And that's what matters."

The sun was low and orange, about to drop behind the hills to the west, and for one glorious moment David stood in its glow with a warm breeze against his neck and June's hand on his cheek. Then, as she pulled her hand away, he saw a glint of gold on her finger and noticed for the first time that she wore a wedding ring. He had never allowed himself to consciously imagine a romance between himself and June, except for maybe a moment ago when he had daydreamed about kissing her, but that did not stop his heart from sinking behind the hills with the sun.

"Why don't you go get changed into some pants that aren't bloody and I'll go check on the ice cream and see if Sebastian's got the bonfire started."

"Ice cream? Bonfire?"

He was still thinking about the ring on her finger.

"Of course," she said. "It's Sunday. We always have lemon ice cream and a bonfire on Sundays."

He knew he shouldn't ask it, that it would make him sound needy, but without thinking it through he did.

"Will your husband be joining us?"

She looked down at the ring on her finger for a lingering moment before bringing her other hand over to cover it. When she looked back up at him, her eyes were moist.

"No," she said. "He won't be joining us. Although I'd like it very much if he could." Then she reached into her pocket and tossed the last of her seeds in to the ostrich. "I'll see you at the bonfire," she said as she walked away toward the house.

David leaned against the fence to watch her go. And even though there were fresh seeds on the ground to be eaten, the ostrich stood eye level with David just on the other side of the fence, watching her too.

11

"So, she was married?"

I couldn't help but interrupt him to ask.

"Yes and no," he said. "Your generation really has no patience for stories, do they? It must be all those damn video games."

"I don't even play video games," I said. Which was true if you didn't count computer solitaire on slow days at the office.

We were sitting on the hay, and the sun had disappeared from the skylight and a soft rain was pattering on the roof. The horse looked to be asleep. I took my cell phone out of my pocket and checked the time — half past two already.

"Cell phones are the same thing as video games, if you ask me," he said. "Little devices for your pocket that suck your brain out through your eyes."

"Give me a break," I said. "I'm checking the time. Besides, I might want to see if I have a message or two. It happens to be my birthday."

"Your birthday! Well, I don't know whether to be flattered that you're still here or sad that you have nothing better to do than sit around all day listening to a nostalgic old man. Do you have family to get back to, Elliot?"

"No," I said, tucking my phone away. "It's just me. And I'm not very fond of birthdays anyway. So, please go on with your story. You said something about following June off a cliff but you quit before you got there."

"You mean I was interrupted before getting there," he corrected me, grinning. "But the story will have to wait. Give me a hand here, will you, young man?"

He gripped his cane and struggled to get up. I stood and helped him. He dusted off his corduroys and looked around behind him in the hay, as if to make sure he hadn't dropped anything. Then he led me from the stall.

It was raining harder now and we stood in the barn doorway, looking out at the house a hundred yards away.

"I could run up to the house and get us an umbrella if you have one," I suggested.

The old man was standing just inside the door, gazing idly out at the sky. "It really is nice, isn't it?" he asked, ignoring my suggestion to get an umbrella. Then he took up his cane, as if he no longer needed it, and walked out into the rain.

I stood there watching him go. He walked through the downpour as though he was enjoying it. When he was halfway to the house, I stripped off my coat and ran to catch up with him, holding it over his head. The only result of my belated gallantry, however, was to have us both soaked by the time we gained the porch. And as soon as we did, of course, the rain ceased and the sun came out from behind the clouds. I shook my coat out and put it back on.

"How old are you today, Elliot?"

"I'm thirty-three, sir. But I'd really rather not celebrate, if it's —"

"Nonsense, young man," he said, opening the door.

He kicked off his Clarks just inside the door. I don't know why older people love those moccasins, but they do. Maybe because they don't have laces, I thought, as I bent to untie my own shoes. He led me back into the kitchen and made me sit at the table.

"Birthdays are a big deal," he said, opening a cupboard. "And every one you're alive to celebrate is a gift."

I feared he might be planning to make a cake — after his lunch performance I could only imagine the mess — but he didn't. Instead, he took down a box of MoonPies. Then he rifled around in a drawer until he came up with a package of cake candles.

"I don't think thirty-three'll fit," he said. "We'll just do three of them."

He took down two plates and put a Moon-Pie on each, inserting three candles into one of them. Then he went on a quest for a lighter that had him searching nearly every kitchen drawer until he gave up and went into the living room and came back with a long-handled fire starter. When the Moon-Pie was finally in front of me with the candles lit, he stood back and smiled. I was very embarrassed for some reason.

"Wait," he said. "Not yet. I need to get a picture."

I began to protest but he turned too quickly and disappeared from the kitchen again. I heard a door open somewhere and what sounded like boxes being rifled through. I sat and watched the candles, trying to remember that birthday so long ago now, the one where my mother left and never came home. But I couldn't.

By the time he returned with an old Polaroid camera, the candles had nearly burned to their bases and the MoonPie was coated in dripping wax. As he fiddled with the camera, I said, "I didn't even know they still made Polaroid film."

"They don't," he replied. "But I have a stash for important occasions."

"You could probably make a fortune selling it on eBay."

"Selling it where?" he asked.

I was about to explain eBay to him, but then I remembered his take on video games and cell phones and I began to doubt that he even had a computer. That, and the candles were really getting low now. My MoonPie was covered more in wax than it was in chocolate.

"Okay," he finally said. "All set here. Now, you wait until I'm done singing and then I'll take the shot just before you blow them out."

He lifted the camera to his eye and began to sing. And as I was sitting there in that kitchen in front of that MoonPie and its three disappearing candles, with Mr. Hadley singing "Happy Birthday" to me from behind an ancient Polaroid camera, my throat got suddenly sore and my eyes welled up. It was so out of character for me that when he finished singing, I forgot to blow out the candles right away, and instead I just kind of smiled at him as he took the picture. The mechanical click and the whine of the photo sliding out the bottom was a sad but somehow happy sound. Nostalgic, maybe. I don't know. But I'll tell you straight up, I still have that photo and I look happier in it than any other, even though my eyes are wet.

By the time he sat down across from me, the candles had burned themselves out on their own and my MoonPie was now completely covered in blue wax. He set the photo on the table to develop, took away my plate, and brought me a new one. Then he sat down across from me.

"Shoot," he said again, reaching for his cane. But this time it wasn't garnish he'd forgotten; it was RC Cola. He went to the refrigerator and brought us each back a can.

"This was my father's favorite treat," he said, cracking the top on his can and taking a sip. "He grew up in the Blue Ridge Mountains of Tennessee. We drove there together once, to settle his father's estate, and we ate MoonPies and drank RC Colas the entire way. We were both sick for days."

He bit into his MoonPie and crumbs fell all over his sweater. He fished a larger crumb from his bulging pocket and ate it. Then he closed his eyes, as if remembering.

I tried mine. It tasted like a s'more to me, but the flavor brought no fond memories.

"You said it was just you," he said, in between bites. "Does that mean your folks have passed on?"

"Yes. Well, I'm not sure about my mother. She left when I was three. On my birthday, actually. Thirty years ago to the day. My dad died when I was nineteen."

"And you've never been married?" he asked.

My mouth was full of MoonPie, having just taken a bite, so I shook my head fiercely until I could speak. "No, sir. No way. And I don't ever intend to be either."

"Why not?" he asked.

"It's fine for some people, maybe, but I'm not interested in having my heart ripped out through my wallet."

"Is that how your father felt when your mother left?"

"Why would you assume that?"

He shrugged, leaning forward to look at my photo where it lay, developing on the table. "We usually inherit more than just good looks," he said, smiling. "And you already told me you got his small ears." Then he laughed. "But my guess is you just haven't met the right woman yet. Or you have and you just don't know it. Isn't there someone special at least?"

"No, not really. Well, there is this one girl I kind of like. You reminded me of her because she said birthdays are a big deal too. She even found a candle for a cupcake, just like you."

"She sounds like a smart woman," he said.

"Yeah, she is. Estrella's her name."

"I love it," he said. "Spanish name, isn't it?"

"Yeah. It means 'star.' Although I think she's part Scottish or something because her hair has a hint of red. But like I said, I don't have any interest in putting myself in a position to be hurt. And besides, I won't be around here much longer."

"That's right," he said. "I almost forgot about Miami. Well, you'll meet the right girl and come around to settling down whether you want to or not. That's how it was with June and me. Well, I knew it pretty early on, anyway — that we were meant to be together. But she didn't. It took some serious convincing on my part, some of which led us to a jail cell in Spain."

"Arrested in Spain? I'm still trying to figure out why she left men's boots behind on that roof. And where her husband is. And what was going on at Echo Glen. Plus, you haven't even told me yet about this cliff you followed her off."

"I haven't?" he asked. "Boy, I had better pick up my pace if we're going to get it all in before the end of the day. You sure you don't mind spending your birthday hearing all this?"

His question made me stop to think for a second. I didn't say it exactly, but the truth was there was no other place I would have rather been. "Maybe if you let me have another MoonPie," I joked. "Then I'll stay."

He started to rise, which I took to mean yes, so I beat him getting to my feet and brought the entire box over to the table.

"I've got a case of them in the pantry," he said. "So, don't be shy. Now, let me see, where was I? Oh, yes, the hippies, the ostrich, and now the bonfire. Then I promise I'll get to me plunging off that moonlit cliff . . ."

12

If a fire could mirror its maker, this bonfire was Sebastian: bigger than was practical, hotter than was necessary, and barely contained within the borders of the pit. The students sat circled up, riveted by Sebastian as he stood between them and the fire, just beyond the reach of the lapping flames, excitedly waving a cigarette and retelling the tale of how he had narrowly escaped death to tame the wild feathered beast, as if the students had not all stood by hours earlier and watched the events as they had actually unfolded. But they seemed to have forgotten, or they at least appeared willing to accept some embellishment for the sake of entertainment.

In the end, David too suspended his disbelief; Sebastian included him in this yarn by turning to point him out as a hero who had made a selfless contribution to the battle and who, according to his retelling —

and he was really stretching now — had narrowly escaped a severed artery and sure and sudden death. "You risked your life to save mine, comrade," he said as his speech reached a fever pitch, his cigarette waving as if it were a baton and he the conductor of his own flaming orchestra. "We are brothers in courage forever now."

David was glad to be sitting just beyond the firelight so the students couldn't see him blush.

The hippies had invited themselves to stay the night, hoping, as it turned out, to be able to take their ostrich with them the next morning, and they had pulled their bus over beside the barn and were now trickling out in ones and twos to join the others already at the fire.

"You want a hit, man?"

The one with the dreads that they called Clarence sat down next to David. David looked at the offered joint and shook his head. "That stuff makes me paranoid," he said.

"No way, man," Clarence replied. "It opens your mind and lets the moonlight in. And besides, it's not paranoia if they're really trying to get you. The government, man, they send out mind-control waves on the radio and put chemicals in our food.

That's why we live off the grid like we do. You should really join us, dude. There's space on the bus . . ."

He wouldn't let up until David at least agreed to think about joining them "off the grid," and then he rambled on with various other counterculture contrivances and tired theories of conspiracy to the point where David almost took him up on the joint just to make listening more bearable. David was old enough to have lived through the real deal and this Clarence character was about twenty years too late.

He was grateful when June finally appeared at his other side. She had a bag on her shoulder and she was carrying a large wooden tub. She set the tub down in front of her and reached into the bag and handed David a box of old-fashioned sugar cones. "You pass me the cones and I'll scoop," she said.

As if June's arrival had signaled a natural change in the order of things, Sebastian wrapped up his storytelling, the hippie ceased his pontificating, and all got quiet and scooted in closer to the fire, tightening the circle. June removed the tub's lid and produced a pewter ice-cream scoop. When she was ready, David handed her a cone. They worked like this for several minutes —

David handing over cones, June topping them with huge scoops of homemade lemon ice cream and then passing them off to travel from hand to hand around the circle until everyone had one. David noticed a few of the hippies sporting two, but there seemed to be plenty to go around, and everyone was quietly visiting and enjoying their ice cream, so no one much cared.

"This is good," David said, once he finally had a cone of his own. "It's lemony, but I'm tasting something else too."

"That's the garlic," June said.

"Garlic. That's an odd thing to put in ice cream."

"It helps keep the students from hooking up when the fire burns down," she said. Then she chuckled and licked her ice cream. "Actually, it's an old family recipe. I grew up in Gilroy, California, the Garlic Capital of the World."

"I've never heard of it," David said.

"Gilroy or garlic ice cream?" June asked.

"Neither, actually."

"I'm not surprised," June replied. "They're both easy to miss unless you're into garlic festivals. Most people just drive by on their way from the Bay Area to Monterey. Where did you grow up, David?"

"I'm not sure I have grown up," he

answered. "But I was raised just up north, in Bellingham."

"Oh, I know it well," she said. "We've got a reciprocal relationship with a few rescues next door in Ferndale. Nice place. Do you have family up there?"

"Not any longer."

He didn't bother telling her that his mother had just recently passed away. Between the fire and the ice cream, the night was just too nice to drag death into. Besides, David was just beginning to move beyond his grief.

"That's too bad," she said. "About your family." After a lick or two of her ice cream, she asked, "Do you ever get back? To Bellingham."

"Not really," David said. "Although the family house is still there, closed up since my mother got ill. Realtors keep calling me saying they have buyers. I guess one of these days I should go and deal with it." Then, both because he wanted to change the subject and because he had just noticed June's bare feet stretched out in front of her on the grass, he said, "Hey, how come you're never wearing any shoes?"

June looked down at her feet silhouetted in the firelight. She wiggled her toes. "I don't know," she said. "I guess I don't like having anything between me and the earth. My mother used to tell me that if I was going to run around barefoot all the time I should at least look like a lady and paint my toes. Sometimes I try, but I usually get distracted before I finish. But then I always did disappoint my mother."

"Is your family still in Gilroy?"

June shook her head. "Everyone's gone." A few seconds later she said, "Well, that's not entirely true. I have a sister somewhere on the East Coast, but we don't really talk. Our childhood wasn't exactly ideal. *Dysfunctional* would be an understatement. Although we did have a pair of first cousins who got along so well they got married. But seriously, about the only thing I have fond memories of is lemon ice cream."

Clarence nudged David and passed him another joint. This time David took it, but he hesitated. He looked around the fire and noticed that most everyone had finished their ice cream and that several joints and a bottle were making the rounds. The night was just too magical already to want to change it with chemicals, so he decided against taking a toke and passed it on to June instead. June passed it on too.

"You don't smoke?" David asked.

"Oh, I have," she said. "I was growing it

before these kids were born. But as I said earlier, I just prefer to have nothing between me and the earth."

The fire was finally burning down to a manageable level and the logs caved in on themselves, sending sparks circling up into the night. David could smell the burning cedar. He leaned back and rested on his elbow, looking at June. The firelight played on her face, and he could see twin miniature bonfires reflected in her eyes.

"Hey, can I ask you a question?"

"You can ask me two if you want."

"Why did you wear men's boots up to that roof?"

There was a long pause with just the sound of the fire crackling and the quiet murmur of other conversations. Then June said, "They were my husband's."

David was not entirely surprised. He'd been thinking about her husband ever since he caught sight of that ring. He sat for a moment, quietly wondering if she said *were* instead of *are* because the boots were gone or because the husband was. But he didn't need to think long because June went on to explain herself without his asking.

"They were never his really," she said. "I mean he never wore those particular boots. I get them at thrift stores. They just represent him to me. It's a charm."

She must have seen the question while it was still on David's lips, because she explained.

"You know, a good-luck trinket. A superstition. Something jumpers do. Some wear necklaces made from parachute pins. Some chant mantras. I knew one guy who pulled out a handful of hair and let it go before he jumped just to check the wind. He jumped so much he tore himself bald and had to start reaching into his jumpsuit, if you catch my drift. Anyway, with me it's boots. Size nine. Just like my husband wore."

"So, your husband's not around anymore?"

"No" — her gaze drifted off into the fire — "although sometimes it feels like he is. He's the reason I got into skydiving to begin with."

"Was he a skydiver? Is that how he died?"

"I said he wasn't around," she replied. "I never said he was dead."

David straightened slightly.

"I'm so sorry. I didn't —"

June ripped out a tuft of grass and threw it at him.

"I'm only playing with you, darling. He's passed on. And there's no need to say you're sorry either. Everyone says that. He died twenty-five years ago in a motorcycle accident."

"Twenty-five years. And you still wear his ring?"

"Geez, I know I just said not to tell me you're sorry," she said, "but I didn't mean for you to jump all over me about still wearing his ring."

"I'm sorry," he said, "I didn't mean —"

She laughed. "See, now you've gone and said you were sorry again." She held up her hand and looked at the ring on her finger, turning it to catch the fading firelight. "I guess I just never had any reason to take it off," she said. "And it hasn't seemed like twenty-five years, just like life going by one day at a time."

"Fair enough," David said. "Maybe that's the difference between death and divorce, though, because I couldn't wait to get mine off. I had gained some weight — I used to be heavier, if you can believe it — and it was stuck on. But the day those divorce papers came I spent four hours in the bathroom with a jar of Crisco and bottle of Dawn. I damn near lost my finger, but I got it off."

"Was she that bad?" June asked.

"Worse. She left me for the husband of a

164

friend of ours because she wanted a boy and he already had four with his current wife. They have some weird three-way relationship and parenting thing going on. Anyway, I don't want to know anything about any of it, really. Besides, it's been ten years."

"Wow," she said, "seems pretty fresh for ten years ago."

"Well, maybe it just felt like life going by one very long day at a time."

"Touché, David Hadley," she said, smiling. "Touché."

After a few quiet minutes where they both sat and watched the fire, alone with their own thoughts, David said, "You said your husband died in a motorcycle accident . . ."

"Yes, we were riding together," she said, without looking away from the fire. "When I noticed he wasn't behind me any longer, I turned back and found him with a broken neck. They said he didn't feel anything. Just missed a turn and wound up in a ditch. We'd been together for almost eight years, but we'd been married less than two weeks. One hell of a honeymoon, right?"

"It sounds awful. I'm so sorry."

June turned to look at him, a smile in her eyes. "Now you've said you're sorry three times." Then her face turned serious. "But, yeah, it was pretty devastating. In fact, I found myself up on a roof just like you, except I was on top of Half Dome."

"Half Dome, in Yosemite?"

She nodded. "We liked to hike there. That's where we were heading on our rented bikes. His family always blamed me. 'He never would have even been on a motorcycle if it weren't for you,' they said. Or, 'You're the daredevil, not my sweet Anthony. It should have been you.' Nice uplifting stuff like that. So, there I was about to make my in-laws happy when I saw this pair of boots just sitting there on the edge of the cliff. All alone, like someone had fallen out of them or something. Or left them there for some reason maybe, I don't know. Who can say? Sometimes when I'm in the city I'll see a pair of shoes in the street or on the sidewalk. Sometimes just one. But I always wonder what the story is behind them. There has to be a story, right? People don't just go around abandoning shoes.

"Anyway, these boots were my husband's size and they looked like some he might have worn. And then I swear he was standing there with me. He said what I told you. He said, 'June, you can't change your mind halfway down.' He was always saying stuff like that. 'You can't peel the same clove of garlic twice,' or, 'You can't be a little bit pregnant.' "

"So, you didn't jump," David said.

"Not that day. I tried to argue with him. Or with the boots, I guess. I told him I wanted to join him, wherever he was. But he said, 'No.' When I insisted, he said, 'Then at least do it with a parachute, just in case you change your mind.' So I bought a used parachute and read up on how to use it. BASE jumping was still pretty new and I couldn't find much about it, but then I was planning to die anyway, so what did I care, right?"

"So, you just jumped without any training or anything?"

"I don't advise it," she said. "Especially since I became an instructor later. But yes. I went back up to Half Dome with a used parachute I wasn't even sure had been packed correctly and had never used. And I brought those boots along too. They looked so lonely sitting there by themselves that I took my shoes off and put them beside the boots. Sometimes I wonder about the person who found them, my shoes and those boots. Must have looked like the rapture had happened."

Here she paused. The fire had burned down quite a bit now and her face was cast in shadow, hiding her expression.

"Please don't leave me hanging," David pleaded. "What happened then?"

"Then I just jumped."

"But what was it like? When did you change your mind about dying? I mean you obviously used the parachute because you're here."

"You really want to know what it was like?" she asked.

"Yes," he said, "I really do. I've been wondering since that day on the roof."

"It's a hard thing to explain to someone," she said. "You really need to experience it for yourself. Once my feet left that ledge, I had no decisions to make but one: release the lead chute and live, or hold it and die. I felt so free. Free from responsibility. Free from my past. Free from my future, if that makes any sense. I even felt free from grief. And it felt so good I didn't want the feeling to end, so I released the chute. Turns out landing a canopy is better learned from experts and not books, especially if you're going to do it on rocks while not wearing any shoes. It took me all night to hike out with a badly sprained ankle and cut feet, but I couldn't wait to do it again."

David sighed. "I'd love to feel what you described. All my life I've been carrying around this weight. And I don't mean this few extra pounds, either. I mean the weight of everything you mentioned. You know, regret and guilt and all that. Anyway, it's been so long I can't even remember what it was like before, without it."

David was propped up on both elbows, with his arms on the grass, and June reached out and laid her hand on top of his.

"You're on your way, David. You'll find your freedom. I know you will."

It was a simple gesture, and a simple statement, but it somehow made David choke up.

"Thanks," he said. "It's just so hard to let some things go."

"No," she said. "It's holding on that's hard. That's why it hurts so much."

They fell silent then, and David realized just how quiet it was. All of the hippies and most of the students had drifted off, presumably to bed, or maybe to other more private places to do what young people do. Others were napping or just watching the fire, lost in their own thoughts. The moon was full, and David and June sat together watching it rise above the treetops. He could have sat there like that for a slow eternity — June's hand on his where it lay on the soft grass, the dwindling fire warm in front of him, the night air cool at his back. But moments are special because they don't last, and she eventually rose and took up her ice cream tub.

Before she left the fire, though, David saw her walk over to Sebastian and whisper something in his ear. Sebastian got up and followed her away toward the house. David couldn't explain why, but he felt a sudden and profound sadness. He had no right to feel jealous if they were an item. He should just be happy to have friends, shouldn't he? A man like him. He wasn't entitled to find love. Not dumpy old David Hadley.

He was suddenly aware of a throbbing ache in his leg; the painkiller was wearing off. And it was Sunday, so he had missed an entire week of work already. He had been planning to call in sick again, but now he thought he'd get up early and leave. He didn't need a certificate from stunt school anyway. Who was he kidding? A little late for a midlife crisis, isn't it? he thought. Then the old voices came back. "And here you are acting like a jealous schoolboy at the age of fifty-one. Grow up, David." His mood had changed so fast he had whiplash.

He rose from the dying fire and walked back to the bunkhouse feeling more alone than he ever had. Which he thought was odd since he was sleeping beneath the same roof

170

as a dozen other aspiring daredevils, even if they were half his age. But David didn't want to feel alone any longer, and he did something that surprised him, something he hadn't done since he was thirteen. Before he climbed into his cot, he knelt down beside it and said a little prayer. He wasn't a religious man, per se, and he wasn't sure Who he was even praying to, but he did it with his whole heart.

"Dear God, Whoever You are, wherever You are, please help me let this feeling of being a failure go. I don't need it, and it has never done me one bit of good. Just show me what I need to do, if You would. Just give me a sign. Thank You. Oh, and please tell my mom and my dad that I say hello. Also, please look after everyone in this big old world and make sure they're safe. At least for tonight. And I know I'm supposed to forgive my enemies so I forgive that damn prehistoric bird that *You* made for what worldly purpose only *You* could know. Thanks. Hallelujah and amen and all that."

Then he crawled into his bunk and pulled the old wool blanket over himself. He must have fallen fast asleep too, because the next thing he knew he was being shaken awake in the dark by June. He couldn't see her, but he somehow knew who it was just the same.

"What's wrong?" he asked, sitting up in his cot.

"Keep your voice down," she said. "Put your shoes on, grab your coat."

He did as he was told. He could see her crouched near him like a shadow as he sat on his cot in the dark, tying his shoes.

"Where are we going?"

"Shh . . . no talking," she said. "The others are sleeping."

When he was ready she led him from the bunkhouse out into the moonlight. It was bright enough to see without the aid of her flashlight, which she carried but didn't turn on. June glanced back over her shoulder with a conspiratorial look on her face and the moonlight sparkling in her eyes. She looked like she was seventeen. And he felt about the same age, in a good way.

The bonfire had been built back up with fresh wood, and David saw Sebastian silhouetted against the flames as he stoked the fire with a stick, sending swirling clouds of embers up into the night. He thought the fire was where they were heading, but June passed it by. She passed the house by too, taking him over the creek on a wooden bridge. When they entered the trees she

172

switched on the flashlight and shone the beam ahead of them on a path into the wood.

"Where are we going?" David asked, still whispering even though they were already a long way from any ears but their own.

"Don't you like a surprise?"

"No," he said, "I'm an accountant. I use the map on a box of chocolates, and I always read the last page before I begin a book."

"That explains a lot," she said, laughing. "I understand about the chocolates, because nobody wants to bite into one of those orange cream thingies by surprise. But I disagree with you entirely on books. I never read the last page."

"Then how do you know how things end?"

"That's the whole point," she said. "If you don't read the last page it never ends."

The path steepened, following the creek up. He couldn't see it but he could hear it above their footfalls. And what a beautiful sound it was too — water running over smooth stones and two pairs of conspiratorial feet following a flashlight beam up a dirt path into the unknown. His leg was hurting a little, but not enough to slow him down, and when the path leveled off, he came up and walked alongside June.

"So, aren't you going to tell me where we're going?"

"Higher," she said. "If you can keep up, that is."

Then she took off jogging. At first, he let her go, watching as the flashlight bobbed in the darkness ahead and assuming she would slow or turn back. But she didn't, and soon he was walking by himself in near blackness. He was jogging in the dark to catch up, fearing that he had lost her entirely, when she scared him half to death. She was sitting on a stump beside the path and just when he came up even with her she turned the flashlight on with it pointed up beneath her chin, creating a floating ghost face in the dark.

"You sure gave this old heart a start," he said, panting to catch his breath, although more from fright than from fatigue. Climbing all those stairs along with this past week at stunt camp had already done wonders for his health, and he possessed more endurance than he even knew. "Where does this path lead?" he asked.

"It leads right to the Center of the Universe," she said.

"You do know that the universe is still expanding, don't you?"

"I should hope so," she replied, an exaggerated expression of seriousness on her still-illuminated face. "But it must be expanding in all directions equally because Echo Glen, which is just ahead, is the Center of the Universe. You'll have to see it someday. I named the sanctuary after it because there's a waterfall there that comes down a sheer face of granite and if you call out a wish it echoes it back to you as if it's already come true."

"It only works with a wish?"

"I'm not sure, to be honest. I've never shouted out anything else. Why would you? But right now we're going up. Way up. Come with me, David Hadley."

She took his hand and led him off the main path onto a steep switchback. The new path was narrower, the going root-strewn and rough, so David fell in behind her and focused on his steps and his breath. They climbed for what seemed like a very long time, and he could tell they were gaining altitude because the air was getting cooler and the trees thinner. He caught glimpses of the moon between the high branches of wind-bent firs, and when they came up on a high ridge, the moon followed them through the trees like a giant eye seeking them out on that dark mountain, intermittently washing June's profile with its silvery light. Oh, the old devil moon, David thought; it shines on everyone equally, but it shines on no one so beautifully as it does on June.

Soon, the trees thinned, the trail widened, and June switched the flashlight off and they walked together side by side in the moonlight. After the exercise of climbing, and with the cool night air on his flushed cheeks, David felt so good he ceased caring where it was they were even going. At least he did until the trail terminated at the edge of a cliff, and he saw the glider there waiting.

It sat perched on the cliff ledge like a giant moth, its pale wings spread out against the dark abyss below, its aluminum frame glinting in the moonlight.

"Whoa," David said, coming to a sudden halt. "How'd that get up here?"

June stopped short of the glider and turned around. "Sebastian and I carried it up and assembled it for you. And you don't want to have to carry it back down, trust me."

"For me? I don't understand. I don't know how to fly that thing."

"That's why we're going together, silly."

"Um, that must be a thousand-foot drop right there."

"It's a ramp slope down, actually. The drop comes about thirty feet farther out. And it's fifteen hundred feet at least. We climbed higher than you think."

He shook his head. "This is crazy."

"You told me you wanted to know what it felt like," she said. "This will give you a taste. Haven't you ever dreamed of flying?"

"I've dreamed of falling too."

"Oh, falling's not a problem."

"It's not?"

"No. When you're falling there's only one thing that can harm you."

"You mean the ground?"

"Yes," she said. "And even it can only harm you once. It's holding on that's the problem. Holding on will hurt you a thousand times, again and again. I want you to let go of all that fear and see what it feels like to really live. What do you say, David?"

He hesitated, looking at the glider and the cliff.

"I can't make you do it," she said. "You have to decide."

Remembering his prayer, David looked up at the stars and thought: *You* must have some kind of sense of humor because this is not what I had in mind and *You* know it.

"And you'll be with me?" he asked. "You'll handle all the controls?"

She nodded. "All you'll have to do is enjoy the ride."

"And you've done this before."

"All the time. We teach lessons up here in the spring."

The moon was right in front of them, hovering out there above all that darkness, and as David looked at it his heartbeat stabilized and his spirit slowly filled with peace. He had stood that day on the roof ready to jump to his death, and now here he was standing on a cliff about to jump into his life. He already felt more alive than he ever had before, and he owed it all to June. If she told him he could flap his wings and fly he should leap off this cliff without question and give it a try.

"I'll do it," he said. "I want to fly with you."

June hopped up and down and clapped her hands. "Hip hip hooray!" she said. "David Hadley's decided to live today. Come here and let me fit your harness."

She retrieved a bag from beside the glider and took out harnesses and helmets. She geared him up carefully, using the flashlight to inspect every buckle and clip. Her small, strong hands tugging and tightening the straps made him feel somehow very safe.

Once he was all set, she put her own harness on, quickly and efficiently, as if she'd done it hundreds of times. Then she led him to the glider and clipped him in.

"Okay, lie down," she said. "Let's do a hang check."

He went prone and let the harness take his weight. It felt similar to flying on the wire, but more comfortable because the harness actually fit.

"You're locked in," she said, going through a verbal checklist. "You've got a main. You've got a backup. Lines are clean. Now my turn. Locked. Main. Backup. Lines. Okay." She unclipped the glider from the carabineer that had fastened it to the cliff. Then she stood David up beside her and lifted the glider by its guide bar off the ground. "Now," she said, "just hold on to me and run. I'll be right here beside you."

"How far do I run?"

"Until your legs lift off and you're kicking air."

"I'm pretty heavy; what if it doesn't lift?"

"Then just keep running until we run right off the cliff."

Oh, that's reassuring, he thought, the sarcasm audible even in his mind. But he didn't say anything. He just took a deep breath.

"I'll count three," she said, "and then we'll

step, step, and run. Got it?"

"Got it," he said. "But give me a moment first."

"You just tell me when you're ready."

But David knew this was the type of thing for which you could never be ready. It was more like something you did when you had fully internalized "Oh, what the hell!" as a kind of personal philosophy. June was holding up the glider, and David's arm was around her waist. He laughed to himself. This is a hell of a length to go to just to get your arms around a girl, he thought. He was talking to the teenage boy he had morphed back into as he came up that mountain trail, and he realized that it was the first time he had let himself talk to or even think of that kid since the accident. And so it was that standing on a cliff clipped into a hang glider with June, bathed in the clean light of a full moon, David Hadley began to heal a wound that had haunted him for thirty-eight years.

"I'm ready," he finally said. And when he said it he meant more than just flying. He was ready to live again.

"Oh, good," June said. "This thing was getting heavy. Okay now, just relax and enjoy the ride. Here we go. One, two, three — step, step, run."

They ran together down the steep slope, a

mismatched pair of smiling fiftysomething kids beneath a giant moonlit wing. The glider rose up, the harnesses caught, and suddenly David was running on nothing but air. By grace or by God he didn't know, but they were flying. They were flying right into the moon.

"Woohoo!" David shouted into the wind. "I'm flying, June. I'm really flying."

They were hanging side by side beneath the wing and she turned to look at him. "Yes you are, David," she said. "You're flying and I'm proud of you."

"Thank you, June. Thank you."

He was almost crying now, it was so beautiful. He felt as though he were among the stars. Weightless and free; at long last a guiltless reprieve. The moon lit the hills and glinted off the distant river. Sweeping out beneath them he saw the valleys and the fields. He even saw Sebastian's bonfire, just a little spark way, way below. And had he had better vision, he might have even seen Sebastian himself standing in front of the fire and smiling as he watched them cross the moonlit sky above, sailing out into the night like two wide-eyed adventurers, together in joint harness, suspended beneath a common wing borne on the winds of hope.

13

He was staring off out the kitchen window, but I could've sworn by the faraway look in his eye that it was that moonlit sky that he was actually seeing and not the afternoon rain falling on the fields.

"We landed right there," he said, pointing out the window. "I'll never forget it either. Gliding in, my feet brushing the tops of the grass, touching down. She had hardly unhooked me and I was hugging her and thanking her. I had never felt so alive or so happy in my life."

"Sounds like a pretty epic experience."

"You really should try it sometime."

"Hang gliding at night?"

"You might start with a tandem flight during the day. I think they still offer them at Cougar Mountain. That's closer to you anyway. I'm assuming you live in the city."

"What gave me away?"

"Your wingtips."

"You mean my shoes?"

"When you took them off coming in from the barn I noticed the soles were sidewalk worn. From walking to work, I assumed. Mine used to look the same way. I lived on Pill Hill."

"I live in Belltown."

"Well, we might have ended up neighbors then if I hadn't been seduced away from the city by Echo Glen."

"Don't you mean seduced away by June?"

"Oh no," he said, shaking his head. "June never needed to seduce anyone. I fell for June the moment I laid eyes on her. Everyone did. You will too. June was just being June, rescuing me the same as she rescued everyone and everything she ever met that needed a second chance."

"Okay, you're really stringing me along now," I said. "I know you already think my generation has no patience, but how did you two finally get together?"

"I see you're like me in that you like to read the last page first. But I'll get there, I promise. I'm just telling you the story as it happened, young man. I do appreciate you taking the time, Elliot Champ. Especially on your birthday."

"It's no problem. I'm enjoying it, actually."

"And I haven't forgotten about that twenty grand I promised you could earn either. I'm getting to it as well, but storytelling is like everything else: the older you get, the longer it takes. And right now I'm due for a little bathroom break."

He used his cane to stand himself up, and then he shuffled off down the hall. I almost reached for another MoonPie, but I'd had three already, so I picked the Polaroid up off the table instead. I know it sounds silly, but the photo made me a little sad about my childhood. My father was never big on taking pictures, never even owned a camera that I knew of, and this Polaroid of me was the first birthday photo I ever had, outside of some clown at the office posting something the year before on the Foreclosure Solutions Facebook page. But that doesn't count. I slipped the photo into my pocket and stood to stretch my legs.

The painting I had noticed earlier caught my eye again, the one with the waterfall. It occurred to me that it must be Echo Glen. It looked just as June had described it to David in his story. And now I knew where that path led, the one I had seen through the living room window, just on the other side of the creek. It led to Echo Glen. I wondered if the old man would let me go up and see it sometime. You know, if I ever came back for anything, maybe to help him move or something. Don't think I was getting sentimental, though. I'd done it before. Helped people move. If you wanted to close deals, you had to do what you had to do. Besides, it was a better way to spend a Saturday than out golfing with the jokers from my office.

I had wandered back into the living room and was looking out the window at the creek and the trail beyond when Mr. Hadley finally came looking for me.

"There's nothing like sitting on the toilet for ten minutes because you're too old to stand," he said. "I should have taken them up on the catheter."

"Okay, a little too much information," I said. "But thanks for the mental image."

"Oh, you'll find out eventually, young man. If you live long enough, two things are guaranteed to happen: you lose people you love, and going to the bathroom slowly takes over the hours left in your dwindling days. Haven't you ever seen the line for the bathroom at a funeral?"

"No, I guess I never gave going to the bathroom much thought."

"You will. You have a lot of time to think about these things sitting on the toilet, I'll

185

tell you. About the only thing that has me questioning the existence of God is the fact that He or She decided to thread the urethra through the male prostate gland. That and cable news. Who would design such stupid things? Should we sit in here and get back to the story? That chair there is the most comfortable."

I don't know why he thought that old chair was so comfortable. If he ever sat in it himself he'd die there, it was so hard to get out of. "I think I'll sit on the couch," I said.

"Suit yourself. Can I get you tea, or maybe another RC Cola, before we start?"

"No thanks," I said. "After our little chat about prostates I'd like to hold off on using the bathroom for as long as I can."

"Sorry about that. Those MoonPies get me on a sugar high and I start blabbering. I'll probably be snoring in another ten minutes or so. So where was I? Oh yes, seducing June. Well, after hang gliding I found the courage to knock on her door the next morning. I even made her laugh with a very clever accountant joke. Would you like to hear it?"

"Sure," I said. "I'd love to hear an accountant's take on humor. Unless it's something silly like why is number six afraid of number seven."

"I don't think I've heard that one," he said.

"Six is afraid of seven because seven eight nine."

It took him a second to get it, then he laughed. "That's pretty good."

"What do you mean? It's terrible."

"Well, if you think that's terrible," he said, "I'm definitely not starting the story with mine. How about we begin instead with the hippies waking up Echo Glen by blasting that ungodly bus horn and rounding up their missing fellows by screaming out a roadkill announcement . . ."

14

David staggered out from the bunkhouse, thinking it was some new playlist on Sebastian's wakeup speakers he was hearing. But it was altogether too early to be getting up for stunt lessons, and not even Sebastian could have dreamed up an alarm like this.

The bus horn was blasting and Clarence, the hippie who had offered David the joint the night before, was hanging from its open door and repeatedly shouting, "Hidy-ho! We gotta go. Roadkill on the radio. Hidy-ho! Hidy-ho! We've got roadkill on the radio."

The door to Sebastian's hayloft apartment burst open and he stepped out onto its balcony wearing a robe. He yelled something but it was impossible to hear over the honking. He reached inside his apartment and grabbed his bullhorn and used it to shout down to Clarence over the noise.

"What's all this racket down there,

comrade? Some of us are trying to sleep."

Clarence said something to someone inside the bus and the honking stopped. Then he looked up at Sebastian. "Roadkill, captain," he said. "You wanna come along?"

"Come along where? What's this talk about roadkill?"

"We got a dead deer on the police scanner, man. Someone hit one out on Dansville Road. We gotta get out there before animal control. We gotta get it while it's fresh. Living off the land, man. Gettin' while the gettin's good."

While he was talking, Sebastian stood gazing down on him, mumbling something privately and shaking his head. He appeared to David almost like a disappointed father looking down on a child.

"You live off the land all you want, comrade, but don't you dare come back here with some dead deer to skin. *Me comprendes?* June will not have you scaring the other animals."

The kid shrugged. "Whatever you say, captain. We would have shared the meat, though. If it's a good-sized deer it'll last us a week."

By this time other hippies had begun appearing from the bushes and the trees, heading for the bus — some of them in various

189

states of undress that led David to believe they had been sharing more than just joints the night before — and they all looked bedraggled and cold, shivering in their rags. When the last of them had boarded the bus, Clarence leaned out again.

"Hey," he called up to Sebastian. "Is there any chance we could get our bird back, man? We don't kill nothing ourselves or anything like that, but I'll bet my head that thing lays some serious eggs."

Sebastian turned without answering and disappeared into his apartment.

Clarence glanced at David, who was standing nearby, watching. "Guess that's a no," he said. "Sure you don't wanna join us, man? Living the dream."

David shook his head. Clarence shrugged and withdrew into the bus. The door closed, the engine started, and the bus pulled away. But for all their rush to leave, it hardly moved above an idle as it rolled down the drive. And it was rocking something awful too, as if maybe those on board were fighting, or possibly dancing. Who knew?

It honked one last time and David watched its taillights disappear into the gloom. He would see that bus some ten years later parked on four flat tires alongside the river several miles up the road. He stopped to say hello then, and to let them know that the ostrich was healthy and doing fine. But he found that only one aged and tired hippie remained, and although he resembled Clarence, if it was in fact him he'd long since boiled his brains, and he remembered nothing about an ostrich or even Echo Glen.

With the bus gone and the ranch quiet again, a few students wandered off to the showers while the others drifted back to the bunkhouse to catch whatever little bit of sleep was available to them before Sebastian's speakers blasted them officially into the third and final week of stunt camp. But having no desire to be violently woken twice in the same day, David stood outside the bunkhouse in the dim light of dawn, just breathing the clean country air and listening to the quiet whisper of the creek. He had been away from work for the longest stretch in probably twenty years, and it felt really good. Maybe his crazy ex-wife had been right about his needing to take a vacation after all. David smiled. He had not thought of his ex-wife without resentment since their divorce, but when he'd thought of her just now he'd felt nothing but peace.

David noticed the lights were on in the house and something gave him the courage to go up. June answered the door with wild hair and an afghan blanket wrapped around her shoulders. She had reading glasses on and a pencil stuck behind her ear.

"You look more like a hippie than the ones who just left," David said.

"Oh, is that what all that racket was?" she said. "They're not really hippies, though. That bus has been trolling around these parts for years, picking up the county's disgruntled youth. Most of them grow out of it eventually. Would you like to come in?"

"If you don't mind. I thought maybe I could use your phone to call my office. They'll be expecting me if I don't."

"Sure," she said, stepping aside to let him enter. "I've got coffee on."

She brought him in and showed him to the phone. It was on a desk that sat in front of a bay window in the living room. The window offered a view of the creek. A desk lamp was turned on as if June had been working there recently, and the desktop was strewn with paperwork and mail. A ten-key calculator had a tape two feet long hanging from the roll.

June went to retrieve coffee and David dialed his office. He was hoping to get voice mail for his boss's secretary since it was so early, but she answered. David instinctively began coughing and speaking in a low, raspy voice.

"Hi, Lindsay, I'm afraid I'm not going to make it in again." *Cough cough.* "Yes, yes, it's very bad. Contagious." *Cough cough.* "Wouldn't want to infect anyone. Yes, maybe out all week. No. No need to call and check on me. Okay. Charlie can handle my quarterlies that are due." *Cough.* "Thanks."

When he hung up and turned around, June was standing behind him with two mugs of coffee. She handed him one.

"Maybe instead of stunt school you should enroll in real acting lessons," she said, grinning. "That was really good. I thought for sure you might die before you had a chance to get off the phone."

David blushed. "I know it's silly, isn't it? But I really do have weeks of vacation time saved up, so I don't feel too bad."

"Well, you should use it," she said, raising her eyebrows as if lecturing him. "Working to make a living is noble. Working to avoid living is tragic." Then, after taking a sip of her coffee, she said, "Hey, you said you were an accountant, right? Do you have any professional advice on how I can turn around a struggling stunt camp located eight hundred miles from Hollywood and make a small fortune? Me and the animals would thank you."

"Well, in my professional opinion, as an accountant, to make a small fortune in your line of business is easy. All you need to do is start with a large fortune."

He laughed at his own joke, but June didn't appear to think it was very funny.

"Come on," he said. "That was a pretty good joke."

"Maybe for an accountant," she said, shaking her head. Then she giggled. "Okay, it was pretty good. And true too. If you only knew. Money. Ha! What's it good for?"

She was standing close to him and she smelled like lavender. He noticed she wasn't wearing any shoes again and he wondered if he should have offered to take his off at the door. For some reason David felt suddenly nervous. He sipped his coffee, nodding to the cluttered desk. "Looks like maybe I caught you working."

June sighed, waving her hand at the desk as if wishing it away. "I'd rather be out in the barn with the animals. And you can tell by my growing pile that that's where I've been too."

"What's in the sack?" David asked. "Fan mail?"

He was referring to a large black-plastic

garbage sack sitting on the edge of the desk and stuffed with what looked like letters and other mail.

"Yeah, right," June said. "*Fan mail.* That's a laugh. That's how I pay my bills."

"Those are all bills?" He almost choked on his coffee.

"Yes. Some of them are several months of the same bill, of course. I feel so bad about having to decide which ones to pay that I just put them all in the bag. Then I blindly draw them out and pay them one at a time until I'm out of money."

"You pick which bills to pay out of a hat?"

"Out of a bag, but yes. That way it's random chance, you see. And when the bill collectors call, I just explain it to them, and I tell them that they're in the same bag with everyone else. Sometimes they get nasty, but then I threaten to not put them in the bag at all. Susan down at the feed store got pretty smart and started sending duplicate bills to increase her odds. But they're pretty good about floating us down there. They love animals as much as we do."

"You do realize that I'm an accountant and this is driving me crazy, don't you? How do you balance your books? How do you keep track of your debits and credits? Pay taxes? Plan?"

"I keep a checkbook, silly. I'm not completely helpless."

"Do you want a hand?" he asked. "I could organize all of this for you in no time. Put it on a ledger spreadsheet that you could easily look at and understand. See everything. Maybe things aren't as bad as you think."

"Maybe they're worse," she said.

"Not knowing is worse."

She looked to be considering his offer, so he pressed her.

"Come on, I do this for a living. I could even call some of the bill collectors and get them to freeze interest. Saying you're an accountant goes a long way sometimes, you know. Although I'd be doing this strictly as a personal favor, since I don't keep up on my CPA license."

June looked at the cluttered desk. "When would you have time even? You're already calling in to work sick."

"I'll start today. Right now."

"What about stunt class? I think Sebastian's doing fire again today."

"My eyebrows are just growing back. Plus, we both know I enrolled in stunt camp pretending to be a reporter just so I could talk to you, as embarrassing as that sounds to say out loud."

There was a pause while June considered,

looking at the piles of paperwork on the desk. They heard the music come on the speakers outside as Sebastian woke up his students.

"I hate that he does that," she said, shaking her head. "It's not good for the animals. Especially not for the horses. But he means well. He has a good heart."

"What do you say about me helping?" David asked, not letting her change the subject. "I'd really rather not have to set myself on fire today."

She sighed. "Sebastian will be disappointed."

"Sebastian will understand. He has a good heart, you just said so yourself."

"Okay, but only if you let me pay you."

David laughed. "Pay me how? Are you going to put me in the bag?"

"No," she said, sticking out her tongue. "I'll pay you in glider lessons, and I'll pay you in food."

David toasted her coffee mug with his.

"You've hired yourself an accountant." Then he rubbed his belly and added, "But I'll warn you, you rarely see skinny accountants for a reason."

June smiled. "Good. I've got cinnamon apples baking in the oven right now, and I make great lemon garlic ice cream, as you know."

15

"You sly old dog, you. Pretty darn smart working your way into the house with the old 'I'm an accountant and can help you with your bills' routine."

"Hey," he said, grinning, "you have to shake the milkshake God gave you."

"Shake the milkshake. Is that an old accountant expression or something?"

"No, it's from the song. You know: *My milkshake brings all the boys to the yard.*"

He sang the line, holding his fists up and shaking them from side to side, as if he were doing the milkshake booty dance, even though he was sitting. I almost fell off the couch laughing again. "Where did you learn that?"

"*Mean Girls*," he said.

"*Mean Girls* the movie?"

"Cable news isn't the only thing I watch, although Lindsay Lohan's on there a lot too these days. It really is a shame. I hope she keeps it together this time."

"You know what, Mr. Hadley," I said, sitting back and shaking my head, "you really are an onion, you know that? Each time I think I've got you pegged you peel off another layer."

"Well, you know what happens when you keep peeling an onion," he said. "Eventually you don't have any onion left."

He laughed, but then his laugh worked into a nasty cough again. He bent over in his chair and appeared to be struggling to breathe. This time I did get up, and I rushed over to see if I could help somehow. But I had no idea what to do so I stupidly patted him on the back, as if he were a choking child.

"What can I do?" I asked. "Can I help somehow?"

His breath was labored and wheezy, rattling in his lungs, but he finally sat up enough to look up at me, signaling by waving his hand that there was nothing to be done. I stood there over him while he caught his breath.

"Can I get you something?" I asked.

"Maybe another RC Cola," he said, straining to speak.

"How about some water?"

When I came back from the kitchen, his

breathing had improved. He fished a pill container from his big sweater pocket and picked out a couple of tablets and swallowed them.

"Thank you," he said. "I'm sorry you had to see that."

"Are you okay?" I asked, hesitating before taking my seat again on the couch.

He sighed. "Yes and no. But I will be. We all will be." Then he looked up at the cat clock on the wall and squinted. "Would you mind telling me the time, Elliot?"

"Three twenty-two."

"Oh, boy," he said, "I had better get moving with the rest of this story then."

"You had just started organizing June's books."

"Oh, yes." He sipped his water and nodded. "Although she didn't really have any books to organize. Just piles of papers. And she was right, it was worse than she even thought. You have to understand June had a lot of animals here at that time. She had maybe seventeen horses then. Almost all of them saved from racetracks. Plus Rosie, who had just arrived, and who you met. But she also had goats. Sheep. A mule even, if I recall. Now she had that silly ostrich, of course. And there were so many dogs and cats you couldn't count them.

"She was the catchall, you see. The last resort. Every other rescue within a hundred-mile radius knew June couldn't turn an animal away, no matter how low on money she was. It's the only reason she had started the stunt school. It had been Sebastian's idea. He had left Los Angeles, where they had worked together on films years before, and he needed a place to stay, so she took him. She was struggling for money and he suggested using the property to run a stunt school, trading on their reputations to get students. It was their third or fourth session that summer when I arrived."

"So, June was a stuntman then?"

"Stuntwoman. She's even in the Stuntmen's Hall of Fame. You didn't think it was really Roger Moore parachuting off that cliff in *The Spy Who Loved Me,* did you?"

"Roger Moore?"

"James Bond."

"Oh, you mean Daniel Craig."

"Oh, boy. I forgot how young you are. Let's just say June was an early BASE jumper. Maybe among the first. They claim the first was a guy jumping from El Capitan in 1966, but June never told anyone she'd jumped off of Half Dome in the same park a full five years before that. She was very humble about her accomplishments. In fact, besides me now, you're the only one to even know the identity of the Barefoot BASE Jumper."

"They never found her out?"

"No," he said. "Never. It wouldn't matter now, of course, but June would rather be anonymous."

"But you still haven't told me how you two finally hooked up."

"You're lucky I watch enough TV to understand your euphemisms, young man. But since you asked, I'll tell you. It all started after the graduation ceremony when I saw her bathing naked in the creek . . ."

16

A lightning storm had set the hills northwest of Echo Glen afire, sending great plumes of smoke up into blue summer skies. The fire department cut the electricity while they fought the blaze, and at night the flames reflected off the undersides of the clouds so brightly that it looked like the apocalypse had descended over the valley.

June spent long nights in the stables calming the horses, which seemed to smell and fear the fire. Her days were spent caring for the other animals, and in the evenings when she wasn't in the stables, she was hard at work in the kitchen, cooking by candlelight on the old propane stove. And not just for David, but for the students too. They received neatly packaged lunches plus a hot meal at the end of each day, but David had never thought about who must have been preparing them until he saw June doing all the work. She had a few volunteer helpers who came and went, working mostly with the animals, but David got the impression that the time they had to offer was limited, and he overheard one of them breaking the news to June that she would be leaving soon for college.

David himself had been busy putting the finishing touches on June's books, having dug through years' worth of poorly kept records, working out figures by hand once the power was cut. He was still waiting to present her with the bad news, however. He had tried several times to bring it up, but she seemed to know it was coming and kept herself so busy he could never get an audience with her for more than a few stolen moments here and there.

But for the first time in ages David was enjoying his work. It felt good to be doing something helpful for someone else, and he was sitting at that desk and looking out at the creek when he had a sort of small epiphany: maybe all this time when he'd been looking for some way to help himself, all he had really needed was to get busy helping someone else. Maybe that's the secret June had discovered; maybe that's why she cared for all those animals the way she did. She offered David a guest room, but he made sure to return to the bunkhouse with the students each evening. They razzed him a little, calling him the teacher's pet, but only in good fun.

That Sunday was the third and worst day of the fires as the students gathered outside the bunkhouse for their graduation ceremony. There would be no Sunday bonfire, since a burn ban was being enforced countywide, and there was no ice to be used for June's famous lemon ice cream, but she made a blueberry pan cobbler on the propane stove and they circled up around the fire pit just the same. The graduation ceremony consisted of a speech from Sebastian, delivered from the platform of the scissor lift ten feet in the air, thankfully without his bullhorn. He said things like not to keep your eye on the goal because then you'd only have one eye on the path. He said to become one with your performance.

"And above all else," he told them, but he was looking at David now, "always be brave."

As he lowered the scissor lift after his speech, the students readied the bucket of water they had collected from the creek. David got the impression that he knew it was coming, but he played along and acted surprised when they doused him with it anyway. He really did have a smile that caught on like a yawn. He walked off dripping, returning moments later with a damp diploma for each of them. He had even made one for David.

They were all sitting around the unlit fire pit, eating blueberry cobbler with their hands and watching the setting sun paint the smoky clouds in glorious shades of pink, when the cars began coming up the drive. One by one, they'd pull up and stop, and then a student would get up and go around and say good-bye to everyone, paying special attention to Sebastian, whom everyone had grown to love, before climbing into the car and waving one last time as it pulled away. This caravan of farewells went on until Sebastian was standing in the drive watching the taillights of the very last car disappear into the dusk. He walked back to the fire with his head hung, his countenance clearly forlorn.

"Well, another stunt camp comes to a close, comrades," he said. "I'm afraid this might have been our last."

"Why would it have to be the last?" David asked.

But neither Sebastian nor June answered him. They both just looked up at the sky as if the answer were there somewhere in the burning clouds. And David knew anyway, since the answer was really on the ledger he had prepared.

"I think I'm going to turn in," Sebastian said.

"Good night," June replied. "I'll catch you on the flip side."

When June and David were alone, David brought it up.

"We really need to go over your finances, June. I've been trying to get a moment with you."

"I know," she said. "But not tonight, darling. Let's enjoy tonight. It's always so quiet when they leave. And the clouds are so pretty. Scoot over here. Watch them with me."

She was sitting with her back against an old log and her legs outstretched, barefooted of course. David scooted over to sit beside her and they watched the last of the light drain from the clouds. The fires had moved downwind, but you could still see them reflected in the sky. It was a very warm evening, maybe the warmest of the summer so far.

"I hope everyone's all right," David said, referring to the fires.

"It's mostly timberland that's burning," June replied. "As long as the firefighters stay safe, it should be okay. Lightning's been around a lot longer than we have. Plus, they'll be some great quaking aspen groves in a few years."

David looked around at the ranch. "It really is beautiful out here. I almost hate to return to the city."

"Oh, that's right," June replied. "You have a job to get back to. I'm always reminded on these last days of camp that the real world still exists. I watch the cars drive away and I wonder where they're all going. Where they'll end up. They're all so young. Don't get me wrong, I'm glad to be staying here. There's nowhere else I'd rather be. But sometimes it's lonely. And sometimes I think it's a shame we don't get to live a hundred lives. Do it all. See everything."

"Maybe we do," David said. "Maybe Shirley MacLaine's not as mad as a fish in a raincoat like they say. Maybe reincarnation could be true and we're all thirty-five-thousand-year-old spirits."

"No," June said. "On second thought, one life is enough. Unless I could come back as a horse. I wouldn't mind living the life of a horse. But a wild one in a place without fences."

"I would have thought you'd choose a bird."

She looked at David with a smile in her eyes. "That's the thing about people, darling; they never do quite what you think they'll do. It's what makes humans absolutely impossible and absolutely interesting at the same time. Like you. I never would have guessed you'd stick it out and be the last one here."

David looked at the rolled-up certificate in his hand.

"Well, I'm an honorary graduate, I think, since I pretty much skipped the final week."

"Don't sell yourself short, darling; you really are a remarkable man."

"Because I jumped over a burning car or because I was dragged through a pile of manure?"

"No, because you were stuck in your life and you did something to change it. That takes courage. It really does." Then she laughed. "And so does taking on an ostrich. How's your leg, by the way?"

"It was a scratch really. The last stitch fell out by itself in the shower yesterday."

"That sounds nice right now," she said. "A cool shower. Too bad the power's still off and the well pump's dead. Hey, there wasn't any money left in my accounts for a new generator, was there?"

"Do you really want to know?"

"No, let's go over it tomorrow. If you don't mind staying one more night," she added. "You might need to get back."

He had already missed two weeks of work and really should have been getting back. But what was one more day? he thought. Besides, it felt good to be alone with June for once.

"No," he said, "it's no problem. I was hoping to stay. I have a little more work to do to finalize your books. I can have it ready to go over with you in the morning."

"Good," she said, standing up and brushing the grass off her pants. "I'm going to go check on the horses. I left a lamp burning in the living room. There's a guest bedroom all made up in the house. You can sleep there. The bunkhouse is too big and too lonely for one person."

David sat on the grass and watched her walk down toward the stables. She faded like a beautiful ghost into the dim red light that seemed to be coming from the clouds themselves. David was suddenly struck by how lonely he already felt. The thought of leaving made him sad, and he could not quite picture what it would be like returning to his life in the city. He pushed the thought away, telling himself he still had tonight. Then he rose and went up to the house to finish his work.

He was at the desk an hour or so later, working by the light of a kerosene lantern, when movement outside the window caught his eye. He held the ledger up to shade the lantern's glare from the window and he saw June standing beside the creek. What was she doing? he wondered. Then, without warning, she peeled her shirt off over her head and dropped it on the ground. She was facing away from him, but he could clearly see her naked back in the dim rubicund glow.

With a trembling hand he turned the lantern down to improve his view. He could now see her so clearly through the window that they might as well have been in the same room. His jaw dropped when she bent to pull down her pants, then stood and stepped out of them. She was now wearing nothing but her underwear, and the reflected light was so dim that it seemed to David as if her skin itself were glowing pink against the backdrop of dark trees beyond the creek. David felt things stir in him that he had not felt in many years, and this stirring made him feel at once lustful and guilty, shameful and dirty, and oh, so very, very alive.

June waded out into the creek and sat

down in the water. Then she leaned her head back, letting the current sweep up her hair. She arched her back so that her ribs and her breasts pointed up to the burning sky. David felt his hand instinctively moving up his thigh. Then the guilt won, and he was overcome. He stood to leave but was glued to the window by some power beyond his control. June rose from the water and stood in the creek, looking straight back at the house and him. He wasn't sure if she could see him or not, the lantern having been extinguished, but embarrassment flooded over him just the same. He turned and left the window. Then he left the house.

Twenty minutes later he was lying on his cot in the dark when he heard the bunkhouse door open. She smelled like the outside when she sat down on the edge of his cot — he would never forget that. Before he could say something stupid, which he very well might have, she leaned down and kissed him. David's hands rose to touch her and he realized she was naked. The feeling of her bare flesh sent an electrical current from his fingertips to the very center of his spine, and he pulled her to him and kissed her more deeply.

She felt small and delicate in his clumsy arms, like a thing too precious to be handled. The world ceased its spinning, at least for him, all its turning having led to this very moment — this embrace, this kiss — and he said a silent prayer that he would always be gentle and loving and generous with her. This prayer seemed necessary moments later when his army surplus cot collapsed beneath their combined weight and only his belly broke her fall. They laughed together in the dark.

"Should we go up to the house?" he asked.

"No," she said, kissing him again. "It's too far. Take me to the hay and ravage me like a wild animal would."

So much for her being delicate, he thought. But he did as she had asked, standing and picking her up with strength he hadn't known he had, carrying her over, and laying her down in the hay. Just enough red glow was coming in through the high hayloft window for him to see the outline of her face, and he caressed her hair and her lips. Then it occurred to him that they should have the talk, although he hated to spoil the moment.

"I don't have any protection," he said. "I'm supposed to be sterile. I mean, I couldn't have a child with my wife, but the doctors said there was always a slim chance."

She laughed, reaching up to place her palm against his cheek. "Oh, darling, you're so cute. I'm fifty-three years old and we're not making any babies tonight."

"Hey," he said, "it happens sometimes. Even at our age."

"Between your sterility and my hysterectomy, if we produce a child there had better be three wise men bearing gifts outside in the morning. Now stop talking and make love to me, please, for the love of nature."

Never before had David heard a more welcome plea, and so for once in his life, he gratefully shut his big mouth and did as he was told.

17

The morning sun slanting in through the hayloft window woke David first. They were lying on the hay and June's head was on his shoulder, her arm flung over his bare chest.

He looked at her face; she was so peacefully asleep that she appeared almost childlike, with her hair splayed out on the soft golden hay. Then she opened her eyes, and there was that smile that had simultaneously captured his heart and saved his life that day on the roof. A rooster crowed somewhere outside.

"Isn't that a lovely sound," June said.

"Much better than waking up to one of Sebastian's mix tapes," he replied.

She laughed. "I know, right? But that won't be happening any longer. I'm not doing any more stunt camps."

"Why not? It seemed like the students all loved it."

"Well, we were turned down for the insurance renewal, for one thing. That, and Sebastian needs to go back."

"Go back where?"

"To where he's run away from."

"You mean LA. Why'd he run away?"

"That's his story to tell, darling, not mine. But right now I'd like to make you a deal. You promise to hold off your accounting report until I've had at least two cups of coffee and I'll make you a big country breakfast. I've got some eggs and bacon left from the stunt camp supplies to cook before they go bad in the icebox."

"I don't know," he said, "I feel bad about eating bacon."

"Oh, it's okay," she said, "this is Canadian bacon."

"Canadian pigs don't count?"

"Of course," she said. "Pigs of every nationality count. These are slaughtered on old man Lou's farm and no one does it more humanely than he does. What I meant, though, silly, is that it's leaner. I thought you were worried about the fat."

David glanced down at his belly. "What are you saying?"

"Nothing. I like your belly."

"But you admit I have a belly?"

"I should hope so," she replied, reaching down and rubbing it. "Otherwise how will any woman ever find her way into your heart?"

"Is that why you're offering me breakfast?"

He thought he saw the smile leave her eyes. He knew he had seen correctly a moment later when she spoke.

"David, I don't want to give you the wrong impression. I'm not really at a place in my life where I'm interested in a long-term relationship."

"That's fine," he said, lying. "I'm not really looking for one either."

"Good. Then we can just let last night be what it was: two adults making each other feel good." Then she leaned up and kissed his cheek. "And you did make me feel good. Very, very good. Now, let's go see about some coffee and some bacon."

He had a hard time focusing on their conversation over breakfast. All he kept hearing was her saying, *"We can just let last night be what it was."* But it wasn't just two adults making each other feel good, at least not for him it wasn't. It was something much deeper than that. And David knew it because he knew he would be content to simply be around her the rest of his days without ever getting to make love to her again. He just felt right when she was near, as if just the sound of her voice could somehow fill the void that had haunted him most of his life. Now he wished he could go back to that pile of hay and wake up earlier and just hold her for a little while. Instead, he was watching her finish her second cup of coffee and wondering exactly how many more minutes until it was time for him to leave both her and Echo Glen. He was still wondering this when Sebastian walked in, followed by the three-legged Labrador.

"*Hola,* comrades," he said.

"Look who smelled bacon," June said, feeding a scrap from her plate to the dog.

"I smelled coffee," Sebastian said. "Although I'd give anything for a *café con leche* and a sweet roll. You Americans eat like farmers."

June ignored his comment, biting into a piece of bacon and smiling across the table at David.

"We're just fueling up because David here is about to deliver the bad news about my finances. Aren't you, David?"

David went over and got the main ledger and brought it back to the table. Sebastian poured himself a cup of coffee and joined them.

"Well," David said, clearing his throat, "you want the good news or bad news first?"

"Good news," June said. "It's always best

to soften the blow, I think."

"The good news is I found a way to trim your monthly budget by nearly half. I got several creditors to agree to freeze interest and take a minimum monthly payment."

"So, no more bills in the bag?" June asked.

"No more bills in the bag. Also, you have Echo Glen set up as a nonprofit, which is really smart, I might add."

"My old accountant helped me do that. He's not nearly as smart as my new one, though," she added with a wink, "and he's moved away."

"Well, he was right to have you do it. But you're not using it correctly and it's costing you a lot in unnecessary taxes. You can lease back the property, which you personally own, to the nonprofit and make all your housing expenses, including your entire mortgage, tax deductible. Of course, the mortgage is past due and that's not good."

"Is that the bad news?" June asked.

"No, that's hardly the bad news," he said.

June gripped the edge of the table with both hands. "Okay, I'm ready."

"The bad news is you're bankrupt."

"We are? I mean, I am?"

"Yes. It looks like you have some income from a pension, plus the few donations you get for the nonprofit, but that all together with the profit from the stunt school is still far lower than your minimum expenses."

"I told you we need to do another stunt camp," Sebastian said. "I know we can get more students, with or without that newspaper article."

"We don't have insurance any longer, Sebastian."

"Maybe David here can help us find some," he said.

"That's hardly the point," she shot back. "You need to return to Tinseltown and you know it. I can't have you here knowing that you're just being silly and running away from where you should be."

"Sebastian doesn't run away from anything," he said.

"Oh, come on, Sebastian, how long have I known you? And stop talking about yourself in the third person. We're all friends here."

"Maybe," he said, "maybe not." He stood and dumped his coffee out into the sink. Then he turned to David and reached out his hand. "It has been my pleasure to meet you, comrade. As long as the sky is above your head, the world beneath all our feet will be a better place." Then he bowed and walked out.

"You're being kind of hard on him, don't you think?" David said to June once Sebastian was gone.

June sighed. "Maybe. But I care about him a lot, and he sometimes needs tough love. And I guess I do too. Thank you for the work you've done, David. I really appreciate it. Is everything there in the ledger? I think I'll look it over this week and give my situation some thought."

David set the ledger on the table and patted it with his hand. "It's all in there for you. You might want to have a real CPA look at it, since my specialty is really auditing inventories. If you do find someone, and he or she has any questions, my number and everything is on the first page. Home and work."

Then both of them seemed to sense that the conversation had come to a close, and they rose and looked at each other across the small table.

"I guess I should get going," David said. "Work will be wondering if I'm alive."

June nodded but didn't say anything.

She came around the table to him, and for a moment he thought she was going to shake his hand, which would have broken his heart, but she hugged him instead. He bent to smell her hair. It might have been a silly thing to do, but he wanted to commit her scent to memory. She smelled of laven-

222

der and hay.

"Thank you, David," she said, still hugging him. "You've been a blessing to have around these last few weeks." Then she pulled away and looked up at him. He would have sworn she looked as sad as he felt, but he couldn't be sure if it was over their parting or the depressing news he had just delivered. "I'll miss you, and I know Sebastian will too."

He wanted to tell her that he'd miss her too. He wanted to say that he didn't want to leave. He wanted to find the courage or simply the words to somehow tell her how he felt. What he said was, "I can't even imagine what it will feel like to sleep in my own bed."

"Probably pretty good," she said.

He nodded, but not convincingly so.

She followed him to the door and said good-bye. Then she stood on the porch and watched him go. His car was parked in the gravel lot behind the bunkhouse and it was a long walk with her eyes on his back. He stopped before rounding the corner and she was still standing there watching him.

"I hope to see you again, David Hadley," she called. "But not on any roofs, okay?"

He smiled and waved. She waved back. Then he rounded the bunkhouse corner.

Before he started his car, he closed his eyes and made a secret wish. When he pulled out, he thought she might still be on the porch. But she wasn't. The porch was empty and the door was closed. He sat looking at it for a minute or two before he pulled out and drove away from Echo Glen. He looked once in his rearview mirror, just in case his secret wish had been answered, but only the eyes of a curious ostrich and an old three-legged Labrador followed him down the drive.

18

He looked so damn sad telling me about leaving June and Echo Glen that I couldn't help but think he was saying good-bye to them all over again.

"I can't believe you just left," I said. "I mean, shouldn't you have told her how you felt or something?"

"I thought you didn't believe in love," he said.

"Well, I don't. But things obviously worked out for you two. I mean, you got married, right? How did that happen? And what was Sebastian running from? And how did she manage to save Echo Glen?"

"You ask a lot of questions," he said. "That's good. It means you're listening and you have a curious mind. But we're losing daylight, so how about I keep going with the story and I think your questions will all be answered for you soon enough. And then we'll get to my proposal for you."

"Fair enough," I said. "So, you had just left Echo Glen."

"I remember. I might be old, but I'm not senile. And how could I ever forget? It ripped my heart out when I left . . ."

David's life was waiting for him just as he had left it, which was a problem when one considers that his world had grown too big for his small routines and tiny apartment.

He returned to the office on Tuesday, after having missed two full weeks and a day, but everything was different. Instead of passing his desk as if it didn't exist, his coworkers would stop and look at him with curious expressions. All day he heard pithy lines welcoming him back from people who had hardly ever acknowledged him before.

"Wow, you look different, David. Really different."

"You ought to bottle that flu you had and sell it as a youth serum, that's what I say."

"Did you lose a lot of weight? It looks like you did. I always say I'm just one good stomach flu away from fitting into my graduation suit again."

"You look tan. Are you sure you weren't convalescing in the Caribbean?"

At five o'clock he changed into workout clothes in the office bathroom and went to climb his stairs, hoping it would bring some sense of normalcy back to his day. But it didn't. He hardly broke a sweat now, and when he reached the top he had no desire left to even check if the door might be unlocked. He felt as though he had outgrown his life like a hermit crab does a borrowed shell, walking around naked in a world that no longer fit. He walked up the hill to his apartment without even glancing at the liquor store, and he sat in front of a turned-off TV and tried to re-create his time at Echo Glen on its blank screen. And he thought about June too. A lot.

He remembered her scent, always lavender mixed with a hint of the outside. He recalled with perfect clarity her tight-lipped laugh and the crow's-feet that surrounded her smiling eyes. Later, he went down to the convenience store and bought a pint of lemon sorbet, just to try to re-create the night he had sat beside her at the fire. But it wasn't the same and he tossed it out after only a bite, retiring to his bed to see if he couldn't revisit their lovemaking in his dreams.

But dreams eluded him, as did any sleep. Even her socks no longer comforted him, and why would they, for had he not held the woman herself in his clumsy arms, and had he not felt her lips pressed against his own?

In the morning he watched the news as he got ready for work, and when they broadcast an update on the containment of the forest fires in Snohomish County, complete with aerial footage shot from a helicopter, he stared at the screen, hoping to catch a glimpse of Echo Glen. He was haunted by the image of June wading naked into that creek, and it struck him as peculiar that the most important moments in one's life often passed unrecognized as such at the time. He wished he had stood at that window longer; he wished he had gone to her instead of letting her come to him.

The week passed as David worked with a renewed energy, hoping to lose himself in the very spreadsheets he used to hate. He climbed his stairs, sometimes twice, and he walked home at the end of each day and did his best not to think of anything at all. At this he failed, and he thought nine hundred thousand times an evening about June.

Saturday morning he got in his car and drove out of the city. But he did not take the exit for Echo Glen. Instead he passed it by and drove farther north, into his past, to a place he had long since forgotten all

228

about, or so he liked to pretend.

The house was there as if nothing had happened. As if his mother had not gotten sick and moved to a care center closer to him; almost as if his father had not died in the accident all those years ago. The yard was mowed, thanks to a neighborhood kid to whom David sent a monthly check, and the flower baskets were planted with purple geraniums by a thoughtful neighbor who knew David's mother had loved nothing more than seeing hummingbirds visit her porch. This small gesture wet David's eyes and reminded him to believe in the general goodness of people before choosing to see the bad.

He parked his car and got out. He stood on the porch and looked out at the street he used to roam on his bicycle, riding long into warm summer evenings until the streetlights came on one by one and he heard his mother's call to come home. What he wouldn't have given to hear that call again. Or perhaps in a way he had, for here he was. He opened the door and went in.

His mother had done little to change the house since he had left it for university at the age of nineteen, and he had done nothing since she left it the year before for the care center. It was a time capsule filled with memories, memories and photos of a once-happy family that had been ripped apart on a cold November night.

David went into the living room and stood looking at the old carousel rooster that they had driven that evening to pick up. It was a sad reminder, but one that neither he nor his mother could ever bear to sell. One of their first customers when they had reopened the shop wanted to buy it. His mother quoted an outrageous price, and when the man agreed to pay it, she changed her mind and told him it actually wasn't for sale. They brought it home the next day and it sat in their living room, a reminder of what David had done. It had not been restored, as had been his father's plan, but was in the exact condition it had been when the wrecking crew recovered it from the ditch. How could a stupid rooster come out unscathed, David wondered, while his seemingly immortal father was suddenly nothing but a lifeless figure whose son cried over him on a cold November road, begging him to wake up? His mother reassured him that it wasn't his fault, but although his mother was an honest woman, David in his teenage wisdom knew she must have been lying just the same. He remembered that day as if it were yesterday, which for him, in a way, it was.

His father had come home excited. His business was American antiques, but his hobby was restoring carousel figures. He had spent much of his adult life tracking down the fate of the figures from a scrapped carousel in the town where he had grown up in Tennessee. And he had finally located the one he had been looking for. It wasn't the bucking horse or the prancing panther that all the other boys had raced to claim before the rides began. No, for David's father it was the old rooster. He said it reminded him of his own father, who loved roosters so much he would sketch them.

After locating it in an old antiques shop just a four-hour drive away, over the mountain pass in Leavenworth, he had written the shop's owner and struck up a deal to buy it. And so he and young David set out to pick it up.

David would never forget how happy his father had been when he set eyes on that old rooster again. It was as if he were reliving his childhood, running his hands over the old wood, the flaking paint. The man had it mounted by its pole in a metal stand, and as soon as they had sealed the deal and he had been paid, my father climbed up on top of it and sat on that rooster like a kid.

David had never seen his smile so wide. And he was still smiling hours later when he asked David to drive so he could get some rest. They said because he wasn't wearing a seat belt he likely died instantly, and David liked to think that maybe it was true. Maybe he died with that smile still on his face, he thought.

David left the living room and went into his old bathroom and looked at himself in the mirror. He saw a boy looking back, and he reached out and brought his hand to the glass, as if to caress the boy's cheek. He wanted to tell the boy that it wasn't his fault. That he was not to blame. But he couldn't. What he did manage to say was something the boy had desperately needed to hear.

"You'll be all right," he said. "Everything will turn out okay, I promise."

And in that moment a weight he'd been carrying dropped from his back. At long last he could find no guilt in that face, only the sadness of a boy who had lost his father too soon. He knew he owed this newfound ability to forgive himself to Echo Glen and to June, and he made a decision on the spot to honor the gift he had been given with a gift of his own.

He was no longer looking upon the boy's

face in the mirror. Instead, he was seeing the man that boy had become. And for once, the man was smiling. He was still smiling when the Realtor knocked on the door.

"I was wondering about that old rooster," I said.

He had paused to take a drink of his water. He looked over at the rooster where it stood by the window, almost as if coming back to the room from a deep reflection and seeing it anew. "Objects are important," he said. "They remind us."

"Sometimes I wish I had something of my father's."

"You didn't keep anything?"

"There wasn't much to keep. The only thing he collected was wine, and he drank himself to death on that. About all there was left were bills and a giant antique wine cask with about five thousand corks in it. I don't even know why he saved them. Although looking back, maybe I should have at least kept that cask."

"What did you do with it?" Mr. Hadley asked.

"I loaded it on my old rusted wagon, the same one my father used when I was a boy to deliver his wine orders, and I towed it with my bike all the way down to the bay. I thought maybe I'd make a nice gesture of dumping the corks into the water and watching them float away. But it turned out to be a huge mistake."

"Why? What happened?"

"It's embarrassing."

"Well, you don't have to tell me then."

"No, I'll tell it. I've never told anyone before, though. What I did was I dumped the corks into the water. All of them. Then I sat back on a rock to watch them bob in the tide and float away. But I wasn't the only one watching. A flock of seagulls saw them and came wheeling over from the piers and started diving and eating the corks. At first I thought it was funny. But then I saw one choking and I realized it had a cork stuck in its throat. Aren't they the dumbest birds? But anyway, dumb or not, all that wine had killed my old man, but I'd be damned if I'd let it kill a bunch of seagulls too. So I waded out into the water and started collecting all the corks.

"There was no way, though. There were too many. I got maybe a couple hundred of them, but that's about it. Well, plus a pretty bad case of pneumonia. I only stopped because someone had seen me and thought I was either crazy or trying to hurt myself, or both. I was crying pretty good and splashing around, chasing away seagulls and throwing corks up onto the bank, when a coast guard skiff eventually came over and ordered me out of the water. I wouldn't get in the ambulance unless they agreed to take my bike, but I forgot to mention the old wine cask and I never did go back for it."

When I finished Mr. Hadley just looked at me from his chair, as if he were waiting for more. But there wasn't any more to tell. He wasn't laughing either, even though I had hoped it would be funny.

"You know what," he eventually said, "June would have really liked you."

I blushed a little, but I didn't say anything. What can you say to a thing like that?

"So you don't have anything from your childhood?" he asked.

"Not really. Just an old photo of my dad from a log-splitting contest he won, and one of my mother that she sent after she left. And I have that old clipping of my dream condo in Miami, of course, but let's not get into that again."

That made him laugh. "Okay," he said, "I'll let up on Florida. They did give us Key lime pie after all. And they have manatees. Who doesn't like manatees?"

"It's good to see you coming to your

senses," I said jokingly. "But let's get back to your story. I think you were about to list your family home for sale."

"That's right, I did. And I spent that night there in my old bed after I'd listed it too. It was the last time I ever slept under that roof, and I swore I could hear my father out in the living room listening to the eleven o'clock news. It was a nice sound to fall asleep to. The next day I left to see June . . ."

19

It was Sunday afternoon by the time he pulled into Echo Glen, and he saw no sign of either Sebastian or June. The truck they shared was gone, and the house was closed up and quiet. David parked anyway and walked down to the stables. As he passed the ostrich pen, the big bird lifted its head and followed him with its curious avian eyes.

"Easy, boy," David said. "We called a truce, remember?"

He found Rosie in her stall, gnawing unenthusiastically on hay, and he reached into his coat pocket for the apple he had bought from a roadside fruit stand on his way.

"Hi, girl. You remember me?"

She lifted her head and licked his outstretched hand, signaling that she did. He couldn't help but wonder if a blind horse could recognize voices the way a blind person could. Or perhaps each hand had a particular taste. He held out the apple, and after a few curious licks, she sucked it up into her mouth and crunched it loudly.

"Isn't that the most beautiful sound in the entire world?"

June was standing in the entrance to the stable, smiling. The open doorway at her back cast a nimbus of golden light around her so that she appeared to David to be an angel called into being by the sound of a horse eating an apple, or perhaps simply by his own silent desire. June joined him at the stall and reached out to rub Rosie's head.

"She likes you," she said. "So far she's been pretty skittish with people. Even the vet had a hard time getting her to settle down for her shots."

"Maybe she should have shown up with an apple instead of a needle."

June laughed. "There's truth in that." Then she looked at David and he thought he saw a hint of sadness in her eyes. "How was your week?"

"It was okay," he said. "How was yours?"

She shook her head. "Not good. I got some bad news."

"About Echo Glen and finances?"

She didn't answer his question.

"Do you have time to take a walk?" she asked. "I'd like to show you something."

They crossed the creek together on the footbridge and walked into the wood. The shade felt nice. When they reached the point where David thought he remembered turning off to go hang gliding that night, he started to take the breakaway path but June gripped his arm and stopped him.

"I haven't forgotten I owe you another lesson," she said, "but right now I'd like to show you someplace very special."

The path she led him up wound through old Doug firs, taking them slowly higher on gentle switchbacks until David could just glimpse the fields and house below them through breaks in the trees.

"Is this all part of your property?" he asked.

"This is nearly the edge of it," she said. "We're surrounded by state land, but fortunately because of the creek they don't lease for logging near here. What I want to show you is just ahead, around the bend there."

They walked together the rest of the way in silence, at least until they rounded the corner into a glen and David impulsively said, "Whoa! It's beautiful."

He was standing next to June and looking up into a narrow mountain glen. The headwaters for the creek ran through the center of the glen, fed by a waterfall tumbling over a wall of moss-covered granite. There was a break in the surrounding trees the width of the glen and the sunlight illuminated the dewy moss, turning it into a carpet of sparkling green. There was a low hill beside the pool at the base of the waterfall with a lone oak tree growing on its crest. The oak's thick leaves filtered the light, green and gold, onto the mossy hillside below.

"It's absolutely stunning," David said, drinking in the view.

"This is Echo Glen," June replied. "Come on, I'll take you to my special place."

She took his hand in hers and led him farther into the glen. At the base of the hill, June kicked off her shoes. David did the same. Then they walked barefoot together up the hill. The moss felt cool and soft beneath David's bare feet. When they reached the tree, June sat down with her back against the trunk and sighed as if releasing every care she had ever had in the world. David sat beside her, and together they watched the waterfall. It was not loud — the water ran low in the summer — but the sound was as soothing as any David had heard.

"Why is there no English word for that

sound?" he asked, almost to himself. "The sound of a waterfall spilling into a pool. Or is there one and I just don't know it?"

June appeared to agree, closing her eyes and saying, "There ought to be a hundred words to describe it."

Yes, David thought, there should be a hundred words at least. But there ought to be a hundred more to describe it heard in the company of someone you love.

"If you yell a wish at the waterfall from right here it echoes back," June said, opening her eyes. "And then it comes true. I know because this is where I sat when I wished for this place to be my home. I suspected then what I know now, that this is where I would spend the rest of my days."

"How did you find this place?" David asked.

"I came here to teach hang gliding for a summer. An old couple owned the property, but they had both moved to New Hampshire, where they later passed away, and the hang gliding school was leasing the property from their children, who also lived on the other coast. I got in touch with them and bought the place on the spot."

"Was it your plan to make it an animal sanctuary?"

"No," she said, shaking her head and smiling. "That was an incremental accident. I was dividing my time between here and Los Angeles, working down there whenever I could. Then one by one, I seemed to come across animals in need. Or maybe they came across me. I don't know. But here I had all this property and these old barns and stables sitting empty. So I started taking them in. Then word got out and the phone began to ring. Before I knew it, I had way too much responsibility here to spend much time in LA, plus falling down for a living starts to get old. That's when I officially founded Echo Glen."

"When I was doing your books it looked like the nonprofit was pretty well capitalized initially," David said. "You must have had a big donor to start with."

"We did." She chuckled. "That big donor was me."

"You did this all with your own money?"

"Why not? I had been fortunate, hadn't I? Being paid pretty well pretending to be big-name stars, jumping out of airplanes or burning buildings. Did you know I once crashed a Shelby Mustang wearing a mustache and a wig? Anyway, this seemed like as good a way as any to give back. You can't see it now, but we've helped a lot of animals over the years. Nursed them back from the brink, placed them in homes. I'm proud of what I accomplished and I wouldn't change a thing."

"Even though you're out of money now?"

"What's money good for if it isn't used for good?"

They sat quiet for a while, watching birds flit between the trees and listening to the murmur of the waterfall. After a while, David reached and took June's hand in his.

"I have to tell you something," he said. "Remember how I told you about my family house up in Bellingham? How Realtors kept calling me to deal with it? Well, it seems like Californians are selling their homes for a lot of money and retiring up there, and the old place is worth more than I thought. I finally listed it yesterday. And when it sells I should have enough to pay off your mortgage here."

When he finished delivering the good news, he looked over at her, hoping to see the smile that he had come already to love. But all he saw was confusion in her eyes. She released his hand and turned to face him.

"I can't take your money, David. It's out of the question."

"Why not?" he asked. "You take donations for the sanctuary all the time."

"That's different and you know it."

"How is it any different?"

"Those people can afford to part with the money for one thing. You have your own retirement to think of. You don't want to end up with nothing like me."

"That's my choice, not yours. And didn't you just say money wasn't good for anything unless it was used for something good?"

"Don't do that, David. Don't turn my own words against me like that."

"Fine, but I'm still donating the proceeds when the house sells."

"No." She said it like she meant it. "I'm not accepting it, David. When people pledge money they do it in amounts they can afford. And they do it for the animals, not because they're expecting something in return from me."

"What's that supposed to mean, June?"

She opened her mouth to reply but appeared to change her mind, getting up instead and walking over to stand by herself and look off toward the waterfall.

Then she said, "We should be getting back."

David stayed seated.

"I can't believe that you think I'm doing this expecting something in return, June. What, just because we had sex?"

"I don't know what you're doing it for," she said, still looking away.

"Maybe because I just want to, June. Can't that at least be a possibility?"

She turned and walked back, standing to look down on him. Her eyes were wet and she was shaking her head.

"You don't want to fall in love with me, David. You really don't."

"Who said I was falling in love?"

"Are you telling me you're not?"

Now David looked away. "Maybe I already have," he said. "I don't know." Then he turned to look up at June again. "But you don't get to decide who I fall in love with, June. If you don't love me back, that's your business. My love doesn't require it. And neither does my gift."

"You hardly even know me."

"That's bullshit, June. How well does anyone ever know anybody? I knew you the moment I saw you on that roof. And I think you knew me too."

"Come on, David . . ."

She walked off a few paces again, standing at the hill's edge and looking down into the pool with her arms crossed. David got up off the ground and went to stand beside her.

"Listen, June." His voice was gentler now,

almost resolved. "I know I'm just a dumpy old accountant, not some Hollywood hotshot. It doesn't take a genius to know that some suicidal slob you met on a roof isn't exactly the world's greatest catch. I know this. And I know I don't deserve someone like you. And that's fine, too. I'm not asking for anything. I'm really not. You've done enough for me already."

"That's silly, and you know it," she said.

A few quiet moments passed between them. Then he asked, "Which part?"

"Which part what?"

"Which part is silly?"

"All of it," she answered. "But especially the part about you being dumpy and not deserving me. I happen to think you're very attractive. Don't laugh; it's true. And besides, I've had quite enough of Hollywood and its hotshots. But this isn't about that, David. There are things about me you don't know. Hell, there are things about me I didn't even know until recently. So let's just let it go for now. All right?"

He wanted to push the conversation, but something in the tone of her voice was almost pleading with him to let it go, so he did. He couldn't bear to see the pain that was in her eyes.

"Will you still give me that glider lesson?"

246

She looked down for a moment, and then the smile he had longed to see crept back into her eyes.

"Fine," she said. "But I won't have you talking nonsense about giving me your money while I'm a captive audience a thousand feet in the air. No funny business. Promise?"

"No funny business. Scout's honor. Can't I at least grope you a little in the harness, though?"

She laughed. "I usually charge extra for that, but seeing as how you've already paid, it's okay. But we better get moving. We'll have to carry the glider up, and we're losing daylight fast. There isn't any moon to fly by tonight."

They walked down the hill together and quietly reclaimed the path. When they had left the glen and the sound of the waterfall behind, David stopped.

"What's the matter?" June asked.

"Wait here a second," he said. "I forgot something."

She looked confused but agreed to stay put while he turned and jogged back up into the glen. He never would know for sure, but he suspected then, as he did many years later long after it had come true, that from where she stood waiting for him on that path she must have heard the wish he hollered at the waterfall come echoing back.

20

He stopped the story there and reached for his cane. Then he rose from the chair and walked to the window and looked out. When he spoke again, it was almost as if he had forgotten that I was there and was talking instead to himself.

"The sun was setting when we launched the glider, but it wasn't that cool yet. It was still July for God's sake. Yet she was shaking like a leaf in my arms when we landed." He shook his head. "And all I cared about was me, me, me, and how good I felt at the time. I didn't think anything of it. I didn't even offer her my jacket, not that it would have helped. I had no way of knowing, did I? It never occurred to me before, but she must have known already. She must have known."

"Known what?" I asked. "What was wrong?"

At the sound of my voice he seemed to come to with a jolt, turning from the window. He looked momentarily confused, glancing around the room, and then to me, as if he had to think about where he was.

"I was hoping to finish the story before we lost our daylight," he finally said, "but it appears my timing was a little off. I think it's time we take a walk, if you're up for it."

"But it's still raining," I said.

"You don't look like you'll melt, young man. I'm pretty sure I've got some galoshes that will fit your feet, and we can bring along the bumbershoot."

"Bumbershoot?"

"Umbrella," he said. "I've got a big one."

It turned out he was wrong about the galoshes. They wouldn't stretch over my shoes. Instead he found me an old pair of rubber muck boots, far from a perfect fit but large enough to do the trick. But while he had been wrong about the galoshes, calling the umbrella big was absolutely accurate. I wasn't sure whether it was a golf umbrella or some kind of gag gift, but it looked like it was meant to be stuck in a picnic table and was large enough and sturdy enough to protect a small family from a hurricane. The damn thing was heavy too.

"Do you usually carry this umbrella yourself?" I asked as we left the porch and walked around behind the house.

"Lord no," he said. "This is actually the first time I've used it. I won it from the golf store in a radio raffle. You should have seen the box they sent it in."

"Well, now I see why you call it a bumbershoot; I'll bet you could use it for a parachute in a pinch."

He led me across the creek, over the old footbridge, and up the path into the wood. The rain thundered loudly on the big umbrella and our boots plashed in puddles on the path. As we walked deeper into the forest, the trees blocked the worst of the rain and the pounding on the umbrella quieted to a patter, allowing us to talk.

"You're taking me up to Echo Glen, aren't you?"

He nodded. "There's something there you need to see before I can explain my predicament and my proposition."

"Good," I replied. "I was worried there for a minute that maybe you had a little hang gliding adventure planned for us."

He laughed. "I wouldn't do that to you. My flying days are far behind me now. Besides, the only person I ever took tandem was June. We had one last flight several years ago. Hot summer day, lots of thermals, we stayed up for over an hour. You should have seen her smile. It really was beautiful."

We walked quietly for a while after that. Partly because the rain falling through the trees created a solemn feeling in me, and partly because Mr. Hadley began to struggle as the path inclined. He had brought along his cane and was leaning on it more and more, his breathing becoming labored and his pace slowing considerably. Looking back now, there was no way he should have been climbing up that path — although when I casually mentioned that maybe we should turn back, he told me that no hitch in his step could keep him away. He said he'd gone up every day, rain or shine, for five years. And once we got there I understood why.

I heard the waterfall before I saw it. Then the trees cleared overhead and the rain returned to the umbrella canopy as we rounded the bend and walked into Echo Glen. The result of the rumbling waterfall and the rain pelting the umbrella was that I could hardly hear myself exclaim, "Whoa!"

Echo Glen was even more beautiful than I had imagined it. A narrow cut in a sheer face of granite cliff, over which the waterfall spilled into a pool, with the gorgeous, clear-water creek weaving through the glen. Then I saw the moss-covered hill and the oak tree.

Many of the tree's leaves had fallen, but those that remained were reddened a startling shade.

I couldn't tell whether he was waiting to catch his breath or maybe saying some kind of prayer, but Mr. Hadley paused at the base of the hill and bowed his head for a moment. When he did finally start up, I followed behind, holding the umbrella and preparing myself to catch him in case he slipped. But I had nothing to worry about because the surefooted old dodger mounted the hill like a goat. I came up beside him and stood looking down at the leaf-covered mound. I knew what it was, of course, even before he knelt to brush away the fallen leaves.

The humble stone was inscribed with these words:

HERE RESTS
JUNE LOUISE MCLEOD-HADLEY
MARCH 3, 1933–OCTOBER 10, 2010
HER SPIRIT HAVING RETURNED HOME,
"JUST BEYOND THE SECOND STAR TO
THE RIGHT AND STRAIGHT ON TILL
MORNING."

It was a simple headstone with a simple message that was not lost on me after having heard her story. But still, she hadn't passed until 2010, which meant there was a lot of story left to hear. Mr. Hadley was kneeling beside the grave with his hand on the stone and his head bowed, and I stood quietly by, holding the umbrella but not wanting to disturb him. He eventually went to rise but wobbled on one knee and fell over and sat beside the grave. My initial instinct was to help him up, but then I didn't want him to feel embarrassed, so I sat down beside him on the wet ground and propped the umbrella up between us.

"I was just about to sit down for a rest myself," I said.

He smiled, obviously aware that I was full of shit. Then he put his hand on my arm as if to thank me. The rain pelted the umbrella above our heads and the waterfall poured down into the pool. It was kind of nice and kind of sad.

"Isn't it a beautiful sound?" he said.

"The waterfall or the rain?"

"Both," he said. "All of it."

"It's nice," I said. "Although I prefer the sun to the rain."

"That's right," he said. "Mr. Miami. I'd almost forgotten. But sunshine doesn't have any history. You know where it comes from, anyway. Not so with the rain."

"Sure you do. Rain comes from a rain-cloud."

"Yes, but how did it get there?"

"How did it get there? Well, I'm no meteorologist or anything, but I did take basic environmental studies. I think it's called the hydrologic cycle. It evaporates from the oceans. Because of the sun, I might add."

He nodded. "Fair point, about the sun." Then he wagged a finger. "But you said yourself it's a cycle. That means each of those drops could have come from anywhere, you see."

"What do you mean?" I asked.

"Follow one drop with me. Come on. Try it. There. That big one that just hit. See it?"

"I see a bunch of them."

"Exactly," he said, raising his eyebrows like a proud professor. "A bunch of drops raining down onto an untouched glen, dripping off our umbrella, joining others in a clear mountain creek, swelling the rivers, and finally pouring into the sea to join all the other drops waiting there in that vast pool of experience, each molecule with a story of its own."

"You're saying each raindrop has a story."

"It's possible, isn't it? Each person sure does. And just think of the places and the people each raindrop might have touched. There. That one. Maybe it quenched Joan of Arc's thirst while she carried her banner in Orléans. Or that one. A sacred drop, perhaps. Could it have landed like a prayer on the upturned face of our Man on the cross? Another, humbler drop. This one watered a field of poppies in Spain. This one fell on my sweet, sweet June on our wedding day. I watched it drip down her cheek. I tasted it on her lip when we finally kissed after saying 'I do.' No, it's not just a cycle, young man. It's an echo, I tell you."

"Is that why June named this Echo Glen?"

"Yes," he said. "Our lives echo. Love echoes. And that wish I yelled all those years ago echoes, right here, along with our love story that unfolded when it came true — the love story that lies beside the waterfall with my dearly departed June."

I looked over at the stone beside us, and for a moment it almost seemed as if there were three of us sitting on that hill together, watching the waterfall and the rain.

"I know you told me not to say I was sorry," I said, "but I am sorry about your wife's passing. I would have loved to have had the chance to meet her."

He patted my arm. "She would have loved to have met you too." He was quiet for a while. Then he said, "She wasn't sad, you know. Not in the end. She died with a smile on her face. She couldn't say it, but I think she knew she was going home. And she knew I'd be joining her there soon."

Somehow a falling leaf had gotten past our umbrella and was clinging to Mr. Hadley's damp hair, and as he mentioned his someday joining her, his position next to his buried wife with leaves already landing atop him was not lost on me.

"Does it make you sad to think about it?" I asked. "Dying, I mean."

As soon as I'd said it, I realized how inappropriate it seemed. But I guess I just never felt comfortable asking my own dad this kind of stuff, and I was curious. Plus, I really had grown to like Mr. Hadley, and the idea of his dying made me really sad for some reason. But he didn't seem offended. He just thought for a minute, then looked directly at me as he spoke:

"I don't know if this answers your question — and I've never much cared for unsolicited advice, so forgive me this one time for offering it — but I'll tell you this, young Elliot: one lifetime is enough when you spend it in love. Yes, it's this old man's opinion that a life lived for love is a life well spent."

I've never been a big believer in signs and all that junk, and after everything that's happened I'm still not, to tell you the truth, but I'm not exaggerating even a little when I tell you now that as soon as Mr. Hadley uttered that sentence — well, the rain suddenly stopped and the sun dropped below the clouds, and an absolutely beautiful rainbow from the mist began rising above the falls. If it wasn't a sign, it sure was impeccable timing. And it was a big bonus to finally set that huge umbrella down for a bit.

"Hey, Mr. Hadley," I said after a while. "Can I tell you something?" He looked at me and nodded, so I went on: "This has been both the strangest and the best birthday ever, and I'm glad it was me who got your letter."

"Well, don't speak too soon," he said. "You haven't heard my proposal yet."

"I'd like to hear the rest of your story, actually."

He looked a little surprised. "You would?"

"Yes. Like what was going on with June? And how did you two save Echo Glen? And you mentioned something earlier about being arrested in Spain. I'm really curious."

"I knew you'd fall for her," he said. "Everyone falls for June. Maybe we should head back, get inside, dry off, and then I'll tell you the rest. I'm afraid this wet moss has either soaked straight through my pants or I've had an accident sitting here. Give an old man a hand up, will you?"

21

We were halfway down the path when he fell. I didn't even see it happen. I was strolling along ahead of him like a mindless idiot, using the closed umbrella as a walking stick, and if he shouted or made any sound at all I didn't hear that either. All I remember is sensing that he was no longer following behind me and turning back to see him lying on the path. I dropped the umbrella and rushed to his side.

"Mr. Hadley, are you okay? What happened?"

He was lying facedown, and it looked as if he was struggling to breathe. I got my hands beneath him and turned him over, gripping his shoulders and helping to sit him upright. He was surprisingly light, and I noticed that he was actually wearing several layers of clothing, including the thick sweater, which made him appear much bigger than he actually was.

"Are you okay? You're having trouble breathing."

"I'm fine," he said, gripping my forearm.

He sounded anything but fine. His voice was raspy and strained, his breathing labored and shallow. The contents of his sweater pockets had fallen out onto the path when he took his spill, and I used my free hand to gather up his things and put them back: notebook and reading glasses, a pen, a small bottle of pills, replacement hearing-aid batteries, several wrapped peppermints, and an old photo.

"Is this June?" I asked, looking at the photo.

He reached out and pulled my hand closer so he could see the photo, even though there were no other photos in his pockets and I knew he didn't need to identify it. I think he just wanted to see her, the old romantic, sitting right there on that dirt path, disheveled and muddied like some old rugby player refusing to quit the game. He took several deep, calming breaths and seemed to feel better after looking at her image.

"That's my June," he said. "Isn't she beautiful?"

"She is striking. I see what you mean about her eyes. They're smiling right off the photo. But why is she wearing a matador costume, and why is there blood on both your hands? I can't see her killing bulls."

"Oh no," he said. "That's fake blood. Dye, actually. She'd never kill an animal for sport. Although we did eat bull stew at our reception. No, this was what June wore for our wedding. I joked that if she was going to keep that bloody matador costume on for the ceremony, I'd dress up as the bull. We were married right there by the *jefe de la policía* who had arrested us just twenty-four hours before."

I was glad he seemed to be feeling better, but my legs were getting tired squatting beside him in the path.

"Well, let's get you back and you can tell me all about it," I said. "Here, let me help you up. You must be freezing. These old corduroys are soaked through."

"I can't promise that that's rainwater either," he said. "I'm sorry to be such a burden. I really am. I'm sure this isn't how you envisioned spending your birthday."

"I'll hear none of that. Lean on me. Or do you want your cane?"

"Who needs a cane when I fall so gracefully?" he asked, grinning. "But what about the umbrella?"

"It's not raining now."

"I won that in a radio contest, you know."

"I'll come back for it."

The sun had set by the time we made it back to the house, and he was shivering in my arms. I got him inside and sat him in his chair. Then I lit the wood stove.

"You usually build this thing up yourself?" I asked. "How do you get the wood inside? Maybe you should have a heat pump installed."

I realized my mistake the moment I said it. Here I was on a pre-foreclosure house call to evict the old man from his property, the property where his wife was buried, and I was dumb enough to be suggesting improvements to his heating system. Fortunately, when I looked up to apologize, he was already asleep in his chair.

Once I had the stove going good, I slipped out and went back up the trail for his umbrella. It was quickly getting dark and I had a hard time locating it. I might not have if it hadn't been so damn big. As I made my way back toward the house on the dusky path, the sound of the murmuring creek was carried to me on a soft breeze. I took in long breaths of cool pine-scented air, smelling the sap and the rain, and reflected on my life for the first time in a long time. Was it visiting June's grave that had me reflecting? Maybe it was Mr. Hadley's stories. It could even have been that it was my birthday, I don't know. Maybe it was an early midlife crisis. Is there a one-third life crisis that happens to people?

I stopped just on the other side of the creek and looked at the house. White smoke was rising from the chimney into the slate-colored sky, and the lamplight made the living room look warm and cozy. I could just make out Mr. Hadley sleeping in the chair where I had left him, and I wondered how many nights these last few years he had sat there alone, looking out at this creek, thinking about his wife. I wondered what their life had been like here before she died. Mostly, I wondered how in the hell I could even go through with trying to get him to leave.

The teapot atop the wood stove was whistling when I entered the house. I ran to take it off before it woke Mr. Hadley, but he was already awake. He looked around the room, as if wondering how he had gotten there, and then he looked at me where I stood in front of him holding the steaming teapot.

"Who are you?" he asked.

"I'm Elliot Champ, sir."

He patted his breast pockets, as if searching for something, perhaps his notebook.

But then he seemed to remember, letting his hands drop into his lap.

"Oh yes. I'm afraid I've taken a nap. That happens sometimes. Why am I all wet?"

"You fell, sir. On the path."

He either didn't hear me or he ignored my comment.

"I took a nap once down at Clancy's, and Lisa tried to tell me I'd passed out. She said people don't nap at coffee counters. I don't go there anymore. Not because of Lisa or anything, though. I had to give up driving. Was I dreaming, or did we visit Echo Glen?"

"Yes, you took me up there," I said. "You fell on the way down, don't you remember?"

"That explains why I'm all wet," he replied. "At least I hope it does. Hand me my cane there, will you, young man? I'd like to go freshen up."

I set the teapot down and retrieved his cane for him.

"How about I make us some tea," I suggested. "And then, if you're feeling up to it, maybe you can continue your story."

"Okay," he said. "There's Smooth Move in the kitchen cupboard, just left of the stove. Maybe you could cut us up an apple too. I need to take my medication."

When he came out again he was wearing furry slippers and a bright-red paisley-patterned robe. Without all those layers of clothing, he looked much thinner than he had before, but he appeared to have recovered from whatever had been causing his coughing fits.

"I didn't know I was being hosted by Hugh Hefner."

"Hugh who?" he asked. Then he looked down at his robe and laughed. "Oh, this old thing. June ordered me this robe from a catalog. She claimed it was supposed to be blue, but then decided to keep it because she said my face matched the fabric I blushed so much the first time I put it on."

"I put your tea on the table there next to your chair."

"Thank you." He lowered himself into the chair. "That stove heats the place pretty well, doesn't it?"

"It reminds me of the one we had in our house growing up. Well, it was more of a trailer than a house, but it had a nice stove. Once a week my dad would borrow the company truck and bring home mill scraps for us to burn. Sometimes, if it was really cold, he'd order a real cord of wood and pay me a couple bucks to split it."

"That's good work," he said, "splitting wood is. Makes a young man strong. But it's a skill you won't be needing in Miami,

I'm afraid."

Uh-oh, I thought. Not this debate again. But I refused the bait, smiling and shaking my head instead of responding.

"Listen, Elliot," he said. "You've been patient enough with me, listening to my story and spending your whole day here. Let me cut to the chase and make my proposition so you can go home and think it over." He reached into his robe pocket and took out his notebook. "Let's see, you said you needed twenty thousand dollars to get that condo, is that right?"

He was right, but I didn't answer him. I wasn't in the mood to hear his proposal just then. I knew I'd probably have to turn him down on ethical grounds, whatever his pitch was, and that would be hard for me to do. Also, I feared once I did tell him no I wouldn't get a chance to hear the rest of his story, and I was really curious about what eventually happened to June.

"You know what," I said, "why don't we wait on the proposal part for a bit. I'd rather not leave now anyway. I'll just hit traffic going into the city. Maybe you can tell me the rest of your story first. You know, how you saved Echo Glen and how you proposed to June. You need to explain being arrested in Spain and that matador costume."

"Oh you've been too kind already," he said. "I wouldn't feel right keeping you."

"No, I mean it. I want to hear the story. You wouldn't turn down a request from a man on his birthday, would you?"

"You really want to hear it?" he asked.

I nodded. "Yes, I really do."

He smiled. "June would have liked you. Have I told you that already? I have. Sometimes I repeat myself. You're a good egg, Elliot Champ. You know that?"

I felt myself blush. "My dad used to call me a good egg."

"Well, your dad was right," he said. Then he returned the notebook to his robe pocket and pulled out an old newspaper clipping. He held the paper out for me. "Since you want to hear more, you might as well read this. It's an anonymous letter to the editor I wrote about my stunt camp experience."

I took the letter and read it.

Dear Editor:

Who knew impersonating a newspaper reporter could be so life changing and so fun? I have hung from the rafters of an old barn dressed as Peter Pan, flown a glider through moonlit skies, and jumped a burning car. I have fought an angry ostrich and lost; I have fought my

268

own fear and won. You see, just an hour and a half northeast from Seattle, in the Center of the Universe, is a place called Echo Glen. This animal sanctuary/ Hollywood stunt camp saves the lives of desperate animals while changing the lives of courageous men and women desiring a career in stunt acting. Here you can get an adrenaline rush and a thousand-watt jolt of feel-good juice at the same time, because the profits from the stunt camp go to the worthy cause of caring for animals in need of a safe and healing place. And that's just what they'll find at Echo Glen. I know because I needed the same thing and I found it there too.

Your paper was invited to attend stunt camp, or at least write an article on it, but no one ever showed. This was good news for me, as it created an opening, but terrible news for your readers, who have been denied learning about this magical place. Please consider writing a story about Echo Glen, or at least asking your readers to donate to this worthy cause.

To donate or make inquiries, please reach out to June McLeod or Sebastian Villarreal at Echo Glen Animal

Sanctuary/Echo Glen Hollywood Stunt School, at 772 1/2 Whispering Willow Lane, Darrington, WA 98241.

Sincerely,
Peter Pan
(If Peter Pan ever grew up
and became an accountant.)

"It's a good letter," I said, once I had finished reading.

"Thanks. I sent it to the *Times* first, and then to the *Post-Intelligencer,* in case they wanted to print it and embarrass their competition. I thought it might drum up some publicity for the camp and for Echo Glen. Plus, I was trying to impress June. I'm not ashamed to admit it either."

He took the letter back, refolded it, and slipped it into his robe pocket.

"Well, if you're serious about wanting to suffer through more storytelling you had better get yourself some tea. And I should get a bite to eat so I can take my medication."

"Oh, I forgot your apple. I already cut it up."

I didn't tell him I had even squeezed lemon juice on the slices so they wouldn't brown, just like I'd seen him do. I went into the kitchen and retrieved the plate of apple slices from the refrigerator and brought them back in to him.

"Did you get something?" he asked. "You can have a MoonPie if you want."

"Oh, I'm fine. I had some water. Thanks."

He ate a slice of apple before fishing the pill bottle from his robe pocket and washing one down with a sip of tea. Then he leaned back in his chair with the plate of apples in his lap.

"Okay, well, where was I? I think I had just told you about June taking me up to Echo Glen. Yes, that's right. I had listed my home and offered her the money."

"But she refused to accept the gift," I said. "Didn't she?"

"Yes, she did. And I believe she would have refused it again if I had let her. But I had other tricks up my sleeve . . ."

22

David's realtor called him at his office that Wednesday to say she had received two offers already on the house. He had been willing to let it go when he listed it but had never considered that the parting might come so soon.

The offers were similar, except he thought he recognized the last name on one of them.

"Van Buren," he said. "As in Gloria Van Buren, the nice woman who taught science and math at the middle school?"

"I'm not sure," the Realtor said. "But Bill is a teacher, and so were his mother and grandmother."

David could not believe that the grandchild of one of his teachers was in a position to buy his childhood home. By what dark magic do days turn into years? He shrugged off the thought and told the Realtor to accept the Van Buren offer, agreeing to drive up after work to sign it.

On his way back from Bellingham that evening, he almost took the exit that would have led him toward Echo Glen. But he didn't. It was all he could do to keep his hands from turning the wheel as he passed. He knew if he saw June he would be unable to contain the news, and he knew if he told her he had sold his family home she would only restate her refusal to accept his gift.

Staying away from Echo Glen and from June proved to be one of the most difficult things David had ever had to do. The home sale took forty-five days to close, and every hour of it crawled by at a pace that was painfully slow. His mother had always been fond of saying that a watched pot never boils, and he assumed this sage wisdom applied to home sales as well, so to pass the time he threw himself into his work, climbing to the top of the billable-hour bonus board for the first time in his history with the firm. It was all smiles passing his desk now.

He took to the stairs again too, jogging up them every day after work and pausing at the top step to look at the locked door and smile. He smiled because of how far he had come from that hopeless man he had been, and he smiled because it was there on that roof that he had first met June. He knew now what he only guessed then, and he was determined to somehow win her heart. And although he suspected paying off her mortgage was not the greatest of strategies, he felt he needed to get it out of the way before he could pursue her romantically, with motives she could no longer question.

Despite the painful waiting to see June, it was the nicest summer David could remember in Seattle. He never once turned on the TV. Instead, he opened the windows and sat in his living room long into the warm August nights, sipping iced tea and listening to the neighborhood kids break dancing on the corner to ghetto blasters pumping out electric beats. And all the while he thought about June.

He could have picked up the phone and called her, or even gotten in his car and driven out to Echo Glen. But he did neither, choosing instead to relive in his thoughts the one night they had shared in that barn, recalling a thousand times her smiling eyes when she woke in his arms. Maybe he chose the fantasy because he was afraid that if he pursued her she would deny him, shattering the illusion that had him soaring through the summer. For it was this illusion that lifted his spirits ever higher, day by day, until he had nearly convinced himself that she would be sitting at Echo Glen, just waiting to receive him and the news of his chivalrous generosity like some damsel in distress waits for her knight to gallop in on his white horse.

When it finally came down to closing day, David arrived in Bellingham early, driving a rented truck. He planned to load up the few remaining things he had asked his Realtor not to let the estate salesperson take, the most cherished of which was his father's carousel rooster. It proved too heavy for him to lift by himself, however, and none of the neighbors were home, so he drove to the local hardware store and picked up a day laborer and offered him twenty bucks to help him load it.

It was a strange feeling seeing it tied down in the truck bed, just as it had been when he and his father had left Leavenworth to take it home all those years before. But although seeing it made him miss his father all the more, it no longer brought up any guilt. He dropped the laborer off with a thank-you and an extra twenty just because, and then drove to the escrow company to sign his final paperwork.

"Now, you're sure you want the proceeds used to pay off this loan at Seafirst Bank," the closing agent asked him for a third time.

"Because that loan's in a different name and once the funds are sent you won't be able to retrieve them."

"Yes, I'm sure," David said.

"And you're aware that there might be a gift tax?"

"It's well within my lifetime exemption," David said. "I am an accountant after all, you know. The little that's left over you can anonymously donate to Echo Glen Animal Sanctuary. I wrote the address there on your form."

He left the escrow office with an envelope of paperwork two inches thick and a smile just as wide. Ever since his mother had gotten too sick to live alone and he had moved her nearer to him, he had often wondered how he could ever part with his childhood home and the memories it held. He thought he'd never be able to sell it, despite his mother's pleas for him to do so, since he was footing much of her bills. But all he had needed to let it go was a worthy cause that wasn't his own.

Before leaving town he stopped by to pay his respects to his mother and father, where they rested together beneath the green grass of Lake View Cemetery.

"I miss you both very much," he said, choking back tears. "But I'm glad you're together again."

It was strange, but even though he had visited his father's grave every weekend growing up, and had buried his mother just several months prior, now that the family home was gone this felt more like closure than any other time before.

"I'd like to thank you for raising me to believe in love. For a while I didn't think it was out there, but now I see it was right under my nose the entire time. It was in our house. I hope to someday be as lucky as you two were."

The sun had dropped behind the hills by the time he arrived at Echo Glen. He parked in front of the house in the pink twilight. He was knocking on the door when he heard someone call his name. Sebastian was standing in the stable door with a shovel in his hand and muck boots up to his knees.

"You're just in time to help me shovel shit, comrade."

David came down from the porch and walked toward him. "I thought maybe you'd gone back to Los Angeles," he said.

Sebastian looked away for a moment and shrugged.

"June isn't here," he finally said.

"Do you know when she'll be back?"

Sebastian leaned the shovel against the

stable door and put his arm around David's shoulder. "Let's go sit down together and have a chat, comrade."

He took David up the stairs to his hayloft apartment. It was David's first time seeing inside, and it was nothing like he would have imagined: a simple cot, a beanbag, the hi-fi system that woke the stunt camp each morning, and an enormous poster of Steve McQueen.

"Is that McQueen's signature?" David asked.

Sebastian nodded. "The King of Cool. I apprenticed on *The Great Escape*. He did so much of his own driving I hardly had a chance to work. Read what he wrote."

David read it aloud: " 'All the courage in the world in a man, and that man my friend.' "

Sebastian smiled. It was clear that he was very proud of this inscription. He pulled the beanbag over near the bed and patted it, indicating that David should sit. Then he opened a small refrigerator and produced a large jar of sangria. He filled two small glasses and handed one to David. Then he sat on the bed and toasted their good fortune.

"Salud y amor y tiempo para disfrutarlo."

David was not certain of the translation,

but he drank to it anyway. The sangria was good. Not too sweet, not too strong.

"So do you know when June will be back?" David asked.

Sebastian lit a cigarette but didn't answer. He blew out a lungful of smoke. "We read your letter in the newspaper," he said. "It was very nice. Unfortunately someone sent it to friends of ours in Hollywood and now I've been found out."

"Found out? What exactly are you running from?"

Sebastian stood from the bed and walked over to the Steve McQueen poster and looked at it. David didn't know what to do so he sipped his sangria. Eventually, Sebastian turned around. He looked to David to be ashamed.

"I am a coward," he said.

"No you're not," David replied. "You're the bravest man I know, and I've seen you take on a dinosaur bird to prove it."

Sebastian dropped his head. "You don't know me, comrade. I came here because I was running away. June was kind enough to take me in, as she does with all things that are weak and helpless."

"But you're no charity case. What about stunt camp?"

He paced the room now, waving his

cigarette as he spoke. "The stunt camp was my idea. I pitched it to June when I learned of her money troubles. But my real motivation was fear. I wanted a reason to stay. You see, comrade, I am hiding from the truth. There is someone I love very much in Los Angeles but I am too afraid to make this love public. I was given an ultimatum and I ran. I ran because I am a coward."

He flopped onto the edge of the bed and hung his head. He had a burning cigarette in one hand, his glass of sangria in the other, and he looked to David to be the very picture of defeat. Especially beneath the proud face of Steve McQueen.

"You can tell me," David said. "I won't judge you."

"You won't?" he asked, raising his head.

"No. I don't have any problem with anyone being gay. And I doubt Hollywood would care much either."

Sebastian shook his head. "No, comrade. I am not gay. That would be easier to explain. My lover is a young woman. An amazing woman. The only woman for me. But, you see, she is Jewish. She has made me the ultimatum to marry her or end our affair, and I ran like a coward."

"But why run? What's the problem? Who cares if she's Jewish? Didn't Jewish immigrants found Hollywood?"

"It's not Hollywood I'm worried about," he said.

"Then what are you worried about?"

He sighed. "My mother."

"Your mother. How old are you?"

"I am forty-two. Why?"

"Because that seems a little old to be worried about what your mother thinks."

"You don't understand how it is, comrade. We are a very Catholic family. It would ruin her."

David thought this sounded somewhat melodramatic, but he didn't say so. Instead he got up and retrieved the sangria and refilled their glasses. Sebastian thanked him and lit another cigarette, scooting back on the bed to lean against the wall.

"You'll do the right thing," David said.

Sebastian nodded. "I hope so."

They sat quietly for a while, drinking their sangria. Sebastian blew smoke rings. After a time, he said, "I did not bring you up here purely to confess for my own relief. I brought you because it is you who needs to find his courage now, my friend."

"What do you mean?"

"I mean that June needs you. She is not one to ask for help, but she really needs you."

"I know she does," David said. "That's why I'm here. My home sale closed today and I used the proceeds to pay off her mortgage. She at least has some breathing room now to make a fresh start with Echo Glen."

Sebastian nodded gently. The look on his face appeared to David to contain a mix of admiration and something that might have been pity.

"That is a very nice gesture, comrade. But I'm afraid it's not financial help right now that she needs."

"What is it then? How can I help? I'm here."

"You're here, yes. But June is not."

"Well, where is she?"

Sebastian didn't answer right away. He downed his sangria. Then he held out his glass and said, "You had better fill us up again, comrade. Then I'll tell you all I know."

23

There were heat waves rising off the tarmac when the plane touched down. David shrugged his backpack over his shoulder and deplaned. He was prepared to answer questions about the purpose of his trip, but the immigration agent simply stamped his passport and said, *"Bienvenido a España."*

It was a nine-hour train ride from Madrid to Santiago de Compostela, and David dreamed about June most of the way. There was something about the rhythm of the rails that lulled him to sleep. And after taking a red-eye from Seattle to London seated next to a crying infant the entire way, then nearly missing his connecting flight, he needed the rest.

David spotted him the moment he stepped off the train. Now he knew why Sebastian had said he couldn't miss him, for the two cousins looked so much alike, David almost believed Sebastian had played some trick on him and come to meet him himself. But that was impossible, since Sebastian was taking care of Echo Glen for June.

"*Hola,* comrade Hadley."

He even spoke like Sebastian. His name was Jose Antonio and he had driven over six hours from Aranda de Duero to meet David and start him on his journey. He handed David a map, a scallop shell for the outside of his pack, and a staff that he referred to in Spanish as *suerte bastón,* which David looked up in his English-to-Spanish dictionary later and decoded to mean "lucky walking stick."

"Have you walked the Way of St. James?" David asked as they climbed into Jose Antonio's tiny Fiat.

"No, *señor*" — he shook his head, patting the dash of his car — "Camino de Santiago is good for pilgrims, but no walking for me; I have a *carro.*" Then he laughed. "I hear my cousin is paid to crash them. Only in America."

When they arrived at the cathedral, the number of travel-weary pilgrims funneling into the ancient building surprised David. "If there are this many people on the path," he remarked, "how am I ever going to find June?"

"Easy, comrade," Jose said. "Just walk the

Way in reverse and you'll run into her. If she left from Pied-de-Port ten days ago, you should meet each other in a week or two."

"A week or two?" David repeated.

"Maybe less, maybe more."

"But aren't there many routes? My book says there are. What if she took a different one?"

Jose shrugged. *"El que busca encuentra."*

David would look this up later too, and while it was a nice saying, he could only hope it would turn out to be true.

They had lunch together in a café. David battled his jet lag with several latte-like concoctions that Jose called *café con leche.* When lunch was through, David took out the Spanish pesetas he had exchanged traveler's checks for at the Madrid airport, but Jose would not allow him to pay for their lunch, no matter how insistent he was. David eventually surrendered, accepting the Spanish hospitality with a hearty thank-you. Then Jose walked David to the cathedral. It marked the end of the Camino de Santiago for every other pilgrim, and the beginning for David.

"Buen Camino," Jose said with a bow.

Then he shook David's hand before disappearing into the crowds. Armed with little more than his lucky walking stick and a

285

heart full of hope, David turned and set out against the tide of tourists, walking into the wild unknown.

June had been walking for ten days already, and still she could not bring herself to accept the news that she knew all too well to be true. She took comfort in the solitude of her journey, however, and she had always wanted to walk the Camino de Santiago.

It was not by chance that she had become such close friends with Sebastian. She had always loved Spanish culture. She met Sebastian on a Hollywood film set and they spent many Southern Californian nights together, sharing chilled wine and talking about the beauty of northern Spain, where Sebastian was originally from. And now here she was, having walked from the French Pyrenees into España, passing through the quiet countryside with only her thoughts and the distant, hollow tonking of grazing goats' bells to keep her company.

She had stopped in Pamplona for a day, searching out the ghosts of characters from a great American novel she'd read as a girl, a book that had left her forever fascinated by the dichotomy of human beauty and cruelty represented in the slow artistic torture of bulls by brave and graceful toreros. But it was off-season, at least in Pamplona, and there were no bulls and no ghosts, other than those that had followed her. And these ghosts were equally beautiful and cruel. For such are all our memories, she thought, locked in the grip of the past, the rough edges polished by the tides of time. Is there anything as conducive to nostalgia as walking? she wondered as she strolled the Spanish highlands, thinking about her life.

"An inward-looking eye sees nothing worthwhile; vain and self-indulgent reflection produces only more suffering."

That had been her mother's favorite saying. And although it may have been the only thing about which her mother had been right, June knew it was high time for her to look at her past if she had any hope of finding the courage to continue on, and if one wants to wrestle with ghosts, what better place to start than with dear old Mom?

Her mother had nearly been forced into being a whore, or so she would always claim whenever June or her sister would complain about the labor they were made to do. "And working in the field is hardly whoring," their mother would add. But it wasn't just *a field;* it was many fields. The land was leased, the water rights rented, and the tools and machinery mortgaged. Try as they might, their family could not squeeze enough garlic out of the ground to ever get ahead. The only bright spot to these long days laboring were the Mexican migrant workers whom June got to interact with. It was here that her love of the Spanish language had been born.

Her sister was always in a world of her own, and as far as June knew she never said two words she didn't have to say to any of the field workers. She hardly said more than that to June when they worked together long into the autumn evenings, peeling garlic side by side. But June loved the migrant workers like she might have loved the brothers and uncles she didn't have. They'd usually break for lunch in the shade of an oak or an old cottonwood, and June would walk like family among them, swapping her meatloaf and bread for *pollo* and tortillas, telling them stories she'd make up about talking cloves of garlic that went hunting vampires in the night, learning jokes from them in Spanish as trade. When she was older and had become interested in boys, she had a string of failed first dates and could never understand why until one of the field workers informed her that it might be the scent of garlic. He gave her a bottle of perfume he had planned to send home as a Christmas gift for his sister. She had smelled garlic her entire life; how could she have known?

For all the hours she and her sister put in, their stepfather matched them hour for hour at the local bar, drinking and gambling away the profits of their labor. And each evening when the girls came in from working, their dinner was waiting. But they would have to eat it alone. Their mother spent her evenings at the old piano, playing melancholy tunes in a minor key that mirrored the mood of their home. For all her lecturing to the girls about not looking back, their mother wasted her life away lamenting a lost chance to play professionally, and the house seemed always to be infused with the soft keystrokes of regret. Some rare nights even now, as June drifted off to sleep, she could hear that piano playing still, just down the stairs of her memory, beneath the sad portrait of her mother that hung forever in her mind as a reminder to live for the moment and to never forget the value of a smile.

June and her sister were physically close growing up but emotionally a million miles apart. June would have thought their shared suffering would have brought them together, but as she grew she learned that some pain wants to be experienced alone. Her sister was a year older and by far the prettier of the two, and their drunken stepfather would sometimes come to visit her in the sisters' shared room. June would lie in the dark, listening to the quiet struggle and whispered threats. She cursed him in her prayers, wishing for his death, but would always regret not finding the courage to do something. Especially after her sister had finally run away for good, leaving June to take her place in the darkness that filled that farmhouse bedroom. The eve of her sixteenth birthday she followed her sister's lead and left. Unlike her sister, however, she never looked back.

June got a call from her sister years later, while she was living in Southern California, to tell her that their mother was gone. Their stepfather was dead too. Murder-suicide, her sister said, but June never did bother to ask who had killed whom. It didn't really matter, she figured, although she could probably guess. There wasn't much in her family's old farmhouse to leave — debt overshadowed their final tragedy — but what little there was they had left to Ingrid, and that was just fine with June. She was a substitute English teacher three hundred miles away by then and she skipped the funeral, saying she'd make it down some other time to pay her respects. But she never could bring herself to go. Her stepfather did not deserve her forgiveness, and try as she would she could find none for her mother either, for despite her private grief, June was sure that she had known.

It was that same year when she had first met Samuel. He was a teacher too: history and home ec, which seemed a strange combination to June. But what wasn't strange was the way his dark eyebrows arched perfectly above his kind and gentle eyes. He had been just the man June had needed to meet, and they were engaged before he could even save enough for a ring. June said she'd marry him right then without one, that they should save the money for a home. But he insisted they wait and build a nest egg first. He taught that summer and all the others to follow, driving a berry bus to supplement what he already had set aside, until he could buy her a proper ring and a home. Both were simple but perfect, a small rambler in the burbs and a small princess-cut diamond set in a plain gold band. He had put that ring on her finger, saying, "Until death do us part." It was on her finger when his motorcycle went off the road and she found him in that awful ditch. It was on her finger when she jumped off Yosemite's tallest cliff. And it was still on her finger all these years later as she walked the Camino de Santiago, wondering if she had denied her heart love all these years to honor his memory or to keep herself from having to truly live. For death had parted them, hadn't it? And had she not been chasing her own death a little with every jump, with every stunt?

The funny thing was, she could no longer remember his face. She couldn't be sure when it had finally faded. It had just stayed there in the past as her life went on, his features polished smooth by all that time until his memory was just a feeling. She had to laugh a little at her own sentimentality. If he were still alive, she mused, they could probably run into one another on this very path and neither would recognize the other, she having forgotten his face, he not knowing how much hers had changed. But here his death had haunted her all these years. It seemed strange how something so brief could cast a shadow so long.

These were a few of the many thoughts keeping June company on her walk. She was desperately trying to prevent them from adding up to something that felt like regret. She refused to fall into her mother's brooding trap. Not me, she thought. I'd risk love over loneliness every time. I'd choose life instead of death, wouldn't I? Isn't that what I preach?

She stopped for the night at a roadside *albergue.* Here at least she could stave off her loneliness by sharing a meal with fellow pilgrims, renting a soft bed to rest her weary head.

David was so out of place it almost made sense that he was walking the road in reverse. But still the faces of the pilgrims he passed hid little of their confusion over his direction of travel. It didn't help, of course, that he was stopping each of them and making them look at June's picture, asking if they had seen her anywhere along the way. Most just shook their heads. A few younger men, mostly from European countries, smiled and said they wished. "She's a foxy older lady, mate. I'd remember running into her." But none had seen her on their travels.

He ran into what would become a repeated problem the very first night. The roadside *refugios* and *albergues* were meant for pilgrims traveling the Way of St. James, and they asked for a *credencial,* which David understood to be a sort of passport that was stamped at each township or village along the route. The trouble was he didn't possess a passport, not having departed from a traditional starting place, and because he was walking in reverse it likely would not have mattered if he had. It took many pesetas, much pleading, and lots of awkward translating from his pocket dictionary, but they would usually find space for him after waiting for the last of the pilgrims to arrive.

Surprisingly, he was little fazed by the hard cots and close quarters, having become accustomed to the sounds and smells of other sweaty bodies sleeping nearby during his weeks at stunt school. Since he was the last to be given a bed each night, before turning in he crept through the rooms peeking at each sleeping face with a flashlight cupped in his hands. This led to a few uncomfortable encounters but no sign of June.

The farther he traveled along the path, the sparser the pilgrims he encountered, and he found himself walking for long stretches of time with nothing to do but question his having come. What if June didn't want to see him? he wondered. What if she wanted to face things alone? Wasn't that her right? Who was he to come all this way just to interrupt her journey?

But Sebastian had seemed worried enough to beg David to go. He said she would welcome his company. And even though she had initially rejected it, he thought she'd also accept his having paid off the mortgage at Echo Glen as a bit of welcome good news. So David had agreed, but he had not told Sebastian his other reason for wanting to come and find her. You see, with paying off Echo Glen out of the way, there was something else David wanted to propose.

24

"You went all the way over there to find her and propose marriage, didn't you?"

He looked at me from his chair with a twinkle in his eye. "I may have," he replied. "But you seem awfully interested for someone who doesn't believe in love."

"Oh, come on. That's not fair. What I said was I didn't believe in it for me. But I'm curious why June left to walk the Camino to begin with. I mean, why was Sebastian so worried about her? Was something wrong? You have to tell me."

I wasn't trying to cut him short, but his storytelling had been punctuated with coughing fits, and I feared he would wear himself out before he got to the end.

"I'll make you a deal," he said. "You add some wood to the stove there, then give me a hand up out of this chair before I fall asleep, and I'll show you."

I looked out the window. It was fully dark now.

"Maybe going on another field trip isn't such a good idea."

He laughed. "Don't worry," he said, "I think I can make it down the hallway where we're going without falling."

After I had stoked the stove back to life, I helped him from his chair. It was clear his energy was waning, as he could no longer rise by himself, even with the aid of his cane. I wondered what he would have done had I not been around. Slept right there in his robe, I guess. Once on his feet, however, he shuffled quite quickly down the hall on his slippers.

He led me to a door and opened it. When he snapped the light on, I saw it was a small corner bedroom with a window overlooking the creek. It had been converted into a kind of studio, and it was immediately clear that the studio had belonged to June. The walls were hung with more watercolors, and an easel with an unfinished canvas stood near the window. But it wasn't the easel that drew my attention — it was the wheelchair sitting next to it. It was a power chair with leg and chest straps, and it was parked beside the easel with its seat raised to an almost standing height, as if waiting for June to return any moment to her brushes and paint.

"You asked about the watercolor of Echo Glen in the kitchen earlier," David said. "That was one of June's first. She claimed she took it up because in her condition no one would dare tell her she wasn't any good, even if it were true. But she was quite the artist, getting better even as things deteriorated."

I had been wondering about the wheelchair ramp covering the steps ever since I had arrived that morning, and now I understood. But I was more curious than ever about how she had come to be in the wheelchair. I couldn't help but think that June had gone off to Spain to do something dangerous and that that was why Sebastian had wanted David to go after her. My curiosity finally got the better of me.

"Why did Sebastian want you to go after June so badly?"

The Gypsy Moths," he said. "Among other things."

"The Gypsy what?"

He led me over to a closet and opened it, pointing to a blue-nylon suit hanging from a hook. It appeared to be one of those flying-squirrel-looking suits that daredevils use.

"Hey," I said, "I've seen those wingsuits on YouTube."

"Well, this was 1986, so YouTube hadn't been invented yet," he replied. "And neither had wingsuits. June worked on a film in the late sixties that involved experimental ideas for flying, and this was a prototype that she had continued to improve on. She took it with her to Spain, along with her parachute. That, combined with the bad news, was why Sebastian was so worried and insisted that I go after her. He would have gone himself, but he had promised to care for the animals."

"So, she had planned to jump there?"

"Yes. At Montserrat, after she had walked the Camino."

Then I noticed the matador costume in the closet. The one I had seen in the old photo that Mr. Hadley carried in his pocket — the one he told me she had worn on their wedding day.

"But you found her, didn't you? You got married. That's the matador costume from the photo."

He nodded. "I did find her. And lucky for me, we did get married."

"And you still let her jump in that crazy bat suit? After you were married and everything?"

"It wasn't up to me to let her do anything," he said. "Married or not, June was her own woman and made her own choices. Thankfully, she chose not to test that crazy suit."

"So, she never used it?"

He shook his head. "It's just a nostalgic movie prop."

I turned around and looked at the wheelchair again, now thoroughly confused. "So, what happened to her?" I asked. "I mean, if she didn't jump, why bring me back here and show me the wheelchair?"

"Because you asked me why she went to Spain."

"Why did she go to Spain?"

There was a pause before he answered, during which I saw him looking at the empty wheelchair. When he did answer, his voice contained no emotion that I could detect.

"Parkinson's," he said simply, with an air of acceptance.

"And that's why she went to walk the trail," I muttered, finally understanding. Then something dawned on me. "So, that must have been the bad news she had just found out when she took you up to Echo Glen, wasn't it?"

David sighed. "All the help she gave

300

everyone else and she couldn't bear the thought of ever needing a little help herself. She was just fifty-three. That's young for Parkinson's, but she was already experiencing tremors and other symptoms. It terrified her. She couldn't imagine a life without flying, without all the athletic things she loved to do."

He turned to look back into the closet at the suit again, speaking now almost to himself.

"I sometimes wonder if she would have flown that suit if I hadn't shown up begging her to marry me. I never asked, but I doubt it. It would have been a suicide mission for anyone, let alone someone in her condition." He shook his head. "And she didn't want to die. She was more alive than anyone I had ever met."

"So, she never jumped again?" I asked.

"Just one time. The day before our wedding, wearing this."

He laid his hand on the matador costume.

"She jumped wearing that?" I asked. "Okay, now you need to finish this story for real or else I'm going to start calling you Hitchcock instead of Hadley."

"What's a young man like you know about Hitchcock?"

"I know he's the master of suspense. Or

301

at least he *was* until you came along and kicked him off his throne."

He laughed, shutting the closet door.

"Okay. Let's go back and see if we can't wrap up this little tale of ours. Sleep seems about all I do well anymore, and with it getting near my bedtime I'd hate to pass out on you."

I didn't bother mentioning that he had already fallen asleep on me twice. Instead, I glanced once more at the empty wheelchair and followed him from the room. On our way back to the living room, I noticed a framed picture on the hallway wall and stopped for a better look.

"Is that June?" I asked, recognizing her from the photo.

"That's my June. And that's me beside her, smiling."

"That's you?" I asked, leaning closer. "You look different."

He laughed. "That's what age does." Then he pointed to a handsome Spanish man, holding up a shiny plaque. "That's Sebastian. This was taken at his induction into the Stuntmen's Hall of Fame. June never could get them to change that silly, chauvinist name."

"So, he made it in after all. That makes me happy. And who's this woman holding his hand?"

"That's his wife."

"I guess he went back for her then."

David nodded. "He asked me to be his best man. He said we were comrades in courage, and that my running off to Spain to marry June had given him the push he needed."

"Whatever happened to him?"

"What happens to all of us eventually. He died. Always a man of action, he saved a girl from drowning during Hurricane Katrina. She begged him to go back for her dog and he did. He was a brave man. He really was. Let's get back to the story."

25

He saw her first from a long ways off. He knew it was June by her gait. She had a way of walking with her body leaned slightly forward, as if always marching against a gentle wind. He had noticed it before while watching her at Echo Glen.

David had been in Spain searching for her now for eight days, and he had spent many a lonely mile daydreaming about what he might do if he actually found her. He had always imagined himself running to take her in his arms, declaring his undying love for her by saying something profoundly poetic, and then sealing their shared fate with a kiss. But to his surprise, as soon as he saw her he sat down on a low stone wall beside the path. Maybe because he was tired, or maybe because even after all of his daydreaming he still had no idea what it was he wanted to say. In the end, he needed to say nothing.

The wall he was sitting on crested a low hill and he watched as she strode up the path toward him. Her pack was enormous for her petite size, and it stuck up at least a full foot above her head, giving her the appearance of a child carrying an adult on her back. Her eyes were downcast, looking at her feet, and it occurred to David that between his disheveled hair and a week's worth of beard she likely wouldn't recognize him even if she were to look up and spot him beside the path. But when she was still a good ten paces away, she seemed to sense his presence, coming to a sudden stop. Then she lifted her head and let her eyes settle on him where he sat.

"My oh my," she said, showing no sign at all of surprise. "It could be all this walking in the sun, but you sure remind me of a man I once slept with."

"Is that so?" David said. "This man you speak of must have been very handsome to attract such a gorgeous woman."

"Very much so," she replied.

"Was he any good in the hay?"

Her eyes broke into a smile. "A lady never tells."

"Oh, don't be coy with me now. I must know."

"He had some moves," she said.

"Although I'd imagine with a little practice he might even improve."

"Is that an offer?"

She shrugged off her pack and carried it over and leaned it against the low rock wall he was sitting on. Then she sat beside him and sighed, looking down at her boots. When she finally spoke again, her voice was quiet.

"I suppose I should have made Sebastian promise not to send someone as his proxy too. He told you, didn't he?"

David nodded. "But he didn't send me as a proxy. I came on my own, June. I wanted to see you."

"It's a long way to travel just to see someone."

"Not really. Not when that someone is you."

"Oh, David . . ."

She looked up at him but her smile was gone, replaced by a look of sad concern. David couldn't tell if it was concern for herself or for him. He feared the latter and began to think he had made a terrible mistake by coming. Perhaps she had really wanted to be alone.

"How long have you been searching for me?" she asked.

"A week or so. I set out from Santiago de

Compostela."

June nodded. "Walking it backwards, eh? Very contrarian of you, darling. I like it."

"How about you?" he asked.

She looked back down the path up which she had come. "Seems like forever," she said, but David could not tell if she was talking about the Camino de Santiago or something else.

They sat quiet for a while. A breeze came up and stirred the tall grass beside the trail. A bird called.

"June, do you want to talk about — ?"

"Why don't we ditch this trail," she said, cutting him off. "I'm afraid it's a bit more touristy than I thought."

"But don't you get a certificate when you complete it?"

"That's what I mean," she said. "Plus, we have completed it, darling. We did it together. You walked the part I didn't."

He hated the idea of not getting to spend some time alone with her after having come all this way.

"I took a full three weeks off from work," he said, "despite my boss's threatening to fire me. If we ditch the trail, what would we do instead?"

She shrugged. "I don't know. We could set out to tickle every horse in Spain. Maybe

307

find a rainstorm and wait for a rainbow to slide down. We could walk into the night and climb the stars to swim in the Milky Way."

"That's quite a list," he mused, looking at her beside him and asking, "but are horses really ticklish?"

"Oh yes," she replied. "Isn't everyone?"

She leaned over and buried her fingers in David's side, tickling him. He laughed, pretending to fight her away.

"And where would we go to do all this?" he asked once he had regained his composure.

She reached into her pack and removed a map, spreading it out on her lap. "I think Sebastian has family in Aranda de Duero. We could walk there."

"Jose Antonio. He came to meet me in Santiago."

"Look at you," she said. "Here I've known Sebastian all these years and I finally get to Spain and you've gone and beat me to meeting his family. What's he like?"

"Sebastian."

"No, Jose. What's he like?"

"He's like Sebastian. You can hardly tell the two apart."

"Well, I understand he works in a winery, and to tell you the truth, I could use a little

Spanish vino. So it's settled then." She stood and took up her pack. "We'll cut away from the trail southeast, and we should be there in a few days."

There was a lot left unsaid, but David figured it could wait for now. He was just happy to have found her and to be walking by her side, regardless of where they were headed. And after eight days' hard trudging, the idea of a soft bed and some Spanish wine sounded damn good to him. He shouldered his pack and followed her down the hill.

The rainstorm caught them out in the open, on a country road at the edge of a field. One moment they were walking beneath the hot Mediterranean sun, the next they were being pelted with huge raindrops as wave after wave bounced like sheets off the road ahead of them. Streaks of lightning split the sky to the north, and the rumble of thunder reverberated above the hiss of falling rain.

"There!" June said, pointing to a barn at the far edge of the field. "Let's wait it out."

They climbed the wooden fence and ran like Olympic sprinters for the barn. David felt the sense of excitement that comes only from running for a reason, and he felt the wet grass giving way beneath his feet and the cool rain hitting his face. It felt good. In fact, he hadn't felt so good in possibly all of his adult life. June had a fair lead and she disappeared into the shadowy barn ahead of him. David joined her just as a peal of thunder echoed across the valley followed by a deluge of rain the likes of which he had never before seen. They were both panting to catch their breath through broad, dripping smiles.

"I haven't run like that since I got chased by the police for stealing a calendar."

"Why would you steal a lousy calendar?" June asked.

"It was on a dare," he said. "And not just any calendar. A calendar with Marilyn Monroe in the nude."

"Oh, I didn't know you liked them buxom."

"I was seventeen," he replied. "I liked them naked. There's one I've got my eye on now, though, and I'd call her petite."

June laughed. "I've been called a string bean by my mother, and tiny enough to fit into a car's glove box on movie sets, but never petite. I rather like it. Makes me think of petite sirah."

"That's twice now you've mentioned wine," David said. "You're making me wish we had some."

310

June grinned, shrugging off her wet pack. "You didn't think I'd come unprepared, did you?"

The rain was pounding down on the old tin barn roof and David removed his pack and changed into a dry shirt. His pants were soaked through as well, but he was too shy to change them in front of June. They hung their wet things up on old nails to dry, carried their packs to a dry corner of the barn, and sat down to drink and eat and watch the rain.

"Sorry, no wineglasses," June said, passing him the bottle.

"This is better," David replied. "There's something very romantic about sitting out a rainstorm and sharing warm wine straight from the bottle. Don't you think so?"

"Romantic, eh? Hmm. Now you're starting to sound a lot like that man I told you I used to sleep with."

"Used to *sleep* with? I thought you said *slept* with before, as in once."

"Well, maybe I just imagined the other times," she replied, reaching for the bottle and letting her hand linger just a moment on his.

They sat quiet for a while, eating trail mix and sipping their wine while watching the rain pour off the roof in sheets.

"I love the sound of rain," June said. "It makes me feel like there's nowhere to be and nothing to do. As if the entire world has agreed to take a break when it rains. As if time stops. As if everything is okay and always will be. I wish it would rain forever."

David thought he heard a hint of sadness in her voice when she said she wished the rain would last forever, and he suspected she was really talking about her fear of what lay ahead. He reached his arm around her and pulled her to him. She let him, leaning her head against his shoulder.

"Nothing lasts forever, does it?" she said.

"No," he answered, "nothing does. But maybe that's what makes some experiences special. I know I'll always remember sitting out a rainstorm in Spain with you. Plus, there are other wonderful things to experience yet."

"There are?" she asked, looking up at him.

He smiled at her. "Yes, there are."

"Like what?"

"Well, let's see: how about the whinny of a happy foal? That's got to be a close second to this."

"Oh, I miss my horses," she said. "I wish I could save them all. And dogs and cats and cows too. I never met a cow that didn't seem gentle, have you?"

"You can't save everyone and everything, June. You've got to let yourself have a life too. Besides, who will save you?"

There was a moment of quiet, and David wondered if she was ready to talk about why she had fled to Spain.

"Give me something else," she said. "Another sound that can compete with the sound of rain."

"Okay," David said, "what about a newborn baby's first cry?"

"That's a lovely sound."

"Or water running over smooth stones. Or how about carolers on a cold December night? Or I know, how about the sound of your lover's step on the stair after being apart?"

"Oh, those are good ones," she said. "How about smells?"

David took a moment to think, looking out the open barn door at the rain. "Let's see, smells are harder. Okay, how about the way grass smells after it's been cut in the spring? Or pine trees in January. I can smell them now. Or a warm bakery on a winter's morning. Who doesn't love that smell?"

"I love them all," June said. Then she snuggled into his shoulder and pulled his arm tighter around her. "What about tastes

though? The bakery has my mouth watering."

"Hmm . . . you want tastes, huh? Lemon
ice cream on a hot summer evening comes
to mind. Or honey straight from the comb.
Have you ever had that? You have. How
about salted butter and blackberry jam on
fresh sourdough."

"You're killing me," she said, laughing.
"That trail mix was manna a moment ago.
Now it might as well be sand."

"I can stop if you want me to."

"No, no, go on. But give me touch now."

"Touch?"

"Yes, like the way silk feels on naked skin."

"Well, I couldn't speak to that one," David said. "But I like the thought of your
naked skin. Let's see. Touch. Okay, how
about the sun on your cheeks on a cool fall
day and a warm hand to hold. A hot tub
near the ocean. A down comforter on the
couch when you're not feeling well."

June closed her eyes, drinking in his
descriptions.

"Give me sight now," she said. "What's
the best thing in the world you've ever
seen?"

"Okay. The best thing I've seen. The look
of streetlights in the fog, especially in San
Francisco. Mount Rainier on a clear Seattle

day. A desert sunset. Sunrise over a misty lake. The allure of a lonely canoe paddling toward you."

"Those are all so great," she said. "You're a pro at this and I feel so much better already. What else? Give me more."

"I'll tell you what the best sight in the world is, if you really want to know. Do you?"

"Yes, I do. Tell me."

"Your face in the morning, the way I saw it in the barn at Echo Glen, after we made love."

"Oh, come on," she said. "My old mug."

"I swear it's the best sight in the world. Your face in the morning. Every morning. Forever."

"Really?"

"Really."

She turned her head to look up at him. Her eyes weren't smiling this time, but they weren't sad either. They had a guarded vulnerability in them, a kind of innocence perhaps. It was something altogether new, and it made David want to hold her tight and never let go, no matter what the world might put them through. He realized then that he had loved her all along, maybe before they had even met. He would always love her, he just knew. His eyes welled up, although he was not sad at all.

"Marry me, June."

"What?" She seemed to have not heard him, or maybe she'd heard him and couldn't believe what he had said.

"Marry me."

"Oh, David . . ."

He thought he saw a flicker of fear in her eyes. Then she looked away. He could have sworn she'd glanced down at the ring on her finger. She sat still with her head against his shoulder, just looking out the barn door and watching the rain. The thunder had passed but the sky was growing darker.

David began to feel silly for having brought up marriage at all. He hadn't planned to do it, at least not right then. He hadn't even told her yet that he'd used his house sale proceeds to pay off Echo Glen, and now he couldn't tell her. He didn't dare risk the chance of having her feel like he was trying to buy her love. He wasn't, of course. He would pay it off again a thousand times, even if she said *no,* or *hell no,* or *no way am I marrying a babbling buffoon of an accountant like you.*

"June, I'm sorry."

She looked up at him.

"I shouldn't have brought it up."

"Don't say that."

"Sometimes I don't think is all, and then the rain and the wine and, I don't know, maybe it's just Spain."

"So, you wouldn't want to marry me if we were back in the States?"

"No, no, I meant maybe it was Spain that had me opening my big mouth at the wrong time."

"I rather like your big mouth," she said.

"You do?"

"Yes, but I wish you'd stop using it to talk and kiss me."

"Really?" he asked, taken aback by her invitation.

June laughed, stretching up to kiss him. She tasted of wine and rain, and her hair smelled of the outside. David pulled her closer and deepened their kiss, never wanting to let it end. He remembered her telling him back at Echo Glen that sometimes a kiss is just a kiss. But no way was this just a kiss.

26

"So, her kiss was her answer?"

"No," he said, shaking his head. "Her answer came the next day, although it was even less direct than a kiss."

"You're killing me with suspense, I swear. But your lists of smells and tastes made me hungry. Any chance of a bite before we go on?"

"Well, let's go see what we can rummage up in the icebox. I think I have some Hungry-Man dinners."

I gave him a hand out of his chair again and we went into the kitchen. Now that I had seen June's wheelchair, I began to notice how things were set up to accommodate her around the house. A cabinet had been removed and there was a second, lower counter, with a smaller sink built out next to the one where I had washed dishes after lunch. I had just assumed it was a vegetable sink, or whatever those little ones are that you sometimes see. I also noticed that the phone was mounted low on the wall, and seeing it reminded me of the call about a cemetery application. I began to have suspicions about Mr. Hadley's plans and his proposal for me, but I didn't ask because I didn't want to know just yet.

"These things still seem like magic to me," he said, turning on the old microwave. "I remember when I first saw one at the local fair. Heated a hot dog right before my eyes. Now your phone can probably cook one. June hated the thing. She said it sucked all the taste out of food. But she never tried a Hungry-Man Salisbury steak or she would have changed her tune. Did you know Salisbury steak is named after the doctor who invented it? How can it be bad if it was invented by a doctor?"

I'm not sure where this burst of energy came from, but he kept up talking about what it must have been like to know your legacy was naming a steak to help people eat fewer carbs, only to have them serve it with mashed potatoes and gravy, as he set the table with a knife and fork, even pouring a glass of milk for me. When the meal had finished heating, he set it down in front of me. "There you go," he said.

"What about you?" I asked.

"Oh, I never eat this late. My medication makes me nauseated. Besides, I'm still stuffed up on MoonPies. No, you eat and I'll talk. Otherwise I'll have to make you up a bed for the night and finish tomorrow."

He retrieved his cane from the corner and lowered himself into the seat across from me. I tasted the Salisbury steak. He was right: it was damn good.

"I remember right where I left off this time," he said, "because I had just been kissing my sweet June. But for the sake of your young ears and decency I'll leave out the two times we made love that night, once to the sound of rain pelting the old tin roof and once to the sound of crickets long after the rain had stopped. I'll start instead the next morning, when I woke to an entirely different kind of kiss . . ."

David was still dreaming about June when he felt her lips on his. Or was it her tongue? He reached up to touch her cheek and his fingers felt coarse hair instead. Drowsy and confused, he opened his eyes and tried to make sense of her elongated face. Then he screamed. June was lying next to him, and she opened her eyes and began laughing, as if being woken by donkey kisses was just the funniest thing in the world. David scrambled to his feet and stepped away from the beast, cursing and spitting onto the ground.

"He was just being friendly," June said, sitting up and scratching behind the curious animal's ears.

"Friendly? That thing had its tongue in my mouth."

"They like the salt," she said, reaching for her pack and fishing out a bag of pretzels.

"How do you know it's a he anyway?" David asked as he watched the donkey eat the offered pretzels from June's palm.

"Uh, those," she said, pointing to its dangling testicles. "Plus he kind of sounds like you when he eats."

"That's not funny," David said.

June laughed. "I'm sorry, I couldn't help it."

After taking turns freshening up and doing their business behind the barn, they ate a cold breakfast of jerky and trail mix before loading up their packs and hitting the road.

"That crazy mule's following us," David said.

"El burro catalán," June replied.

"What's that?"

"It's not a mule, it's just big like one. It's a Catalan donkey. They may be extinct someday."

"Well, why's he following us?"

"Maybe he wants another kiss," June teased.

"More likely he wants the pretzels in your pack," David replied. Then he had an idea. "Hey, instead of cutting back to the road, can't we keep going south across this field, as a kind of shortcut?"

June stopped, quickly consulting her map.

"It's definitely a more direct route, but it will be slower going through this wheat than it will be on the road."

David grinned. "Not if we've got help with our packs."

Five minutes later they were walking together hand in hand like two carefree lovers out for a morning stroll as the donkey followed along behind them, carrying their gear. Between both packs, the combined straps had just reached around its girth. David was quite proud. But despite the pleasant walk and the levity of their morning wake-up surprise, David's proposal in the barn the evening before weighed heavily on his mind. He was acutely aware that June had not answered him yet. Plus, the way she had glanced at her wedding ring when he had mentioned marriage had not been lost on him.

The wheat field they were crossing eventually terminated at a wooden fence on the other side of which was a red poppy field that stretched away as far as the eye could see. The vivid Spanish sun was fully up now, warming the damp poppies, and a haze of evaporation was rising from the field, giving the vermilion vista an otherworldly appearance.

"Looks like this is the end of the line for you," June said, removing their packs from the donkey.

She offered him a handful of pretzels as payment for his services, and then she and David climbed over the fence and started off across the poppies. The field was very flat, and when David looked back a full half an hour later he could just make out the donkey still standing at the fence, watching them go.

"Animals sure do love you," David said. "Although I think you may have spoiled him with those pretzels."

"Maybe," she replied. "But I like spoiling the men in my life."

"*Men?* Should I be worried?"

"Not unless you're the type that gets jealous easily. Are you?"

David smiled. "No. And maybe it's you who should be worried anyway, since it was me the donkey was kissing."

June laughed. "Touché, darling. Touché."

"You've said that before to me. It's kind of cute."

"Touché or *darling?"* she asked.

"Both," he answered.

"Well, you might not know this but I'm a first-rate fencer. And *darling* is something I picked up from a marvelous actress on a New Zealand movie set. That's the glorious thing about Hollywood. It lets you reinvent yourself."

"Do you ever miss it, being in Washington?"

"No. Echo Glen is home."

They walked then without talking, just the sound of their feet sweeping through the poppies, driving out clicking grasshoppers from their path. David considered telling her that he had paid off Echo Glen with the proceeds of his home sale, giving her at least one less thing to worry about, but decided against it even though he knew she had a lot on her mind.

"June, I'm here to listen if you want to talk about it."

"These poppies seem to go on forever, don't they," she said, stopping to consult her map.

It was obvious to David that she was not yet ready.

"We're running low on water too," he said, draining his water bottle, then opening his backup and offering it to June.

As David slathered himself with sunscreen, June produced a compass and checked their direction. Then she held up her hand and sighted the sun, comparing her findings to her map. She looked to David like some kind of medieval pilgrim making her way to an important port — perhaps she was Agustina de Aragón herself, the Spanish Joan of Arc, off to chase away Napoléon with just her courage and a basket of apples.

"I might be going about this assbackwards," David said, "since I let my silly proposal slip last night, but have I told you yet how much I love you?"

June looked up from her map. Initially there was shock on her expressive face, but then her eyes seemed to crease almost involuntarily into their signature smile. She looked back down at the map, and David swore he saw her blush.

"I love you too," she said quietly.

But her quiet declaration was more than enough for David, and he smiled like a boy who'd stumbled onto gold, he felt so good; in fact, he skipped a step, nearly dancing a little jig right there among the poppies.

It took them two more hours' walking to find the road. The poppies ran right up to the edge of it, and as June consulted her map, David stood watching a strange ritual play out on the asphalt.

There were power poles running along the far side of the road, and on the cables strung between them were perched numerous black birds of a variety unfamiliar to David — large enough to be crows, but with red beaks and red toes gripping the thick lines. The fields were seething with grasshoppers, hidden beneath the poppies, and these birds had found the perfect way to hunt them. As unlucky grasshoppers made attempts to cross the road, the birds would wing down and snatch them up in their red beaks before flying back to the wire and swallowing them. One after another, these cunning hunters from above picked off the grasshoppers.

"It's hard to know who to root for, isn't it," June said, looking up from her map and noticing the feeding frenzy.

"What do you mean?" David asked.

"Well, it all depends on your perspective, I guess."

"My perspective?"

"Exactly," she said. "Standing here it's easy enough to observe impartially. But if we were up on the wire, I'd bet my head we'd be rooting for the birds to eat their fill."

"But aren't the grasshoppers pests?" David asked.

"To the wheat farmer, maybe. But the birds are also pests, unless there are grasshoppers to keep them away from the berry fields. It's easy, of course, to hate any group when you lump them all together instead of looking at each as an individual."

"An individual grasshopper, you say, huh?"

She nodded. "It's impossible to hate anything when you identify with its struggle."

"You really are a modern philosopher in hiking boots and a parachute, you know that? Because whatever you just said sailed right over this accountant's thick head."

"Nonsense," she said, "you're just not looking. Let me show you." She grabbed his arm and pulled him to the ground beside the road, making him lie down on his belly. "Now look from this perspective and tell me what you see."

"I see the same thing I saw while standing: grasshoppers jumping into the road and birds picking them off."

"Okay, good. Now select just one

individual grasshopper and follow its progress."

"Pick one?"

"Any one. And try to see it as an individual."

"Okay, there." David pointed to one that had just hopped a good two feet into the road. "I like that one."

It hopped again, unseen. Then another leap, followed by a flicker of passing shadow, a click of beak, and it was gone.

"Shoot!" David exclaimed.

"See," June said, "you were rooting for the grasshopper because you're down on its level."

"Now I've got to see one safely across," he said. "I feel responsible. Like a grasshopper crossing guard or something."

"You might be going a bit far now," she said, laughing.

"Let's follow that one there," David said, pointing. "I have a good feeling about it. I'll bet a peseta he makes it."

"I hate to bet against him," June said, "but deal."

They watched as David's grasshopper hopped across the hot pavement. One jump, two. Then a third. It was in luck, it appeared, as was David, because the birds were distracted by something and chattering loudly on the wire. The grasshopper jumped again. And again.

"It's almost across," David said, getting excited. "Go, little fella, go! You can make it. I'll share my winnings with you if you do."

It made a final leap to the far edge of the roadway, safe at last from the beady eyes above. David had just declared victory and was attempting to collect when a bicycle tire appeared as if from nowhere and flattened the grasshopper into a black smudge.

"Hey!" David shouted, standing up and pumping his fist in the air. "You killed my grasshopper, you little scalawags."

The bicycles stopped and two boys looked back from their seats with wide-eyed and curious expressions on their tanned faces, as if wondering from what hidden hole beside the roadway this yelling lunatic had emerged, barking at them in a strange language neither understood. June stood up and hailed them reassuringly in Spanish, saying what sounded an awful lot to David like an apology and her reassurance that they should ignore her partner. While he fished out his pocket dictionary, she walked to them and showed them the map and spoke in broken bits of local dialect, much too quickly for David to look up. The boys shook their heads and pointed back the way they had come, with wide, way-long gestures.

"What are they saying?" David asked, flipping through his book unsuccessfully.

"They say we must backtrack to the main road. They say it is five hours by car, two days on foot, one day on bicycle."

David opened his pack and traded his pocket dictionary for his wallet. "Ask them how much for the bikes."

"You want their bicycles?" June asked.

"No, I want a soft bed in Aranda de Duero. The bicycles will help us get there."

"What's the hurry?"

"My aching back from a week of rock-hard cots and last night on the dirt floor of a barn."

"I thought you enjoyed last night."

"Very much so," he said. "But I'd still like a soft bed and some good food."

"You ask them yourself then," June said.

The boys looked on from their bicycle seats as he and June bantered, following their conversation with turning heads.

"Fine. Tell me how. My Spanish is no good."

"*How much* is *Cuánto cuesta.*"

David turned to the boys and pointed at the bikes, asking, "*Cuánto cuesta?*"

They looked at one another, confused. David opened his wallet and held out pesetas, pointing at the bikes again. The boys shook their heads. David added more bills, but they shook their heads to this offer as well.

"I don't think they want to sell," June said.

"But I must be offering them twice what these old things are worth. Look at the rust."

"Maybe they don't care for money," June suggested.

David tucked the bills away in his wallet. Then he held out his wrist and showed them his watch, pointing from it to the bikes. The boys seemed confused, so he took the watch off and handed it over for inspection, again signaling that he would like to trade for the bikes. The boys turned away and looked at the watch, whispering to each other in private consultation. Then they turned back and nodded, dismounting their bikes.

June marched over and snatched the watch away from them and handed it back to David.

"What are you thinking?" she asked. "You can't trade your watch for those old bikes."

"Why not?" he asked.

"Because I said no."

"It's my watch, June. I can do with it what

I want."

David handed the watch back to the boys, but June quickly snatched it away again, this time putting it in her pocket. The boys looked at each other and shrugged, either greatly amused or just highly confused; David couldn't tell.

"June, what's going on?" he asked. "You're acting strange. That watch isn't even special to me. And it's only gold plated."

She crossed her arms. "It's not about the stupid watch, David."

"Then what is it about, June?"

"It's about everything."

"That doesn't make any sense."

"Oh, it doesn't?"

"No. Don't you want to get where we're going?"

"You know what doesn't make any sense?" she retorted, raising her voice to nearly a shout. "I'll tell you. You coming all the way to Spain to hunt me down like I'm some runaway kid when you have a life of your own to be living back in Seattle. That's what doesn't make any sense."

"I came because I wanted to see you, June."

"No, you came because you were worried about me, David. You came because you feel sorry for me, don't you? Go ahead, David, lie to me and tell me it isn't true."

She was yelling by this time, and the boys watched with raised eyebrows as they stood beside their bikes, holding them upright with white-knuckle grips on the handlebars.

"That's silly, June. I don't feel sorry for you. I love you."

"No you don't."

"Yes I do."

"I have Parkinson's, David."

"I know, June."

"Do you know what that means?"

"Yes," he said, lowering his voice and nodding. "I know what it means."

"I'm not sure you do."

"I'm trying, June. I might not be able to get on your level exactly. I mean I can't imagine how it feels to be you. But I checked out a book on Parkinson's and read it on the airplane. I know what can happen, but there's lots of hope too."

"I won't be some charity case, David. I won't, I tell you."

She was crying now. David wanted more than anything to reach out and hold her, to comfort her, but he didn't dare risk making her feel any more vulnerable than she already did.

"No one's asking you to be anything but yourself, June. Your wonderful, beautiful, kind, giving self."

"What if I don't want to be beautiful and giving and kind anymore, David? Did you ever think about that?"

"Then don't be. It doesn't change a thing for me, June. I love you. You have a lot to offer, no matter what difficulties lie ahead. There's no reason to walk through life alone when there are people begging to share the journey with you."

"People like who?"

"People like me."

June wiped a tear off her cheek with the back of her hand. "More like crawl through life now," she said.

"Then I'll crawl with you."

There was a moment of silence between them. The boys were quietly watching from beside their bicycles. The birds had even fallen silent, watching from their wires.

"Did you mean it?" June finally asked.

"Mean what?"

"What you said last night. What you asked me."

David nodded. "I did."

Another tear rolled down June's cheek, but her eyes creased ever so slightly into a smile, and she let this one go. She looked down at her left hand. Then she reached with her right and twisted the ring from her finger and handed it to one of the boys. *"Comercio esto para las bicicletas."*

The boys turned away and looked at the ring together, inspecting the small diamond and quietly consulting each other again. Then they turned back and nodded, stepping away from the bicycles and holding them out. David looked to June. He wanted to protest her parting with the ring, but something told him not to, and he stepped up and wrapped his arms around her instead. She hugged him back, leaning her head against his chest. They stood there embracing for a full minute, the boys looking on from beside their bicycles. How strange these foreigners must have seemed to them.

Eventually, David and June collected their packs and strapped them on, each of them taking up a bicycle, mounting their seat, and thanking the boys in Spanish before they pedaled away together. David glanced once over his shoulder, expecting to see the boys still standing there watching from the road. But all he saw was a distant glimpse of flailing elbows and churning legs as they ran the other direction toward home. He looked over at June, pedaling a steady pace beside him. His heart swelled with happiness. They'd made it this far; they'd make it through, no matter what. They had love. And love was enough.

He looked ahead at the empty road and enjoyed the warm sun on his neck and the cool breeze against his face.

"I haven't forgotten that you still have my watch in your pocket," he said. "I want it back."

"No way," she replied. "You were ready to just give it away, so it's mine now."

"And what exactly are you going to do with a men's Seiko Automatic Chronograph?"

"I plan to pawn it to help raise money for Echo Glen."

David let them pedal for another minute or two in silence before he looked over at her again and said, "Why don't we pawn it for wedding rings of our own instead, since I already used the proceeds from my mother's house to pay off the mortgage on Echo Glen."

"You did not."

"I did."

He half expected her to argue with him over it, but tears welled up in her eyes again and she met his gaze long enough to smile a silent thanks. Then, as if to keep her from crying again, she stood up from her bicycle seat and took off ahead of him, pedaling fiercely and shouting back over her shoulder, "Last one to Aranda de Duero has to buy the wine."

27

"You can't stop there."

"I need to rest, young man. It's nearly nine and I begin to fall apart around then. You don't want to see it, trust me."

He used his cane to hoist himself up from the table, taking away my empty plate.

"But you haven't told me about the wedding yet. And what about that matador costume? How does that figure in? And being arrested. Come on, I want to hear the rest of the story."

"I'll tell you the rest when you come back."

"You want me to come back?"

The idea of returning made me happy. I was really growing fond of Mr. Hadley, and it occurred to me that if he wanted me to come back it was possible he was also taking a liking to me.

"You'll have to come back to collect your money," he said.

Uh-oh, I thought; now things were going to get real. I had honestly forgotten why I was there to begin with. It seemed more like visiting an old friend by now than a pre-foreclosure counseling visit. I couldn't even remember where I had left his file. In the living room? On the couch? The barn maybe? I knew I hadn't taken it up to Echo Glen in the rain.

"Maybe we should call it a night," I suggested, rising from the table. "And since you're tired you can wait to tell me your proposal until I come back. How's that sound?"

"Sit down, please," he said. "I'd like to tell you now, while you're here. It won't take long."

He opened a drawer beside the phone and removed a thick manila envelope. Then he carried it over and laid it down on the table in front of me. "Take a look in there."

I sighed, reminding myself that this was, after all, my job. If he wanted to talk about his foreclosure, I'd have to let him. I opened the envelope and pulled out a stack of papers, quickly looking them over. There was a map of the property with new boundary lines drawn at the southeast corner, and an application to separate off a tiny sliver of land.

"I'm not sure I get what all this is about," I said.

"This is what I need you to help me with."

"But what is it, exactly?"

"It's a short-plat survey to spin off the piece of property where June is buried. Just the northeast corner of Echo Glen."

"I see that, but why?"

"The bank is foreclosing — as you well know, since it's the reason you're here — and there's nothing much I can do about that. I'm embarrassed about it, for sure. But maybe you can understand that mortgage brokers were calling and sending letters all the time at the height of the market, offering easy loans and nearly free money, or so it seemed."

"I know," I said. "I was just getting into the business then. I wanted to help people buy houses, not foreclose on them."

"Well, I knew at the time that it was too good to be true, me being an accountant and all. I never would have done it, except June was getting worse by then and there were new experimental treatments that our insurance wouldn't cover. I took out the loan, despite her protests, and we spent the money on bills here, and on sending her to Portland for treatments. I was able to buy her a better wheelchair and build the ramp."

"Did they work?"

"The treatments? They helped some. But you know how things turned out. And now I've accepted that the property is lost, and I'm ready to leave here. But there's a problem."

He looked up at the painting of Echo Glen on the wall and sighed before going on.

"I buried June up there in Echo Glen, as was her wish, but I did it without the proper paperwork. Apparently Washington State only lets you inter someone on private property if the property is designated as a cemetery."

"That's what this form is about?"

He nodded. "I need to make this happen, Elliot. I need to ensure that June can rest in peace forever where she lies."

"So, that's why you told me the story."

"That's why I wrote that letter and invited you, or Mr. Spitzer, I thought, out here for this chat. And yes, it's why I told you our story. You needed to know how important it is to June and to me that she stay buried here."

"Okay, I'm with you," I said. "What can I do?"

He reached and sifted through the paperwork. "I need you to get your bank to sign off on this."

I looked it over. "A quitclaim deed?"

"Yes, releasing their interest in the portion that will become the cemetery. Then I need it filed with the county. In return, I'll agree not to fight the foreclosure and I can be out of the house as soon as two or three weeks."

"Where will you go?"

"That's not important right now. Will you help me?"

"Well, our company only contracts with the bank, and this is a bit of an unorthodox settlement for us to make. Usually we just offer a cash incentive for people to leave."

"I'm not looking for any money," he said. "In fact, hold on just a moment . . ." He reached into his robe pocket and produced his notebook and glasses. "Let's see," he said, putting the glasses on and opening the notebook, "you said you needed about twenty grand to have enough for your Miami condo down payment, is that right?"

"Yes, that's right. Right around that much."

"Well, how about you do the legwork to get this paperwork signed and filed, and I'll pay you twenty-five thousand dollars for your trouble. That's your down payment plus a little something extra. Sound fair?"

It sounded more than fair. It sounded downright generous.

"I'm sorry, Mr. Hadley, but as tempting as it is there's no way I can take your money. It would be a conflict for me."

He frowned, looking at me over his reading glasses. "Are you sure? It's a lot of money."

"Yes, it is. And you should use it to settle into a new place. There's no need to offer me any money for my help. I'm happy to do it for free. And besides, it's my job."

His frown lifted into a hopeful smile. "So, you'll do it then?"

"I'll sure try. I can't guarantee anything, but it's a tiny part of a big parcel you're asking them to split off. Plus, I'm seeing a way that I might be able to pitch it as a positive."

"How would you do that?" he asked.

"I'm guessing that once I make the bank aware that there's someone buried on the property they might have some issues when it comes time to sell. The only thing banks hate more than losses are liabilities. But if the burial spot is spun off into a separate parcel then there's nothing to disclose."

Mr. Hadley grinned. "I like the way you think, young man. Bravo! I knew you were right for the job the moment I opened the door this morning and saw you."

I smiled, happy to have made him proud,

but also relieved that his proposal was actually something I could try to help with. I think he felt relieved too, because he leaned back and sighed.

"You're sure you won't take the money?"

I shook my head.

"Well," he said, "it's a big favor you're doing me and I'll really be in your debt if you pull it off. I'm in your debt just for trying. You're a good man, Elliot. June would have liked you."

I got the feeling that this was his way of telling me that he liked me, and it made me blush a little. "Thanks, Mr. Hadley. I really like you too."

I thought he might correct me again and tell me to call him David, but he didn't. He just sat there in his crimson robe and smiled at me. There was an awkward moment between us, neither seeming to quite know what to say to wrap up such a long and personal day spent together. He looked beat, as if the day had taken a lot out of him. Realizing how late it was, I figured I should bail and let him get some rest.

"Oh shoot," I said, looking at my phone. "It's gotten late. You think I could use your restroom again before I go?"

"Of course," he said. "You know where it is."

When I returned to the kitchen from the bathroom, he was stirring the contents of a plastic bucket with a spoon.

"I put the papers back in the envelope for you there," he said, nodding toward the table. "I was hoping you could take this warm mash to Rosie on your way out. She needs her pain medication, but I'm too tired."

"Do I need to feed it to her?"

"Just set it in front of her, she'll know what to do."

He followed me to the door. After I had put on my shoes and jacket, he handed me the bucket.

"I know you say you won't take the money, but I'd like to thank you somehow, Elliot."

"It's no problem," I said. "I'm happy to help. It's my job."

"No," he replied, "not just for that. I'd like to thank you for listening. It meant a lot to me to tell our story to someone."

I wasn't sure why, but I was suddenly overwhelmed by a desire to hug him good-bye. But then I had the bucket of mash in one hand and the envelope in the other — and besides, men don't really hug. Not like women do, anyway.

"It was my pleasure, Mr. Hadley. Getting to listen to your story is more than thanks enough. It's been a great day."

I moved toward the door, and he opened it for me. I was halfway to the barn when I heard him call after me.

"Happy birthday, Elliot."

I turned around and looked at him, standing in the open doorway. I had forgotten all about my birthday.

"Thanks," I called back. "Now shut the door before you let all the heat out."

He laughed. "You sound a lot like June."

"I take that as a compliment," I said, smiling.

He nodded. "As you should. Good night, my friend. Please drive safely. Deer around these parts like to jump out at you for fun, I swear. And thanks for feeding Rosie. This old head needs to hit the pillow. Good night!"

He waved one last time before shutting the door.

I stood for a moment in the drive, just listening to the quiet and feeling the cool air against my cheeks. The clouds had cleared and the stars were out. I couldn't remember a time when they had looked so close, perhaps because I was far away from all the light pollution in the city. I made myself a promise to get out in nature more. Go camping or something when the weather warmed up in the spring. Or maybe I'd be in Miami by then. I wondered if you could see the same stars from there.

The barn was dark and it took me a minute to find the light switch. When I did, only a single dim bulb blinked on at the far end of the barn, near Rosie's stall. It seemed like ages ago already that Mr. Hadley and I had come out here in the rain to deliver warm apples after our own lunch. When I reached the stall, Rosie was fast asleep on her side. I set the bucket of mash down beside her head and turned to leave. I was exiting the stall when I stopped and turned back, sensing that something was wrong.

I knocked on the door for a full five minutes before finally giving up. Not a single light was on in the house, leading me to think that Mr. Hadley must have already turned in and gone to sleep. Who knows, maybe he took his hearing aids out. I decided I'd call in the morning to let him know.

The car was cold, so I sat for a minute to warm it up. But the truth was I didn't want to leave. I finally put the car in Drive and pulled away, the sweep of my headlights illuminating the property that I had seen for the first time just that morning but would never see the same way again. It's funny how things look different once you know their history.

I saw the wheelchair ramp built over the porch. I saw the barn where Rosie lay, her spirit now running in the fields of whatever dreams a blind horse has of heaven. I saw the old barn where David and the others had bunked for stunt camp, above which Sebastian had temporarily lived with his bullhorn and his Steve McQueen poster. I saw the old fire pit, nearly hidden now behind the tall grass — the fire pit where David and June had first shared lemon ice cream while being harassed by hippies; the fire pit where they had later flirted with one another when stunt camp was through. At least I assumed it was the same fire pit, but it didn't really matter, I guess, because all of it faded into blackness as my headlights passed by and I pulled away and left the Center of the Universe behind.

You sure could say it had been an interesting day. But it had been much more than that, really. It had been a sad but uplifting experience. An honor to hear Mr. Hadley's story, in a way. And above all else, it had been one hell of a birthday.

28

I make it a personal policy to never go to Finnegans on Friday nights — too many amateurs; too much drinking — but this was one night I made an exception. I just couldn't go home to my apartment. Not after the day I had just had, followed by the lonely drive into the city from Echo Glen.

"Hiya, handsome."

As soon as I heard her voice I knew it was exactly what I needed to hear. And it was probably why I had come too.

"Hi, Estrella. How are you? Busy in here tonight."

"That's Friday for you," she said. "What'll ya have? It's on me, since it's technically still your birthday."

I glanced at the clock: eleven fifteen p.m.

"You don't happen to have any RC Cola, do you?"

She shook her head.

"I didn't think so," I said. "How about a

club soda with lime."

"Getting wild tonight as usual I see," she joked, taking down a glass and scooping it full of ice. "You hungry?"

"No thanks. Say, you ever had a Moon-Pie?"

"What's a MoonPie?"

She handed me my drink, and I handed her the Polaroid that Mr. Hadley had taken of me blowing out my candles. She smiled, looking at the photo. "I haven't seen a Polaroid photo in ages. You look happy here, but that's a funny little cake."

"They're popular down south, I think."

"Polaroids?"

"No, MoonPies."

"I thought you said you were from around here."

"I am. I grew up in Belfair, unfortunately."

"Oh, come on," she said. "Belfair's not that bad."

Not that bad, I said. "What do you know about Belfair?"

"We lived in Bremerton through my sophomore year of high school. My dad was in the navy."

"Okay, but it rains all the time and you know it."

"Yes, but that's why it's so green." Then she smirked, adding, "Of course, you won't have to worry about that once you move to Miami."

"Florida gets rain," I said, shrugging.

She laughed. "In the form of hurricanes."

What does everyone have against Florida? I wondered. "You sound like a client I spent all day with."

She handed me back the Polaroid. "Well, you have wise clients then."

"I'll miss this place more than the rain anyway," I mumbled.

Someone called from down the bar, distracting her. She held up a finger, then turned back to me. "What's that now?"

"Nothing. You've got customers."

"It's all right. They can wait."

"I just said I'll miss this place when I move to Miami."

"Miss Finnegans? Really?"

"Not Finnegans so much. But, you know, seeing you."

"I said I'll be right there," she called down the bar. "I'm sorry," she said. "Come again?"

And this was why I didn't come in on Fridays.

"I'm fine," I said. "I'll just watch TV."

"That infomercial for a silly home paraffin wax kit's been running all night again. I can't find the remote."

"I like soft feet. Maybe I'll pick one up."

She laughed. "You sure you grew up in Belfair and not Bellevue? Okay, Mr. Soft Feet. I'll be back to check on you."

As soon as she was gone I was lonelier than ever — even though the bar was crowded with laughing people blowing off a week's worth of steam. Usually I spent Friday nights at home, watching *Seinfeld* reruns. Sometimes I'd walk to Pacific Place and see a movie by myself. Very rarely I'd have a date. But tonight I had a lot on my mind, and none of those options sounded any good.

It seemed like ages ago that I had left Seattle to drive out to Echo Glen, but it had been just that morning. It was less than twenty-four hours ago, in fact, that I had sat in this very seat, watching this very TV, and that silly depression-pill commercial had come on, reminding me of Mr. Hadley's letter and those crazy bird stamps. Amazing how tiny things like that can really rock your world.

I wasn't quite sure whether it was Mr. Hadley himself or his story that had gotten to me most. I was fascinated by his wife. Attracted to her even, in some strange way, and I found myself wishing I had lived the story instead of just having heard it. I guess you could say I was falling for June. I wondered what it felt like to hang glide off of a cliff into the moon. I found myself envisioning a poppy field in Spain. They're red, right? Isn't that what he said? Crimson maybe. Anyway, I was all mixed up. And I was sad too. Sad for Mr. Hadley's losing his property when it meant so much to him; sad that June had passed away, even if she had lived a long and fulfilling life; and sad that I would never find anything like the love those two shared. Not that I was looking or anything.

As I sat there thinking, I began to hate my job. I knew damn well that somebody had to do it, but did that somebody really need to be me? Some sorry sap works the execution lever too, but that doesn't make it a job I'd ever do. Who the hell was I to kick these people out of their places with a check from the bank and big fat f-you? Sure, I sometimes helped them move. And I'd absolutely help Mr. Hadley too. I'd do what he had asked at least. I'd cash in every favor I'd stored up to get his quitclaim signed and his short plat pushed through. But what if there was more I could do?

"Just one minute left, better make your last birthday wish." Estrella sat down at the empty stool beside me and nodded toward the clock. Then she smiled. "Gee, fella, aren't you going to offer to buy a girl a drink?"

"Buy you a drink. But aren't you working?"

"You looked like you could use some company so I got Tom to cover for me. He's closing anyway."

"Okay, sure. I'd love to buy you a drink then. What'll you have?"

"I'd like a hot chocolate."

"One hot chocolate coming up."

I raised my arm to get Tom's attention, but Estrella pulled it back down, biting her lip and shaking her head.

"We don't serve hot chocolate at Finnegans, silly."

"But I thought you wanted —"

"And I do. Let's go to Dilettante on the hill. They've got Viennese cocoa to die for and they're open till two."

It was drizzling again outside when we left Finnegans, so we took my car, which I had parked nearby instead of walking.

"I guess this means you don't like me," she said, looking out the window as I drove.

"Why would it mean that?"

"Because you only ask out girls you don't like, remember?"

"Yeah, but this is different."

"How so?"

"I didn't ask you; you asked me."

She laughed and we rode the rest of the way in silence.

Dilettante is a trendy late-night dessert spot on Capitol Hill, serving everything from double-sized portions of their famous homemade rice pudding to double chocolate truffle martinis. It's a great place, but you could easily wake up the next day filled with double regret. We snagged a quiet, candlelit booth in the back and looked over the menus.

"Oh, aren't you a cute couple," our server said, arriving at our booth with such speed he had to check himself on the booth back, as if he were on roller skates.

"Oh, we're actually not —"

He waved my comment away. "I'm not telling, handsome. What happens at Dilettante stays at Dilettante." Then he turned to Estrella, saying, "This one is a real romantic. You want your usual, sweetie?"

Estrella nodded. "Extra chocolate shavings, please."

"And how about you then, Romeo?"

"I'll have the same."

"Two dark chocolate Viennese coming up."

As soon as he was gone, I turned back to

355

Estrella. "You must come here a lot."

"Sometimes," she said. "I just live a block away."

"Ah, I see. So this was a ploy to bum a ride home?"

She grinned. "Yes, because it's so hard to hop a bus up the hill I have to seduce a new customer every night for a ride. It's tough being a poor defenseless woman in the big city."

"All right. I'm sorry. You know I didn't mean it like that. But you did just say you were seducing me, for the record."

"Of course. Dilettante is where I seduce all my men."

"Great. That sure explains the 'This one is a real romantic' comment from our server."

"That's just Georgie being Georgie. It means he likes you. But let's get back to you. Tell me about your day. You looked a little down when you came in."

"I did? Maybe I was down, I don't know. I had the strangest birthday. But you don't want to hear about this."

"Yes, I really do," she said.

So I began telling her about my day. From my drive out to Echo Glen that morning and meeting Mr. Hadley, to his tale that unfolded throughout the afternoon and into

356

the evening. I was in the middle of his and June's budding love story at stunt camp when Georgie breezed by to drop off our hot chocolates with a wink, fortunately in too much of a hurry to stay and chat.

"Oh, this is good," I said, tasting mine.

"Isn't it heaven?" she replied. "I was addicted to them for a while, but I've managed to cut back to one or two a week. You must have noticed all the weight I gained, since you come in to Finnegans all the time."

"No," I said, shaking my head, "I never noticed. Which is strange since I've spent so much time there at the bar counter stealing glances at your ass."

She blushed, looking down at the table and biting her lip coquettishly, as she sometimes did. A dab of whipped cream remained on her lip, making it even cuter than usual.

"I can tell you're the type of boy my mother always warned me about," she said. Then she looked up at me with sexy, half-hooded eyes and added, "Fortunately for you, I never listened."

I was lost for words, but I know I blushed for sure.

"Now, get back to the story of David and June," she said. "I was really enjoying it."

So I went on, filling her in on everything Mr. Hadley had told me, although with much less detail and clarity than he had recounted it with. It was strange, but Estrella and I knew very little about each other, and yet here we were bonding over someone else's love story. By the time I got to the part where Mr. Hadley had left me, with the two of them engaged and in love, despite her Parkinson's diagnosis, riding off toward Aranda de Duero together on bicycles traded for with June's ring, Estrella was cradling an empty mug with tears running down her face.

"It's so beautiful," she said, shaking her head. "Everyone should find true love like that. The way he went after her all the way to Spain. It makes my heart ache. What happened?"

So I told her I hadn't heard about the wedding yet, but I filled her in on June's being buried at Echo Glen, and about how Mr. Hadley had asked me to help push the paperwork through so he could dedicate it as a cemetery.

"He even offered me twenty-five grand."

"Wow," she said. "That's a lot of money."

"I know it is."

"What are you going to do?"

"I know what I'm *not* going to do. I'm not

going to take his money. But I will help him."

"See, I knew you were sweet as pie, despite that too-cool-for-school loner attitude you saunter in with all the time."

"I do not saunter."

"Do too. Three nights a week, same thing: 'Club soda with lime and a menu, please.' Even though you always order the chicken Parmesan sandwich."

"I love the chicken Parmesan sandwich."

"Apparently."

"I think we've talked enough about me," I said. "I'd like to hear about you. But first I'm getting us another round."

"See," she said, "now you're addicted too."

I flagged down Georgie and ordered us two more cocoas. Then I settled back in my seat to hear about Estrella.

"Oh gosh," she said. "I don't know where to start. What do you want to know?"

"Everything."

"I'm afraid you'll have to settle for the brochure and not the book, since it's getting late. Let's see, I already told you I grew up in Bremerton and that my dad was in the navy — they live in Seward Park now. My mother makes quilts. She enters them in contests and wins. She sells them on a website I helped her design. I love cats, but my only pet is a betta fish named Bernie that I've had for five years. People think fish don't return affection, but they do. What else do you want to know?"

"What's one thing you couldn't live without?"

"Chocolate," she said, grinning. "And books. Next."

"Okay, something you're good at."

"Puzzles. Especially landscapes."

"Something you're bad at."

"I'm horrible at caring for houseplants. I kill one a month it seems, but I refuse to give up."

"Your favorite thing to do on a Sunday."

"Visit my parents for dinner and a game of Scrabble."

"Scrabble?"

"I'm a Scrabble champion. At least against my parents."

"So, they're still married?"

"Thirty-two years and counting. Theirs is a real love story, not unlike the one you just told me, minus the BASE jumping and hang gliding and all that. My father works on planes, but he says only a fool or a soldier would jump out of one."

I blew on my chocolate, mumbling almost to myself. "This is really challenging my worldview."

"What is?" she asked. "The cocoa?"

"These love stories. That's two today."

"That's right," she said, nodding. "You're the guy who doesn't believe in love. What did you say the other night? It's fun at the beginning, but bites you in the end. Someone's been hurt a little, I'd say. Tell me, Elliot, who was she?"

"Who was who?" I asked.

"The girl who broke your heart."

I shrugged, looking down. "My mother, I guess."

As soon as I said it I wished I hadn't. But something about Estrella's face made me want to pour out my past, wounds and all. So I told her. I told her about my mother running out on us. I told her about my father's passing. I even told her about my childhood obsession with moving away to someplace sunny, realizing for the first time as I said it that perhaps I had somehow connected my childhood sadness with the rain that seemed always to fall outside my bedroom window.

When I finished, her expression was a mix of tenderness and pain. As if my story had hurt her somehow. But she didn't say anything, which was kind of nice. Sometimes you just want someone to listen because there's nothing to say.

"You know what I just now realized?" I said. "I've spoken about my childhood exactly twice in my entire life. And the first time was this morning with Mr. Hadley. What a birthday."

"I'm glad you chose to share it with me," she said.

And she seemed to actually mean it too.

"And now I understand why you always order club soda, and why you had that glass of wine last night to honor your father's birthday tradition. He sounds like he was a character."

"He sure was. The tree-topping sommelier of Belfair. But he had some funky ideas about life and love."

"Well, maybe he did the best he could."

"You know what," I replied, feeling my mood suddenly lighten, "he did do the best he could. And that was enough."

We were looking across the table at each other when Georgie swung by with our check, since it was coming up on two and the place was about to close. Estrella reached for her purse, but I beat her to it and handed him enough cash to cover the bill plus a generous tip.

"This one's a keeper," he said when I told him to keep the change. Then he winked at

Estrella before taking off on his closing rounds.

"You could have let me treat since it's your birthday."

"It's not my birthday any longer," I said. "And that's just fine with me. Come on, I'll give you a lift home."

"I'm only a block away."

"Then I'll walk you."

"You don't have to do that."

"I know. I'm not doing it because you need an escort. I'm doing it because I want the extra time with you."

She smiled.

The rain had quit and the night was clear and cool with just a hint of coming chill in the air. It smelled like fall. We could hear laughter echoing in the empty streets as we walked, other Friday-night celebrants heading for home.

"So, what are you studying at UW?" I asked.

"Did I tell you I went there?"

"I'm a mind reader."

"You are? What am I thinking right now?"

"How incredibly handsome I am."

She laughed. "Oh my God, you are a mind reader."

"Seriously though, I overheard you talking to the other bartender at work."

"Oh, you've been eavesdropping too, not just staring at my ass. It's good to know your interests are more than primal. I'm working toward my master's in psychology."

"Uh-oh, are you one of those women who have a *DSM-4* beside your bed all highlighted with your exes' diagnoses? Wait, is *diagnoses* even the correct plural of *diagnosis*? I forgot I'm talking to a Scrabble champion."

"It is," she said. "I'm impressed."

"Not bad for a community college kid, eh?"

"I'm more impressed that you know what the *DSM* is. But we're actually on version five now. My plan is to be a high school counselor, not a practicing psychiatrist, so you don't have to worry. And no, I don't diagnose the men I date."

"Would you ever consider dating a really handsome but slightly neurotic foreclosure counselor from Belfair?"

We had turned off Broadway by then onto a residential street, and she stopped on the dim sidewalk and looked at me. She cocked her head slightly and smiled. "Even though he's on his way to Miami?"

She certainly had a point there, especially after my stupid speech the other day about only dating women I don't like. I was searching for a response when she leaned in and kissed me on the cheek. Just a quick peck, but it caught me by surprise.

"Maybe," she said. "But unlike you I only date men I actually like. Thanks for walking me home."

She turned and walked away from me, through a gate and up toward an old Victorian house turned apartments. I hadn't even realized we had arrived — maybe because I didn't want the night to end.

"Hey, Elliot," she said, turning back.

I was still standing there, thinking about that kiss. "Yes?"

"I had a question about the story you told me. About Mr. Hadley. It's none of my business, but I was thinking since he offered you all that money, maybe there was some way he could use it to save his house instead. It's such a lovely story between those two. It would be a shame for him to have to move."

"That's a good question," I said. "I'll find out."

"Okay," she said, lingering there a moment longer. "Maybe come by the bar and let me know how it goes."

"You know I will."

"And thanks for tonight. I had fun."

I was thankful for being far enough in the

shadows that she probably couldn't see me blush. "I had fun too. Good night, Estrella."

Then I turned and walked back to my car alone, kicking leaves and thinking about a hundred million things all at once, but for some reason, still smiling.

29

The phone rang fifty times before I quit counting. What kind of person doesn't have voice mail, or at least an answering machine? But of course I knew the answer to my own question.

It wasn't raining, so I went for a jog. It's a great way to connect with people in the city. When you're out walking, no one ever says hello. I think they're afraid you might stop them to talk or something. And people are way too busy for that. But when you're running, other runners, and occasionally walkers, will nod at you and smile, sometimes even tossing out a quick greeting as you pass them by. I think they know you won't slow down and ask them for more than their simple hello.

After my run I sat on a bench at the waterfront sculpture garden and watched the ferries travel back and forth across the sound. For two hours I sat and thought. I thought a lot about Estrella. I knew the night before had softened me some, but I was still unwilling to change my position and let myself get wrapped up in love. And besides, I didn't even think she liked me that much. And why would she? What did I have to offer? The only place I was going was Miami. But what I found myself thinking about even more than Estrella was Mr. Hadley and his story.

I had to know how things had finally come together for him and June. Did they have a happy life together when they returned from Spain? Before things turned too bad, anyway. It sure seemed like it from all the paintings she did. More than anything, though, I didn't like the idea of his being surprised when he delivered Rosie her daily apple. But then he wasn't answering his phone.

"Just drive out there, Elliot," I told myself. "Quit being a chicken."

A woman walking by on the path in front of my bench saw me talking to myself and quickened her pace. It made me laugh, after having joked the night before with Estrella about the *DSM-4*. What would she say if she could only see me now? I wondered, sitting there debating with myself. But somehow I knew what she'd say. She'd say to drive out and see Mr. Hadley.

There was a truck and flatbed trailer parked in the drive when I arrived. I knocked on the door, but no one answered. Then I heard a tractor. When I turned around on the porch to look, I saw a backhoe working at the tree line at the far end of the property, beyond the barn.

It was a nice sunny fall day, but the damp grass still soaked my shoes as I crossed the field.

"Hey there!" I waved to get the driver's attention.

He was pushing dirt into a large hole, and when he saw me he lifted the bucket and turned the engine off.

"Howdy," he said, touching the bill of his cap.

"Do you know where Mr. Hadley is?"

"The old man? I'm not sure. He walked me out here to show me where to dig. I asked him if he wanted me to come and get him before I put it in the ground — sometimes they like to say a few words or something — but he said no."

He paused to gaze off toward the house.

"Funny thing is he told me he had to go somewhere and tell someone that her favorite horse had died, but then I never did see him leave the house."

"Thanks," I replied. "I know where to find him."

He touched his hat. "Righty-oh."

I heard the backhoe start up again as I walked away.

I saw him as soon as I rounded the bend that led into the glen. He was sitting beneath the oak tree on the hill, next to June's grave. His back was to me, but because the waterfall was running lower today without the rain, I could hear that he was talking. I knew it was June he was talking to, and the thought of it melted my heart. I just couldn't bring myself to interrupt him. I turned and walked back the way I had come.

I was sitting on the back porch an hour and a half later when he came limping slowly down the path. He was having trouble walking, even with his cane. Still, the way the path was worn I could tell he hadn't lied when he'd told me he went up to Echo Glen every day. He was halfway across the bridge when he saw me. I thought he might ask me why I was there but he didn't.

"You came back for the MoonPies, didn't you," he said.

"Maybe," I replied. "But I also brought you some tea." I held up the box. "A Stash sampler. You can't be drinking that Smooth

Move all the time or you'll never get off the pot."

"Son, when a man's almost eighty years old the toilet is his throne. That's why us old folk always have padded seats. Come on inside and I'll put some water on to boil."

It felt strangely familiar inside the house, considering I had only been there for the first time the day before. As if it were more a homecoming than a second visit.

Mr. Hadley took the tea sampler into the kitchen and put water on to boil. "Seems awfully hard to choose with so many flavors," he said, looking at the box.

"I like the Chai Spice."

"Chai Spice it is then."

After he had taken down two mugs and put the tea bags in, he opened the drawer beside the phone and handed me his foreclosure file. "You left this here yesterday."

"Thanks," I said. "That's a rookie mistake that'll get you fired in my business. Did you read it?"

He shook his head. "It wasn't mine to read."

"You could have read it and not told me."

"Is that what you would have done?"

I shrugged. "Maybe."

"That's because you young people are

loose with the truth. My generation gets a stomachache if we lie."

I hadn't thought about it before, but he had a point. The truth did seem to be a somewhat pliable enterprise for my peers and me. Especially in my line of work. I made a mental note to try to be more honest, even with the little things. And as long as I was being honest, I felt I should confess something.

"Mr. Hadley, I hope you don't mind, but I shared your and June's love story last night with a friend of mine. With that girl from the bar I had told you about. The one I kind of like."

"The one with the beautiful Spanish name."

"That's her. Estrella. Anyway, I didn't mention anything about June being the Barefoot BASE Jumper, since you said I was the only one who knew. I hope that's okay."

He was fiddling with the teapot but I thought I saw him smile. "It makes me happy to think that you found our story interesting enough to share."

"Oh, I did. And she did too. That's why I came back. We have to know what happened in Spain. Or at least that's one of the reasons I came back. I wanted to tell you about Rosie, but I see you already know. I tried to tell you last night."

He gazed out the window in the direction of the field. "That's Mr. Thorpe's son out there with the digger. I had him bury her beneath her favorite live oak. She used to stand beneath it for shade in the summer, smelling the air and feeling the breeze. It's strange that you can bury a horse on your property no problem, but you need a silly cemetery permit to lay your wife to rest on the same land."

He looked very tired and very alone standing there in the light of the window. The silence was interrupted when the teapot began whistling. He went over to the stove and filled our mugs.

"Can I ask you something, Mr. Hadley?"

"Sure, Elliot. But please, call me David. It's my belief that our spirits don't age and mine is too young to be called Mister."

"Sorry."

"No need for sorry."

"Okay. What I wanted to ask was . . . well, instead of going to all the trouble of getting the bank to sign off on that short plat in exchange for you leaving, why don't you try to save your property from foreclosure instead?"

"I don't understand what you mean," he said, handing me my mug of tea.

"Well, since you have twenty-five thousand to part with. You did offer me that much, didn't you? Why don't you let me try to negotiate some kind of mortgage modification that will allow you to catch up and keep the property?"

"I'm so upside down in this place," he said.

"But what if they'd lower the payment?"

"I'm afraid that's not possible."

"Why not?"

"Correct me if I'm wrong, but there's no incentive for the bank to sign the quitclaim unless they're getting something in return. And my agreeing to sign over the property in lieu of foreclosure is our bargaining chip, you see."

"Yes, but what if I could somehow get them to do both?"

"Oh, I doubt you could do that."

"I can be very convincing."

He sighed, looking around the kitchen. His eyes settled on June's painting of Echo Glen.

"No," he said, "I think it's almost time for me to leave this house anyway. No sense in dragging it out. And besides, the money I had intended to pay you with is tied up right now." He looked back at me, a serious expression on his face. "Let's just focus on getting the short plat signed, if it's all right with you."

"Sure. But I just thought —"

"Enough of that talk," he said, cutting me off. "Didn't you say you wanted to hear the rest of the story? Let's take our tea into the living room and I'll tell you. I think I left off with that crazy wife-to-be of mine racing me to Aranda de Duero on a rusty bicycle. I wanted a pillow and she wanted some wine."

30

With his watch still in June's pocket he couldn't say for sure what time it was, but it must have been well after one in the morning when they finally pedaled into the sleeping streets of the old Spanish town. It was so quiet in the square he could hear the pigeons cooing and rustling up in the old stones of the church they stopped in front of to rest and get their bearings.

"I don't think I've ever been so tired before in my life," David said, offering June his water bottle.

"I'm surprised these old bikes held up," she replied.

"Frankly, I'm surprised these old bones did," David said with a laugh. Then he looked around at the deserted square, a few gas lanterns casting pools of light onto the cobblestones. "You'd think there'd be an inn or a hotel, wouldn't you? Where did you say Jose works again? In some underground bodega off the main square here somewhere?"

June nodded. "There's supposed to be a network of old Roman cellars all beneath the town." She opened her pack. "Sebastian gave me an address. Although I'm sure they've long since closed."

"Let's find it and wait for them to open," David suggested. "I could lie down and sleep right here on the street."

The square was dark but they eventually found the address above the door of a tiny street-level shop. They had propped their bikes against a wall and were just sitting down on the curb out front to wait for morning when the shop door opened and someone came out. June stood to chase after the shadowy figure. David followed.

"Disculpe," she called. *"Habla usted inglés?"*

The figure turned around, and they saw that it was a man wearing a hooded cloak. *"Sí, señorita,"* he said.

"Can you tell us where to find Jose Antonio Villarreal? He's supposed to work here in a bodega and the address we were given is for the shop you just came out of."

The man glanced around nervously, eyeing David and June with suspicion. Then he gestured toward the shop door. "Just go inside and down the *escalera, señorita.*

You'll find him."

He turned without another word and hurried away into the shadows. Once he was gone, June leaned up onto her tiptoes and kissed David passionately on the lips.

"What was that for?" he asked.

"Just in case we get murdered," she said.

Then she grabbed his hand and pulled him toward the shop entrance.

It was dark inside, but a lone candle was burning in a glass urn against the far wall where a little door stood open and a set of steps led down into the gloomy depths. They could see lights and shadows moving below, hear the quiet singsong murmur of hushed voices speaking Spanish. They looked at each other and shrugged. David took the lead as they descended the stairs.

At the bottom of the steps a stone passageway led to an open cellar door. Inside the cellar were several men and women standing around a tall table, looking intently at something on the tabletop. The cellar walls were lined with racks of wine.

"Jose, is that you?"

At the sound of David's voice Jose spun around. There was a flash of surprise on his face, followed by recognition and a quick smile. "Señor David."

"I'm afraid I lost your lucky walking stick."

378

Jose waved this away. "Something lost, something better found. This must be June." He grabbed her by the shoulders and kissed her on each cheek. Then he did the same with David before gesturing grandly for them to enter. "Come in, come in. Join us. Juan, get down two bottles of the 'seventy-eight. Let's celebrate the safe return of our comrades."

They were introduced to the others and within minutes all were standing around the table, drinking wine and chatting like old friends. A platter of cold tapas was produced, and David snacked heartily on fresh cheeses and stuffed olives, hungry after their long ride. The table had a map spread on its surface. In the center of the map was a bullring.

"What's the map for?" he asked.

"Ah" — Jose sighed — "this is *plaza de toros,* where the festival is taking place tomorrow. We are planning a protest but have just been informed that the *policía* are erecting a perimeter this year. We won't be allowed within two hundred meters of any entrance, subject to arrest."

"What are you protesting?" David asked.

"The torture of bulls, of course, my comrade. They say it is rich in tradition and we say tradition is no excuse not to change.

There are other ways now, besides. They can dance with the bulls. Jump over them. But no torture, no blood."

June seemed to take an immediate and keen interest in this disobedient endeavor, looking very closely at the map and asking Jose what exactly they had planned.

"We want to make the spectators aware," he said. "We want to make a statement about how inhumane it is."

A woman at the table who appeared to be Spanish but spoke with an Australian accent held up a matador costume and several vials of red dye. "We had planned to lie in front of the entrance covered in fake blood while a matador walked among us, as if proud to have slain his fellows. Let them see how it would feel if the victims were people instead of bulls. But now, as you can see, that plan is shot."

"We don't mind being arrested for the cause," Jose added. "However, there is no point if we are nabbed before we can even get near the bullring. No point."

"Well, this is all very interesting," David interjected, "but I was thinking maybe we could find a bed to rest in. If it's not too much trouble. It's been a hell of a long day."

"But of course," Jose said, setting his wineglass down and straightening his posture as if ashamed to have been caught slacking on his manners. "I will take you to my place at once."

But June was paying them no mind, looking intently at the map instead. She glanced back up at the matador costume.

"That thing looks like it might fit me," she said.

The Australian woman glanced at the costume in her hand. "I think it would, yes."

David did not like where this was going. "June, what are you up to?"

June looked at David, a mischievous grin forming slowly at the edges of her mouth. "Are you up for a little adventure, my love?"

"Oh gosh. Maybe after I've had some sleep."

June turned to Jose. "I might just have an idea if you know someone who has an airplane."

The big doors stood open and the crowds were funneling through, buying beers and renting seat cushions on their way into the bullring. David was nervous, silently chastising himself for even allowing June to go through with this little stunt. But June would be June, and he had been so tired the night before after walking halfway across Spain, followed by their bike ride, that he would have agreed to almost anything in exchange for a soft place to lie down and a real pillow.

"You sure she'll be okay?" David asked Jose.

"She'll be fine, comrade. It is understood that we will do something every year. The worst they do is hold us in the *cárcel* until the festival is through. Two days. It's a small price to pay."

"Two days in the hoosegow sounds like a pretty high price to me," David said. "Especially every year."

"Perhaps," Jose replied. "But still a much smaller price than the one paid by the bulls."

David could think of no argument to counter this, so he sucked up his worry and followed Jose toward their seats.

The open-air arena was infused with a strange energy — excitement for sure, but with something else vibrating beneath the surface as well; jubilation laced with blood-lust, perhaps. David himself had never seen a live bullfight from the stands, and the way things were to work out, he never would.

They had paid for *barreras* tickets in the *sombra* section — ringside in the shade — giving them a clear view of the open-air arena and the blue sky above. As the grandstands filled, David glanced around, recognizing several familiar faces from the bodega the night before. He felt a shiver of excitement run up his spine, as if he were an important agent involved in some urgent and subtly brewing conspiracy. He felt it even more when Jose palmed him a vial of red dye.

Wait for the band, he reminded himself, wait for the band.

As the seconds passed, his nervousness grew. The stands were nearly filled now, and legs and elbows pressed into David, adding to his anxiety. There was a rail in front of them, and on the other side of the rail was a sunken alley that circled the ring. There were several offset splits in the wall wide enough to provide access into the ring for the banderilleros and other costumed assistants to the toreros who were now gathered in this alley, looking out over the wall into the empty ring.

David was about to ask Jose how June would be able to time her entrance, since there was no way she could hear the band, but before he could get out the first word, everything seemed to unravel at once.

First, several uniformed officers stepped out in front of the stands and scanned the crowd. One of them recognized Jose, saying something to his partner and pointing.

"Mierda!" Jose said. "I've been spotted." He nudged David and passed him his vial of dye, saying, "It's all up to you now, comrade. Good luck." Then he took off, shouting, *"Con permiso! Con permiso!"* as he leaped over legs and knees, running the length of the grandstand and disappearing into the vestibule that led out of the arena. The officers gave chase.

David was now sitting there alone with two vials of dye when the band began playing a lively marchlike *pasodoble* tune. He knew this was his cue, but he was frozen with fear and confusion. He heard shouting and saw several of his fellow conspirators hopping down into the alley and making for the slits that led into the bullring, stripping off and casting aside their shirts along the way, men and women both. Their backs were marked with messages deriding the cruelty of the art. The band played on, oblivious, as the protesters successfully gained the ring, pouring their vials of dye onto their now-naked torsos and falling to the arena floor in the poses of wounded animals — seven in total, missing only Jose and David. And, of course, June.

Her timing could not have been more perfect. It was so perfect, in fact, that David sat watching the sky with wonder over how she had managed it. Her parachute was silhouetted against the sun as she turned tight spirals above the ring, dropping altitude and descending fast. As she came closer into view, the crowd saw her gold-embroidered matador costume and began to "ooh" and "ahh," assuming, or so it seemed, that this was an untraditional but planned part of the performance. She was still falling as the *policía* poured into the ring, running for the bloodied protesters with dangling handcuffs. But when they noticed June they froze in midstep, eyes glued to the sky above as she swooped down and came in on her final approach, flaring the canopy and touching down with the choreographed grace of a theater toreador entering the stage on wires. The police stood watching, amused and confused, possibly even wondering themselves if maybe this wasn't all part of the act.

June shrugged off her chute, pulled out a wooden sword, and rushed to the prone and writhing protesters one after another to pretend-slay them. The crowd cheered louder; the police officers looked around for direction. David watched all this from the stands with a sense of unease. His unease turned to angst when the big doors opened, and his angst to horror when the bulls rushed in — six of them in all, each thundering out into the arena with tossing horns and angry eyes.

Without thinking, David stood and hopped the fence and dropped down into the alley, racing for the nearest entrance into the ring. By the time he got there it was sheer pandemonium, with police rushing for the exits and brave banderilleros charging in past them with pink capes to distract and corral the confused bulls. David could not find June. Her parachute had been caught on the horn of a bull and was being dragged around the arena, its yellow smiley face a taunting image circling the mayhem, but she herself was nowhere to be seen. David moved through the waving capes and the rushing animals without fear, obsessed with his search for June. He did not find her. But fortunately, she found him just in time.

A particularly large bull was heading straight for David from behind, and June gripped his arm and wrenched him out of its path not a second too soon. The bull's side brushed his thigh and the wind stirred by its passing parted and fluffed his hair. When he looked at June she was smiling with exhilaration.

"I've never felt more alive," she shouted

above the noise. "How about you?"

David was caught off guard by her question and paused to take in the scene. The entire bullring was melting down around them. One of the bulls had jumped the fence and was flushing costumed assistants from the alley into the ring like circus clowns running for their lives. Several bulls had been corralled by banderilleros but were resisting being forced back into their pens. June's torn and shredded canopy trailed by, still being dragged by the circling bull. And the spectators were all on their feet now, on tiptoes or pressing into aisles for better views, cheering and shouting with delight at each wild turn of events. Strangely, the band played on through it all, as if the entire mad enterprise were the sinking *Titanic* and they its loyal musicians determined to go down with the ship.

"You know what," David said, "I do feel alive."

Then he noticed the two vials still in his hand, forgotten in all the excitement, and for reasons he would never quite understand — perhaps due to adrenaline, or even simple elation at living on the edge with the woman he loved — David peeled off his shirt as the others had done, popped the tops off the vials, and dumped the red dye over his bare chest. Then he scooped up an abandoned cape and began taunting the passing bulls with it, shouting at the top of his lungs as he had seen done in old movies, *"Olé! Olé!"*

To his surprise this worked, and an energetic bull veered toward him. He stepped aside with a wide flourish of the cape and let it pass — a middle-aged matador, born again in the *plaza de toros* of an ancient pueblo in Spain. The crowd cheered him on, their eyes glued to David as he stood shirtless in the ring, holding the cape. Never before had he truly stepped onto life's stage, and here he was now in its very center.

He looked over at June. She was standing several paces away, watching him. Her eyes were wide with surprise and she was smiling with pride. And he knew in that moment that she loved him. Really, truly loved him, as he had already loved her from the moment of their first meeting on that roof. And he also knew that they were meant to share the rest of their time together as husband and wife, and that they would someday lie side by side in eternity, happy to have lived lives worth living, happy to have found love worth sharing.

They came together and kissed. And

although the crowd was cheering them more wildly than ever and the mayhem was still swirling all around them, for the few moments their lips were locked the world contained only them. June opened her eyes and smiled. Not a guarded smile, but a true smile from the corners of her mouth to the very edges of her eyes. The doubt she had carried seemed to be gone without a trace, and David was sure he saw acceptance and hope now written on her face.

June glanced over his shoulder and her expression changed to one of concern. "Drop the cape," she said. "Let's go now."

He began to protest, enjoying the moment too much to let it end, but then he followed her gaze over his shoulder and saw for himself the bull standing several feet away, blowing and stomping and preparing to charge.

The cape had hardly hit the ground and they were running at a mad dash for the fence, holding each other's hands all the way. They were relieved when they squeezed through the partition into the safety of the alley.

"We pulled it off!" David said, hugging her.

June smiled up at him. "Yes. Yes, we did."

Of course, no sooner had they cleared the

arena exit than they were nabbed by waiting police and slapped with a pair of handcuffs each.

31

"I can't believe you went to Spain and fought real bulls in a real bullring with a real matador's cape! You really are the man, Mr. Hadley, you know that?"

Mr. Hadley looked very tired, but he managed a grin.

"And then there's June," I said. "Skydiving into the ring like she did. What a wild pair you two were. So that's how you got arrested then. And it explains June's matador costume in your wedding photo too, I guess. But how did you go from being put in handcuffs to being married? I want to hear it all."

Mr. Hadley sighed. "I could spend the entire afternoon boring you with details, but the short answer is June."

"But how? What did she do?"

He started to answer but was seized by another coughing fit, as he had been several times during his story. He took a minute to catch his breath and then went on to explain:

"It turned out the hooded man we had met the night before — coming out of the bodega, you remember — was the *jefe de la policía.* He had a soft spot for the suffering of bulls himself, you see, although he would not publicly admit this. He had been there to warn Jose and company that they were to be arrested if they protested. This battle between them had been ongoing for years, as you might have guessed. Hell, maybe it still is. I don't know. Excuse me."

He looked like he was going to cough but didn't, pausing instead to sip his cold tea. Mine was long gone.

He continued: "Anyway, at first we were labeled *taurofobos,* or detractors of the festival, and were held overnight in the jail. They even threatened us with stronger charges. However, the investigation turned up a guilty bull handler who had released the bulls into the ring to punish the protesters. The funny thing was the crowd had loved the show. Many said it was the best festival in all their years attending. And somehow, June won over the chief while being interrogated, and the two of them hatched a plan to claim that the entire stunt hadn't been a protest but an elaborately orchestrated proposal.

"I found this out when the chief came to release me from my cell, saying that he himself would be marrying us that very evening, the final day of the festival. June kept the matador costume on to keep up the illusion. She never did tell me how she had convinced the chief to let us go. Although I couldn't help but notice as he administered our vows that he was wearing my gold-plated Seiko."

"What about the bulls, though? And Jose and the others?"

"The others were set free as well. The bulls were not so lucky. The bullfight went ahead as planned while we were in jail. In fact, at our reception the next evening they served bull stew. But what can you do? It was their culture, not ours. For that one night we let it go. Dancing instead, drinking and singing with the throngs of people who came to celebrate the end of the festival and our wedding."

His gaze drifted off for a moment, as if he were lost in the past, reliving the memory.

"June was glad to read in later years that many places had moved to outlaw bullfighting altogether, including Barcelona. I'm not sure where things stand in Aranda de Duero. You win such wars yards at a time, not miles. But right now I'm afraid I'm very tired, young man. I need rest. Would you mind terribly if we called it a day?"

Even though I had been hoping to hear more, he did look tired. His face was pale and his posture slumped.

"Of course," I replied. "I'll leave you to it. You've been more than generous with your time already."

I rose and took up his loan file, which he had returned to me, pausing before heading to the door.

"Mr. Hadley," I said, "I'm going to get your quitclaim signed and your short plat filed if I have to personally camp outside the bank manager's office to make it happen. We'll make sure June gets to rest in Echo Glen forever."

He was still sitting in his chair, looking up at me, and tears welled up in his eyes and he gently nodded his head. When he spoke, his voice was choked with emotion.

"You're a good man, Elliot Champ. A good man."

Then he tried to rise from his chair but was unable to on his own. I reached out my hand and pulled him to his feet, helping to steady him on his cane. He followed me to the door, moving very slowly. I lingered to look at the paintings, keeping his pace so as not to make him feel like he was lagging behind.

When I stepped out onto the porch, I noticed that the truck and tractor were gone. Only a slight mound of fresh earth stood out against the trees at the edge of the field.

"I hope to have some info for you as early as next week," I said. "Should I call first or just stop by?"

"Come anytime," he said. "Except for Tuesday afternoons when the van picks me up for the clinic. Otherwise I'm here."

"Okay." I hesitated. "You sure you're all right, though? I mean, do you need anything?"

He waved my offer away. "I'm fine. Don't you worry about this old man. A lovely home health care worker comes by to check on me three times a week. Even delivers my organic groceries." He glanced around, then added in a conspiratorial tone bordering on a whisper, "She doesn't know, but I order the RC Cola and MoonPies from Amazon."

"They sell those things online?" I asked.

He managed a chuckle, lifting a brow. "What don't they sell online?"

"I hadn't figured you for a computer man."

"I'm not," he replied. "I have Internet TV.

I shop during commercials."

By Wednesday I was the most popular man in the office. First, because I had two twenty-four-packs of double-decker chocolate MoonPies on the shelf behind my desk. Second, because I was handing out leads left and right since my head just wasn't in the foreclosure business. In fact, my mind was everywhere but, moving instead between Spain, Echo Glen, and even Seattle in 1986.

Every time I walked outside the office building I'd look up and see the Columbia Center hovering high above the city, the very rooftop where David and June had first met. I almost began to doubt parts of his story, but a quick trip to the public library turned up the articles on the Barefoot BASE Jumper. It felt kind of good to be the only person other than Mr. Hadley who truly knew her identity. As if I were somehow connected to that story and that era, even though I was only four years old and drinking wine from a bottle in Belfair at the time.

I had made some progress on getting the servicer to sign off on Mr. Hadley's quitclaim deed. Anything that would speed up getting the delinquent loan off their books was good for the big banks, still scrambling to improve their balance sheets so they could loan and loan again. That afternoon I was at my desk killing time — lost in the YouTube rat hole, watching BASE jumpers and bullfighters — when the call came in. The bank had agreed to the terms and had signed off on the deal. They were sending the paperwork over by courier for me to have Mr. Hadley sign.

I went into Finnegans that night hoping to see Estrella. I wanted to fill her in on the rest of David and June's story, and I guess I also wanted to get her advice too. It felt good to be helping Mr. Hadley protect June's burial place and all, but the deal with the bank called for him to sign a deed in lieu of foreclosure and vacate the property within thirty days. Where would he go?

"It's not your problem," a little voice kept saying in the back of my mind. "Just get the deal over with and move on."

But that didn't seem right either. Unfortunately, Estrella wasn't there to help me sort through the noise. It was her night off. I realized I didn't have her number, which seemed strange. Why hadn't I asked for it? I considered going to see if she was at home, making it as far as driving to her neighborhood before deciding that an unannounced pop-by seemed a little forward. I stopped into Dilettante for Viennese cocoa instead. Maybe I had even secretly hoped I'd bump into her there, but I didn't. I guess some nights you're just meant to be alone.

I'll admit that it did briefly occur to me that perhaps I should spend less time working and more time meeting people. But what's the point of making friends if you're moving away soon? Well then, I thought, downing my cocoa and looking at the booths filled with people, maybe you'll make more friends in Miami anyway.

"Now, you're sure you want to sign this?"

It was the third time I had asked him.

He looked at me over his reading glasses and nodded. "You got everything I asked, and I thank you for it."

"You haven't told me yet where you'll be moving."

"Maybe I'll move in with you," he said, winking. Then he finished signing the agreement.

Neither of us spoke. We just watched the steam rise off of our untouched tea. I think we both sensed that today was a day for business and not a day for stories. There was a kind of finality in the air. Eventually, he reached for his cane and stood himself up from the table. He was moving much better today. He looked rested. He walked over and leaned his cane against the wall. Then he reached and took down June's painting of Echo Glen.

"I want you to have this," he said.

"There's no way. I couldn't."

"You seemed to really like it, and it would mean a lot to me knowing that someone looks fondly at it from time to time. It would have meant a lot to June too."

"But what about you?"

"Oh, I've got the real thing to look at."

"Yeah, but you won't in three weeks. I'm planning to help you move, by the way. And don't even try to tell me no. It's part of the service I provide my clients at no charge."

"Is that right?" he asked, smiling.

"That's right."

He looked around the kitchen for a moment, as if quickly inventorying his things, or perhaps preparing himself to say good-bye. His face was serious when he looked back to me.

"I might just take you up on that," he said.

Then he held out the painting, and I stood to take it from him, lifting it up and looking at it in the light coming through the kitchen window. It really was a gorgeous watercolor. I carried it with me to the door. Standing there in the foyer preparing to say good-bye again, it was hard to believe I had knocked on his door less than a week before.

I don't know what came over me, but I set his file down on the floor and leaned the painting carefully against the wall. Then I hugged him. I knew at the time it was a silly thing to do, but he didn't seem to mind. He even hugged me back.

After I had the painting stowed carefully in the backseat of my car, I looked back to see him still standing in the doorway.

"I'll record the short plat with the county and bring the docs out to you so we can apply for that cemetery license," I said. "Until then try not to eat too many MoonPies."

"It's impossible to eat too many Moon-Pies," he replied.

I shook my head, disagreeing. "I've been scarfing them all week. They taste like heaven but they're hell on your guts."

He laughed. "That's why you need the Smooth Move."

"You call me if you need anything, okay? Anything at all. Even if you want some help negotiating a lease or looking at properties or something. My car here gets good mileage and I love just driving people around."

He smiled, nodding that he would. Then he held up his hand in farewell. He was still standing there, leaning on his cane and watching from the doorway as I pulled away.

32

"It's more than a little unconventional," the county clerk said, "but I think we can let it slide."

"I appreciate it. I really do."

"It's just that we usually need to see easements for ingress and egress before we can push a short plat through."

"I'm glad you're making an exception."

"I help where I can." He sighed deeply, as if his authority was a burden nearly too heavy to bear. He continued sorting through his logbook as he spoke: "I'm putting it in as nonconforming, of course. We'll call it a family plot since your Mr. Hadley here owns the dominant property too. He just better hope he never sells it."

"I'm sorry, what was that?"

"We had a fella in here split himself off a parcel for a gold mine before he sold to his brother. Thought he was being real cute. Was sure he'd hit the mother lode and was gonna keep it all to himself. Heh! Greed. But he hadn't thought of any ingress or egress easement either, and when his brother figured him out, well, he refused to let him cross onto his parcel. Stood guard with a twelve-gauge. As fate would have it, the only other access was a goat wall, a sheer granite cliff on top of which was state forestland. I'll be damned if that silly son of a sap didn't fall four hundred feet to his death trying to rappel into his parcel and his precious mine. Funniest part was he had no will and no kids and his brother got the parcel back in probate. I merged the two again like it had never happened. But a thing like that will surely teach a fella the importance of ingress and egress."

My mind was beginning to turn in a direction I didn't like. "So, let's say someone did buy this other property," I said. "The main parcel. Like let's say the bank foreclosed and sold it. Could someone be buried in this cemetery parcel later or would they need permission from the new homeowner?"

He glanced at the map, shaking his head. "I suppose you could hike up over Whitehorse there and down into the gully, but that's one hell of a trek hauling a body. That's why I say it's good it's a family plot on family land." He stamped the short-plat document and turned and put it on the copier. "You want one copy or two?"

"Better make it two," I said.

I had an ache in my gut all the way out to Echo Glen. And it wasn't from the Moon-Pies either. The clerk in the recorder's office had left me with an earful of stories and a sinking feeling. How was I ever going to tell Mr. Hadley that we had failed to anticipate a way to get him access to and from his wife's plot? This new bit of bad news meant that once he moved, not only was it possible that he could never visit June again, but he also had no guarantee that he could be buried there next to her.

I racked my brain the entire drive, searching for a way to fix the situation. I knew the bank would never sign off on an easement. While carving off a sliver of land had no real effect on the property's overall value, recording a permanent access easement across it would. Plus, it could call out the fact that someone was buried on the adjacent parcel, whereas there was nothing to disclose as things stood. And now that I had hand-delivered the bank Mr. Hadley's signature on the deed in lieu of foreclosure, they had no incentive to do anything. I wasn't sure how badly Mr. Hadley might take the news, but I was fairly certain his response couldn't be good.

He didn't answer the door, even after I knocked several times. I headed around back, assuming he was up at Echo Glen visiting June again. But something stopped me before I hit the bridge. It could have been just a gut feeling, or it could have been that I heard the TV. I went back and peeked through the bay window, past the rooster and into the living room. The TV was on, blaring out the ever-late-breaking news, and Mr. Hadley was slumped in his chair, with his chin on his chest.

Was he breathing? I couldn't tell.

I rapped on the window. He didn't respond, so I rapped again, louder. Still nothing. Now I was getting concerned. I took out my cell phone and dialed his number. I heard the phone ringing in the kitchen as I looked through the glass, but still he didn't move in his chair. My pulse quickened; my neck began to sweat. I tried the back door but it was locked, so I ran around to the front. That door was locked too. Next I tried the kitchen window, but it was jammed with a wooden dowel that would only allow it to open an inch or two. I circled the house, trying every window I could reach. They were all either locked or painted shut. When I returned to the back of the house, I was out of breath and panicking. Another look confirmed that Mr. Hadley remained slumped lifelessly in his chair.

"Screw it!" I peeled off my jacket and wrapped it around my hand. Then I punched out the window and cleared the glass shards from the frame. I hoisted myself up and rolled into the house, coming to rest at the rooster's feet. I scrambled up and ran over to him, kneeling in front of his chair and gripping his shoulders. He fell limply into my arms. Then his head jerked up and his eyes popped open.

"Are you all right?" I asked breathlessly.

He looked at the broken window, the glass on the floor. Then he looked at the blaring TV and back at me. He appeared disoriented and confused. His face was flushed.

"Mr. Hadley. Are you okay? Should I call for help?"

I held him there in my arms, ready to carry him to my car and rush him to the ER. Where was the nearest one? I had no idea. Could I remember CPR? *Remember?* I'd only ever seen it in movies. Before I could decide what to do, Mr. Hadley reached up and carefully removed one of my hands from his shoulder. Then he reached past me to the table beside his chair. He picked something up and tucked it into his ear. He repeated the process in the other ear, adjusting the hearing aid volume. Then he looked at me and said, "You must have really missed me."

"Missed you?"

"Yeah, I've never had anyone break a window and climb into my living room just to give me a hug."

"This isn't funny, Mr. Hadley. I think maybe you've had a stroke or something."

"Why would you think that?"

"You seem dazed and confused."

"Wouldn't you if you fell asleep to Wolf Blitzer and woke up being shaken by someone who'd broken into your home? I thought maybe I'd dreamed myself right into the broadcast."

"I was worried," I said.

He laughed. "As am I."

Then I realized how silly the situation really was. Here he had simply dozed off without his hearing aids in, and I'd jumped to the conclusion that he had up and died in his chair.

"Would you mind if I turn the TV off?" I asked.

"Please," he said. "I'm not sure why I ever turn it on."

I reached for the remote but it wouldn't work.

"The batteries are dead," he said. "That's why I took my hearing aids out. I was too tired to get up."

I rose and switched off the TV. The silence was a nice change from all the urgent jabber and debate.

I looked at the broken glass on the floor.

"I better clean this up," I said. "Do you have a dustpan?"

"With the broom in the kitchen pantry."

He insisted on helping me sweep up the mess. He found a roll of duct tape and some cardboard boxes and we patched the broken window. Then we stood back to look at our work.

"I'll have someone come by and fix it tomorrow," I said. "I'm really sorry."

"Let the bank fix it," he replied. "And don't you be sorry. Old Sebastian would have praised you as a man of action. A comrade in courage. Plus, it tells me you were concerned."

"Well, I don't want anything to happen to you."

"Come and sit down with me," he said. "It's time we have a real talk. There's

408

something I need to tell you."

"Okay. There's something I need to tell you too."

Instead of the kitchen or living room where we usually sat, he brought me into June's studio. He said he felt like she was in that room more than any other and he wanted her to sit in on our chat. There was a daybed in the corner with a wingback chair next to it. Mr. Hadley lowered himself onto the bed. I sat in the chair.

"There's something I need to get off my chest," he said.

"No, let me go first."

I was afraid that whatever he might have to say could only make what I had to tell him even worse.

He nodded. "Okay then."

"I have some bad news."

"You do?" He looked immediately concerned. "It's not about the short plat, is it? It went through okay I hope."

"No, it's not that," I said. "It's recorded. I even filed the deed transferring the new parcel to the Echo Glen nonprofit. That's not it."

"Well, what is it?"

"The problem is something we overlooked. I don't know quite how to say this, Mr. Hadley, so I'll just spit it out. They made an exception on the short plat since this cemetery is a family plot, but we didn't include any easement for ingress and egress to access it. And even if we had tried, I doubt the bank would have gone for it."

"That's okay," he said.

"Maybe I'm not being clear. We really screwed up. Once the bank sells this place off, you won't be able to even visit June without the new property owner's permission." I choked up a little, swallowing before going on. "What's worse is I can't even guarantee that you'll be able to be buried next to her when your time finally comes."

He must have seen that I was struggling because he leaned forward and placed his hand on my knee. "It's okay, Elliot. It's fine."

"It's not okay. Here I thought I'd done this great thing but now you have to leave in thirty days — almost three weeks now, actually — and you won't be able to go up and see June like you're used to. Maybe you could just sneak onto the property. But people get shot doing that. And hell, the new owners could put up a gate. Or have dogs. And then what's even harder to swallow is someday when it's finally time —"

"You don't have to worry, Elliot. Everything's fine."

I paused to catch my breath, realizing that my mind was running nearly as fast as my pulse was racing. "What do you mean everything's fine?"

He sighed, glancing over at June's empty wheelchair. "You don't have to worry because I'm not moving out."

"You're not?"

"No."

"But I don't —"

"I'm not moving out because I plan to die here, Elliot."

"I don't understand. You're supposed to be out at the end of the month. We signed a deed in lieu of foreclosure."

He patted my leg again. "You're not hearing me," he said. "I won't make it that long."

"Oh, come on. You're not dying. I mean we're all dying, right? But not soon. You could live a long time yet."

He shook his head gravely. "I'm dying and I'll be buried next to June before anyone can sell this place."

I didn't believe him. I didn't believe him because what he was saying made no sense, and I didn't believe him because I didn't want to believe him. Mr. Hadley dying? No way.

"Get out. You're pulling my leg."

"I'm much sicker than I look, Elliot. I've

been battling cancer for years. It's moved from my liver to my lungs."

"Cancer. Really? What about surgery?"

"I'm already missing half my colon and various other bits and parts I won't bother you about."

"Radiation then. Chemo."

"Been down that road. The simple fact is I'm dying, Elliot. And the truth is I'm okay with it. I'm tired. I'm tired and I'm ready to be with my June again. She died on this daybed while I sat in the chair you're in now. She liked to look out at the creek and the trail that leads up to Echo Glen. I plan to die the same way before the month is out."

My jaw was quivering and my knee was bouncing beneath his hand. I had to get up. I stood and paced the room.

"I don't understand," I said. "Is this a joke?"

He watched me, shaking his head. "It's time for me to rejoin June."

"*Rejoin* her. That sounds poetic, Mr. Hadley, but what if there's nothing after this life? What if this is it?"

He shrugged. "I don't believe that, and I don't think you do either. But if there is nothing else, I'll be with June in Echo Glen. And just being near her is enough for me."

I stopped pacing and faced him now, grasping for hope. "Okay, but you can't possibly know when exactly you're going to die. No one does. It can't work like that."

He nodded. "Yes, it can. The doctors have given me very little time, Elliot. And this state allows people in my position to be prescribed assistance in deciding when the time has come."

"What do you mean *prescribed*?"

"I'm sorry, Elliot. I know this is difficult."

I walked over to the window and looked out at the creek and the path. The story he had told me, the trip up to Echo Glen. He was dying and he wanted to be buried next to June, but he was losing his home. He needed the bank to sign off on a quitclaim so he could make Echo Glen an official cemetery so they could lie undisturbed. He had planned this whole thing, playing me like a fool.

I turned around to face him again.

"So, you used me? You knew all along that you're dying and this whole thing was a ruse to get me to do your bidding."

"It wasn't a ruse, Elliot. I just didn't tell you everything."

"Yeah, I'll say not. What was that you said to me the other day? That my generation is loose with the truth. Look who was a pot calling the kettle black. You're a liar, Mr. Hadley. A damn liar."

"Elliot, that's not fair."

I knew he was right, but I didn't care. "How could you, Mr. Hadley? How could you draw me in with your story? How could you make me like you? How could you make me fall for June? How could you do it only to tell me she's dead and you're dying? It's not fair!"

I was nearly in tears by then, and he rose from the daybed and came over and put a hand on my shoulder.

"I'm sorry, Elliot. I needed help and I didn't have anyone. If you hadn't taken up my cause, it's likely that I would never have been able to be buried next to June. I couldn't risk that. And you have to realize that I hadn't yet gotten to know you. I was expecting a greedy hustler to show up. Some fast-talking foreclosure rep from the bank that was threatening to throw me out. I was writing to a Ralph Spitzer, if you remember."

I looked at June's empty wheelchair sitting beside us. I had never even met her and yet I loved her in a way. Maybe I loved Mr. Hadley too. I never would have believed it had someone told me this, so I don't expect you to believe me now, but it's possible to miss someone you've never met. And it's possible to miss someone who isn't even gone yet too. That's how I felt about Mr. Hadley and June. I missed them both.

"Are you really even struggling to pay your bills?" I asked. "Or was that just part of the ploy to force the bank's hand?"

"I'm not that conniving," he said. "My being broke is for real. My social security hardly covers the bills. I've been selling off my stamp collection to keep myself in MoonPies."

"What about the twenty-five thousand you offered me?"

"That was real too. And I'd still like to pay it to you. I just didn't mention that it's coming from a life insurance policy."

"But they don't pay on suicide . . ."

Just saying the word made my stomach turn.

"That's a myth," he said. "It's a term policy I've had for a long time and it's way beyond the two-year exclusion period."

"Well, I still don't want it," I said. "Give it up to charity or something. Use it to pay someone to bury you or manage the cemetery or something."

"Actually, that's another reason I wanted to talk to you."

He had a serious look in his eye, and the

tone of his voice made me listen up.

"Talk to me about what?"

"I have another favor to ask."

33

"Can you believe he asked that of me?"

It was late. Two empty cocoa mugs stood between us on the Dilettante table.

"Well, you said he doesn't have any children, right? Maybe you two were brought together for a reason."

"For me to be the executor of his estate?"

"Well, what did you tell him?"

"I said I'd think it over."

"You should do it, Elliot. He wouldn't have asked unless he thought you were the right person."

"But I buried my father already, Estrella. By myself. At nineteen. This isn't something I needed dropped on my plate right now."

"You sound upset."

"I am upset."

She sighed, reaching for her empty mug and gripping it in both hands as if it still might provide some warmth. "It sounds to me like you're going to miss him."

"I didn't say that."

"You didn't need to."

"Well, of course I'll miss him. And I don't understand why he thinks he needs to take this pill. It's suicide."

"What if he's in a lot of pain?"

"I know he's terminal. I made him show me the forms he filled out for the Death with Dignity Act. It was so surreal. You know what the form's title was? 'Request for Medication to End My Life in a Humane and Dignified Manner.' Can you imagine signing your name to that?"

Estrella looked down at the table and shook her head.

"You know what worries me the most, though? I feel like maybe he's scheduling his own death just so he can be buried next to his wife before the bank throws him out. I believe he's dying, but can't he do it naturally?"

"Maybe," she said. "Or maybe he's so alone or in so much pain that another month or two isn't appealing to him."

"I intend to try and get him more time so he doesn't need to take those stupid pills. There has to be a way. They can't possibly hold him to the agreement and make him move if he's dying. No one's that heartless."

"Maybe he needs support, not saving."

"There have to be laws against throwing a dying man out."

"You can't fix everything."

"What do you mean?"

"It's not our job to save the people we love, Elliot. It's our job to love them through whatever it is they're going through. Maybe he just needs someone to be with him while he makes this final transition. It can't be easy alone."

"Maybe you're right. But I didn't say I loved him."

"You didn't have to say that either. It's obvious that you do. And who could blame you? I haven't even met him and I already love this guy."

"Would you like to?"

"Like to what?"

"Meet him."

She looked down into her empty mug. "Would you like me to meet him?"

"I told him I'd come out this weekend, but to tell you the truth, I'd rather not go alone."

She looked back up at me and smiled. "Then I'd love to meet him."

The drive seemed longer than usual, even though I'd done it now several times. Estrella sat beside me, watching the trees get lashed by high winds that sent the last of their golden leaves whirling across the highway in gusty dervishes that seemed to dance all the faster as we blew past.

I cracked the window and lit a cigarette.

"I didn't know you smoked," Estrella said.

I blew a lungful at the cracked window and watched it get sucked out into the gray morning. "I don't."

"I don't either," she said. "Can I have one?"

I handed her the pack.

She lit a cigarette and inhaled, immediately coughing out the smoke and waving her hand in front of her face to fan it away. She tossed the cigarette out the window.

"Guess you weren't kidding," I said.

"I haven't smoked since trying it in high school. It's just as bad as I remember. And you shouldn't smoke either."

She reached and snatched the cigarette from my mouth midpuff and tossed it out her window too. Then she crossed her arms and looked at me to see if I'd protest. I wanted to appear upset, but I couldn't help but smile.

"I'm not really a smoker either," I confessed. "I only bought them the other day. I'm not sure why. I was walking past the 7-Eleven and saw a group of friends smoking together. They looked like they were having fun."

"It's 2014," she said, "people should know better."

"It's been a rough week for me at the office."

"Why's that?" she asked.

"I don't know. My head just isn't in it. I went on just three sits and I left every one of them without a deal. Two I told to apply for mortgage modifications, the other I told to sell their house themselves since they seemed to have equity."

She looked at me, confused. "What's wrong with that?"

"Nothing," I answered, "as long as you don't mind going without a paycheck. You may not know this, but I'm very good at my job. Or at least I used to be."

"Did you ever think maybe you're just worried about all this stuff with Mr. Hadley?"

I was beginning to notice that she had a way of always cutting right through the crap. I liked that. For a guy like me it was important. I could bullshit myself for days before I'd stand up and face something.

"I feel like I'm going to a funeral," I finally said.

"Me too," she answered. "But let's make the best of it. I'm looking forward to meeting him."

He opened the door to greet us even before we got out of the car. He was wearing his corduroy pants and knitted sweater, the same ones he'd had on the first day I'd arrived.

"He doesn't look too bad," Estrella said, eyeing him out her window before opening her car door.

"He puts on a good show," I said.

And I was right too. His cane was nowhere to be seen as he welcomed us in like old friends. He hugged Estrella, winking at me over her shoulder to let me know that he approved.

"Elliot told me you were as smart as paint, but he said nothing about you being as gorgeous as a spring day too."

I closed the door behind myself. "That's because I'm an enlightened twenty-first-century man who doesn't objectify women, Mr. Hadley. So enlightened in fact that I would never use a saying like 'smart as paint.' "

He laughed. "If it was good enough for old Captain Silver, it's good enough for me."

Estrella smiled at his literary reference. "Never mind Elliot, Mr. Hadley," she said, "I rather like being complimented by men. Although let's hope your stories and motives are truer than the old one-legged sea captain's were."

"Ah," he said, "I see you've read Stevenson."

"Of course. He's one of my favorites."

Then Mr. Hadley reached out his arm in a theatrical pose and recited a line of poetry: *"Under the wide and starry sky, / Dig the grave and let me lie: / Glad did I live and gladly die, / And I laid me down with a will."*

Not to be outdone, Estrella finished it: *"This be the verse you 'grave for me: / Here he lies where he long'd to be; / Home is the sailor, home from sea, / And the hunter home from the hill."*

And just like that, they had hit it off. So much so I could hardly pry them apart for the next two hours.

Mr. Hadley gave her the tour, showing her the carousel rooster in the living room, the paintings in the kitchen, June's studio with its view of the creek. He even made sure to show her the bathroom, pointing out his pink-padded toilet seat. She commented on his sweater and he blushed, telling her that June had knitted it for him. Then Estrella

423

told him about her mother's quilting and about her fond memories of knitted scarves for Christmas.

"Oh, June loved Christmas too," Mr. Hadley said.

"Show her the wedding picture," I suggested.

So he did, along with the matador costume in the closet. Estrella wanted to see more pictures of June, so the three of us sat down together on the couch and looked through his photo albums. It was like picking up where Mr. Hadley had left the story off and getting current with the rest of their lives together at Echo Glen.

There were lots of photos of June, mostly around the farm with her animals, and in each one her spirit leaped off the page as if she were there in the room with us, not only alive, but more so than any of us three would ever be. And as her physical condition deteriorated in the pictures over the years, this look of wonder never left her eyes. There was a great image of her and David dressed up in 1920s formalwear while floating down the river on inner tubes. David held an umbrella over them to shade them from the sun while June dangled her feet into the water and sipped a can of old Rainier Beer. Her timeless smile haunts me still. Later, there were photos of June in her wheelchair, painting.

Estrella asked about a photo of June reading to a child in a hospital bed. Mr. Hadley told us that as her condition worsened it was harder for her to spend as much time caring for animals — being largely confined to the wheelchair — so as they wound the animal shelter down, she took up visiting the Everett hospital and reading to children in the cancer ward. She always read them the same book, he informed us: *Peter Pan.* He suspected this was both because she loved the story so much and because it was the one book she had completely memorized and could recite word for word even as her ability to read was slowly stripped away by the advance of her disease. He would later read it to her himself, he told us, after her voice had finally gone, leaving behind only the smile that never seemed to fully disappear from her eyes. In fact, the last image in the album was a photo taken by someone else of her lying on the daybed in her studio, looking longingly out the window at the path that led to Echo Glen. David slept in the chair beside her with a copy of *Peter Pan* on his lap.

He lingered on this photo before closing the album, his fingers gently resting on the page as if he might be able to reach into the past and touch her once again. I saw tears well up in his eyes, but I couldn't tell if he or Estrella saw mine.

"She was a magical woman," he said, almost to himself. "A magical woman indeed." He closed the album and looked up at us. "She loved this life right up to the very end, but she had no fear about leaving it behind. She thought it all one big adventure. I buried her with that book so she'd have Peter and Wendy to keep her company until I could join her. You know, Elliot, I ended the story where I did because I wanted my life here with June to remain private. But the truth is she was such a mighty spirit no one person could ever hope to keep her to himself. And it would be a crime to try anyway.

"I'll never forget the afternoon I came home early from an accounting job I'd taken in Marysville — finally deciding Seattle was just too far to drive — only to find her in the stables frozen in a corner. She couldn't move a muscle and had been there most of the day. I knew she had been downplaying her symptoms to spare me worry, but I had no idea how much. I carried her to our bed, crying the whole time. 'Why her?' I asked, begging God to answer me. 'Of everyone in the world, why her, why her, why her?' You know what she told me later that night when she finally came around? She looked at me and smiled, asking, 'Why not me?' That was my June."

When Mr. Hadley finally closed the album, there wasn't a dry eye between us. But we were all smiling despite our tears. Then he took up a binder that he had brought out with the albums from his room. At first, I thought it was another photo album, but it wasn't.

"Now I have some things for you to sign, Elliot," he said, pulling out several documents and handing them to me.

There was an article making me the trustee of Mr. Hadley's living trust, and another making me an officer and stockholder in the Echo Glen Corporation.

"Don't get too excited," he said. "There's no real money in the company or the trust. You won't get business cards either. This is the entity that will own the private cemetery. It's just a formality. A bothersome bit of red tape that will allow you to file for the cemetery license after I'm gone."

I don't know why I hesitated, but I did. Seeing my name on official documents made me nervous. Not because of the responsibility so much — I'd handled similar arrangements when my father had passed — but because it implied that Mr. Hadley would not be around to fill the role himself.

"I still plan to pay you that twenty-five thousand I offered you from my life insurance," he said, apparently sensing my hesitation. "No one should do anything for free."

I shook my head. "I'm not taking your money, Mr. Hadley. I'm happy to do it." I picked up the pen, filled in my address, dated the documents, and signed them. "There," I said, passing them back, "now I'm the proud owner of a cemetery."

I glanced over at Estrella and she smiled.

Mr. Hadley put the forms back in the binder.

"The rest of this in here is stuff you might need after I'm gone," he said, patting the binder in his lap. Then he paused, looking at Estrella. "Is this okay to discuss?" he asked.

"Go ahead," she said. "It's fine with me."

He carried on: "My birth certificate. My will. Insurance policy information. There are bank statements, as sad as they are. And there's contact information for the home burial people who will prepare my body here at the house. I put Mr. Thorpe's son's contact info in the back. He'll dig the grave. Make sure he doesn't try to bring that digger up there and ruin the whole hill. He's lazier than his dad was but he's a good man. Just ask him to dig it by hand."

It seemed strange to hear him talk about having his own grave dug, but if it was at all strange to him he didn't let on.

"That should be everything," he said. "Everything except the death certificate." Then he turned to Estrella. "I used to be an accountant, you know."

She smiled. "Yes, Elliot told me."

"I do have one question," I said. "Let's say thirty years from now I pass away —"

"Thirty years?" he asked, cutting me off. "More like ninety years the way medical science is moving."

"Okay, sure. But in however many years, when I pass, who will be responsible for the cemetery?"

"Be a fun project maybe for your grandkids," he answered.

"What if I don't have any kids?"

"You'll have kids," he said. "I can tell."

"You can?"

"Well, no. But I can tell you'd be a good dad."

"Really? I've never thought about it."

"Most men don't until it happens," he

said. "But yes, you would. Don't you think so, Estrella?"

She nodded. "He'd make a great dad."

"You're lucky I'm a married man, Elliot, or I might just try to steal this one away from you. She's a keeper." He closed the binder in his lap. "But there's nothing to worry about with the cemetery. June and I will be pushing up grass on the hill, blanketed in waterfall mist and fallen leaves. Forgotten to the world, as it should be. This is all just a formality to get them to issue a license, and then you can forget about us and let us be."

We all sat quiet for a minute, the weight of what we had just been discussing settling in. I could hear the cat clock ticking on the wall. It was past noon already.

"You know what I would love?" Estrella said. "A chance to see Echo Glen. Elliot showed me the painting you gave him and it looks so beautiful."

"That's a great idea," Mr. Hadley said. Then he turned to me. "Would you mind taking her, Elliot? I've already been. And besides, I could use the time to make us all some lunch."

I knew it had sapped a lot out of him to go through the photo album and the documents, and I'm sure he had been worn out even before we started after showing us around the house. But I think he mostly didn't want Estrella to see him struggling up the path with his cane. He was a sweet man, but he was a proud man too.

"I'd be happy to walk her up and show her," I said. "But I thought maybe we'd all go out to lunch. I can drive us. There's a great little diner I passed by just in Darrington."

He looked surprised at my suggestion, and I thought for sure he would turn it down. But he nodded.

"That's Clancy's old place, before he passed on and his lazy kids sold it off to some clown. I've not been, but I doubt they have anything nearly as good as a Hungry-Man Salisbury steak dinner with home-style mushroom and onion gravy. But I'll go along if that's what you two want."

"How about you, Estrella? Diner or Hungry-Man?"

"Hmm . . . ," she said, thinking. "I kind of feel like pie."

Mr. Hadley raised an eyebrow. "The Hungry-Man includes a chocolate brownie."

"As tempting as it is," she said, "I vote for the diner."

He nodded, accepting his defeat. Then he

plucked up his energy and rose from the couch to return the photo album and the binder to his room.

"You kids have fun. I'll be waiting when you get back."

It was the first time we'd held hands, although I'm not sure which of us made the move. It just seemed like halfway up the path our hands kind of came together. The wind had died down and the sun was peeking through the trees. It felt nice, even though it was a chilly fall day.

"I really like Mr. Hadley," Estrella said.

"Yeah, I could tell. It's pretty clear he really likes you too. And you know what, so do I."

"Uh-oh," she said. "Is that why you just let go of my hand? Because you only date girls you don't like, remember?"

"No, I let go of your hand so I could get a head start."

"A head start on what?"

"On racing you the rest of the way."

I took off running ahead of her up the path.

"Hey!" I heard her call from behind me, closing in. "That's not fair. You cheated."

She was faster than me and had passed me by before we gained the bend that turned in to Echo Glen. When I arrived she was standing there looking up at the waterfall.

"It's so beautiful," she said breathlessly. "I can see why a person would want to spend forever here."

"Come on, I'll show you where June's buried."

We climbed the low hill to the oak tree and stood looking down at the headstone together. Estrella read it out loud.

" 'Just beyond the second star to the right and straight on till morning.' It's from *Peter Pan,* isn't it?"

I nodded. "I'm not surprised it was her favorite story. She kind of reminds me of Peter Pan a little. I wish she were still around to sprinkle some of her fairy dust on us. Wouldn't it be fun to fly the way she did?"

"Well, let's hope she's in Neverland never growing old."

I pointed to the space beside the stone. "I guess that's where Mr. Hadley will be buried. It's strange to think about, isn't it? That he's here now, but soon he'll be down there. It seems cold and lonely and impossibly horrible."

"Oh, I don't know," she said. "Maybe you're looking at it wrong. It looked to me like they had great love and a great life, and that's more than most people ever have. Besides, I'll bet it's nice here when the sun comes out and warms the grass."

"Maybe," I said. "But I still plan to talk him into waiting. I met with a real estate attorney and she thinks it might be possible to force the bank to accept a deed-for-lease situation, as long as he can make the original mortgage payment. That way he can stay as long as he needs."

"But I thought he couldn't afford the payment."

"He can't. But I can. At least long enough to give him some time. I've been saving for awhile."

"Yeah, but that's for your condo, right?"

I shrugged. "Miami isn't going anywhere."

Estrella put her arm around my waist and leaned into me. We stood that way watching the waterfall together.

"You know what, Elliot," she said, "you're a good man."

"Yeah, everyone keeps telling me that."

I didn't mention that this whole situation had made me question the kind of man I really was. I'm not so sure a good man would go around earning his living by offering financially strapped people cash for their house keys.

We broke off the main path on our way back and hiked up to the bluff where June had taken David to go hang gliding into the moon. It was really high with a really amazing view. You could just see the house at the edge of the tree line, a spire of white smoke standing like a feather from its chimney, and you could see the fields and barns beyond.

I could almost picture it as Mr. Hadley had described it being that night, with a big swollen moon and Sebastian down there somewhere standing beside his crazy bonfire. If he hadn't told me the story, who would be left to remember? Does it even matter? Does there need to be a photograph or a record for a thing to have happened? I thought about all the quiet, undocumented moments that must flare and fade forever from the face of humankind's vast experience. Moments made even more special because they belonged to only those who had experienced them. Moments like this one for me.

I put my arm around Estrella and pulled her into me. She felt warm in the cool air of the high cliff. She rested her head on my shoulder, and I smelled her lavender shampoo, smiling to think that she used the same scent as June.

"Would you ever go hang gliding?" I asked her.

"I don't know," she said. "I suppose I would if I trusted the person I was getting into the harness with."

"Yeah, me too."

We stood for another few minutes, taking in the view.

"We better get back and wake him up," I said. "I'd bet the lunch check he's nodded off in front of the TV."

34

He was waiting for us with his coat on and his hair combed when we returned. He almost seemed like a nervous kid heading off to school. He had surrendered his pride, though, and he used his cane as we walked together out to my car. He tried to sit in the back but Estrella insisted he take the front passenger seat instead.

"I haven't been out to a restaurant in years," he confessed once we were buckled in. "Well, unless you count the hospital cafeteria."

It was fun driving with all three of us in the car. It felt like a family outing. Estrella and Mr. Hadley challenged each other to name the various types of trees that we passed, and I only had to correct them once when they both agreed on a western hemlock that was actually a grand fir.

"Look at you," Estrella said. "Taking us both to school."

"Hey, I might not read Stevenson, but I'm a logger's son."

It was too late for lunch and too early for dinner, so the diner was nearly deserted. It appeared as if the hostess was also the cook, and she smiled at us from behind the grill as we entered. "Three for dinner and the show?" she asked.

"Yes, please," I said. "But what's this show bit all about?"

"Haven't you all ever been to Larry's Out-of-This-World Scramble House? If you haven't, you're in luck, because Larry doesn't usually work on Mondays when the fish are running."

"But today's Sunday," Estrella said.

"I know. He usually takes Sunday off to get a head start on not working Monday. But he's here today. And that means if you can eat without laughing your meal is free."

She brought us to a booth and sat us down with menus. There was an enormous mounted lobster hanging on the wall above our booth and the plaque read: WORLD'S LARGEST SHRIMP.

Larry made his appearance a few minutes later. He had the world's worst toupee, a mustache that curled at the ends, and a smile that curled just as wide. His cheeks were red.

"I see we have three siblings for brunch," he said. "Who's the oldest so I know where to deliver the check?"

Mr. Hadley raised his hand, but Estrella pushed it down.

"He's buying," she said, pointing at me. "He lost a bet."

"Welcome to our little diner then. We call it Out-of-This-World because we opened a location on Mars, but it just didn't have any atmosphere. Hey hey!"

He looked to us for a laugh. We only smiled, determined to get our meals for free if we could.

"We offer breakfast anytime, and our house specialty is French toast during the Renaissance. Ha!"

He paused again, but we all just smiled again.

"I can tell I have my work cut out for me. Tough crowd here. It's hard to appreciate good humor on an empty stomach, I guess. How about we get some food going for you?"

We all decided that breakfast sounded pretty good. I don't know why, but there's something homey about breakfast for dinner on a cold fall day. Mr. Hadley and I both opted for the French toast, with him adding, "Extra whipped cream and extra

Renaissance for me, please!" while Estrella decided on Swedish pancakes, saying that since they served breakfast anytime she'd like hers served during the Enlightenment. This made Mr. Hadley smile. Larry chuckled, and I could tell he wished he'd thought of it himself.

The windows were already getting dark, but the diner was nice and warm, with bright yellow lights and the scent of butter and bread. We made small talk, as if we were just three friends out for an ordinary meal. There was no way any of us could have predicted how it would end.

Larry came by with a big glass of orange juice for each of us. We told him we didn't order any juice but he said nonsense.

"It's fresh-squeezed by my pet gorilla every morning. Try it. I promise you it's out of this world."

When our breakfasts arrived they were enormous. Estrella and I dug in, but I noticed Mr. Hadley hardly ate any of his; he mostly just picked at the whipped cream. While we ate he told us a story about how June would always order two eggs with her breakfast, one scrambled and the other poached, because she never could decide which she preferred. He said they had a really rude server in Oregon once, so June

440

told him they had poached the wrong egg and sent her breakfast back.

When we had finished eating, Estrella had her heart set on pie. She was torn between marionberry and apple. She just couldn't decide.

"Apple's good with cheese melted on top," I said.

"I know," she replied, "but marionberry is great warmed up with a scoop of vanilla ice cream. Which would you order, Mr. Hadley?"

"About all I can eat is the ice cream anymore," he said, "the berry seeds get caught in my bridge. But let me teach you a little trick my father taught me." Then he hauled a quarter from his pocket as if he had brought it along just in case. He tossed the coin and caught it, slapping it down on the counter and covering it with his hand. "Heads or tails for apple?" he asked.

"For apple," Estrella said. "Hmm . . . how about tails."

He lifted his hand and it was in fact tails.

"Shoot," Estrella said. "I really wanted marionberry."

Mr. Hadley smiled, winking at me. "See, the trick works every time. Could you excuse me, Elliot? I need to use the boys' room."

I let him out of the booth, helping him up and handing him his cane. He thanked me. Then he noticed the mounted lobster and leaned a little closer to read the plaque.

"Heh!" he said. "If that's the world's biggest shrimp, the gorilla who squeezes his orange juice must be his wife."

Then he shuffled off toward the restrooms in the back.

"The poor man hardly ate anything," Estrella said once he was out of earshot.

"I know. Maybe we should order him some ice cream."

Larry came by and Estrella ordered her marionberry pie and a dish of vanilla ice cream for Mr. Hadley, just in case.

"Okay," Larry said. "But you haven't laughed yet, so let me try one last time. I hardly have enough business to be giving out free meals. Now, you two look like a nice young couple, so I'll tell you about the pair who came in last week to celebrate their silver wedding anniversary. I asked them what their secret was. You wanna know what they told me?"

"Sure," I said. "Lay it on us."

"They said their secret to a happy marriage was that they always make time to go into the city for romantic dinners."

Estrella smiled. "How nice."

"Isn't it?" Larry replied. "They do it religiously two days a week. The husband goes on Thursdays and the wife goes on Fridays. Bada-boom!"

This time Estrella couldn't help but laugh.

"Got ya that time!" he said. "One marionberry à la mode and one vanilla double scoop coming up with your check."

When he brought the desserts over I wished I had ordered pie of my own. It looked that good. Estrella saw me eyeing hers so she offered me a bite from her fork.

"That might just be the best berry pie I've ever had."

"Yes, but is it out of this world?" she asked.

"I think I'd need another bite to be sure."

She laughed. "Is it rude not to wait for Mr. Hadley?" she asked. "Maybe you should go check on him."

"He's fine," I said. "He spends a lot of time in there at home too. It would only embarrass him if I went to check."

Estrella told me I had to name the song playing on the kitchen radio if I wanted another bite of her pie. When I informed her that I didn't listen to country music, she told me she wouldn't share her pie with a philistine who didn't appreciate Jim Reeves. I tried to steal a bite while she wasn't looking, but she caught me.

"Maybe you should eat Mr. Hadley's ice cream," she said. "It's almost all melted anyway."

"You know what?" I scooted out of the booth. "I'm gonna go check on him. I'll just let on that I had to use the restroom."

"I know what you're up to," she said. "You're just trying to get out of the check."

"No," I said, pulling out my wallet and laying down a card, "I honor my bets." Then I leaned over the booth and kissed the top of her head, saying, "Even though it would have been on the house if you hadn't laughed. I'll be right back."

That girl really is something, I thought. She had me smiling all the way to the bathroom. My smile disappeared the instant I opened the door and saw Mr. Hadley on the bathroom floor.

"Help!" I shouted, leaning out from the bathroom but not wanting to take my eyes off of him. "Call an ambulance now!"

It was the longest ten minutes of my life, sitting on the floor holding him, checking repeatedly for his faint pulse. He was so light and so limp in my arms I almost felt like I was holding a doll.

We followed the ambulance to Providence

hospital in Everett, doing nearly eighty the entire way.

"I should have checked on him sooner."

"You didn't know, Elliot," Estrella said.

"I should have been more aware."

"Elliot, this is not your fault."

"It was my idea to go to the diner."

"Come on. That had nothing to do with it."

"He'll be okay. Right? I know he's going to be okay."

Estrella grabbed my free hand and held it, which reassured me some, but she didn't say anything. I focused on the ambulance lights ahead of us and drove like a man trying to outrun death.

It was a long time waiting before we could get any information from anyone, other than general reassurances that they were taking care of him. We sat in the lobby and tried to take our minds off what had happened by watching the people passing through. You see a pretty good cross-section of society hanging out in a hospital lobby. I guess disease and death are democratic.

Eventually, a nurse came to get us. He looked about twelve to me, but what do I know. He was nice at least.

"Mr. Hadley is stable and awake now," he said. "We'd like to keep him overnight, but he's insisting on going home."

"Is that a good idea?" I asked. "I mean, after what just happened. He must have had a stroke. Or a heart attack."

"None of that." The nurse shook his head. "Mr. Hadley fainted. He has low blood pressure and it appears he took too much of his pain medication. Has he been complaining of more pain lately, or has he been unusually active?"

I glanced at Estrella before answering. "Maybe. I know he was walking around without his cane and stuff."

The nurse shrugged, as if to say *What can you do?*

"So, he'll be all right, then?" I asked. "He's fine?"

The nurse looked back and forth between Estrella and me. "You're aware of Mr. Hadley's condition, aren't you? I mean, he has told you?"

"He's told us he plans to kill himself," I said, hoping maybe if I exposed his plan now the nurse could help me talk him out of it.

"There's nothing suicidal about that man," the nurse said, "I'll vouch for that. I was a witness on his competency form. He's been entertaining us all around here for a long time and would keep it up forever no doubt, if he could. And everyone wishes that that were the case, trust me. There aren't many patients loved here more than Mr. Hadley."

"So, there's no hope, then," I said. "Nothing we can do?"

"There is hope," the nurse said. "Hope for quality time with people he loves. Hope for a peaceful transition. Some days will be better than others, but the symptoms will continue to get worse until the cancer runs its course or he decides he's had enough. So, yes, there is something you can do. You can be with him. Make him comfortable. Make him feel loved. Help him die with dignity. That's all any of us can do now."

I'll tell you what, he might have been young, but he was a hell of a nurse. I looked at Estrella. She had tears in her eyes. I felt like crying but I didn't. Instead, I reached for Estrella and pulled her to me and hugged her.

"Is he really demanding to be taken home?" I asked the nurse, still hugging Estrella.

"You know Mr. Hadley," he replied. "Says he has an appointment to keep with his wife tomorrow. It'll be an hour or so yet before we can discharge him. I'll send you home with some pamphlets on pain management and palliative care. We have one on what to expect at the end of life too. I'm assuming you're taking on the role of his primary carer."

Primary carer. I looked at Estrella, then at the nurse.

"I am?"

The nurse glanced up from his clipboard. "I asked him if it was okay to speak with you about his medical records before coming out, and he said you were not only the executor of his estate but his best friend."

Now the tears did well up — so fast, in fact, that the nurse's face blurred right there in front of me in the bright hospital hall.

It was late by the time we returned to Echo Glen. If there were stars out, I didn't see them. My mind and my eyes were on getting Mr. Hadley from the car safely into the house.

I offered to go in and get the wheelchair but he insisted on walking himself. I helped him as much as he'd allow. Estrella went ahead of us and opened the door. He was groggy from whatever the hospital had given him, so I walked him down the hall toward what I assumed must be his bedroom. It was the only room left in the house I hadn't been in yet, and as soon as I opened the door I realized the pains he'd taken to conceal just how sick he really was.

There was an oxygen machine on a cart next to the bed. An IV with a bag of saline and coils of tubes stood next to it. The dresser top was littered with pill bottles. It almost looked like a hospital room right there tucked away in the back of that old farmhouse. His pride was either greater than I had thought or he just preferred to keep the evidence of his deteriorating condition contained within his bedroom.

I helped him lie down, taking off his shoes and covering him with an afghan.

"Can I get you anything?" I asked.

"Not unless you've got a time machine hidden in your pocket," he said. He looked very tired. "You've done enough, Elliot. Thank you. And please tell Estrella I really enjoyed meeting her today. She's a keeper, that one is."

He smiled and closed his eyes.

"She's a great girl, that's for sure. I'll tell her. Do you need some tea or water or anything like that?"

He didn't answer because he was already asleep. I tucked the blanket around him and crept out into the hall, closing the door behind me. Estrella and I sat around the kitchen table, wondering what to do now. It was pretty late. Past ten for sure.

"I'm gonna stay," I finally said. "You take my car since you have class tomorrow."

"Where will you sleep?" Estrella asked.

"On the couch. That way I can keep the stove going and check on him every once in a while. That nurse gave me enough pamphlets to keep me in reading material for a week."

"I don't know," she said. "I don't like the idea of leaving you out here all alone without a car."

"I've got my phone. I can call a cab when I'm ready to head home. I'll probably stay a day or two at least."

Estrella glanced at her watch. "Okay, but I'm coming back tomorrow. I'll see if my mother can follow me out for a ride home in case you're not ready to leave. She'll insist on bringing you some home-cooked food anyway. You'll see what I mean when you meet her."

It was clear she didn't want to leave, but it was getting late and she hadn't exactly signed up for today's misadventures when I'd invited her out to meet Mr. Hadley.

I walked her out to the car and we hugged by the door. For a moment I thought she might kiss me, or maybe I thought I might try to kiss her. I wanted to, sure, but it didn't happen and that was okay. It had been a long and emotional day and it didn't feel right to make this that kind of good-bye. But the hug felt really nice anyway.

She got in and spent a few minutes monkeying with the mirrors and adjusting the seat to fit her height.

"The brakes can be touchy so don't slam them. And look out for deer. They like to jump in front of your car for fun out in these parts. You know what, I never even asked if you knew how to drive."

"Of course I do," she said, smirking at me. Then she pretended to search beneath the dash. "Where's the thing to shift the gears?"

"It's an automatic," I said, playing along.

"Uh-oh. I only know how to drive rigs with a dog leg and a clutch. What's a poor country girl to do?"

"Get out of here," I said, closing the car door.

She rolled down the window, leaning her head out. "Call me if you need anything, okay? Even just to talk."

"Sure thing, counselor. But no talking or texting while you drive. Now get on, I'm freezing out here."

She smiled and pulled away. I stood and watched the taillights disappear down the driveway. It's a strange feeling to watch your own car drive off. Like your life is going on without you. Which is kind of how I felt anyway with Estrella gone.

35

The sound of blaring music jolted me awake. I got up off the couch and walked down the hall and opened Mr. Hadley's door to find him sitting on his bed singing along to "Dancing Queen." His shirt was off and a tube was running from the IV pump into a port in his chest. He froze when he saw me. Then he reached to the bedside table and switched the music off.

"Good morning," he said. "I'm either really high right now and am imagining you or this is really embarrassing."

I hooked a thumb over my shoulder to indicate the living room. "I slept on the couch."

"What about Estrella?"

"She drove herself home in my car."

He nodded. Then he glanced at the old tape player on his bedside table. "I guess all we're missing is Sebastian with his bullhorn and we could go out and jump burning cars today. June loved Abba. I'm more of a rock-and-roll man myself."

"You seem to be feeling better this morning."

He looked down at the port in his chest. "This port was for chemo," he said. "It's funny to think that I made it through the sixties without touching anything stronger than pot, and now here I am hooked up to an IV drip of Dilaudid with methadone mixed in for good measure. Some breakfast, eh? Oh well, it makes watching *Good Morning America* interesting at least."

After he got dressed and after I had eaten a bowl of stale cereal from his pantry, we spent the morning watching TV and laughing together at all the stupid things that seem to be so important to everyone else in the world. Mr. Hadley was really funny when he was loopy. He had a take on everything . . .

"You know, these elections are sheer lunacy. It's like a bunch of turkeys lining up to vote for Thanksgiving . . .

"If I were rich, Elliot, I'd leave a scholarship fund to buy every one of these kids a belt . . .

"This Viagra in these commercials has to be one of the worst things to ever happen to women . . ."

It really was a riot, until his meds began to wear off. I could tell it was happening because his energy seemed to wane, and his gaze would drift from the TV to the floor. The look on his face hinted that he was fighting off pain. He was coughing a lot too. It became clear to me just how hard it must have been for him to spend all those hours telling me his and June's story. And now I knew what all those pills he was popping were for.

He hadn't eaten yet that I had seen, so I made him some tea and melted butter in it when he wasn't looking. Why not? The pamphlet said that high-fat foods were a good way to get needed calories quickly, and it all ends up in the same place anyway, right?

I called my office and let them know I'd be out all week and asked to have my cases reassigned. They weren't happy about it, but I would have been hard-pressed to care any less. It wasn't like the clients would miss me — whether it was I or some other suited swindler knocking on their door to hustle them out of their houses, what was the difference? I just didn't much feel like going on any foreclosure sits right now.

Mr. Hadley napped, waking late afternoon in much better spirits. He took some pain medication and managed to eat an apple with a glass of Ensure mixed up from an awful-smelling powder. Then he put his coat on and headed for the door.

"Whoa, where are you going?" I asked, looking up from the pamphlet I was reading. It's funny how protective you can feel of someone once you've watched them sleeping.

"I'm going to see June, of course."

He said it as if it were the most obvious thing in the world to do, and I guess after all he had been through while still managing his daily visits, it was.

"Hold on," I said. "I'll come up with you."

We didn't talk much, enjoying the sounds of the creek and the forest instead. It wasn't raining, but it had gotten suddenly cold and there was a definite bite in the air.

"Is Estrella coming back with your car?" he asked when we were about halfway up the trail. "If not, I'll spring for a taxi to take you home."

"She's bringing the car back tonight," I said.

"Oh good. She's a sweet girl. And smart one too. I really think June would have liked both of you."

"Her mother's coming to drive her back home since I'm staying here with you."

He stopped on the path, eyeing me. I turned to face him.

"What?" I asked.

"You've done too much already, Elliot. Much too much. I'm very grateful, but you have a life to get back to."

"I'm staying," I said, "and that's all there is to it."

He leaned on his cane and eyed me. "Do I have to force you to leave?"

I smiled. "You already know I'm not above breaking in through a window."

"I could call the police."

"Don't forget that I'm the executor of your estate with a power of attorney. I'll have you declared incompetent."

He laughed. "It wouldn't take much to prove that."

Then he continued walking on up the path. I followed.

"If you really plan to stay," he said as we walked, "I insist that you let me make you up a bed in June's studio. I have an air mattress I used to sleep on in there. It's quite comfortable."

"I can agree to that."

"There's more. I insist on buying groceries, now that I no longer have a mortgage payment to make. A growing young man like you can't live on frozen dinners and

MoonPies alone."

"I can agree to that also."

"And you'll have to put up with being woken by Abba. Occasionally a little Lynyrd Skynyrd too."

"Wow," I said, "Lynyrd Skynyrd, look at you."

"And you'll need to promise not to try and talk me out of what I plan to do. That's most important of all."

"I don't know if I can promise that, Mr. Hadley."

"You have to, Elliot. I'm not ready yet, but there will come a time soon when I am. I don't want it to be a fight. I know you think I'm doing this because I was being foreclosed on, but you're wrong. I held off writing that letter as long as I could."

I took in a deep breath of cold fall air, mulling over his request. I didn't want to make a promise that I couldn't keep, but I didn't want to upset him either. It wasn't my right to tell him how to live or how to end his own life.

"I'd be honored to stay with you through the process," I said. "Whatever that looks like. No argument, just love and support. That's what someone should do for his best friend."

He kept on walking and never took his

eyes off the path, but I could tell that he was smiling.

Mr. Hadley was asleep in his bed when Estrella and her mother arrived. It was getting dark and the resemblance between them was so striking that when I opened the door and saw her mother standing there with an armload of casserole dishes, I mistook her for her daughter and leaned in to kiss her on the cheek.

"It's nice to meet you, Mrs. Ackerman," I said, realizing my mistake as soon as I saw Estrella behind her removing a duffel bag from the trunk of my car.

"Oh!" she said, looking surprised by my kiss. "It's nice to meet you too, Elliot. Estrella says very nice things and I know they're true because we raised her to never lie. I whipped you up some of Estrella's favorite dishes."

I took the casseroles from her and stepped aside to invite her in. Estrella followed, lugging the duffel. I went to kiss her on the cheek but she turned her head and our lips brushed each other. It was a little awkward but kind of nice too.

She held up the duffel. "I figured a day or two might turn into more, so I brought you some stuff to wear from my dad's closet.

It's all brand-new. Mostly Christmas gifts from me he refuses to wear. He swears Dockers are high fashion. I brought you a toothbrush and stuff too. Don't worry, it's not my dad's."

We all sat around the kitchen table and ate dinner together. I got the feeling they had already eaten but wanted to be polite. One of the dishes contained a pizza-pie casserole, and I could see why it was Estrella's favorite. I liked her mother. Not only did they look alike, but they acted a lot alike too.

After dinner we all had tea.

"Are you sure you'll be okay out here by yourself?" Mrs. Ackerman asked as I walked them to the door.

"I'm not by myself," I said, smiling. "But yes, I'll be fine, thank you. And thank you for the food too."

She hugged me. It's hard to explain how exactly, but it was a mother's hug and it felt good.

"Those dishes are refillable," she said. "You just call when they're empty and we'll bring more."

Once her mother was outside on the porch, Estrella pulled me to the side. She wrapped her arms around my waist and looked up at me. She was smiling, but it was a sad kind of smile.

"He's lucky to have you to keep him company," she said. "I have to work tomorrow night but I can get Tom to cover me on Wednesday. I'll borrow my mother's car and come and hang out with you two. Maybe I'll bring along some games for us all to play."

"As long as you don't bring Scrabble," I said.

Then she bit her lower lip like she does, and I knew that she wanted me to kiss her. Which was more than fine with me because I'd been thinking about it since we hugged good-bye the night before. I leaned in and brought my lips to hers. We were kissing when her mother pushed the door open.

"Estrella, I almost forgot —"

"Mom! A little privacy, please."

Her mother blushed, quickly handing me a book before stepping back outside and pulling the door closed.

"Sorry," Estrella said. "How embarrassing."

"Not for me," I replied, leaning in and kissing her again.

She tasted like spearmint and honey. Maybe because of the tea she'd had after dinner. I'm sure I tasted like pizza pie, so I guess I'm lucky it's her favorite.

I saw them off from the porch, waving good-bye as they pulled away. When they were gone, I stood there for a minute longer just looking out over the barn and the field and the tree where I knew Rosie was buried. I had almost forgotten the book in my hand. I was worried it might be a downer about grieving but it wasn't. I could just read the title in the twilight, and when I did it made me smile — *Peter Pan and Wendy.*

36

I knew the day would come when he could no longer visit June, I just didn't think it would come so soon. It was the morning of my eighth day sleeping on the air mattress and I woke up late. Usually I could count on a wake-up call from across the hall as Mr. Hadley rocked his IV to the oldies. But today there was silence.

I found him still in bed, his eyes half open and his breath coming intermittently and rattling and wheezy in his chest. He had been sleeping more and more, his energy fading with each passing day, but he had always managed to rally in the morning. Not today. When he saw me he tried to smile, but I could tell he was in a great deal of pain. I cleaned his chest port with sterile gauze, as his home-care nurse had taught me to do, and inserted the IV. The methadone and morphine were supposed to keep the chronic pain at bay; the other narcotics were designed to act fast when he experienced breakthrough pain.

I spent the morning sitting on the bed with him, watching YouTube videos on my phone. He liked anything with animals. We watched a few hang gliding videos too. In the afternoon I came back from using the bathroom to find him standing in his robe holding on to the side of the bed. I didn't want him to feel helpless so I fetched him his cane. It just wasn't happening. He took two steps, then stopped, spinning a slow circle around his cane until he almost went down. I scooped him up and put him back in bed. He hardly weighed anything.

"Can I get you something?" I asked.

He was pretty doped up but he looked straight up into my eyes and said, "June."

"How about we shoot for tomorrow."

He shook his head and made like he was going to get up again. It nearly broke my heart. Then I had an idea.

"I'll make you a deal. You stay here and rest and I'll walk up there and take video. Then I'll come back and we'll sit and watch it together, okay? It'll be just like you've gone yourself."

I'm not sure he understood me, but tears welled up in his eyes and he rested his head back on his pillow.

It's hard to explain why, really, since I don't normally get all sentimental and stuff, but I had tears in my eyes too as I set out across the footbridge with my phone held out in front of me. Something about seeing the empty footpath passing by there on the screen, as if Mr. Hadley had already vanished and I were filming his ghost walking up to Echo Glen.

When I got back and had recharged my dying phone, we sat on the bed and watched the entire video together. And that's the only way he would ever see Echo Glen again until he was buried there. I thought about carrying him up once — since he was so light — but he had developed a strange fear about going much of anywhere farther than the bathroom by then. And even getting that far required my help.

He grew restless at night, staying awake and staring at the ceiling while picking at his sheets. I'd sit beside the bed and read him *Peter Pan.* I must have read the entire book three or four times through, but it seemed to help him relax.

I thought perhaps I should go home for a little while, get some things of my own to bring back, but I just couldn't get myself to leave. Estrella came by on the evenings she didn't have to work, delivering more of her mother's meals. She even brought a dandy quilt Mrs. Ackerman made for Mr. Hadley. She'd help me clean up around the house or do laundry, and then we'd eat something and sit together and play board games on the kitchen table. She brought Monopoly one night but it reminded me too much of my job. We didn't talk too much about what was happening with Mr. Hadley; we didn't talk too much about what was happening with us. We just hung out and made small talk mostly. And to tell you the truth, that was more than enough.

We'd hug when she got there and hug again when she left. We even kissed good-bye a few times. I knew there was more between us that needed to be explored, but everything seemed to be on hold. It's a strange feeling waiting around for death. There's a kind of silence that enters the house. I can't really explain it, but you probably know what I mean.

When he asked me to open the dresser drawer I kind of knew what I would find. It was still a shock though. Maybe because it was so innocuous looking.

It was lying in the drawer by itself. A simple prescription bottle just like the others scattered about the room. The only difference was the sealed safety cap and the warning on the label. Pentobarbital, it was called. Ten grams. Just enough to end a life, I guess. I felt like I was holding a bullet or a bomb. The directions said to drink it on an empty stomach followed by something sweet to help keep it down. I put it back and shut the drawer. He wasn't ready yet, but when he was he wanted me to know where to find it.

I sat on the edge of the bed and we looked at each other for a long time without talking. I got the feeling he was sad, but not about dying. I think he was sad for me because he knew I'd miss him. He had not been out of bed for several days, and it had come to my cleaning him. I know it embarrassed him but it didn't bother me at all. The home-care nurse had taught me how on one of her visits, and how to shift his position in the bed with pillows to keep him comfortable. He hadn't eaten anything solid in a long time, but she said that was normal and okay.

The hardest thing was his breathing. I would sit in the dark in a chair beside the bed and listen to it. It sounded like he was choking or drowning. Surprisingly when he was awake this didn't seem to panic him at all. I thought a lot about my dad while sitting in that dark room. I don't know why. Maybe because he had died so suddenly and I hadn't had any time to really say good-bye. They had taken him away already by the time the mill manager came out to the floor to tell me. I didn't even get a chance to see him until I looked at him in the casket.

I was sitting in the chair beside Mr. Hadley's bed one evening when I had one hell of a surprise.

"You know how to whistle, don't you, Steve? You just put your lips together and blow."

When I heard it I thought maybe I was dreaming.

"Steve," I said. "Who's Steve?"

"Humphrey Bogart," Mr. Hadley replied from his bed.

He hadn't been talking for days so it shocked me.

"It's from *To Have and Have Not,*" he added. "It was the first film my father took me to see."

"I've never heard of it," I said.

"I've got it in a box around here somewhere on VHS. You want to watch it?"

I couldn't believe my ears. Not only was he talking but he sounded like his old self again too. I turned the lamp on. He was sitting up in the bed.

"Sure. We can watch it."

I couldn't move the TV into the bedroom so I brought my air mattress into the living room. Then I carried him out and propped him up on it with pillows. He told me where to look for the VHS tape and I found it. By the look of the thing he'd watched it many times before.

"Do we have any MoonPies left?" he asked.

It was hard as hell not to get my hopes up. The pamphlets had done their job, though, and I knew this didn't mean he was getting better. But it didn't mean I couldn't enjoy the time with him either.

We sat and ate MoonPies and drank RC Colas like a couple of kids staying up beyond their bedtime because their parents are away. We both had smiles on our faces and chocolate rings around our lips. When the movie was over I asked him if he wanted to see another. I guess I didn't want the evening to end. But he didn't. He said he had just wanted to see Lauren Bacall one last time. Plus, he was looking tired again.

When I reached for the remote to rewind the tape he laid his hand on top of mine.

"There's something I'd like to tell you, Elliot. Something that might not be fair of me to say, but I need to say it. When June passed it wasn't easy. It wasn't easy because I was alone."

"You're not alone now, Mr. Hadley."

"I know," he replied, giving my hand a squeeze. "Thank you." A few quiet moments passed. "I only have one regret in life, Elliot," he said. "And that's not bad for a man my age. I only ever kept one thing from June all the time we were married. I had hoped that maybe someday we'd adopt a child. I always wanted a son. I never told her though. I didn't want her to think I'd missed out. This may sound silly, but I want you to know that my one regret is not a regret anymore."

His eyes were all wet and his chin was quivering like he might cry. He went on.

"I'm not afraid to die, Elliot. I've got my new best friend to see me off and the love of my life waiting for me. That's better than any man can hope for."

I was trying not to cry myself now. "I'm going to miss you. I really am."

"I'm going to miss you too, Elliot Champ. You just make me a promise that you won't be alone. I won't feel good about leaving otherwise."

I thought I understood, so I nodded.

"I'm in no position to lay advice on you.

But I can boil seventy-nine years of experience down into this: Find yourself someone worthy of your love, and love her with all you've got. It's the only thing that's worth a damn in this life. That and maybe love like this." He smiled and squeezed my hand again.

Now both of us were crying, but neither of us bothered to dry our eyes or pretend we weren't. It was what it was. We lay back on the air mattress together for a while, just staring up at the ceiling, side by side. I think some people go their whole life without feeling what I felt lying there holding Mr. Hadley's hand. It's hard to even talk about how much I loved that man.

Nothing lasts forever, and grace in the form of a midnight reprieve was no exception. His coughing returned and so did his pain. I carried him back to his bed sometime before sunup.

The dresser drawer was closed still, but we both knew what lay there waiting. At least we had told each other how we felt.

It was a clear, cold Thursday afternoon when he finally told me he was ready. I had just returned from my walk up to Echo Glen, and I guess I kind of knew because I had told June he'd be joining her soon.

When I sat down to show him the video he squeezed my hand and pointed at the drawer.

It was a heavy drawer to open. But it was harder watching him suffer. I took the bottle into June's studio, loosened the lid, and set it on the windowsill beside the daybed that overlooked the creek and path up to Echo Glen. Then I went into the kitchen and poured a warm RC Cola into a glass and put it there beside the bottle. Each step, each movement, was a solemn one.

When everything was ready I went back and unhooked his IV, picked him up, carried him into the studio, and laid him on the daybed. I made him comfortable with pillows and blankets from his room. Then I sat in the chair to wait. He was looking off out the window at the path, almost like he couldn't wait to get up to Echo Glen and his wife again. I wasn't sure if he wanted me to stay in the room, but then, without taking his eyes from the window, he reached out and felt for me, his hand landing on my knee. We stayed like that for a long time.

The sky grew darker, the creek and the path dissolving into the twilight. As the light faded from the room, the features of Mr. Hadley's face faded from my view, and the last thing I saw was a remote kind of smile.

I bowed my head and prayed.

I'm not sure when in the night he passed. Exhaustion caught up to me, and the relief of his decision made it okay to finally rest. I fell asleep there in that chair — the first real restful sleep I'd had in a long time. When I woke there was just a hint of gray in the sky and Mr. Hadley was gone. His body was there on the daybed, but he was somewhere just beyond the second star to the right and straight on till morning, probably flying that old hang glider into the full moon with June.

I felt like I should be sad but I wasn't. As scary as it must have been for him, he had danced me through it like a pro. From the day his letter had arrived on my desk to this moment right now. I didn't notice until I stood up and stretched my legs that the bottle still stood on the windowsill, untouched. He had timed it perfectly, the sly old dodger. He'd set the stage but in the end it was June who had called him home.

Now all there was left to do was make a call of my own so that I didn't feel alone. I'd honor my last promise. That and find his farewell binder. I was sure everything I might need was in there. After all, he used to be an accountant, you know.

37

I was the only one left on the hill as the grave was filled in. But I wasn't alone. Estrella was not far off, standing between her mother and father beside the waterfall, their hands linked as they watched for signs of rain in the cloudy sky above the glen.

They had come to pay their respects, but mostly I think to support me, since they knew it would be hard to say good-bye to Mr. Hadley. And I suppose it was in a way, although I felt as though we had already said all there was to say.

As Mr. Thorpe's son piled on the last shovelful of dirt and packed it down, I was not so much sad as I was relieved that his long suffering was over and that he and June could now lie side by side forever in peace. I thought about that day in his story when he had come up here with June, the day she told him that if he shouted a wish at the falls that wish would come true. And his wish had. I was looking at the proof.

Then, when a drop of rain landed on the fresh mound of earth, I thought about the afternoon Mr. Hadley and I had come up here in the pouring rain. I thought about sitting right here where I'd just put him in the ground, beneath that huge umbrella, and listening to him tell me about the beauty of each raindrop and the stories they held. He said everything was a cycle, and he said everything had an echo. And I know now that he was right about that too, because his and June's love story would forever echo in my heart.

Mr. Hadley had not wanted a stone, and it was his only wish that I didn't follow. It was a simple slab of marble picked from a local quarry. The mason had inscribed it for me on site.

HERE RESTS
DAVID JOSEPH HADLEY
JANUARY 22, 1935–NOVEMBER 14, 2014
WHOSE WISH WAS ANSWERED HERE
IN ECHO GLEN, WHERE HE RESTS
NOW FOREVER BESIDE HIS BELOVED
WIFE, WHO TAUGHT HIM TO LET GO
OF HIS FEAR AND FALL INTO HIS LIFE

We all ran together down the path toward

the bridge that led to the house. None of us had thought to bring an umbrella, and the rain had come all at once, almost as if on cue to chase us away so that David and June could be alone at last.

We were soaked by the time we reached the house. I built up a fire in the stove and we sat in front of it to dry off and had tea while I told Estrella's parents funny stories about June and Mr. Hadley. Her father was quiet but very nice. I liked him. It felt almost like we were a family, which scared me a little.

Estrella wanted to stay behind with me, but I couldn't be sure when I would be going home. I had lots of odds and ends at the house to take care of yet. I saw them off in the driveway.

"I know you have a lot on your plate right now," Estrella said after our third hug good-bye. "But I'd love to see you. You know, away from all this. Maybe call me when you get settled back in your Seattle place?"

I told her that I would, and I meant it too. I just had no way of knowing at the time that when I saw her next it would be to say good-bye one last time.

I watched them drive away, feeling much the same way as I imagined Mr. Hadley must have felt when he'd stood on this porch to watch me go. And then I was just as completely alone as he had been too, there in the very center of the universe.

He had been an accountant to the very end, and every one of his accounts was current if not already closed. Except the mortgage, of course, but we had already settled that, and the property now belonged to the bank. There wasn't much money left, but what there was he had left to me. But there was one thing about which he had not told me the entire truth.

His life insurance policy was not valued at the $25,000 he had offered me. It was for four times that amount and I was the sole beneficiary. I used some of it to set up the annuity for the private cemetery, filing for the license on behalf of the Echo Glen Corporation, of which I was now the owner, but that still left me more than enough to get my dream condo in Miami with big bucks to spare. Still, I wasn't planning on going through with it until the call came in.

I've told you I've never been a big believer in signs, but it was hard to deny the coincidence of finally checking my voice mail only to find several messages from my Realtor in Miami asking if I'd gotten the e-mails he'd sent. He'd found the perfect place, and it just happened to be in a building I'd had my eye on. It wasn't a penthouse, sure — there was no way I had the scratch for that, even with Mr. Hadley's gift — but it was a midfloor unit overlooking the pool with a peekaboo view of the baby-blue Atlantic.

I sat looking at the photo in the e-mail for an hour before I decided to call him up. He answered right away.

"Damn, Elliot, where've you been? You just fell off the face of the earth on me, dude. Left me twisting in the tropical winds, my man."

I told him I'd had some personal business to attend to.

"Listen, Elliot, this is the deal of a lifetime. Not like those others I sent. The bank has foreclosed, the place is vacant, and the best part is they'll let you do a lease option. That means you can get yourself set up over here, settle in, and close when you've saved up the last of your dough."

I didn't tell him I had the money to buy it right now.

"I don't know, Kevin," I said. "I'm reconsidering Miami. Plus, I'm kind of tired of tossing people out of their homes."

"Reconsidering? Where are you right now?"

"I'm out in Darrington, on a ranch wrap-

478

ping up some family business."

"Shit. Okay, listen. I want you to walk to the window and tell me what the weather's like right now."

I walked to the kitchen window and looked out. "It's raining. But not hard."

"Not hard. Ha! You want to know what I'm looking at out my window right now? Palm trees and blue skies. Oh, and women in bikinis Rollerblading by. How's seventy-nine degrees sound next to your *raining but not hard*? Think about it. This place won't last long."

I told him I would and hung up the phone. I sat there for another hour with Estrella's number on my screen and my finger on the Call button. I almost pressed it a hundred times.

I was watching from the porch when the van pulled up the drive and parked. The man who got out wore the clinic uniform. He was very friendly. I wheeled June's chair down the ramp and helped him load it into the van.

"It's nice of you to donate this," the man said. "It will be put to very good use."

"It's not from me. I'm just carrying out my best friend's last wishes. They said on the phone you might be able to return the

IV and oxygen machine as well. They're just inside."

When the van left, the house was nice and clean. I had tossed out all the food and built up a bonfire the night before and burned all the old miscellaneous personal papers I had found. I made several trips to the dump and some to the Goodwill. No one ever thinks about what happens to their toothbrush or their slippers after they're gone. I had taken the photo album and some other special things back to my place, which I would probably also be cleaning out soon. Only the kitchenware and furniture and June's paintings remained.

I was in the living room watching the tail on the old cat clock sweep back and forth, waiting for it to meow, when the knock came on the door. It was my second conversation with a Realtor in as many days. I invited him in as if it were my place, which seems kind of strange now that I think about it since the place kind of belonged to him.

"Wow," he said, glancing around, "looks like whoever ends up buying this place is going to be happy to get it fully furnished or pissed that they have to get rid of all this stuff."

"Do you think the bank will auction it?" I asked.

"I doubt it," he said, looking at the papers he had brought along for his inspection. "The place is pretty run-down and it isn't a hot market for houses on undividable acreage right now. Horses are out of style, I guess. They'll probably list it through us. That's what they usually do."

He walked around writing things down on his sheet.

"They told me someone had died," he said nonchalantly. "Looks like we'll need to get a glass guy out here to fix that window."

"Could you do me a favor?" I asked.

"Sure," he said. "I appreciate you cleaning it up and all. What can I do for you?"

I laid my hand on the old carousel rooster in front of the window bay. "If I leave you my number will you call me if whoever buys the place doesn't want this?"

He looked at it with a blank expression, almost as if he were wondering who would want the old thing. "You can take it now if you want to," he said. "All of this is technically yours until you hand me the keys and we change the locks."

"I know. But it's way too big to fit in my car."

"They rent trucks down at Olson's."

"The truth is I might be moving to Miami soon."

"Well, hell," he said, "I don't know if it's true, but I heard that we put a man on the moon. I'm sure we can ship it there."

I looked at Mr. Hadley's father's rooster, remembering his song-and-dance routine when I had first arrived.

"No," I said. "It belongs here. Just call me if the buyers don't want to keep it."

He looked at it again and shrugged. "I wouldn't go too far from the phone."

As much as she loved Dilettante's Viennese hot cocoa, I noticed she hadn't touched hers the entire time I'd been talking. Then again, I hadn't touched mine either. I guess it was a hard conversation for both of us to have.

"Could you have picked a place any farther from here?"

"It's not like I'm leaving the country," I said.

"Are you sure you're not just running away?" she asked.

"Running away? This has been my dream since I was a boy, Estrella. Since way back in Belfair."

"That's exactly what I mean," she said, raising an eyebrow.

"Are you psychoanalyzing me now?" I asked.

"No, I'm just pointing out the obvious. Are you going to tell me that this whole thing with Mr. Hadley didn't dredge up any feelings about your own dad?"

Why'd she have to be so damn smart? It just made this all that much harder on me. "Maybe there's a little truth to that," I admitted. "I don't know. But I have to go, Estrella. When I left Belfair all those years ago I pretty much had the clothes on my back, sixty-four bucks, and that condo clipping that I clung to like hope."

"Well, I hope you find what you're looking for."

I know she meant it, but she still said it with a little heat.

"Maybe you can come visit. You know, fly out. I should be able to make good money out there. I could spring for tickets."

"Come on, Elliot. That's not happening."

"Why not?"

"Because I'm doubling down on my credits in the spring. Then once I graduate I'll be looking for a real job, not slinging cocktails at Finnegans. And besides, this is where I plan to build my life. This is where my family is. Not Miami."

"I could visit here then."

Now she really raised her eyebrow. "Let's just call this what it really is, Elliot. We're going our separate ways."

"Well, you sure seem over it already."

"No, I'm not. This sucks for me, Elliot. I called to invite you to my family's house for Thanksgiving; I didn't expect you to dump me. I really like you."

She looked off out the window for a minute, biting her lip like she did. Then she went on.

"You wanna know something? When you started coming into Finnegans I was really attracted to you. But I didn't think you were the kind of guy I could ever end up with long-term. That's what was so funny when you told me you only dated girls you didn't like. Because I knew what you meant. I'd been hoping you'd ask me out so we could maybe have a little fling."

"Wait a minute. So you're saying I was the guy you didn't really like that you wanted to go out with just for fun. Like I was getting played at my own game."

She smiled. "I didn't know you then. I just thought you were handsome and interesting. But then this whole thing with Mr. Hadley made me look at you differently. And it honestly made me think about my own life differently too. We both deserve the kind of love they had, Elliot. And I intend to wait for it."

"And you don't see that kind of love with me?"

"That's the problem. I did start to see it with you. But it's not possible to see it or you if you're all the way in Miami."

We fell silent then and kind of sat looking at each other. I could tell we were both wondering what to say next. There was this feeling like maybe if either of us said the wrong thing there might be tears. And it felt like we'd both already cried enough.

Georgie swung by and glanced at our untouched cocoas, and then at our faces. "Uh-oh," he said, "this doesn't look good."

Then he crossed his arms and glared at me.

"If you do anything to hurt this young woman, Romeo, I'll personally see to it that you never dine at Dilettante again."

"He doesn't care," Estrella said. "He's moving to Miami."

"Miami? Of all the places. Don't worry, honey, he'll catch crabs on South Beach. Everyone does. The cocoas are on me."

Then he floated off on his imaginary skates.

"You wanna know what's funny?" Estrella said.

"What's that?" I asked.

"We're not really even breaking up since you never actually asked me out on an official date."

"I didn't?"

"No. I asked you to buy me a hot chocolate when you got back from Echo Glen on your birthday, but you never did ask me out. Isn't life a kick sometimes."

She had a point there. Life could be a real kick.

I walked her home even though she said it would be easier if I didn't. It was cold and clear. The frozen leaves crunched beneath our feet and we could see our breath.

"I wonder what the temperature is in Miami," she said.

"Seventy-seven. I checked it this morning."

She stopped and turned and threw her arms around me. For someone who claimed she didn't like me that much, she sure held me tight. It felt really good. I rested my chin on the top of her head and looked at her gate and the walkway that led up to her door. I doubted I'd ever see it again and that kind of broke my heart.

She pulled away and looked up into my eyes.

"Do me a favor, will you, Elliot Champ?"

"You name it, Estrella Ackerman."

"You make damn sure that whoever you end up with deserves you."

She rose up and kissed me on the cheek. Then she turned and walked away from me, through the gate and up to her house. She had just put her key in the door when I laid my hand on her shoulder. She turned around and I saw that she was crying. I took her in my arms and hugged her tight. Then I took her face in my hands and looked into her eyes and kissed her. She was smiling when I finally pulled my lips away.

"You make damn sure he deserves you too."

She bit her lip and nodded that she would.

I never would know if she stood to watch me go or not. I didn't have the nerve to look back. I guess I knew that if I did I wouldn't be able to keep walking.

38

They don't call it the Sunshine State for nothing.

I had been there less than a week and already they were addressing me as the Yankee Screamer at the office. I made the mistake of asking what a Yankee Screamer was.

"You know, one of you Yankees who comes down here and gets so sunburned you scream when you're touched."

Then this joker laid his hand on the back of my neck and I damn near jumped out of my chair. I had to stop myself from punching him. Seems the guys in the foreclosure-counseling business are about the same on either coast. But they weren't that bad, I guess. They invited me out for dinner and drinks after work.

Trouble was nobody in Miami eats dinner until ten, and drinking doesn't start in earnest until around midnight. Who the hell can keep up that kind of schedule? I tried to ignore the ridiculous fist pumping and the strobes and the deafening techno blare, shouting over the noise to the bartender for a club soda. He charged me ten bucks and didn't even give me my lousy lime. It sure wasn't Finnegans.

The condo was nice, though, it really was. It had a big glass door and a balcony that looked over the pool. Of course, every time I looked down there I kept hearing Mr. Hadley's words: *"The sun is nothing but a weapon,"* he'd said. And as an official Yankee Screamer I could now attest to that.

Besides being lonely, the worst part about it all had to be Santa Claus. I was coming home late Saturday afternoon from buying groceries and there was old Kris Kringle himself, ringing his little bell for donations, it being officially the first week of December already. I gave him a couple of bucks, but I'll be damned if he wasn't wearing sunglasses and Bermuda trunks. That's not right. And neither were the neon-pink lights strung on the palm tree in the building lobby.

My new lease-to-own condo had a fancy gas fireplace — although I can't imagine why — and I sat that night on my rented sofa and looked up at June's painting of

Echo Glen, which I had hung above it. It was about the only thing in the place that I owned, and I was beginning to think maybe it was the only thing there I wanted to own.

I realized while sitting there that maybe you just have to achieve some dreams in order to be free of their grip. How many nights had I sat looking out that rain-streaked trailer window telling myself that everything would be okay if I could only manage to escape? I think what that boy really wanted was to escape the sadness that he had tried his best to cover up with pages torn from glossy real estate magazines.

I took out my trusty old condo clipping and held it up. Here I was; the boy had escaped Belfair at last. I flipped the switch to turn the fireplace on, tossed it in, and sat back to watch that tattered old dream burn.

There was a dusting of snow on downtown Seattle, and white lights wrapped the sidewalk trees. I pulled my coat tight and walked down my old familiar street.

The place was almost empty when I walked in. I had no way of knowing if she'd be there or not, but she was, standing behind the bar with her eyes on the door as if she'd been there expecting me the entire time. But if she had been expecting me, you'd never have known it from the way her face lit up with surprise. We locked eyes and neither of us could contain our smiles. I took a seat at the bar.

"What'll you have, handsome?" she asked, still beaming but with a mischievous glint in her eye now.

"Club soda with lime and a menu, please."

"Hey, wait a minute," she said. "I recognize that order. Didn't you used to come in here before?"

"Why yes, I did," I said.

She nodded, squinting at me. "I know you. You're that guy who moved to Miami."

"Well, here I am back."

"Didn't you buy a place there?"

"As it turns out I got a great deal on a run-down old ranch house around here, next to a cemetery I own. And they tell me it should close in time for Christmas."

"Hmm . . . ," she said, twirling her hair on her finger now. "So, that's why you came back then."

I shook my head. "I came back because I thought maybe I'd officially ask a certain someone out on a date."

"Officially? Oh . . . sounds serious."

"It's very serious indeed."

"Assuming this certain girl was to say yes, what would this official date look like?"

"I don't know," I said, meeting her smiling eyes with my own. "How do you feel about hang gliding?"

EPILOGUE

There is nearly a foot of fresh snow on the trail now, and the crystalline pine branches tinkle overhead like wind chimes as I pass. The creek is frozen. A narrow swath of unobstructed twilit sky illuminates the glen. Icicles hang from the trickling falls. The scene is so pristine and sacred — the leafless oak tree, the hill blanketed by untouched snow — that I just can't bring myself to take another step and disturb it. From where I stand I can just make out the two headstones, side by side, so close together they nearly touch.

I'm proud to be the caretaker of this private little cemetery. I'm even prouder to be the caretaker of the love story that rests here. I don't know if I'll be buried here or not. Let's hope that day is still a very long ways off. But I can tell you this much for sure: if you shout a wish in Echo Glen, that wish comes true.

It's almost fully dark now, just enough light reflecting off the snow to make my way. I stop just short of the bridge, on the far side of the creek. A curl of white smoke rises from the chimney. The lights are on. The house is warm. Mr. Hadley's rooster stands at the bay window. I see Estrella beyond it in the living room, trimming our Christmas tree.

I think sometimes life lines up to give you exactly what it is you really need, and on my thirty-third birthday that's exactly what happened to me. My father had done the best he could. But he had left me with a lot of fear and some bad advice about love. And then a very special man came along and taught me otherwise. I can't put it any better than he put it, so here is what he said:

"Find yourself someone worthy of your love, and love her with all you've got. It's the only thing that's worth a damn in this life."

And you know what? He was right.

ACKNOWLEDGMENTS

It was at a café in New Orleans that my editor, Sarah Cantin, asked me what my next book would be about and when she might be able to expect it. All I could tell her at the time was I was working on something special and would be heading off to Spain to jump out of airplanes in pursuit of inspiration. I could sense her concern even though she was kind enough to try to hide it. I would like to thank Sarah now for her gentle encouragement, her insightful editing, and her patient reassurance. Some literary journeys seem far too personal and precious to ever share, but Sarah's deep and immediate love for these characters, along with her enthusiasm for their story, made letting this manuscript go to print just a little easier.

I also need to thank a very special friend who limped into my life at a low time, lifted me up, dusted me off, and taught me how to live again. We made a vow to never harm each other and we broke the vow only once. I did not know it until I had finished writing, but this love story was my way of finally saying good-bye. But then as James M. Barrie so touchingly wrote in *Peter Pan,* "Never say good-bye because good-bye means going away and going away means forgetting." And I will never forget, dear friend. The smudge-faced boy you loved will be forever sitting beside you on that lakeside bench, watching the sun go down on Neverland.

ABOUT THE AUTHOR

Ryan Winfield is the *New York Times* bestselling author of *Jane's Harmony, Jane's Melody, South of Bixby Bridge,* and *The Park Service* trilogy. He lives in Seattle. To connect with Ryan, visit him at www .RyanWinfield.com.

The employees of Thorndike Press hope you have enjoyed this Large Print book. All our Thorndike, Wheeler, and Kennebec Large Print titles are designed for easy reading, and all our books are made to last. Other Thorndike Press Large Print books are available at your library, through selected bookstores, or directly from us.

For information about titles, please call:
  (800) 223-1244

or visit our Web site at:
  http://gale.cengage.com/thorndike

To share your comments, please write:
  Publisher
  Thorndike Press
  10 Water St., Suite 310
  Waterville, ME 04901